Bridget

A NOVEL BY
M.A. HENDERSON

Bridget
By M.A. Henderson

Published by Killer 3Bs, Richland, WA, 99352.

www.ninefruitbooks.com

Library of Congress Catalog Number 2018912569
ISBN: 978-0-9987195-2-8 (trade paperback)
eBook ISBN: 978-0-9987195-3-5

Cover photographs obtained from
Thinkstock (www.thinkstock.com)

Cover design © Spark Design & Communication
(www.sparkdescom.com)

Chapter artwork layout © Spark Design &
Communication (www.sparkdescom.com)

Printed in the United States of America

Bryce – there is a bridge
who can not be burned.

CHAPTER

1

BETWEEN ASPHALT AND TURF

The freeway meters out punishment to all, irrespective of whether or not they be faithful to its rules. For by its will, time is siphoned off and exhaust spit back with a carbon-monoxiousness that poisons away peace. There is no camaraderie within its painted lanes… just cruel competition. The weak, the harried and the ill-prepared are forced to the side. Only the fast and fit survive. To every driver, the freeway steals, kills and destroys… yet it is still the quickest way to get about LA.

Bridget descended the on-ramp with a tense, two-fisted grip on her steering wheel. Hunched forward a bit in the driver's seat, she craned her head about in search of an opportunity for entering the freeway's densely-packed line of cars… all of which were moving faster than her fifteen year old Nissan. With the merge lane petering out, she conceded to the need for forcing her way in. Spotting a sliver of space several car-lengths ahead, she floored the accelerator and felt her engine's paltry jolt of power… delivered as it was amidst a more prominent whine of protest. Coming abreast of the opening, she glanced over her shoulder. The driver of a black Escalade had realized her intent and was increasing speed to deny her access. She swerved across the dividing line into the narrow space before him, fully convinced that he would yield simply so as not to risk damage to his expensive car. Once in, she tapped her breaks in moderating to the flow… and received back an angry horn blare in return.

Disregarding the implication – that she had become like everyone else in this metropolis of overly-aggressive motorists – Bridget turned her attention to the next obstacle. To her left… and slightly ahead… was a furniture delivery truck brandishing the much bandied-about phrase 'How's my driving?'. Ignoring the 1-800-no-where number, she slid her car ahead far enough to slip before that truck's grill. Then, in drawing up on the rear of a yellow Cadillac, she throttled around its left side and narrowly squeezed back in front, causing its driver to abruptly break. Committing such trivial highway offenses had become a small price to pay… especially if it meant not having to ride someone's bumper for miles.

She pushed past more vehicles in her constant search for a pathway through traffic. Coming abreast of a big rig's cab, she waited for the precise moment in its oscillatory break-and-accelerate cycle affording her sufficient space, then swerved ahead of it. The maneuver earned her another prolonged horn blast… and in response, she apologetically offered a hand wave into the airspace about her. Returning to the modest cruising speed of ten miles-per-hour over the posted limit, the Caddy, the semi, and all other offended vehicles soon became distant memories… remnants of space and time retaining existence only within the confines of her rearview mirror.

For Bridget, traversing the freeways of Southern California was a simple matter of balancing gains and losses. Gain a lane or lose time… and in the process, a piece of her sanity. She had not always been like this. Once, her attitude toward the road had been more leisurely. But her life no longer had margin for such enjoyment, as constant anxiety and the need for haste overrode all previous driving tendencies… except perhaps guilt. Because she was a citizen of LA, Bridget conformed to its standards, although doing so grated against her nature, leaving her feeling uneasy… and a bit dirty. Ideally, she preferred an existence within the speed limit… or perhaps slightly above as a courtesy to those with whom she shared the road. Most days, she felt as if there was no survival at such meager speeds.

Today was no exception. She was late… and being late had become more than sufficient vindication for adopting the worst sorts of freeway manners. To live a life that did not inconvenience others was impossible… even though she could still vaguely recall a time when such was not the case. Before moving to LA, she would say that much could be made of a person's character based on how they drove. It had been a long time since she last resorted to that adage.

She discarded the thought, as the traffic would not afford the luxury of such contemplation. Having cut off a laundry service van in order to gain a coveted gap in the far lane, Bridget was unexpectedly brought up short by a Hummer.

"Come on! Make up your mind!"

Its driver had previously moved to the right, creating open space for her, but then abruptly returned before she could take advantage. For the first time since entering the freeway that afternoon, Bridget laid into her horn. She would never have done that ten years before. Back then, such expressions were distasteful… nothing more than childish responses at having one's carefully planned out tic-tac-toe pattern taken away. Still… she gave the Hummer one more short toot simply out of frustration at not being able to see around its immense girth. Although she felt it supremely inconsiderate that anyone should own such a monstrosity, what actually irritated her was being made to face the neat little row of white decals on its rear window. The owner's pride in having a happy family comprised of husband, wife, three children and dog unfairly forced upon her a depiction she would never know. Muttering driving instructions at the mega-utility vehicle, she twisted her head away from its honor student sticker to check if her previous spot on the right might present a better opportunity… but that vacancy in traffic was already filled. Nature and the LA driver both abhor a vacuum.

To her, the freeways of Southern California always seemed a disturbingly accurate semblance for the state of her heart. Moving faster than was safe at most times, and at others snarled to a halt amidst so much unnecessary turmoil. Always, she found herself burning, consuming precious energy in rushing about toward some poorly mapped-out destination. The thing she wanted most from life always took a backseat to the conflict she and the city's millions endlessly vied to resolve by getting ahead of one more thing in life. She hated it. Hated existing in a state of being pricked by a conscience slowly growing familiar with offending others. Worse was the feeling of being stuck in the reoccurring predicament of shirking one or both of her all-too-often conflicted responsibilities – her daughter or work. After a decade on the freeway, she no longer sought resolution over such things… only the means to endure a frantic existence.

From bitter experience, Bridget knew too well that living frantic was fertile soil for anger… and LA motorists drove angry. Angry because there were insufficient lanes for the number of cars, angry when construction shut down perfectly good lanes to repair other perfectly good ones, and angry because there was not a special lane just for them. Bridget was angry. Angry that getting about the city took so much out of her. Angry that her daughter did not appreciate the sacrifices being made on her behalf. Angry that her husband had run off with another woman and left her heartbroken. And angry with herself… because she lived life so very thin.

Bridget momentarily veered her car to the left over the shoulder's rumple strip in order to peek about the Hummer. For as far as she could see, there was nothing but a long string of lit brake lights foretelling of an accident… and more delay. Moving back into her lane, she endured once more the jolting agitation of the roadside bumps… and as if timed perfectly with regaining a smooth surface, the dashboard chimed politely at her.

This is just perfect – low on gas!

To her, the needle never seemed to spend much time near full, with the similarity to how she felt being far too obvious. She seldom took opportunities to carve moments out of her day for rest, and frequently found herself without the reserve needed for covering life's unexpected challenges. Having to rush about all the time drew energy out of her in the same way an engine sucked a tank dry. But to drive in LA was to risk living on empty, and having to accept that made her even more angry. And anger, she knew, only fueled discontent. She wanted to be somewhere else. Somewhere peaceful without asphalt or concrete. These days, it seemed the only green thing in her life was the golf course… and she hated the golf course even more than the freeway.

Don't go there, Bridget! Everything you're doing… all you're giving up… it's all going to pay off one day. You'll see. Besides… you're focusing on the negative. Keep your eye on the main objective – getting Blaire through her teenage years. After all she's been through… we've been through… we're all we have left.

Bridget begrudgingly backed a half car-length off the Hummer in conceding to herself that this lane afforded the only chance of making up lost time. She had left work early in hopes of arriving for the start of her daughter's second golf tournament of the school year. Her supervisor had not liked that, but her offer to come in on the next Saturday immediately softened his mood. Nobody wanted to work weekends.

Actually… it had been work and not traffic that was responsible for her missing Blaire's previous tournament, and she was determined not to repeat that same breach of parental duty today. She would gladly give up any number of Saturdays in order to support Blaire. After all, there would only be so many opportunities left to watch her daughter compete… and this particular tournament was to be special. Blaire, a mere sophomore, had been designated team captain. Throughout the work day, Bridget toyed with the implications this good news had for her daughter. Maybe, in the eyes of the coach, Blaire had finally come to a new appreciation for her role on the team. Maybe all of Bridget's efforts at parenting were finally paying off.

At the same time, a voice in the back of her head kept arguing for a more likely explanation. Blaire's distinction had nothing to do with maturity. Even as a freshman, the girl had been a serious challenge to the seniors on the team, and now… a year later… was simply too talented not to be captain.

Bridget navigated her way across three lanes of packed traffic on the Hollywood Freeway in order to merge onto the Five… and eventually to reach the Ronald Reagan. The flow should be somewhat better there, allowing her to quickly make it to the Nottingham golf course. She ventured a quick look at the dashboard clock – she might still make it on-time. Fortunately, this tournament was not far off… by LA standards. Though a mere twenty three miles… as the traffic copter flies… from her downtown workplace at the Desert Valley Credit Union, Bridget considered it nothing short of a miracle if the trip could be made in under an hour. The shotgun start… the only way to get the entire field through the course before dark… would be at two. But even if she could arrive by then, getting to whatever tee Blaire was assigned would take more time.

With mere minutes to spare, Bridget pulled into the clubhouse parking lot with a strong sense of something being off. There were far too many parking spaces available and no school buses on hand. She quickly rationalized to herself that those were instructed to park elsewhere. Unfortunately, the course's tranquil pro shop struck her as an even stronger omen of ill. To her, the start of a high school golf tournament could best be described as a riled-up beehive – a constant hum of activity accompanied by the occasional sting of some poor teenager's emotions run amok. There were always clusters of golfers buzzing about, making last minute purchases while their coaches trailed behind fretting over what it would take to get them out on the course so the tournament could start on time.

This pro shop, however, only had a lone attendant behind the counter chatting it up with two elderly golfers. As she approached, it was evident that all three had nowhere to go and plenty of time to get there. So she butted right in.

"Excuse me… sorry to interrupt… but I'm here for the ladies' high school tournament… the one with Valencia High. Have they teed off yet?"

She cringed as the men grimaced to the course representative… right before moving out the door. That clerk, in contrast, stared back blankly.

"Umm… no… they've not teed off… but that's because we're not hosting a women's tournament until next week… or maybe you mean the high school men's one tomorrow?"

"No, it's ladies. My daughter assured me it was here today."

He produced a clipboard from behind the counter and flipped through several of its attached sheets before turning the result toward her. The page was a flier listing various dates set aside for high school tournaments.

"We put these up for the regulars so they'll know when the course is unavailable. See there – next Tuesday." He pointed to an entry labeled 'High School Ladies Tournament, 2 to 7.'

Her sinking feeling, first brought on by the absence of school buses, had reached its fullest depth. She was in the wrong place and would be incredibly late for Blaire's tournament… maybe even miss it altogether.

"I can't believe this. She definitely said it was here… I'm sure of it. You wouldn't happen to know where it is?"

"Sorry, lady… no idea. Why don't you just call her?"

"Oh… she'll have her phone off."

Bridget could not bear to explain that it made little difference whether Blaire's phone was on or off. Despite having spent extra on a family cellular plan with extended minutes, her calls to Blaire almost always went to voicemail… and without the courtesy of a reply.

"How about if I look it up for you on the web?" He briefly turned to a computer on a back table. "They're at Richardson Ranch. Know where that is?"

Letting out a small gasp, she responded as much to herself as to him. "But that's got to be over thirty miles away! It'll take forever getting there!"

Fuming on the inside, she caught herself in time to put on a smile and thank the man. Heading out the door, she was already busy in calculating the time required to reach the new destination – near on an hour with the most favorable of traffic.

…and I still need gas.

She spent a considerable portion of this side trip weaving through a seemingly endless line of semis dueling it out in their thinly veiled lane wars that kept Highway 14 all gummed up. Going miles side-by-side with one of these trucks, with another blocking her way forward, was as unnerving as her inability to rationalize how it was that Blaire could repeatedly pass along incorrect information.

Because there's absolutely no way she mentioned Richardson Ranch!

Both the truck traffic and her daughter left Bridget feeling the same way – trapped.

After enduring the extra hour of driving, Bridget pulled into the golf course's parking lot fully resolved to bear the burden of the misunderstanding… if for no other reason than to keep it from becoming another thing that set her daughter off. She was immediately relieved on seeing a side lot strewn with school buses. Checking first with the pro shop, she was directed to a tournament coordinator's booth off the main practice green. Grabbing scorecards for the club's two courses, she headed out to the portable awning where a man was lounging behind a foldable table. His calm demeanor told her all she needed to know – the tournament had been underway for some time.

"Excuse me, I'm looking for my daughter, Blaire O'Connor. She goes to Valencia High."

The man smiled back politely… although it came with slightly raised eyebrows. She consoled herself that it was nothing… probably just his way of greeting someone without words. He was, in no way, judging her for being the kind of parent who always showed up late for her child's events. As he scanned a chart on the table, Bridget breathed in deeply to steady herself.

"Let's see… She's… on the Hillside Course. Her group teed off from four… so they're probably on nine by now. That's back across the road you came in on."

As he cautioned her about remaining clear of play and being alert for errant shots, Bridget put the necessary effort into maintaining a pleasant demeanor. She was, after all, very familiar with the proper etiquette from years of spectating on a golf course. Having thanked him, she moved back through the parking lot and across Richardson Ranch Road, coming to a halt at a safe distance from the field of play. Several girls were coming off the ninth green, and Bridget, recognizing two of them as being from Valencia, asked about Blaire.

"Her group's behind ours… and moving *really* slow. They should already be on the tee… but you know Blaire…"

The two then exchanged a quick look and started snickering in the way teenage girls do when wishing to convey that they possessed secret knowledge about someone's shortcomings.

"Is… something wrong?"

"Oh, she's in a towering funk – again! And this one's like totally epic!"

"Yeah… totally!"

They quickly moved on, exhibiting far less reticence in their continued enjoyment of having delivered bad news to the mother of their least favorite teammate. Bridget's eyes shifted down the fairway to the vacant ninth tee, dreading to find out what it was that her daughter had done this time. Her general feeling of anxiety had increased on hearing fresh words of disparagement about her child. She knew all too well that Blaire was a challenging person to live with, so it should come as no surprise that others shared in the same frustration. Blaire simply rubbed other kids the wrong way. Always had.

Over the years, Bridget had concocted far too many excuses in an effort to explain away her daughter's worst behaviors, so much so that compensation gradually supplanted confrontation as her approach to parenting. She was often hard on herself for not taking a firmer hand, though to do so had its consequences... not the least of which was exhaustion. For Bridget, it had become far easier to avoid the minefield of Blaire's displeasure altogether rather than tread right through. Still... it seemed obvious that the more allowances she made, the more Blaire took advantage. At least in the context of golf, what she saw in her daughter was easily chalked up to her being an intense competitor, playing full-out to win on every stroke. Bridget had therefore decided long ago that Blaire could behave whatever way she wanted on the golf course... for to do otherwise was to pointlessly step into the minefield.

Squinting off at the unoccupied ninth tee box, Bridget's thoughts flashed back to the previous year. Blaire had only been on the team for a month before the first serious issue arose regarding her attitude. Her golf coach called unexpectedly one afternoon to say that Blaire had thrown a fit after muffing a long iron shot out of a bunker during the team's very first competition. Then, to make matters worse, Blaire categorically refused to board the bus at the conclusion until she could master the shot on the course's practice range. The team had been forced to depart without her, requiring Bridget to drive all the way to Oxnard. Despite the obvious inconvenience this posed, what with her having to leave work early and slog her way through traffic, the more infuriating thing was that Blaire could not be made to apologize.

"Mother, you're the one who's always telling me to do my best... so how is it that you can't understand what that takes? I can *never* allow that to happen again."

"You know I want you to succeed, Sweetheart, but... you could have chosen to wait and practice that shot at home. Don't you think that would have been more... considerate?"

Bridget clearly recalled that Blaire had not answered the question. To her daughter, such interactions were games, and not responding was often her way of winning... which usually meant that Bridget bore the burden of losing. In the end, the whole thing became one more humiliating indictment against her performance as a mother. The coach made Blaire sit out of competition for a week, and though Bridget tacked on a restriction of her own, such things seldom made an impression on Blaire. The whole affair concluded in typical fashion, with Bridget ending up rewarding bad behavior by getting the girl her first cell phone… simply to avoid having to worry the next time such a thing happened.

Still looking down the ninth fairway, Bridget noticed a group of girls emerge from around a hedge and make their way to the women's tee box. Even from a distance, she was able to pick out Blaire based on her slender build and strawberry blond hair… not to mention the way she kept herself apart from the other members of her party. Bridget also spotted something of the displeasure in her by the way she seemed to be bouncing the head of her driver off the turf while walking.

That bad mood's because of me – I'm sure of it. She's got to be frustrated with me for not managing my schedule better. Well… I may not be on time, but I'm here. And I'll find some way of being an encouragement… regardless of what her scorecard says.

Bridget glanced down to the small rectangular card she had taken from the pro shop. This hole was a 305 yard par four from the ladies' tee – nothing too challenging for Blaire. From having followed her on countless rounds of golf, Bridget had come to know that her daughter's typical drive would land some fifty yards out on this hole, leaving an easy pitching wedge to the green. Still… she watched nervously as Blaire's tee shot went up and veered slightly off center, and then was relieved to see it end up in a good position on the fairway. The other three girls, noticeably taller and therefore likely upperclassmen at their schools, teed off without coming close to how far Blaire had hit her ball. While tracking the flight of the last drive, Bridget noticed that her daughter was already descending the elevated tee box into the fairway… alone.

Wait for the others, Blaire. At least try to act cordial.

With a degree of disappointment, she followed her daughter's progression down the fairway well ahead of the rest of the group. On reaching the shortest of the tee shots, Blaire moved off to the side as the other girls began conferring amongst themselves. Each in turn took their approach shot, leaving her daughter's as the last one. Blaire then extracted a club from her bag and jogged the thirty-some yards up to the green's fringe. Glancing out to the fairway, Bridget noticed that the other girls were leaning in close with crossed arms, so obviously put out with Blaire for holding up play. Being familiar enough with the game, Bridget knew that taking an exorbitant amount of time to line up a shot was one of those mind games some golfers resorted to in frustrating their opponents.

Sometimes I can't help feeling that everything in life is a mind game to her.

But she also knew that her daughter would do whatever it took to get the shot right, even if it meant that everyone else on the course had to wait. Whether in golf or any other venue of life, Blaire never compromised for the convenience of others.

After studying the approach, Blaire walked back to her ball. It was then that Bridget realized the spot where she stood was in the background of her daughter's line-of-sight to the target. Quickly shifting to one side, she immediately came to a halt as Blaire took up her stance. After a practice swing, Blaire pitched the ball into a loft, delivering it through a series of bounces to within six feet of the pin. Without a hint of emotion as to whether this was considered a good shot, Blaire circumvented the green and deposited her bag on the cart path to the clubhouse not far from where Bridget stood. Hoping it to be an encouragement, she ventured a very subdued four-fingered wave from waist level toward her daughter… but received back a frown accompanied with an ever-so slight wag of the head. There was no misinterpreting the look – Blaire was upset.

It can't be that she's displeased with that last shot, but maybe the round's not going so well. Or maybe those girls are treating her poorly. Or maybe… she's just mad at me.

Still thinking it through, she noticed Blaire mark her ball and take off to the opposite side of the green in a series of pranced strides, obviously doing her best not to tread upon the intended putting paths of the other players. It was, in Bridget's mind, a sour reminder that her daughter was more than capable of thinking about the concerns of others, yet often chose not to. But in this case, Blaire's deference was nothing more than respect for the game itself.

Pushing the unpleasant feeling aside, Bridget did her best to remain at ease as the other girls went about putting out in turns. Irrespective of how many times she had walked a golf course with Blaire, each new occasion made her insides tense up. The feeling, she knew, was in no way connected to a concern over her daughter's performance, which typically outstripped most golfers her age. It was something related to a wholly different sort of scorecard. Golf was Blaire's world and not hers… and no matter how hard she tried to fit in, Bridget could never get any closer than spectator.

As always, she told herself not to dwell on negative things, and instead to focus on how fortunate she was to be the mother of such an accomplished teenager. Blaire had real potential, and not just in the game. From all outside appearances, the girl had it all… looks, intelligence, charm and skill… even if what went on inside was a complete mystery.

Bridget had been staring absentmindedly down at her feet when it occurred to her that she should be enjoying Blaire. In looking up across the green, she found her daughter leaning casually on her putter while waiting her turn – a perfect still-life of youthful beauty and vigor. Quickly shifting her shoulder purse about, Bridget began rummaging within for the digital camera she bought herself as a Christmas present the previous year. Already, she had filled up three memory cards worth of photos of Blaire golfing. She was in the process of discretely bringing the viewfinder to her eye when she remembered – Blaire said no more pictures during tournaments. She dropped the camera back into the depths and re-shouldered the purse.

When it was her turn, Blaire took her time in examining the line to the cup from both directions. Eventually assuming her stance, she took a single practice stroke before putting. Her ball caught the back rim and fell in – a birdie on nine.

The other three girls, having already holed out, took off as soon as Blaire finished, moving as one toward the clubhouse in leaving Blaire to tend the pin. As they came near, Bridget gave them a warm smile and was on the verge of congratulating them as a group for finishing the hole well when she noticed that each girl lowered her head toward the cart path, in no way open to being spoken to. Turning back toward Blaire, who was coming off the green, Bridget quickly shoved the implication out of her mind.

"Blaire, that was fantastic."

"*Obviously*, Mother, seeing as I'm the one who just did it."

Whoa… she's really ticked!

"So… how's your round going so far?"

"On this course?! You've got to be kidding! It's ridiculously easy."

"But that's great for your chances in the tournament… isn't it?"

By way of an answer, Blaire gave a shrug of the shoulders… just before hefting up her golf bag. Deciding to change the subject, Bridget nodded ahead to the three girls who were already crossing the clubhouse parking lot on their way to the back nine.

"So how're the others doing?"

"What others?"

"The other girls in your foursome."

"How should I know? I couldn't care less about them… as long as they stay out of my way."

"Blaire… what's got you so upset? Anything I can do to help?"

"Not likely, Mother. I just so happen to be really pissed at Barksdale."

"Who's Barksdale?"

"The league coordinator for high school golf. You should meet him – just your type. Thinks way too much about giving girls a good experience rather than pushing them."

"Well… there's nothing wrong with that…"

In crossing the road that divided the golf course in two, Bridget imagined for a moment that a pleasant resignation had taken hold of her daughter's expression. Instead, what developed on the girl's face was her typical smile… rich with the false indulgence shown whenever they happened to be discussing the subject of golf.

"Mother… he's a complete jackass. He knows how good I am, and he still refused to group me on the Desert course. This one's got a lower rating and is over 400 yards shorter."

"So that's what's bothering you?"

"Not really. I'll play wherever they put me."

"I don't understand… You just said…"

"What I said was that he wouldn't let me take a cart out to inspect the course beforehand."

Ugh! She's doing that thing again where she expects me to read her mind… and if I point it out, she'll start an argument.

"Umm… Blaire… you do realize that you've played here plenty of times before."

Together, they stepped from the sun-softened asphalt of the parking lot onto the concrete sidewalk leading up to the clubhouse, with the noise of Blaire's golf spikes changing from something dull and muted to that sharp, clicking shrill of scraped metal. At such times, Bridget was convinced that her daughter dragged her feet a bit simply because she enjoyed the sound… or perhaps knew it irritated others.

"Mother, that's hardly the point. How's anyone supposed to play this game without studying every detail of the course beforehand?! Surely even *you* realize that pin placements change all the time…"

With the words came Blaire's all-too-common incredulous wagging of the head. In any other setting, Bridget might have called out the behavior, but now she let it slide.

Just get her through the tournament happy…

"I'm sure you'll do fine despite that. By the way, I'm really sorry for being late. I went to the wrong…"

"You were late? I hadn't noticed. Hey, I need to make sure Barksdale's got my scores right so far. Why don't you wait in the clubhouse and I'll see you when its over."

"But I thought I'd follow you on the back…"

As Blaire was already dashing around the clubhouse to where the organizer's booth sat, her appeal went completely unnoticed. Bridget remained in place for several minutes trying to decide what to do with herself. To be offended by Blaire was such a well-worn experience that she hardly noticed the feeling. In truth, she was irritated that all of her rushing about to get here had been deemed of such little consequence to Blaire. So much coaching had been invested into helping the girl see outside herself. Yet again, all that effort seemed to have been wasted. This frustration, though, was not the thing overwhelming her feelings. The thing taking hold deep inside was a heavy sadness… that her presence had never been considered a pleasure to her daughter.

She moved through the clubhouse and out its back to a balconied overlook of the practice green. Leaning on the railing, she stared down to the tenth tee where Blaire and her party were already in preparation for continuing the tournament. From there, she took several pictures as Blaire teed off, for like an ant tirelessly storing up small kernels of grain, Bridget still had much work to do. She had little more than two years left to amass enough memories of her daughter to sustain herself through what she feared would be a long, cold winter of her life.

She continued to watch as Blaire's foursome made its way out onto the course, their outlines eventually shrinking to mere dots amidst the landscaping. Blaire, she knew, would remain totally indifferent as to whether her mother stayed or left… especially since a school bus was there to return her home. Although part of Bridget felt compelled to remain to the end… if by chance to encourage, sympathize, congratulate, or maybe even celebrate… whatever might please Blaire… she nonetheless turned away and made for the parking lot, too tired to remain there fighting against the feeling of being unappreciated.

On the drive home, her eyes and reflexes were on the traffic, but her mind turned fully to the consideration of her own life. She could see no other purpose to her existence outside that of work and her daughter. She rose early each morning to make breakfast for two, take Blaire to school, and then head to her job in the city. Afterward, she would return home, maybe doing a bit of grocery shopping on the way, or… like today… rush off to share in one of Blaire's golfing activities. There had been nothing else since the divorce. In not too many years, her daughter would be off to college, and Bridget would find herself completely alone.

CHAPTER

2

BRIDGE IT

Third of five, Bridget was born into a lower middle-class family of Milwaukee. The Kwiatkowski children were second-generation Polish-Americans, and as such grew up within a tussle between old country traditions and Western ways of life. Her father had been one of those to disembark at Ellis Island with little in his pockets and his mind teeming with wild notions of the American dream.

Peter (Piotr) Kwiatkowski initially found employment in New York City as a longshoreman, but left for Wisconsin after a few years in order to pursue the opportunity of co-owning a business with a second cousin. The buy-in requirement had been fairly straightforward – he was to marry that relative's sister-in-law. After ten years of the partnership, the cousin moved from Milwaukee, leaving full ownership of the company... along with its struggle for profitability... to her father.

For most of her adult life, Bridget's recollections of her parents were largely that of detached entities contending with each other as much as with the unfortunate caricature imposed upon them because of their Eastern European descent. She knew that neither claimed the other as a friend, yet both seemed not to have had anyone particularly close to them outside the family.

For as long as she could remember, her father daily exhausted himself in trying to keep afloat a floundering plumbing business, completely unaware that the rest of his family had been set adrift. To him, raising children was *babska robota* – woman's work. He had a company to manage, which often was his excuse for avoiding the harsh prospect of an unpleasant wife. Bridget had never known him to be one who bravely faced his troubles at home. Instead, outside of making money by cleaning drains and connecting pipes, he had one overarching fascination in life – Hollywood. Though a mediocre plumber, he rightly prided himself as a true movie buff.

Her mother, owing to a multitude of health problems, also displayed little interest in parenting. Life, she regularly claimed, had betrayed her by having her sold to a man who loved his work more than his wife. While frequently professing herself to be unfairly burdened with the task of tending to five little ones on her own, it was not uncommon for Roksana Kwiatkowski to have done nothing all day other than sit around. By nature, she was a supremely petulant woman, at ease only when connected to her TV in the same way a terminally-ill patient became dependent on an IV for delivering painkiller… drop by drop… one episode at a time. Early on in life, Bridget came to understand that the frail front her mother put on nearly every day was mostly an affliction of mind and heart, and not of body.

More so than anyone else in the family, Bridget grew up aware of the symmetry in the make-up of the Kwiatkowski children. The oldest was a sister, then a brother, followed by Bridget, then a second brother, and lastly… the baby of the family… another sister. Stemming from his enthusiasm for the silver screen, her father chose his children's names from prominent movie stars of his era: Lauren (Bacall), Wayne (her father, not caring for the name John, tried unsuccessfully to get 'the Duke' to stick as a nickname), Brigitte (Bardot), Dean (Martin), and Natalie (Wood). How her own name eventually came to be spelled as it was remained a mystery. Perhaps it was simply that somewhere along she had decided that she did not care for being named after a movie star. Decades later, having experienced firsthand the good and bad of what LA had to offer the world, Bridget would settle into a sad acceptance that her father had spent his life completely deceived by Hollywood's depiction of American life.

Still, in odd ways, all five children could be said to have somewhat lived up to their father's hoped-for associations. By the time Bridget entered elementary school, her older siblings had already enjoyed the heyday of her parent's marriage… before her father's business turned truly sour, and before her mother took refuge in Tab soda, cigarettes and soap opera make-believe. Wayne and Lauren fully consumed the meager stock of their parents' attentions in being treated as lord and lady of the Kwiatkowski household… more-or-less as their namesakes had been regarded during the golden era of Hollywood. As teenagers, these two became largely independent entities disconnected from family life, both eventually moving out to establish lives of their own in other time zones.

Conceived when her parents were well into their forties, Natalie was born the very day Bridget turned nine. As the youngest, this girl grew up during the most turbulent years of the Kwiatkowski family, making her something of a tragic child… or as Bridget often thought, a child most-adept at exploiting tragedy to her own benefit. Her little sister did not drown, as had her namesake, but instead daily submerged the family beneath her ocean of neediness. Nothing could be made to work properly for Natalie. Every chore became the building of the pyramids, every homework assignment was a frontal assault on self-esteem, and every minor disagreement grew into a mountain range of opposition. In all these things and more, Bridget was there to help and console her younger sister, although considerable effort was also expended in offsetting her mother's indulgences. Somehow, everything seemed to click into place for Natalie during her teenage years… after their father had died, and only the girl and her mother were left. She eventually graduated from college and married well, but for reasons Bridget could not quite pinpoint, never seemed to relinquish a childhood resentment toward the sister who had been a second mother to her.

To Bridget, Dean had always been the enigma of the family. In trouble at school and in trouble on the street, he was… in Bridget's mind… a significant contributor to her father's untimely death from stroke. As his namesake had surprised fans by breaking off the partnership with Jerry Lewis in order to seek individual stardom, Dean broke all ties with his family the week after their father's funeral. At sixteen, he ran away from home to chase a rock-and-roll pipe dream. Yet unlike the star he was named after, Dean never amounted to much as a performer, being at best a backup guitarist for third-rate bands. Bridget had not heard from him in many years.

As for herself, she never found there to be much of a similarity to Brigitte Bardot. Unlike that famous French actress, who was glamorous, sophisticated and gushing over with sex-appeal, Bridget considered herself to be rather plain looking… which was fine with her since she most often preferred to go unnoticed. As the family finances had always been tight, she grew up sharing a room, dressing modestly in hand-me-downs, and putting just enough effort into her wavy auburn hair to keep it under control. Perhaps the one thing she came to admire about her namesake was the woman's support for animal rights… not that Bridget was all that concerned with how horses or cows got treated. She simply respected that the actress had given up a prominent career to become a staunch advocate for a cause she felt passionate about. Bridget, herself, was drawn to service organizations throughout her high school years. Having had the opportunity to participate in the Model UN was a particular delight, leading to many fantasies of one day becoming a peace emissary to the nations.

Unfortunately, her home life turned out to be a real-life distortion of those dreams. Due to her place in the birth order, as well as a quiet disposition, Bridget ended up being burdened with a disproportionate share of the household chores, which included many aspects of rearing her younger siblings. She took on these responsibilities out of an earnest desire to help her family, though she was not ignorant of the fact that her parents had willfully relegated their roles to her.

From her perspective, the real authority in the Kwiatkowski household… the higher power everyone yielded to… had always been the TV. On at five every morning irrespective of the day of the week, it ran continuously until midnight with a programming regiment that set the family's routine. Morning talk shows started her school day, and game shows greeted her arrival home. Control of the TV after school was a free-for-all not unlike an encapsulation of *The Lord of the Flies*… and as in that novel with the arrival of adults to the island, so it was with her father's appearance home from work that order restored anarchy. Considering himself the chief vassal of the tube, the news hour and beyond was his domain. Every meal was eaten with the set on, with him commanding the prime viewing spot at the table and all other seats filled in based on the family pecking order. He then would watch all night with zombie-like attentiveness right up until his bedtime. Their weekends started out with Saturday morning cartoon chaos, and then the TV transitioned into a shrine for whatever sport the season held dear. Though in her memory, the bizarre combination of *Lawrence Welk* and *Hee Haw* sometimes supplanted the games… except, of course, those of the Packers.

Despite her family's dedication to TV, Bridget felt that the most devout worship of all was rendered by her mother each weekday from morning to afternoon. Watching soap operas seemed the woman's only purpose in life. Throughout most of Bridget's childhood and teenage years, the Kwiatkowski children would come home from school to find their mother emotionally drained from her daily binge on the intrigues, scandals and heartbreaks aired that day. Household chores and preparations for the evening meal were seldom attended to. Instead, her mother would take to her room for a nap... or to the phone for an extensive review of the day's happenings with a fellow soap opera enthusiast. At such times... or whenever the children were left to fend for themselves... arguments arising or matters requiring an adult's attention would be handled by her mother in exactly the same approach. With a raspy voice brought about from chain-smoking the day away, the woman would commandingly call out one name, always strangely delivered twice in rapid-fire succession.

"Bridget! Bridget!"

By third grade, Bridget had become so adept at attending to her mother's call that the other children, both young and old, turned it into a tiresome, worn-out saying in their household. 'Bridge it, Bridget' was mockingly echoed toward the girl whenever she, as her mother's delegate, attempted to ply her meager peacekeeping skills upon her siblings. It was similarly repeated whenever she was dispatched to perform some service as her mother's private domestic. Bridget willingly endured this abuse in hopes of easing her mother's nerves... strained as they were from the dramas of daytime TV. Besides... no one else ever responded to the woman.

Bridget did not retain many memories from childhood that might be characterized as happy, although there were those that ended up being important in shaping her way of thinking. One of these was a rare occasion when her father took time away from his business to drive the family to the beach one summer Saturday. She could not say how old she was at the time... Natalie was still in diapers and Dean was but a small boy... nor could she recall which of Milwaukee's many beaches it had been. Maybe Bradford... or McKinley... or somewhere along South Shore. Those details were really unimportant. The outing was supposed to be time for them together as a family, but her older siblings disappeared promptly on arrival, somehow finding their way back home later in the evening.

She distinctly remembered having prepared the lunch herself that morning... because it never got eaten. Shortly after getting there, Dean spilt the picnic basket out of the back of the station wagon in his frantic search for beach toys. He got walloped right there in the parking lot... and she was severely scolded for having not packed the thing better. The worst occurred soon thereafter when Natalie started wailing because she got sand in her eyes. Both parents yelled at Bridget again, this time for not taking better care of her baby sister. Everything then somehow transitioned into a shouting match between her parents so savage that her mother insisted on keeping Natalie and Dean in the car with her as a punishment to her father… and then ran the battery down to near nothing in playing music on the radio.

As bad as all that was, the thing that stood out prominently in Bridget's memory about the trip was the determined way in which her father had dragged her by the hand out to the beach and commanded her to build sandcastles. Before leaving her there alone to read his newspaper in the shade, he made a point of telling her that the entire outing had been ruined. He never said it was because of her… though the way he scowled certainly made her feel that way.

She recalled that there were far too many sunbathers on the beach that day for her to continue crying for long. Thinking him serious about the sandcastles, and wanting to please him, Bridget got busy with bucket and shovel. It had been unusually hot that week… at least by Milwaukee standards. She remembered how difficult it had been preventing the gritty sand from drying out. She worked quickly, dribbling her structures with water from the lake, but was never successful in building anything noteworthy enough to risk calling her father over… though she never gave up trying. She repeatedly returned to completed sections with a sprinkle or a pat about the base with moist sand. For what seemed like hours, she did her utmost to keep everything held together, right up until it was time to leave. He never came to see what she had made. The car trip home was filled with her parents arguing over whose terrible idea it had been to go to the beach. Bridget remembered staring out her window, fighting off the tears.

As she moved into her teenage years, with her older siblings gone and her parents completely disengaged, Bridget progressively took on more of the day-to-day management of the household. She did the cooking and cleaning for everyone, and from the time she received her driver's license on, it was she who chauffeured, shopped and ran errands. Even after leaving for college, it was she who strove to keep the family connected. She sought, most unsuccessfully, to gather everyone together for the holidays, and only she commemorated birthdays and anniversaries. She never doubted whether this service to the family was anything other than appreciated. That is… not until she married without a single member of her family in attendance did it fully occur to her how fragmented her childhood had been. Sure, she was prepared for the sadness of not having a father to walk her down the aisle… for he had died years before… nor was the absence of her younger brother unexpected… simply because he could not be found. Yet in the weeks leading up to her wedding, Bridget endured a series of heartrending and humiliating disappointments as each of her remaining family members called to offer excuses for why they could not be present. The worst, by far, was her mother, who insisted that she was far too weak for travel.

Throughout the high school and college years, Bridget never gave much consideration to men simply because she never met one capable of diverting her attention from the one true love of her life – responsibility. In moving into the workplace, her perspective on her appearance gradually changed. She lost weight, began dressing smartly, and daily put extra effort into her hair and makeup. None of this was done in order to attract admirers. In taking a position right out of college with an international manufacturer of furniture in Minneapolis, she simply purposed to be as professional in appearance as she hoped to be in performance. Men began asking her out on dates, though her mind remained fixed on her career. After seven years of working hard, she had distinguished herself in being promoted to the role of regional sales manager.

She met Mitch O'Connor at a company cocktail party. From first impressions, she found him to be charming, an excellent conversationalist, and a quick wit. He seemed as equally enamored with her based on the number of times he found his way back to her during the course of the evening. At that time, he was working as a purchasing agent in the sales team she had recently become the supervisor of, which ensured that their paths would frequently cross. Yet he did not wait for them to run into each other at work – he asked her out before the party's end. They dated casually for several months, throughout which time she gradually became won over by his affection toward her, as well as a devotion to excellence in his career. They saw each other near on every day over the course of four months before he proposed, and were married a half year later.

Having wasted so many lonely nights in pondering over what had gone wrong in her marriage, Bridget eventually came to pinpoint with bitter confidence the first indication of trouble. About two years in, while they still lived in Minneapolis, Mitch began circulating his résumé without informing her. Only after he had accepted a job offer from a major West Coast import-export company did she discover that what he said was a business trip actually turned out to be an interview instead. Naturally, she was both hurt and offended that he chose to exclude her from a matter that so clearly impacted them as a couple. When she confronted him, he reacted as he should – with a sincere apology seasoned by many conciliatory words. So… she forgave him.

In looking back, what angered her most about the situation was how she had responded – in exactly the opposite manner to which she should have. She conceded to him not because it was the best thing for them as a couple, but because of a hidden fear that a domineering spirit must have arisen in her to account for why he had acted in a manner inconsistent with how a loving husband should. She had been making more money than him, with her position in the company having greater prestige. Perhaps she had unknowingly flaunted this. She therefore purposed at the time to put extra effort into showing herself willing to be the type of partner who went out of the way to honor the other's wishes. She quit her job, along with all aspirations of a career, and moved to Seattle with a focus on starting a family. Yet the unspoken thing that remained stuck in her mind was that he had never bothered to ask the recruiter whether there might have been a position for her as well.

When Blaire was born, Bridget had already put away all thoughts of working outside the home. This first child was a step in the direction of an unrealized dream – that of building a loving family. Bridget nonetheless entered motherhood conflicted. Her own mother had passed away after a long struggle with emphysema, with the anticipation of Blaire's birth preventing Bridget from attending the funeral in Milwaukee. There had been a hope in her heart that the presentation of a grandchild to her mother might… in some small way… dispel a bit of the hurt she experienced in growing up with such disinterested parents. In reality, she was fully aware that grandchildren produced by her older siblings had elicited no significant alteration in her mother's mindset. The bond between the woman and her TV remained strong right up until the end.

They were settled into a peaceful apartment complex on Bainbridge Island. Blaire was growing like a weed, Mitch was thriving in his job, and Bridget was ready to expand their family. It was then that a new position offering better pay and more opportunity for career advancement opened up for Mitch in the company's Los Angeles office.

"This is a defining moment for me, Bridget. Just think of it – I'll be at the corporate headquarters from now on. I'm telling you, that's where my abilities will be truly appreciated. So… umm… what say we wait a bit on our plans… at least until we get settled there. Then, I promise, we'll try for a second child."

She was happy for him… happy that he was given a pathway forward to fulfill his dreams. Still… things had been working out for them in Seattle, so why change? She kept that concern to herself, relying instead on Mitch's assurances that he had the family's best interests at heart.

They moved to Southern California when Blaire was not yet two, renting a two-bedroom apartment north of the city in the small community of Newhall. From what Bridget came to understand of Mitch's new responsibilities, which mostly involved management of the company's teak imports from cultivated forests in Central America, his work hours would be based on the business affairs of the field offices. Sometimes he rose early and sometimes he slept in, with many a night spent out entertaining clients. Always, she did her best to support him during what was clearly a critical time in his career… and because his sleep schedule was so sporadic and their apartment so small, she held in check her desire for a second child. Soon, he kept saying, a promotion would come his way, and then everything in life would finally settle down.

CHAPTER

3

LIVING IN THE CITY

There was a brief time in which Bridget would have called life in LA as sweet. Their move had gone smooth enough, and though their place was considerably smaller than their one in Seattle, they were happy. While Mitch's new job had its demands, their weekends were their own to explore the city's abundance in parks, beaches, outdoor markets and amusements ideal for a young family. With Blaire transitioning out of diapers, they began taking extended trips into the mountains, deserts and forests of Southern California. Having identified a few reliable babysitters allowed them to go out more as a couple, which brought back a newlywed feel to their marriage. Everything was special when they were together – even simple things like hanging around the apartment on a Sunday morning sipping coffee and pouring over the *LA Times*.

Bridget was equally excited about where Mitch was heading in his career. With little more than two years into his current position, he called home from work one day to announce that he had been made director over all of the company's Central American and Caribbean accounts. She was elated for him, and suggested right off that they go out as a couple that very evening to celebrate. She found a sitter, made reservations at his favorite Italian place, and then threw herself into getting gorgeous for their night out. They were seated in a secluded candle-lit table, ordered wine, and toasted to his success.

Somewhere between dinner and dessert, the way Mitch spoke about the future seemed to change. Maybe it was the wine taking hold in him, or that she, having settled into a silent warmth over how pleasant the evening was, had completely given over the conversation to him. He spoke little of them as a couple and mostly of himself. This promotion, he said, had been long overdue. It did not matter that the other account managers were more senior than him, as only he possessed the cleverness for helping the company succeed. For proof, they need look no further than how his own clients felt about him. They simply adored him… and why not, as all their accounts were prospering under his supervision. And management… they were simply gaga over his unique ability to bring in new contracts.

"Know what's really amazing, Bridget… I'm barely getting started! I've got so many incredible ideas for growing the company. Mark my words… this promotion is the first step toward my goal of reaching upper-management… and eventually… the very top!"

She listened attentively as he elaborated on plans for climbing the corporate ladder, but also searched her memory, trying to recall a time when they had actually discussed such lofty career aspirations. Sure, they had talked about the work itself, as well as his expectations for advancement, but never had she actually considered the heights to which he was intent on reaching.

"…and I fully expect to be given that corner office I was mentioning before… you know, the one facing out toward the ocean. Anything less would be an insult to my importance, don't you think? I'm telling you, things are finally starting to work out the way they should."

"I'm so proud of you, Mitch. You're doing such amazing things for the company. So… what do you think about moving forward with our plans?"

"Huh? What plans?"

"You know… for a second child."

"Oh, that. Well… we should probably wait a bit longer… you know… until I can get my new work schedule sorted out and get use to the job. Maybe in a year or so…"

They went home that night, paid the sitter, stood arm-in-arm together for a few moments over their slumbering child, and then retired to the privacy of their own room. Later… Bridget did not immediately fall asleep as Mitch had. Instead, she lay wide awake in bed thinking over the evening. The question as to whether she would continue to be a supportive wife never entered her thoughts. She would definitely make whatever sacrifices were needed to help him succeed in his career. That was what families did. Surely he felt the same way. After all, they were so likeminded… and had not that been the thing first attracting her to him? Still… it bothered her that she had not understood the full extent of his ambitions… or maybe she had not listened closely enough to what was truly on his heart.

Just before nodding off, Bridget came to the firm conclusion that the dinner celebration had been a success… despite her unease… owing to the frank nature of their conversation together. With more such candor, she would surely better understand his career aspirations… and he would come to embrace her desire for a second child.

Over the day following their evening out, Bridget replayed in her mind the things Mitch had predicted regarding his future. In no way did she begrudge him of those ambitions. Any wife would cherish the look of pride on her husband's face as he related how the CEO had singled him out as the company's most promising talent. What she did not quite know what to do with was the hunger he displayed for more. She tried to focus on concrete things. His promotion came with a sizeable pay raise that would allow them to finally secure the financing needed to purchase a small house. She should concentrate on doing research into the real estate market rather than giving consideration to words spoken over a glass of wine.

But he said there would be greater expectations on him to entertain clients. He's already out too many nights a week as it is…

That, in itself, had not really bothered her. It was the upbeat way in which he informed her of the fact… as if he was relishing the prospect of more time away from home.

No… it can't be that. He's crazy about us. He's just so excited about the challenges ahead of him.

That would be her, if given the opportunity. She would do everything she could to fulfill her responsibilities. After all, she had gladly given up a thriving career to take on the role of a stay-at-home mother… simply because family always came first.

He might be enjoying the prospect of a higher-visibility position in the company… maybe a bit too much… but he's earned it. Everything he's doing is to support us.

That very afternoon, Bridget loaded Blaire into the car and drove to her favorite outlet mall, then spent several hours in hunting for bargains in men's clothing stores so Mitch could start out as a company leader with a fresh look. She picked out a half dozen dress shirts, then added on a belt and a few ties to match. As a final gesture, simply because she knew he would be touched by it, she threw into her shopping cart a coffee mug embossed with the phrase 'The World's Greatest Dad.'

That evening when he came home from work, she excitedly laid out her purchases on their bed, talking through with him how she thought each might go with one of his existing suits. Then, over the subsequent days, she waited with anticipation for him to wear the first of these new shirts, going so far as to put one out as a suggestion for the next morning. After a week of him opting for things from his existing wardrobe, she gave up trying. The new clothes, like the coffee cup, went neglected on rack and shelf.

On the very next weekend, after coming home hours late from what he said was supposed to be a few quick errands, Bridget watched in silent amazement as he made multiple trips from their apartment complex's parking lot… each time with arms loaded down by shopping bags from the upscale men's boutiques of West Hollywood.

"What's all this, Mitch? I thought you were going to the hardware store."

"I was… but I got the idea from you. You're absolutely right – I definitely need a new look now that I'm on the executive track."

"But what about the things I already bought for you?"

He paused with a smile on his way out for another load.

"Oh… those'll be excellent as backups."

She was mulling over the phrase, trying not to allow it to creep beyond the context of clothing, when he reappeared at their apartment door lugging in a large cardboard box. The images and wording printed on the sides clearly displayed the contents.

"You bought golf clubs?"

"A golf bag too. Bringing that in next."

"But Mitch… you don't even know how to play."

"I've got to start sometime, don't I?! From now on, I'm going to be entertaining a whole new class of clients. The executives from our biggest Latin American suppliers… not to mention our Asian buyers… they all expect to be wined and dined during their visits to LA. But even more than that, Bridget, they come with expectations of being treated to championship-caliber golf – California-style. I really need to get serious about the game if I'm going to continue to impress upper management. You do want that… don't you?"

"Of course I do… but shouldn't you be focusing on…"

"I've already signed up to take lessons and started scouting out country clubs."

"Country clubs?! Mitch, what're you talking about?"

He paused with both hands on his hips, dipping his head forward in a slight wag… which always managed to make her feel stupid.

"You do realize that I'm trying to move into the upper echelon. So it's time that I made some changes to my lifestyle. Higher visibility in the company comes with higher expectations. I have an image to uphold. I thought you'd get that."

In actuality, everything in her mind was muddled in confusion. She was certain that nothing about golf ever came up in any of their conversations regarding his promotion… but why should that be a thing to bother her? Surely his desire to play was just one of those things men did to deal with stress. Everyone needed a distraction. Besides, the exercise would do him good. But joining a country club… that was a whole different matter. He definitely never mentioned that. Though she would certainly not vocalize it, she firmly held that such places were for the rich who had nothing better to do with their wealth than to lounge around all day discussing expensive cars and what private schools their children attended. That was not the way she had been brought up to think. And how could they possibly afford such a thing anyway? Surely he must realize that even his raise would not permit that.

She glanced up to find him in much the same posture as before… except with the slight puckering at his lips that suggested he sensed her thoughts.

"You're not giving this a rest, are you?"

"Mitch… we make important decisions together. That's what married couples do."

"I know that… but this really isn't a 'married couple' kind of decision. It's more of a… professional development thing."

"What's that supposed to mean?"

"Bridget… when a person gets to my level in management, they find that career decisions become… more complex. There are so many factors to be considered. What you don't understand is that club membership is crucial for building connections and improving my social standing… which just so happens to open up all kinds of new opportunities for me. In fact, I'd go so far as to say that being a member of a prestigious country club is critical toward making the next step up in the company. So you see, it's really not an option."

"That doesn't mean we couldn't have discussed it together."

"We're discussing it now."

"Only *after* you've decided on your own what you're going to do."

"Bridget… you're looking at this all wrong. This is actually a great opportunity for you too. You may even find it… enjoyable."

"What're you implying… that I don't know how to enjoy myself?! Because I've got interests in all kinds of…"

"Of course you do! I just meant… it'll be good for us as a family."

Over the next few months, as Mitch concentrated on learning how to play the game, Bridget was relieved that the subject of country club membership did not reappear in any of their conversations. Early on in his lessons, she endeavored to accompany him whenever he went to a driving range for practice… simply to make evident her support for him… but soon gave up the effort as keeping a four-year-old from being a distraction proved impossible.

A sizeable chunk of their weekends was soon dedicated to him golfing… or sitting in front of the TV watching tournaments. He had, at great expense and without including her, done more shopping to supplement his wardrobe with new golfing apparel. After joining a weekly men's scrambler at a nearby public course, every Sunday morning soon became Mitch's time with his new golfing buddies.

"Save the paper, Bridget, and we'll read it together when I get back in the afternoon."

They never did.

He began spending hours at clubhouse bars after his rounds and then, on coming home, spent even more time in meticulously cleaning his clubs and pouring over the morning's scorecard.

Mitch was playing twice a week for near on three months when the subject of country club membership came up once more… this time, in a way Bridget had not expected – in the aftermath of a very confusing phone call. As per the house-hunting approach they agreed upon, she was to do the initial screening of the market. She had been at this for over a week, meeting with various agents and keeping careful track of her inquiries on a notepad in order to brief Mitch on her findings. She had narrowed down the field to three that specialized in mid-to-lower-end housing for young couples, yet was still receiving follow-up calls from others.

"Hello?"

"This is Marty Eggleston from Royalty Properties. You must be Mrs. O'Connor."

"Yes. Thanks for returning my call. Mind holding it a minute while I find something to write with?"

She scrambled about for pen and paper, trying to recall when she had contacted this particular agent and what she might have already told him about their needs. He was not from one of her preferred agencies… though it would clearly not hurt to get another perspective on the market.

"Hi, I'm back. So… let me start out by telling you a little bit about…"

"No need, Mrs. O'Connor, no need. I'm calling to give you the good news – the owners have accepted your offer. Congratulations!"

"I'm sorry... what'd you say?"

"Just got off the phone with the other agent. Your check to cover the earnest money cleared this morning, so you and your husband now have first right of refusal. We've still got a tight window in which to work out the financing, so the three of us should sit down together as soon as possible to go over the numbers."

None of this was making any sense, so it had to be a simple mix-up on the part of an exceedingly busy person.

"Excuse me, but I think you might have us confused with some other couple. We've just started looking... I don't think we've even met yet."

"Not to worry... I'm sure we'll have a chance to get to know each other very soon... assuming you're feeling up to it?"

"Ahh... I feel fine... but what's that got to do with..."

"That's fantastic. Rest easy, Mrs. O'Connor... we've accomplished the most difficult step toward getting you into your dream home. Everything from here on out should go smoothly once... Hey... I'm sorry... I've got another call coming in. What's say you two sort out the when, and get back with me tonight, okay? Gotta go."

He hung up leaving her thinking it was the strangest phone call she had ever received. No matter how good that guy might be as a realtor, there was no way she was going to engage someone that disorganized. She put the phone call out of her mind for the remainder of the day, returning to it in the evening as they sat down for dinner.

"Mitch, you won't believe it, but I had the weirdest call from a real estate agent today. This guy got us completely confused with one of his other clients and wouldn't stop talking long enough for me to help him sort it out. He's probably too embarrassed to call back with an apology. Honestly, I felt really terrible for the guy. He's either new at this, or he's got too many things on his plate. Imagine getting mixed up over something as important as which client it was who put down earnest money. Somewhere out there there's a couple waiting to hear if... Hey, where're you going?"

"I need to make a quick call."

He abruptly jumped up from the table and hurried into the living room. Their apartment, being small, allowed phone conversations in one room to be easily overheard in another... but Blaire chose that very moment to fuss over her dinner. When he returned to the table, Bridget noticed that his mood had changed from tense to reassured.

"That was close. I thought for a minute you might have messed up the surprise."

"What're you talking about?"

"I put down earnest money yesterday on the perfect house. You're going to love it. Good thing I moved fast or we'd have missed out. I know for a fact that we beat out several other serious offers."

He sat across from her with his biggest smile, clearly expecting her to appreciate what he had done. She, however, was almost too numb for words.

"You… did this… without… discussing it… with me…"

"Like I said, I wanted it to be a surprise. I was planning on taking you over as soon as our offer got accepted. Want to head out right after dinner?"

"How much did you put down on this… surprise?"

"Well… the owner insisted on three percent. You'd be proud of me – I tried talking him down to two and a half… because the house isn't particularly large… but he wouldn't budge. Given its prime location… I can't blame him. Like I said, he's had lots of interest in it already."

"How much?"

"How much interest?"

"No – how much did you put down?"

"Forty seven… thousand."

She sat stunned as he went back to eating his dinner, at the same time making funny faces toward Blaire. She waited for something… anything… that might reveal this to be some kind of elaborate prank on his part. Nothing came.

"Mitch, how could you make a decision like this without including me. That's nearly everything we've saved up. Wait… if forty seven thousand is three percent, then… that's… that's over a million-and-half-dollar home. Mitch, we can't possibly afford that… and we'll never get a loan approved for it anyway… not based on your salary."

"Don't worry – I've got it all figured out. I've checked around… the job market's really strong right now, so you should easily be able to find something paying in the mid-…"

"Who said anything about me getting a job? Blaire's not even school age yet… and what about a second child?"

"Yeah… about that… I'm thinking… maybe we should wait a bit longer for…"

She could hear no more of him, and jumped up from the table before making a scene… though slamming the bedroom door behind her felt so good given how angry she was. Throwing herself down on the bed, she began to cry the kind of tears that came more from frustration than from hurt or anguish. He had done it again… excluded her from a major decision that impacted them as a family. He had thought so little of her… and so much of himself… that he could decide alone to throw down tens of thousands of their dollars.

I'm the one who put nearly all of that away before we were even married! I save and he spends.

She grabbed a pillow and began wringing it about in her hands, fully aware that it was his and that she was using it to vent her rage.

What kind of a man makes an offer on a house without consulting his wife?! I'll tell you – one who doesn't respect her! He's never cared about me. It's always been about him. Well… I'm not putting up with it anymore. And I shouldn't have to either. With everything I do for him, you'd think I'd deserve better than this!

She flung his pillow against the headboard, then sat motionless on the edge of the bed replaying the exchange in her mind.

You handled that all wrong, Bridget. You didn't say nearly enough about how he makes you feel. He's the one at fault. You should have stayed at that table and made him break down. You should have laid it all out… how he's always saying 'we' but never really meaning it.

All of a sudden, she tensed up at the murmur of voices beyond the door. Mitch and Blaire were moving down their apartment's short hallway… though the sound of them dissipated as quickly as it had arisen.

What in the world is he thinking? There's no way I ever gave the impression I wanted to go back to work. I want a big family – he knows that. I've said it enough times. I can't stand the thought of going back to work… but what can I do about it? I've got no choice now that he's gone and sunk our savings into a house… a house I've never even set eyes on. I should ask for the check back… say I never agreed to it… I should make him go and beg for it…

For a moment, she strained in listening for anything from within the apartment. She heard only noises from without – the stereo next door spewing out rap music, someone walking about in the unit above, and the rise and fall of a passing siren. Nothing from within.

Who am I kidding… the owner's probably already spent the money. We're stuck. And there's no way a bank's going to grant us a loan that large based on his salary alone. If I refuse to get a job, then we lose all that money. I've got no choice. He knew this. He knew I'd do anything for our family.

The anger resurged within her, except this time she did not pick up a pillow or seek any other form of outlet. She sat powerless on the edge of the bed, waiting for wisdom she knew would never come.

This is all your fault, Bridget… for not standing up to him earlier… for not confronting him with his… selfishness.

A soft tap came to the door, and she was surprisingly thankful for its source simply because it seemed to confirm the very thing she was feeling.

"Bridget… Sweetheart… can I come in? Sugar… you know we need to talk this through."

It was only him, coming to cast his sickly sweet spell of persuasion on her. She could resist that… as well as his meaningless use of pet names.

"Go away, Mitch. I'm in no mood to listen to you."

Tomorrow, she would start looking for work, but tonight she would not give in to him. It would take a whole lot more than…

"Mommy… let me in. Daddy says he's real sorry"

Great! Just like him to drag Blaire into this!

"Bridget, dear, you're upsetting our daughter. Please open up so we can discuss this like…"

She popped up from the bed and made the two steps it took to reach the handle with the full intent of pulling Blaire in and closing him out. Instead, she froze on opening the door. There was Blaire in her cutest set of pajamas – the ones with little gold and purple flowers all over them. Aware that Mitch stood by smiling at the rare accomplishment of having gotten his own daughter ready for bed, Bridget refused to meet his eye, staring down instead at her beautiful child. She knew in an instant that she would do whatever it took to protect her daughter's future. She would give up being a stay-at-home mother and throw herself into a hunt for work… all for this precious little girl.

Over the next few days, Bridget polished up her résumé, then began circulating it to area recruiters and in response to placements in the paper. Within a week, she had received several calls of inquiry… which only went partway in offsetting how horrible Mitch had made her feel. Despite his many requests, she repeatedly declined to be shown 'his house'… as she had already begun to think of it… simply because she was still too angry with him to judge fairly the place he single-handedly chose as their first house together. In fact, she refused to hear anything from him about this place. Yet on the following weekend… one in which Mitch had purposefully forgone all golf activities as his meager form of an olive branch… she gave in to the reality of eventually needing to see the house. Come Sunday evening, he made a call to his realtor, and then drove them on what felt like a most circuitous route through several residential neighborhoods. The house, located on a wide cul-de-sac, turned out to be a rather plain-looking split-level structure with a two-car garage facing the street. Nothing particularly special. Waiting for them in its driveway was likely the man she spoke with over the phone. He seemed so much like any other polyester-cladded salesman that the thought of meeting him came and went between glances at the house. Her mind, however, was on what she needed to know before getting out of the car. Mitch was undoing his seat belt when she reached over to tap his elbow.

"You're in charge of Blaire, got it?"

"Sure."

"Before we go in, I want to know – why this particular house?"

"You'll see… I don't want to spoil the surprise for you."

He then briskly popped out of the car, acknowledging the realtor while unbuckling Blaire from her car seat. The realtor, in turn, greeted her warmly, again asking if she was feeling better… right before launching into a general description of this four-bedroom, two-and-a-half-bath house as they moved together up the short walk. He paused for a moment while fumbling with the lock-box on the front door, then moved aside for her to enter first. A wide threshold opened up onto a sunken living area, the rear wall of which was almost entirely glass. It took her less than a half dozen steps in before she understood exactly why Mitch had selected this house. She stood there staring out the back windows without the slightest ability to generate words worthy of expressing how betrayed and undervalued she suddenly felt.

"What do you think, Bridget? Nothing beats a view of a golf course! And not just any golf course – that's the Piper Mountain Country Club… which I'm sure you realize is one of the most prestigious ones in the area. This backyard looks down onto the 13th tee box. Imagine, one day we'll be able to afford membership… and then I can just walk right out onto the course anytime I want!"

She was in complete dismay… which he clearly mistook as the same kind of wonder he was expressing. She somehow found herself being led through a set of sliding glass doors and across a tiled patio to the back edge of a narrow yard… all the while as he chattered on about how great this house would be for entertaining and what an important statement it would make about him as a junior executive. She kept her mouth shut, as the realtor was tagging along. Mitch went on and on about how he had done research and studied all the options, finally deciding that this house, located on this golf course, offered the best real estate value to them as a family. Nothing else seemed to matter to him. Not the layout of the kitchen… or the size of the bedrooms… or the neighborhood and its schools. Mitch had gone for and gotten what was important to him.

She offered very little in the way of questions for the realtor, feeling that nothing she might ask could make things any better. She was stuck with this house. In the whole drive back to the apartment, Mitch peppered her with all sorts of comments about his dream home, and to each she responded with the fewest words possible, trying to make it so very clear how upset she was with him. He understood none of it, mistakenly ascribing her silence to a concern over the financing.

"You worry too much, Bridget. Relax! I already assured the agent that with you working, we'll be just fine."

"Really?! That's surprising, Mitch… seeing as when you made the offer you told him I was too sick to see the house."

At least that shut him up for the remainder of the trip home.

Blaire went into daycare, and Bridget went back to work. She took a position as a regional sales manager for a national electronics chain. The job turned out to be relatively straightforward – charting projections and issuing weekly reports to the corporate offices on the East Coast. As her new workplace was not too far away, she was able to pick up Blaire and get back home with time to prepare dinner.

For the first few months, coincident with them getting settled into the new house, everything seemed to be working out. Her boss was happy with her performance, corporate was happy with her reports, and the bank was happy that the O'Connors were making their mortgage payments.

Mitch was happy too… happy with his rising status at work, and happy with his life of golf. The very day after they moved into the new house, he proudly announced to her that he had signed the family up for a trial membership at the Piper Mountain Country Club. He then warmly asserted that for the next six months they could enjoy all the benefits of a country club lifestyle without actually having to join. Sure, they would be responsible for monthly dues, but the amount for newcomers was a fraction of what actual members paid. He boasted that he could now play golf anytime he wanted, Blaire could take swim lessons at the club pool… and she could finally make some friends. He kept reassuring her that there was no obligation… they could just walk away after the six months were up. She fully suspected otherwise. When that time came, Mitch took out a loan to cover the forty thousand dollar buy-in fee for club membership. Perhaps he had misled her, or perhaps she had been confused, for she fully thought this to be an equity club… in which case the membership fee could be resold whenever they decided to leave. It was not until years later that she learned otherwise.

The jump in monthly dues itself nearly brought Bridget to her breaking point. She had been looking into her company's options for maternity leave, but now felt it far too risky to take any length of a furlough. Besides, her corporate headquarters had instituted a new 'face-time' policy requiring staff in her position to touch base each month with the store managers located in their territories. Her boss made it clear how badly he needed her to take on this new responsibility along with her existing ones. And since he threw in a sizeable pay raise as an incentive, Bridget began traipsing about the freeways of Southern California three times a week in order to personally visit the eighteen different stores from which she gleaned sales data. It meant longer work days, much of which was spent in her car.

The frustration of not being on hand during Blaire's year as a kindergartner gnawed away at her. Her daughter went from before-school daycare to after-school daycare… all without Bridget being there on a consistent basis. Her feelings of guilt only intensified as Blaire entered first grade. There were so few opportunities for meeting teachers or seeing firsthand in the classroom those things Blaire was learning. Another year went by, and it seemed as a lifetime. Blaire moved into second grade, and the family only occasionally ate sit-down dinners together owing to the difficulty of accommodating their different work schedules… and the unfortunate reality that she often came home too tired to cook. The hours she spent on the freeway, coupled with a steady diet of fast food, gradually worsened both her attitude and her figure.

She still did her best to stay connected to Blaire's schooling by doing the little things… like bringing cupcakes on Blaire's birthday… or volunteering for the PTA… or helping out with weekend fundraisers. She nightly sat with Blaire as the girl did homework, and diligently kept fresh the refrigerator door's displays of artwork, class assignments, and school announcements. Too often, she found that magnets reserved for Blaire were instead being called upon to hold up examples of Mitch's golf accomplishments, as well as notifications of mixers, tournaments, and club meetings. She moved these around to the side… or took them off altogether… yet more golf things always showed up. The refrigerator door soon became for her a passive battleground full of hidden resentment toward the man who seemed to love a game more than he did his wife or daughter.

To her, his energy always seemed to be focused outside the home… on his work or play… and never on family life. He had bought fully into a country club lifestyle consumed with rounds of golf, social functions, and committee meetings. The more time he spent there, the more his thinking changed.

Perception seemed more important to him than substance, with envy, jealousy and pride all too often becoming the lenses through which he viewed his neighbors, co-workers and fellow club members. A culture of debt had also crept in, frequently displayed in his eagerness to enjoy today's pleasures while deferring payment until tomorrow. She tried gentle persuasion, caution, and even firm insistence, yet large credit card charges from sporting goods outlets and various designer clothing stores continued to appear on their monthly statements. Always, he had the same excuse – that golf was an investment in his career, and to do it right, he needed the latest and greatest in the way of everything. Besides, he was the one making the most money so he felt he had the right to choose how it was spent.

She once overheard him at a dinner party telling a few of his golfing buddies about the four 'Cs' in a man's life: career, car, club and clothes. She could not refrain from interrupting in what she hoped would come across as a lighthearted tone to pose a question. Surely there were more important things to consider? The men all laughed, and Mitch quickly rationalized away the moment by saying it was just guy-talk.

"Besides, Bridget, it's not like 'children' fits in phonetically... and there's really no 'C' word for wife."

She was on the verge of offering 'companion' as a possibility when the men quickly changed the subject to golf. One of them made a point of telling her how fortunate she was to have Mitch for a husband, as he routinely won the most money during their weekly scramblers.

"I... didn't know you bet on those things."

Mitch waved it off as nothing more than clean fun, but the sour looks on those standing around told her that the stakes were much higher. She waited until they were in the car on the way home before asking how much he typically wagered. He answered only indirectly with what he must have thought was more reassuring.

"Bridget, you need not worry... I seldom lose. It's all part of my system. I keep my handicap high with Saturday play, and Sunday's golf comes home to pay!"

She had no idea what that meant, except that it sounded less than honest.

It was not the first instance since joining the country club that she felt distant from his way of thinking. The more time he spent there, the more his regard for her seemed to slip away. She tried to rationalize it by telling herself that he endured much stress as a corporate executive in the extremely competitive business of shipping. He rose early on most days and spent many an evening out appeasing some disgruntled client. Yet even on those nights when he was home, there was little in the way of intimacy from him. She could endure that knowing that he loved his family. At least that was what she was hoping… though she could not shake the fear that things were teetering in the wrong direction.

She hated it… an unresolved root of bitterness that kept popping up in her over how things were turning out. Year after year, she put off her dream of having a big family while persisting in telling herself that such a sacrifice was the most noble thing one could do. The voice in her heart always proclaimed otherwise. Soon, the palm trees lining the long approach into their country club, as well as those scattered throughout their neighborhood, became a raggedy symbol of what she was going through. They never changed colors, never dropped elegantly-shaped leaves, and never brought forth buds as a sign of new hope in spring. She despised them for the false sense of tropical ease they gave off. If only it would snow… or even rain hard for a week… then golf would be forced to yield some small portion of the calendar. But the Southern California sun always seemed to shine… and the game would not be displaced. This, she could almost bear, but having to languish upon the freeway while Mitch enjoyed his country club lifestyle bit at her. Her life was being wasted away for his enjoyment… more so lately since he had rearranged his work schedule so he could go in early and be home before Blaire arrived back from school. That should be a mother's privilege. She should be the one there when her daughter stepped off the bus so they could spend quality time together. Mitch was now getting her to himself all afternoon… even taking the girl out on the course with him. But Bridget… once home in the evening… was saddled with the rather unpleasant tasks of contending with Blaire over unfinished homework and making her get ready for bed.

Bridget was not of a mind to dwell on difficult circumstances without taking steps to make things better. She would fix this problem of them living a disjointed family life, and the first step would be dinner. She had it all planned out – the timing, the menu and even a fun family game the three of them could enjoy over dessert. Once Mitch saw how special this time could be, he would surely make it a priority for the future.

She chose the day, made sure there were no conflicts with him, and then turned the details over and over in her mind, making sure everything was perfect. After a quick stop at the store for fresh ingredients, she arrived home from work to find the house empty. Only mildly concerned, as she made it clear to Mitch when he and Blaire should be back from the course, she got to work cooking. The table was set and the meal was soon to be done. Everything was put on simmer as she took to the phone. No one at the clubhouse or pro shop had seen Mitch… which was not all that surprising for a golf course where so many members came and went. She waited fifteen more minutes and tried again… and then again. Nothing.

She made a small plate for herself and went to sit on the back porch, periodically venturing to the edge of their yard in order to peer down on the course. After nibbling away at her special meal, she left their yard and moved down to the 13th tee box. The sun had already set, casting the course into a blend of grays. It was then that she spotted them… two shadowy outlines hovering about a faint glow on the 13th green, with their voices of banter and challenge carrying up to where she stood. She could just make out that a lit candle was in the cup, and they were attempting to 'putt it out.' As she continued to watch and listen, the small light flickered for a moment before being extinguished, followed immediately by both father and daughter erupting into cheers.

"Hey, you two! Come home! You've missed dinner!"

In shouting, she tried to keep her tone calm and cheery, for surely some of their neighbors might overhear. The two waved back and then ascended the slope toward her walking arm-in-arm. What mother would not want such a healthy father-daughter relationship? Surely it was worth the price she was paying, She should be thankful, but instead it saddened her. Their pleasure came at her expense.

As they had eaten pizza at the clubhouse snack bar, she went about putting away the food she prepared, as well as the anger she had at them for forgetting about her special dinner. Everything she ever wanted out of life was to be the mother she never had, in a loving marriage she had never seen lived out, and part of a family connected by mutual respect and care. The pieces were there, but no matter how hard she tried, they could not be made to fit together.

Blaire was in second grade when the girl took up the game in earnest. From then on, Bridget's life became irrevocably immersed within the world of golf.

CHAPTER

4

OUR LITTLE GIRL

As with many first-time parents, Bridget invested considerable effort into recording on film the precious moments of Blaire's infancy – the first solid food, the first tooth, the first steps, the first bubble bath, her first Christmas, and birthday number one... along with all those to follow. Bridget faithfully kept up the effort as her child grew, photographing her playing at the beach, covered head-to-toe in flour as they baked cookies, riding a merry-go-round, holding a sparkler in the Fourth of July twilight, and trick-or-treating as a little princess. Such moments Bridget lovingly sorted, captioned, and displayed chronologically in album after album. Blaire sitting astride a pony, Blaire in her high chair, and Blaire upon her 'big girl potty.' Bridget was there with her camera for the first day of each school year... and the last as well. From kindergarten all the way through elementary school, she diligently sought to preserve every achievement and every milestone.

Because she fully expected her albums to be appreciated throughout the years to come... maybe even for generations... Bridget chose the sturdiest of binders capable of withstanding whatever stress time might beset upon them. These, she covered with fabrics of her own choosing for that personal touch. Before mounting any photo beneath a page's protective laminate film, she added a short note referencing the date and setting, often tacking on a witty caption regarding the significance of a particular entry.

She took much pride in these, regularly returning to the completed editions to enjoy the special memories of family. As the frequency with which she revisited the albums seemed to increase as Blaire grew older, Bridget counseled herself not to think anything amiss in the habit. Only good could come from reminding herself of the joy she had in starting a family. Besides, keeping her memory fresh as to how the older ones were fashioned helped her maintain a consistent style across the years.

Hidden deep within, she maintained a darker, more illusive motivation behind her photography. These albums also served as a secret validation that *her* family would not end up being the failure her parents were responsible for. At those times when she struggled to connect with her daughter, Bridget submersed herself in the girl's baby pictures. Or when her husband's detached tendencies threatened to assail her with associations of her own father's disconnected nature, she would search through the albums for anything suggestive of togetherness… and then latch onto those photos as a talisman against her fears. She would never admit to overindulging in the past at the expense of the present. Considering such a thing only tarnished the loving sacrifice she was making on behalf of Mitch and Blaire… and hopefully all her future children. If anything, she viewed the time spent in reminiscing as a fit strategy for dealing with the occasional concern that her efforts might not be yielding what she hoped for.

As the years went by, she found it more and more difficult to convince either Mitch or Blaire to thumb through an album with her. Blaire had been willing enough as a small child, but not of late… not since Mitch introduced her to the game of golf. That had been years ago, when Blaire was but seven. Now, at ten, the girl shrugged her shoulders in boredom at what should be considered special moments in her life. More and more, Bridget's photographs were of Blaire playing golf… as were the things posted on the refrigerator. In fact, nothing in the way of mother-daughter time seemed to divert Blaire's interest away from the game… not shopping, not museums or concerts, and certainly not the zoo. These days, Blaire never spoke about school, friends, or any interest other than golf.

Bridget was convinced that things were bound to improve as Blaire grew older. After all, her child was still in elementary school… far too young to remain preoccupied with one thing for very long. Soon, with a move into middle school, Blaire would get exposure to new things and develop more meaningful interests. The girl was clearly intelligent enough – every single one of her grade school teachers made a point of saying so. Blaire was amazingly vivacious, and had a gift for amusing people with her smile, a clever word or a cute antic. Everywhere Bridget took her, Blaire was admired.

Yet middle school, when it finally came, brought no change in Blaire. She remained just as fixated on golf… maybe even more so. Bridget began to feel that what she previously thought to be wonderful father-daughter time was actually something altogether different. Mitch had the girl out on the golf course nearly every weekend… and most days after school. Blaire was now speaking openly about her personal knowledge of club officers and employees… and with a familiarity that was highly inappropriate for a child. All that exposure to a country club lifestyle was peaking her curiosity about the ways of the adult world. But Mitch refused to see any of it. He bragged on and on about how the club president thought Blaire was so cute… and how the course pro really enjoyed teaching her… and how his daughter had bested a couple of his golfing buddies in stroke play on the putting green.

Whatever that's suppose to mean…

As far as Bridget was concerned, grown men had no business hanging around a twelve year old girl… no matter how good she was at golf. It was all impossibly wrong… she was losing her daughter to the same thing she had lost her husband – to a game.

For Blaire, there came a day when a notion took hold in her thinking of a difference between herself and others her age. It was not just that so many things came naturally to her, or that the kids she knew were lacking… which they obviously were. She simply came to see herself as being the only one capable of possessing the full package – looks, personality, athleticism and smarts… all in unequaled measures. She was unique.

With this realization also came a freedom she doubted anyone else possessed. She found herself to be completely devoid of those weaknesses that so easily encumbered others, both young and old. Unlike girls her age, she never got worked up emotionally and never lost control. Out on the course, she could go toe-to-toe with the boys, and what she lacked in strength was more than made up for with cleverness. She was also not in the least bit intimidated by older golfers, having already become familiar with their ways. Her father had shown her the game within the game, teaching her how it must be played on the inside in order to become the best on the outside. He said it was of the utmost importance that she not be affected by anything or anyone.

"If you can't be touched, then you can't be beaten."

His advice went deeper into her thinking than he could ever have imagined. She would live this way: be nimble, coordinated and steady on the outside, but cold as steel on the inside. She had already begun experimenting with how she could use a blank stare from her steel gray eyes to bore holes into the minds of other golfers… while at the same time displaying a graceful demeanor to offset and confuse. A sweet word here, a little shoulder shrug there, and a hand placed gently upon someone's back… all that and more could help her gain an advantage.

Her first tournament… at ten… clinched it for her. She was a golfer. More than a golfer… she had real potential for greatness. Although she had not played especially well… not to her standards or her father's… the outcome of that match was not the revealing factor. She found that she was totally driven to win, and willing to do whatever it took. It was now up to her parents to ensure that her skills were fully developed. Her father was the best for helping her continue in the culture of the country club and regular lessons with the course pro, whereas her mother would surely drive her to every regional golf tournament available to juniors.

As she moved from childhood into her preteens, it became very evident to Blaire that a distinctive beauty was on her horizon. Hers would not be the false elegance of so many country club women… or the sickly-sweet innocence of the iconic girl next door… and definitely not the fabled airheaded attractiveness of the Southern California bleach blonde. Blaire would attain something entirely different. She would master a precocious cuteness, with every mannerism delivered for the achievement of an adorability that could… if she so desired… be easily transformed into something even more irresistible. Blaire knew she would grow into all the fullness of womanhood… it was only a matter of time. After all, development-wise, she was already so very far ahead of girls her age.

On their country club's annual President's Night, when awards were conferred for exemplary achievements and service, Blaire was designated by the members-at-large as the Most Promising Junior Golfer. She surpassed kids older than her, both boy and girl, by dominating four consecutive tournaments. At the age of twelve, she stood on stage before hundreds to receive recognition. The club president placed a medal about her neck and on her head a visor bearing the golden emblem of the club's seal, both of which were only conferred upon members who had distinguished themselves above all others in the game.

Later that night, after the ceremony concluded and all but a remnant had dissolved into the parking lot, Blaire was led by her father to the club's Hall of Fame, situated in a room off the main entrance. There, he showed her the glass cabinet where her name would be included with those of past winners. Kneeling beside her and placing both hands on her shoulders, he then told her how special she was in being deemed the most gifted young golfer to have come through the club. This would be the first of numerous awards coming her way if she but fully applied herself to the game. He then meandered off to chat with a board member, likely leaving her there with an expectation that the displays would continue to inspire where he had left off.

But Blaire was not in the least bit captivated by the polished chrome of trophy or plaque, nor was she impressed by long lists of names, framed photographs, or signed memorabilia. Those things collectively defined the club's legacy, but meant nothing to her. Her eyes focused on a single thing – the reflection of a young girl upon a glass surface. Though its form was darkened by the tricks of refraction, the image was nonetheless faithful to its owner, as each bore a ribboned medal about the neck and a visor on the head.

It happened all of a sudden. One moment she was enjoying how she looked with the new honors, and in the next… the reflection became real. Not just real – more alive than anyone she knew. More alive than the father who had just knelt beside her or the mother who had clapped more enthusiastically than anyone else at the ceremony.

Blaire had hardly settled into this discovery when the girl in the glass began to scan her, scrutinizing the visor, the ribbon, and the form of her tangible self. She knew instantly what the reflection was doing – appraising the worthiness of her, as the originator, to offer herself as a blueprint for this glassy self. The illusion became so strong that she felt riveted to the spot on the floor where she stood, spellbound in anticipation of the specter's assessment.

That moment came when their eyes finally locked on each other. As a knowing smile slowly crept over the face before her, starting at the corners of the mouth and eventually spreading all over, she knew the reflection had approved. More than approved. The smile gave the grade that foretold her fortune. This remarkable, one-of-a-kind girl possessed the makings of greatness. And as if to promise it as so, the glass offered her a slight tip of the head. Whatever the future held, it would be of their own making.

Then, both sets of eyes… those within the glass and those benefited by its wisdom… ventured off together in the direction of the lobby where the parents and a few prominent members of the club had collected to relish one final moment of the evening's splendor. The smiles on both girls deepened once more. None of those people, the parents included, could possibly grasp the fullness of all that Blaire had discovered.

CHAPTER

5

THE WAY I THINK

Ants on a sidewalk.

I don't mind them being there. I can even get down at their level to take a look... if I feel like it. In some ways, they're kind of fun to mess with. I can frustrate them by putting things in their way... or tease them with something sweet.

Mostly I like making them do tricks for me... like when they writhe about all crazy-like after I poke them with a stick... or how they thrash around frantically when I drop them in a puddle... until they go still. I can even get them so riled up that they'll fight with each other.

It's so easy to torment ants... which makes them not so interesting after all. Much too stupid and easily confused. Just crawling about aimlessly on my sidewalk. I can step on them anytime I want... though sometimes that's more trouble than it's worth.

Just boring little ants.

But I'm not going to bother looking out for them either. It's not my problem if they get in my way. They're on my sidewalk.

People are ants.

It's on them to get out of my way. Sometimes I want to stomp on those miserably ugly things. So annoying and so pathetic. Guess that's why they have to depend on each other... can't survive on their own... just like ants.

Not me. I don't need anybody.

You know... people are so predictable. Stoke their ego or wound their pride, and they act exactly the way I expect them to. Not one has it in their puny little brains to figure me out.

I exist... but they... I can't say that they do. Not really. I mean... I'm pretty sure they feel pain... like a tortured ant does... but nothing more than that. They're... hollow. There's nothing to them.

Just props on my stage... there for me to arrange, rearrange or discard... whatever suits me. After all, I'm the only one who brings life to them... because without me, they're nothing. I could say they're lucky to be part of my play, but that's giving them more credit than they deserve. Luck's something for only me.

Truth is... they're just things.

Hey... what's this thing they keep calling 'truth' .. as if such a thing was really a thing?! I mean... it's my stage. I can say whatever line I want, and it's always perfectly delivered to talk my way in or out of anything. It's so obvious – truth is nothing more than the making or unmaking of whatever I choose. They just don't get it. It's me who brings life to the words that matter... so there's no such thing as a lie from me on my stage. I know that's true... ha, ha... because with my line they react exactly the way I expect them to. It's so easy to get them to do whatever I want.

Well... not always easy or it wouldn't be fun.

Still... there's nothing like seeing them go crazy over something they know to be so obviously untrue. They end up spending so much effort correcting me... or persuading me... or second-guessing themselves. It's so funny. But in the end... they've got no voice because it's my stage and I hold the script... so they have to accept whatever I say.

I like the way I think.

And why should I be concerned about hurting someone's 'feelings'?! If I snap a twig in two, should I feel sorry for it?! It's just a thing. And why should I apologize to something so fragile? And what's that mean anyway? If I said it, or did it, then that's the way I wanted it to be.

Besides... apologies are for losers. I happen to know exactly how to get around anything I've done. I just smile... give a little tilt of my head... and they think it's so charming. I don't even have to put much effort into it. Act shy and they come gushing all over me.

Totally disgusting.

Actually... I can say 'sorry'... when it fits in with the play on my stage. It's so easy to get them to accept whatever I say... even though it gets really annoying. 'Good morning,' 'good night,' 'please,' and 'thank you' – those things mean nothing. Those are just sidewalk words meant for ants to fool themselves into thinking they exist.

So gullible.

But the thing I absolutely can't stand is when they harp on me about 'responsibility.' I get so tired of hearing them spout out that word. It makes no sense. Things don't own me! Chores don't own me! They get all butthurt when I don't jump up at their feeble commands... or think I'm somehow being precious when what I do matches what they say.

I don't care what they think... if they can think at all.

If there's any responsibility, it's them to me. All that really matters... all that anyone's responsible to... is me. After all, it's my sidewalk and my stage. When're they ever going to figure that out?!

But they're just ants, clueless and boring... and so very slow at getting around to what's really important – whatever I want.

Yeah, sure... there are things I don't have yet. I'm only twelve and a half. I'm still growing and still have so much to learn. I don't even know how to drive a car yet. Bet I could... if I wanted to. But I'll be patient and follow their ant-rules... for now.

But why even bother with rules?! Those are just for normal people to help them get through their miserable lives. I get so tired of them going on and on about how happy they are to show me the right way to do things. I don't need their help. I don't need anything from anybody. I'm all I need now and forever. Besides, they're not here to help me... they're here to do what I say.

'Plan for the future.' Puhhh-leeease! That's just more ant-talk. The future's going to have to plan for me, 'cause I'll have whatever I want out of it – fancy clothes, fast cars, a huge mansion, and lots and lots of money. And I know exactly how to get those things – I just take them! Because anything I choose to take is already mine.

So why should I be concerned about consequences?! What an idiotic waste of time! I don't have to ask 'what if' because I'm not some pathetic little ant who's always making mistakes. Besides... no one can outsmart me!

Oh my god, how can they be so slow and stupid?! Mom and Dad... and all those useless teachers... they actually believe there's things I should learn from them. None of them get it – the whole world's my sidewalk and my stage, and I'll have whatever I want out of it... including all those ants and props doing exactly what I say. They can't help it – they're nothing.

No one else exists... I mean, truly, truly exists... like I do.

Maybe that's why I like golf so much. No idiotic brainless teammates to deal *with. Stroke after stroke, and hole by hole… it's just me and the way I think.*

"Blaire! Come down and set the table. Hurry it up. Dinner's almost ready."

I know that tone – she's feeling overwhelmed. This'll be hilarious! Bet I can eke out a bunch more frustration from her.

"Yes, Mother. In a minute."

"Please don't make me call you again!"

Watch me make you call again. It'll be so easy… like countless times before. I'll never set that table simply because I don't want to. And I shouldn't have to either. That's ant-work. Stuff suited for the likes of her.

What a total cream puff! She's all soft and gooey, inside and out. So easy to squish. But what an embarrassment as a mother! She doesn't even have it in her to see how feeble she is… which is kind of amusing in itself. Like whenever I work her into hysterics. She's got no idea how much I enjoy making her cry.

Not that I can't cry too… I can shed the tear that gets her to break down and do whatever I want. She lowers her guard to me every time. Then I push her to the limit… and beyond.

So pathetic.

Not me! I'm not blinded by fickle emotions. I see the whole stage… every single prop on it. Nothing rattles me… except maybe how annoying her whining gets. 'I really don't understand you, Blaire.' As if she had it in her to. Let her try. Let her swear up and down how much she loves me. That word from her means nothing. Only I understand love. Only I can truly love. I love the greatest love of all. I love me.

I really like the way I think.

CHAPTER

6

FRICTION

Inertia is a property of matter characterized by the multiplicative combination of velocity and mass. Velocity is nothing more than motion, so all objects with inertia are in motion and tend to remain in motion… whereas objects lacking inertia are at rest and tend to remain at rest. Set off in a particular direction, an object in motion will continue as it began… until it encounters another object. An object in motion contacting an object at rest always imparts some of its inertia, with the amount yielded up being equivalent to that which is received… all without loss. This idealized give-and-take conservation of inertia exists in a perfect system entirely closed off from external influences.

Such is never the case. Objects in contact with other objects, rubbing and colliding, produce friction… and friction steals inertia. All objects, irrespective of their mass, are invariably brought to a halt by friction. That is, unless work is done to maintain motion. Only work can keep objects in motion. By definition, work relates to the force required in moving an object. The greater the mass of the object or the distance needing to be moved, the more work that is required.

Work, unfortunately, can never fully compensate for the inertia that is lost to friction. Thermodynamics has a catch – a built-in 'no-win' scenario. The disorder of a closed system *always* increases. The more work required for maintaining inertia, the more the resulting disorder within the system. True…

some parts of a system can be brought into order through work done by other parts, but always at the expense of overall disorder. This disadvantageous consequence comes about as a result of heat given off in the doing of work and heat produced from friction. No conserving measure can bring to zero the amount of heat lost when one object in motion comes in contact with another. And since no system can ever be truly closed, when heat is lost, it is lost forever.

Bridget willingly sacrificed for the betterment of her family. After all, they depended on her. Through her feverish work, the house stayed clean, meals were prepared, dishes and laundry were washed, shopping got done, and the finances were managed. With an eye on her family's emotional state, she strove to meet every need. All this she did while maintaining a full-time job. Most days, she rose already exhausted… and continued that way until night in her frantic effort to keep things in motion. In the perfect world she longed for, her husband would be the loving partner who shared in both the labor and enjoyment of family, while her daughter would grow and mature through a close relationship with her.

In reality, Bridget was burning herself up and wearing herself down with how massive a job it was to keep her small family moving. She was not a confrontational person by nature, believing that individuals who cared found ways of showing it… though she could not help but notice that the other members of her household did not share in this perspective. More often these days, their golf things – their gloves, balls, tees and scorecards – were scattered about the house, and the more chaotic things got, the less willing they were to work alongside her. Yet no matter how hard she tried, she could never close off her house to the influence of the game. All her efforts to move her husband and daughter toward being responsible family members only yielded friction, resulting in a no-win situation in which surrender to work was her only option against complete loss.

Change and choice.
Choice and change.
One comes in response to the other. As rational beings, humans tend to believe that change results from choice. A person appraises a situation, makes a determined act of the will – a resolution – and then sets into motion change. The relationship, however, all too often operates in the other direction. Choice follows change. People change, and others make choices.

From Mitch O'Connor's perspective, his wife had changed. She was supposed to help make him affluent and influential… to build him up as a success. There had once been so much potential in her, but years of fretting had wasted it away. Motherhood had completely changed her. Not that he resented his daughter. Quite the opposite. Blaire made him proud. But Bridget, once appealing, had allowed herself to put on weight, with curves going to all the wrong places. She no longer made an effort to please him in the way a woman should. He could live with that… if only she was not such an embarrassment at the club. She was a pitiful golfer… and looked absolutely hideous in shorts. He could hardly endure being on the course with her… even at couple's mixers, the lowest level of club competition. She tried to hide it, but everyone knew there was no appreciation in her for the game. This was not what his maturing career needed… a wife who had completely lost focus of what was important. She might be willing to accept that the best years of her life were over, but his were just beginning. So… he was making choices.

From Blaire O'Connor's perspective, her parents had changed. They no longer recognized her as the center of the family. They were always bickering over trivial amounts of money or time, and who was supposed to do what. Her father, a marginally decent golfer, had grown lazy of late. His game had flattened out, though his ego had not. There was nothing else to be learned from him since he had not continued to push himself. In contrast, her mother was nothing more than a smothering influence. She was always working, or nagging about work, and had never been any fun. Responsibility was her crutch… a lame excuse to cover over her inability to compete. The woman's plainness was disgusting. Both of them, father and mother, were so very boring. Neither could keep up with her. So Blaire made choices. She would spend as much time as possible on the course, and not associate at all with her parents.

From Bridget O'Connor's perspective, both husband and daughter had changed. They were more distant, less affectionate, less attentive, and completely focused outside the home. They no longer expressed an appreciation for her work, her sacrifices, or the difficulties she embraced in keeping the family together. An attitude of 'you owe us' permeated their behaviors. Bridget was making choices too. She would throw more of herself into strengthening the connections to Blaire and Mitch. She would seek them in those places outside the home where they sought enjoyment. She would become more, not less, involved at the country club and in Blaire's golfing endeavors. She would give more of herself toward building her husband's social and professional ambitions, while at the same time laboring to make their home a haven. Surely they would eventually choose to come back from those other places that so obviously lacked the togetherness she just knew they would come to value.

After six years of country club living, Bridget found that she no longer had the desire for a second child.

CHAPTER

7

THE DUALITY OF GOLF

A well-groomed, richly tended golf course depicts one of the most peaceful sites of green-colored heaven on earth. It is the very embodiment of mankind's management of Nature. A golf course is wilderness subdued, confined and exhibited in grasses cut to four heights – rough, fairway, fringe and green. It is carefully manicured desert sands, their crystalline whites a soothing semblance of snow for the parched artificiality of Southern California. The golf course is well-pruned hedges, majestic oaks, and fountain-bathed waterways. All within is designed for beauty… and danger.

The golf course is an adventure – a milestone-laden theater comprised of nine hole introduction, snackshop intermission, nine hole conclusion, and inebriated clubhouse epilogue. It is *Canterbury Tales* of the tragic, the triumphant, the untruthful, the opulent, the gambler, the jester, the seductress, and the downright weird. Golf is billiards spread over a hundred acres. It is capture the flag played out in eighteen installments, each interspersed with occasional bouts of hide-and-seek. It is round after round of a passive-aggressive boxing match. Golf is spiraling out-of-control failure dotted with just enough success… and the occasional miracle… to keep the player coming back for more. The golf course is both endless pleasure and a true trial of the soul.

The golf course is a temple with many worshippers.
We are the Early Risers. We travel by the morning star to greet the dawning.

The course is ours, and we pioneer the day. Feeling the deepest, we understand the fullest of all that is the glory of the primordial outdoors. Like ancient man, we write as with hieroglyph the day's first imprints of motion upon dew-laden surfaces. Alas… because we know full well that our testament to those who follow is not meant to endure beyond the purge of the sun's emerging rays, we bear fully the burden that remembrance of us must fade, as we are called forth into industry and economy… to our day's labor.

We are the Lords of the Links. Midmorning belongs to us – the time of the most faithful and most devout – the members in good-standing. We are threefold blessed, with health, time and money. The course is ours, and we do not share – we rule. We come primped to worship and to be worshiped, for all that has been tended so carefully has been done for us, according to our wishes. But we are not wholly heartless. Our merry ways on the course eventually carry us into internal conferences held over libations and tall tales. Only then, when we are at ease, do we willingly grant the course to our lessers.

We are the Hearty – the worthy ones. By mid-afternoon, heat has driven away the old, the weak and the lazy, allowing us to claim what is rightfully our own. Temperature is of no consequence to us. We move between sprinkler-lavished spaces as nomads journeying across desert wildernesses… from oasis to oasis. We neither languish nor wilt, and our irreverent mad-cap play is the height of worship to blue sky, green grass, and brown earth. The course is ours, and we revel in it, yielding only at the setting of the sun.

We are the Beleaguered. Our pilgrimage from afar is the truest form of worship. We come in weariness seeking refuge from concrete and steel… from stress and disappointment. Here, we are understood. We are accepted, free to walk in the coolness of twilight. Our meek devotion is rewarded with a morsel of the course's delight as it bestows upon us one last forest green moment of splendor, given as sustenance against the blackness of night and another day of toil. The golf course graciously grants us its respite, and we bow to it in humble adoration.

Early on in their country club experience, Bridget asked Mitch to teach her how to play the game of golf. He started her out easy by explaining the rules and familiarizing her with the equipment, right before progressing to the basics of grip, stance and swing. Through these initial instructions, she paid close attention out of an eagerness to show herself a capable companion in those things of interest to him. Although she possessed no strong affinity for the game… or for sports in general… she nonetheless purposed to attain whatever level of proficiency it would take for him to feel comfortable in having her share in this newfound passion of his.

They soon made their first outing together to a driving range where he tested out her abilities. Her diligent optimism soon gave way to frustration. Short club or long one, big metal-headed thing or one with a highly angled face – no matter what she tried or how hard she applied herself, she could never get her arms to move in sync with how he said her hips should pivot or her feet should shift. The harder she swung away, the more the grip felt foreign in her hands. Nothing she tried consistently produced meaningful contact between club and ball. She quickly found herself overwhelmed with all the little things he kept instructing her to heed, and asked if they could give it up for the day.

They went out again, and still she struggled. The more she failed to do things exactly as he insisted, the angrier he got with her inability to generate anything approximating a reproducible swing. Soon, she was near on tears at the way he kept finding fault with not only her performance but also her effort. After a dozen or so attempts with a seven iron… a club he made a point of saying was the easiest one in the bag… an especially bad swing hacked up an inordinate amount of turf and sent reverberations of pain through her hands, wrists and arms. She looked up in full expectation of receiving sympathy from him, but instead found him shaking his head in disgust. He then proclaimed the effort as hopeless and went about collecting his clubs to leave. It was the first time in their marriage that she sensed from him a deep disappointment in her as his mate.

Not being one to give up easily, Bridget signed herself up for beginner lessons at a public golf course near her workplace. For six straight Fridays, she secretly dedicated her lunch hour toward an expectation that proper instruction from a proper coach would be just the thing needed for her to develop the necessary skills. Unfortunately, as the weeks progressed, she found herself to be no more capable at the game than when she started. At the conclusion of her final lesson, her instructor thanked her for the effort and made a parting point of reassuring her that golf was not for everyone. Very few, he said, possessed the coordination necessary for playing well. She should look on the bright side. She was better off knowing that the game was not for her… at least before she ended up investing too much into it.

For Bridget, trying to play golf amounted to the impossibility of coaxing her body to do what it was incapable of doing. Fish would fly and bats would swim before she could master this game. The humiliation of being confronted with her inadequacy somehow compelled her to do exactly the opposite of what she knew she should. Rather than seek out her own interests and give up on something that was so obviously unsuited for her, she threw herself into becoming a fan of golf... all in a backdoor approach toward regaining her husband's approval. As Blaire's interest in the game began to pick up, Bridget diverted more of her free time toward golf. Nearly every weekend was now being spent in either supporting her husband's passion or in escorting Blaire about the course... something that had to be done anyway since club policy prohibited unaccompanied access to minors.

When Blaire was new to the game, Bridget found that traipsing about the golf course with the girl proved fairly easy... even enjoyable at times. They often ended up spending what she considered to be quality time in hearing about the things going on in Blaire's life... and the walking did her good. Blaire soon took to the game with amazing prowess. With Bridget's time and energy being at such a high premium, more often than not she found herself chauffeuring Blaire about in a cart. That setting proved not to be as ideal as she had hoped. For her part, she ended up having to pay close attention to how Blaire wanted her to drive. The girl was even more obsessive about the game than was Mitch... which only got worse on her becoming involved year-round in junior's competition. Bridget soon found herself constantly constrained by Blaire's golfing rituals. Everything had to be done just right or she risked setting her daughter off. Things got so bad between them that Bridget had to establish a set of guidelines for herself in order to endure their golf outings together.

'Don't speak to her until a hole's completed.'

'Stay behind her at all times, and definitely out of sight whenever she's swinging.'

'Don't offer to help her in any way. She insists on keeping her own score, cleaning her own clubs, and raking out traps herself.'

'Tend the pin only when asked. Otherwise, don't even risk stepping out onto a green.'

'And most important... never, ever make suggestions.'

Bridget soon began struggling with a hidden resentment toward golf. At times, she would go so far as to nurture a notion that the game was... beyond a doubt... the most ludicrous pastime ever conceived. Although Mitch and Blaire openly reveled together about all its intricacies, she held onto a more ridiculous premise as to how it was played. In as few 'strokes' as possible, using an assortment of approved sticks, one was to hit a small ball into an only-slightly-larger-sized hole positioned a great distance away. The supposed challenge to the game was in getting that ball to traverse those distances along narrow pathways festooned with obstacles and hazards. To her, the beauty of a golf course was actually a contradiction, a deception, and ultimately an enemy toward anyone crazy enough to play.

Bridget was not fooled – the golf course was not a place of peace. She saw the fairway rough as the haunt of wayward drives, lost and abandoned. The bordering forests came alive to snatch away the passerby. Quiet ponds were graveyards, flowering hedges became thorny thickets, and sparkling beaches turned deadly quicksand. To her, golf course hazards made no sense... like false flooring on a basketball court... or a marsh in centerfield... or bushes on the fifty-yard line. Then why, she often wondered, would anyone be willing to pay such great sums of money to landscapers, horticulturalists, lawn-and-garden contractors, fertilizer wholesalers, rock-and-sand distributors, and resident greenskeepers, all to ensure that something beautiful hid something perilous? Especially when all that beauty seemed lost on the players.

And another thing – it troubled her deeply that vast expenditures of water were needed to keep everything looking lush... especially in such a parched place as Southern California. It was a travesty as bad as the wasted resources dedicated toward making cemeteries appear tranquil and green when the occupants had clearly lost all ability to appreciate.

Yet the most unpleasant aspect of golf was not its physical contradictions. It was the space upon which the visor hung, the body that filled the polo shirt, and the feet that strode about on spiked shoes – the golfer. Bridget was often tempted to think of golf as a perverse shell game in which beauty was deceptively used to steal contentment, but she more consistently held that the patrons of the game... her husband included... were not the happy lot they claimed to be. Though she generally considered herself to be the type who sought out the best in others, yet all too often what she encountered out there left her mystified. She had seen country club golfers be argumentative, arrogant, petty, superstitious, morose, vindictive, vulgar, deceitful, derisive, drunken, and even sometimes destructive. At their core, they just seemed to take pleasure out of hitting things in the most pedantic of ways.

No small wonder it's not a team sport!

And the vanity!

The golf course and the carnival were clearly the best places to go if one wished to see the bizarrely dressed. Knickers with high socks, eye-popping plaids, stripes and dots worn together, goofy fluff-ball topped hats, tassel-laden shoes, appallingly pleated skirts, and ridiculously heavy sweater vests... all in a clash of colors and fabrics that no decent person would dare be seen wearing on the street.

Outside of the context of the game, Bridget actually considered most country club members to be rather amicable. She had spent many delightful hours socializing with them, or playing cards in spirited and wholesome competition. But get them out on the course, and golf transformed these pleasant people in a manner worthy of Robert Louis Stevenson. The amiable Dr. Jekyll, who would never contemplate pocketing a card, dared within their hidden Mr. Hyde to improve a lie, fabricate a score, disregard a duff, or miraculously find a lost ball. Worse, she knew that the liberty these people demonstrated toward their own play never seemed to spill over toward moderating the rigidity with which they regulated others.

She sometimes pondered on the abuse she had experienced after having alerted a member of Mitch's foursome to a pitching wedge left on the edge of the previous green. She thought it a kind thing to do, but Mitch openly berated her for having 'helped' one of his opponents. Golf just seemed to bring out something dark in him. He would often brag about how easy it was to get into the minds of his competition… positioning his shadow as an irritant, uttering a faint cough at a critical moment, lavishing both false praise and false advice, or going stone cold after someone's remarkable shot. It made no sense.

How did belittling others make one a better player?

He would tell her… most authoritatively… that it was all part of the game, but Bridget was certain he played something wholly different.

Golf simply did not mesh with her way of thinking. She was not a particularly competitive person, either with herself or with others. She valued endeavors that brought balance, harmony, and cooperation to teams… everyone striving for the common good. Yet she was not without understanding. The duality of the game – its beauty and its challenge – was the very thing that captivated golfers across skill levels. The beauty, to some extent, she could appreciate… indulgently false and fabricated though it sometimes seemed… but the challenge never held sway over her.

She had come to see golf as an addiction. A drug that required vast amounts of money, but never quite satisfied. As proof, she needed to look no further than how Mitch frequently burned through the family's discretionary funds in buying the latest things in equipment, supplies and apparel. And time, to Bridget, the most precious commodity of all, was lavished upon a thing… a game… and not on his own family.

She eventually came to understand that there were only two ways to play this game. It was either all out, with nothing else in life but golf, devoting everything to it as Mitch and Blaire did… or as goony-golf on a grander scale, taking nothing seriously, investing as little as possible, having no expectations about the outcome, and simply enjoying the moment. Country clubs were built for the former individuals, while the latter were barely welcome on the most rudimentary of public courses.

Still… she was very careful not to openly criticize the game they loved. She kept her thoughts to herself… even though she had been rained on, burnt up, screamed at, ignored, bombarded (hit twice by errant shots), and bored to tears by golfers as they expounded, pontificated, chided, whined, relived, rationalized and boasted.

To her, golf was the great divide. A person either took up the family pastime with passion or became an outcast like her. The side activities of country club life – tennis, fitness, cards and social events – could never redeem the non-golfer. Value was merited only through skill and dedication to the game.

Bridget had come to accept that the golf course would never be a place for her, though she still endeavored to develop a deeper relationship with Blaire through the time they spent together on it. Their respective differences over the game nonetheless came out on every outing. Such was the case when Bridget once witnessed a father savagely berate his grade-school son for playing in a sand trap. The boy had been using the handle of a rake to draw a mural in a fairway bunker while his father's foursome waited for a green to clear. On passing by with Blaire on an adjoining fairway, she caught a sadly sufficient view of that child's drawing – two linked stick figures… one large, one small… both holding golf clubs in their free hands. Blaire's disapproval echoed the man's embarrassment as he went about conscripting his son to rake out the trap.

"The golf course is no place for babysitting."

In truth, their own roles were reversed. Bridget was trying to connect, and Blaire was only mother-sitting.

CHAPTER

8

SECRETS

It was a constant fascination to Blaire that in one moment she could be the focus of so much adoring attention, and then in the next be completely overlooked. Either way was fine with her. In fact, she preferred it when adults took her for granted, as none ever suspected her of being clever. In their eyes, twelve year olds were just children.

So go ahead and underestimate me. Get sucked in by all my sweetness and turn your back on me. I'm only a little girl... but you lower your guard at your own peril.

Blaire always felt at liberty to go wherever she chose around the clubhouse. In so doing, she was able to freely study the ways of men and women. Not that anyone she ever met had it in themselves to teach her anything. She found out things on her own. In particular, she was very interested in uncovering inconsistencies and exploiting those for a competitive edge... or sometimes just for the fun of it. Mostly, she stored up their secrets, waiting for the perfect moment to use them. Examining the flaws of others up close also helped her weed out the occasional bad tendency in herself, as the absolute last thing she ever wanted was to end up like one of them. That, of course, would never happen seeing as she was far superior to them all.

For as long as she could remember, the ladies' room had been her place of greatest amusement. Far too many women... her mother included... openly shared their insecurities while fretting over their appearance before a mirror, not in the least bit aware of being overheard. They always then acted all coquettish-like on stepping outside.

Totally ridiculous.

She saw the same tendencies played out in the men, even without having access to their private spaces. Of course, girls her own age were the worst... especially in the locker room right before a tournament. Without a clue, they openly shared their misgivings about their abilities, admitted that a parent had pressured them into competing, or gushed over some stupid crush they longed to have accompany them out on the course. Blaire always found ways of twisting those confidences at a critical moment in order to bring down the girl's play.

Through careful observation, she came to learn much about the membership of the Piper Mountain Country Club. She could easily distinguish between those who were financially well-off and those who worked hard at faking it based on the subtleties of how they flaunted wealth. She discovered the ones who had drug habits or struggled with alcoholism. She recognized the men who cheated on their wives... and vice versa... by noting how they acted around their spouses in comparison to when they thought they were unobserved. She knew for certain that Kurt Timmons was happily married... and intent on staying that way... based on the detached air with which he went about his business as the course pro. He was very careful to keep at arm's length the many vivacious females who routinely trolled for his attention. In contrast, she knew that the current club president had his fingers in several honey pots... even though he acted all stately whenever his wife was around.

No one ever suspected her of watching them, yet the surest way to lose Blaire's respect... if such a thing could be said for how she viewed people... was to witlessly become a victim to one of her false fronts. Her mother was one such person. How that woman could repeatedly fall for the same thing over and over was totally beyond Blaire. But her father... he should know better than to underestimate her. After all, he was the one who first taught her to take note of a competitor's weaknesses. He had set her on the path toward greatness, so for him to overlook her abilities was an unforgiveable offense.

For years, it had been his practice to wait for her arrival home from school, and then together they would walk down to the clubhouse. But lately he was parting from her as soon as she entered the front door in his haste to get out on the course. This deviation in routine was both curious and rather annoying, particularly since the club's stodgier members would hassle her if she was found down there on her own. She could deal with them, but having her father turn unreliable was a different matter. More often than not, he would be gone for hours, then turn up late at the clubhouse.. well beyond the time required to finish the back nine. She had come to expect a burger out of him at the snack shop, but now he was showing up after its closing time. When a change in his habits affected her, it was clearly her business to find out. So… she decided to follow him.

On her first day of spy-work, she waited as he descended from their backyard, and then trailed behind him using fairway trees and shrubs as concealment. Everything in his behavior seemed normal. He played the 13th and 14th holes as any golfer might. But then… on the 15th tee… he rested on a bench for a long while, even allowing a foursome to pass in front. Once that group cleared, with no one approaching from the 14th, he got up to the tee with a long iron… another oddity… and sliced his ball into a large cluster of trees just off the fairway. She was amazed that the errant shot did not phase him in the least. He simply collected his bag and moved on. The last she saw of him was as he entered those trees. After twenty minutes, with two other groups having passed through the 15th hole, she made her way into the copse… but found no sign of him.

Well-versed in the ways of golf, she knew his behavior to be beyond unusual… even for a mediocre golfer such as himself. On the next opportunity, it being the following Monday, she made directly for the set of restrooms located off the 15th green rather than tailing him. From that vantage point, she had an excellent view of the fairway and those trees. For that day, and the next, he played through the hole as one might expect, using his driver and avoiding the trees. Both times as he passed by on the way to the 16th tee, she ducked into the ladies' room, and then hustled back to the clubhouse ahead of him. But on Wednesday, it was an iron from the tee into the trees again, followed by his disappearance. She loitered about the restrooms for over an hour trying not to look stupid each time someone passed by. He eventually reappeared onto the 15th fairway when no one was there, finished the hole, and then made a brief stop in the adjoining men's room before heading for the 16th tee. She could hear him through the wall whistling in the self-satisfied manner that always irritated her. He was happy.

She had a notion as to what he was doing with himself, but not why he chose some days and not others. In her mind, though, the most pertinent question was not 'what,' 'when,' or 'why,' but 'who.' She would need a different vantage point for determining that. She would conceal herself in those trees.

The next day, after he left for the course, she rode her bike to the parking lot of the condos that bordered the 15th hole, and hid herself in a narrow culvert that ran away from the edge of the fairway through the clump of trees. Since it was early fall, and still dry, the ditch provided her with perfect concealment from which to view of the trees.

After about thirty minutes, she caught sight of him on the 15th tee but could not tell which club he had extracted from his bag. She soon heard what she was hoping for – not the hollow metallic ping of a driver, but the solid whack of an iron. The next sounds were of his ball rifling through leaves and impacting wood. She kept her head down, and in a matter of no time he emerged into the covering. Without stopping to look for the ball, he walked straight through the trees to a side entrance of the condos. There, he put his hand to a call box and spoke. From her distance through the trees, she could not make out his voice, but clearly heard the sharp click of the door being unlocked. Just before he entered, she noticed him briefly pivot about. On his face was not a hint of nervousness over the possibility of being detected… only anticipation.

Once the door closed behind him, Blaire left the culvert to retrieve his ball. She found it lying in plain sight, easily recognized by the distinctive 'O'C' he typically penned in permanent ink as his means of distinguishing his ball. She picked it up and was staring at the marking when a crazy idea came into her head. Pocketing the ball, she dashed out of the trees and up to the 15th tee box. A party of four had just arrived, and as two of its members were well-known to her, she stayed there pretending to watch them tee off. Her real focus was those condominiums abutting the hole beyond the trees. This complex had four stories, with porches overlooking the golf course. She could see into those on the top floor, and many on the third, but the ones on the lower levels were obscured by the trees. Most of the sliding glass doors on the visible units were curtained against the afternoon sun. Nothing struck her as unusual until her eyes were drawn to a unit on the third level, as someone within had closed the blinds.

Blaire remained on the 15th tee as the foursome departed, making a point of thanking them for allowing her to watch so they might not become suspicious. More parties played through, and she greeted each warmly while maintaining a close watch on that particular porch. The curtains stayed closed.

Blaire eventually moved off the tee to the shelter of an arborvitae hedge and continued to watch. After an hour, the curtains reopened and a woman stepped out onto the porch. She leaned over the railing to scan the

15th fairway in both directions, then returned inside. Minutes later, her father emerged from the clump of trees and continued up the 15th fairway. Just before passing beneath the woman's balcony, he momentarily glanced upward. Any other person on the course would have thought nothing of it, so brief was its duration, but Blaire now knew for certain.

She watched him move beyond the restrooms toward the clubhouse, not even bothering to finish the remainder of the back nine. She had time. He would get a drink or two in the clubhouse bar before coming home. So she leisurely retraced her steps to the drainage ditch to retrieve her bike… all the while plotting a new course forward.

Golf had brought father and daughter together. Golf would now separate them.

CHAPTER

9

COMMITTEE WORK

"I already told you – it's all part of our responsibility as club members."

"Responsibility?! You've got some nerve talking to me about responsibility! I've done my share and more – you know that! I'm already on two committees as it is. So why don't you just do it yourself?!"

"I can't – *you know that!* It's a conflict of interest."

"Yeah, well… you get the interest, and it's me who always gets the conflict."

"Bridget… *please*… for me… take on this committee role. Supporting JIG is really important. You know I'd do it if I could, but I had to resign my position on the rules committee so I could…"

"That's nothing but a bunch of drunk guys engaged in the age-old argument of what constitutes 'improving one's lie.'"

She fully expected her double meaning to make him react, but he just sat there blank-faced… and then plowed on through.

"…run for a place on the board. The bylaws are very clear on that. So if you refuse to do it for me, then at least do it for your daughter. She's the one who'll really benefit."

Bridget was buying none of it. She knew full well that Mitch's request had less to do with Blaire and more to do with him having set his sights on an upcoming vacancy on the Member's Board, a panel of members-in-good-standing who advised the trustees on club business. He had talked about nothing else for the last several months, constantly going on and on about how this springboard role would elevate his standing in the club. He kept insisting that increasing the visibility of the O'Connor family at the club was crucial for positioning him as the best candidate.

She knew full well that 'Juniors in Golf' was the only consistently understaffed committee at the club. Nobody wanted to be stuck on JIG. It was nothing more than babysitting kids on Saturday afternoons while their parents were out on the course. Mitch's angle of her doing it for their daughter's sake was even more ridiculous. Blaire, at nearly thirteen, hardly needed supervision. In fact, the girl's involvement in golf could not be any greater short of moving onto the course permanently. Fortunately, Bridget had avoided being considered for JIG during her seven years as a country club member. Mitch's current persistence, however, eventually wore her out. She caved in simply to put an end to all his begging and berating.

"Thanks, Bridget… this will really help my case. I'll make it up to you, I promise. One more thing… it would look a whole lot better for me in the eyes of the trustees if you were seen as volunteering… you know… rather than being asked. Please call Dot tomorrow and request that you be included on JIG."

If Bridget had to deal with anyone in the club's front office, her preference was that it be Dorothy Sutherland. Aside from being the only woman on staff, Dot… as some commonly referred to her… had shown herself to be more than capable as the part-time administrator responsible for coordinating member activities. Though Bridget would never be so rude as to ask, she had heard about some of Dot's misfortunes. Recently divorced, word was that Dot's ex-husband had repeatedly cheated on her. Word was also that he had been abusive in some way… though nobody seemed to know exactly how. Word was that their marriage had ended bitterly with both parties having spent far too much on legal fees in their rush to get free from each other. Word was that Dot got hired at Piper Mountain without ever having played golf… which impressed Bridget to no end. The club, extending membership privileges to its employees, immediately became this woman's new home. Word was that she had begun work there with three goals in mind: start a career, learn the game, and find her new soul mate. And because Dot was attractive and outgoing, word was to watch out… because this young woman was on the prowl. Fair or not, men seemed overly drawn by the aura, while their wives were put on guard by the supposed stigma. Yet to Bridget's way of thinking, Dot… because of what she had been through… deserved the benefit of everyone's doubt.

The two of them had worked together several times in the two years since Dot started at Piper Mountain, most recently on the local arrangement committee for a men's college tournament. In some ways, Dot reminded Bridget of herself… very capable and highly dedicated to her job… although the comparisons seemed to end there. Dot was a model Californian woman – young, blond, liberal-minded, and well-endowed with both the physical and personality attributes Bridget begrudgingly acknowledged as lacking in herself. Still… the two of them got along well enough. In fact, it was through a conversation with Dot that Bridget first came to learn about Mitch's desire for a position on the board, and it was through Dot that she discovered that his ambitions did not stop there.

"You do realize, Bridget, that being on the board is the first step toward bigger things. Mitch has so much potential. He's practically a shoe-in for becoming club president one day."

"Really? I had no idea he was even interested. Did he tell you that?"

"Yes… well… I guess you two don't get much time to talk."

The O'Connor divorce caught most club members by complete surprise… even though many would later claim to have seen it coming.

The night Mitch walked out on her was by far the most devastating moment in Bridget's life. After crying her eyes out for many weeks, she gradually began to turn herself toward the future. Not being a vindictive person by nature, she purposed… if for no other reason than her daughter's sake… to put on a courageous front and seek an amicable settlement in parting ways. It was Bridget who, on the advice of a coworker seasoned in the divorce wars, proposed that they employ the services of a mediator rather than lawyers. The money saved was the appeal for Mitch, and the faint hope of rapid closure became hers. They entered into negotiations in full agreement on one point – that neither party could endure another day being married to the other.

Unfortunately, the downside to the approach was the mandatory session in which she was compelled to write a biography of their marriage… and then have it read out loud by the mediator. She knew that this task was not imposed in hopes of altering the state in which she found herself, nor was it meant to provide any kind of parting shot. Instead, the mediator assured her that their biographies would help move them forward in the negotiations. For Bridget, re-assembling her mangled memories ended up being far more painful and humiliating than having to hear Mitch's account of how she had proved to be a disappointment as a wife. Although she put little of it on paper, recalling all the ways he had lied and deceived his way through their marriage brought clarity beyond her comprehension. So many overlooked inklings crystallized into a realization of how foolish she had been. The marriage was always about Mitch and what he wanted. Their decision-making processes, their lifestyle, their social circles, the division of labor – everything – had been engineered by him for his own convenience. In each instance, she had agreed to his preferences in her short-sighted… albeit sincere… pursuit of a harmonious family.

All in all, she felt that the entire mediation process was carried off in a surprisingly cooperative vein, especially given that one party had severely broken the heart of the other. They were able to work out issues of custody, property, debt, alimony and fees… all done in as smooth a manner as one might hope for from the best of committee work. The contract was signed, and then the state of California provided its certification. The O'Connor marriage was no more.

As per agreement, Mitch would contribute to the cost of raising Blaire and share in the mortgage payment… up to a point. His responsibilities would cease on the date of Blaire's high school graduation ceremony… whether she finished or not. The house would then go on the market, with any profit from its sale being split evenly. However, the most surprising aspect of the negotiations for Bridget was that Mitch never contended for custody of Blaire… though he was adamant on one point. If Blaire were ever to attend any form of higher education, then he would be completely absolved from making any contribution. This ended up being the only heated point of contention between them, as Bridget took it to be his parting shot at hurting her personally.

She learned six months later that Mitch had remarried and returned to the Pacific Northwest in order to take on his company's accounts in Asia. She fully expected… and very much hoped… to never lay eyes on him again.

For Bridget, the months following Mitch's departure were surreal. Throughout much of that time, she felt like a small boat drifting aimlessly in an ocean of dense fog. She was well aware of echoed noises all about her, but had no ability to discern either their source or meaning. She moved through those days as if riding on the massive upheaval of a dark and angry sea. She had failed. All her dreams of having a happy family got sunk deep within the humiliation and devastation of her abandoned heart.

Yet in other instances, Mitch's absence felt oddly like she had lost a limb… a right arm… with the simplest of skills needing to be learned all over again. She began attending a weekly support group to help her adapt to this lonelier lifestyle. There, she met other women who had been cruelly betrayed, but also encountered those who owned solely the foolishness that led to their divorce. The loss, she was surprised to discover, was the same, not contingent on guilt or blame. Talking through her situation with sympathetic listeners proved helpful… though the passing of a year had not yet provided her with a hint of what life might look like beyond the pain.

She made one very significant change to her life in an effort to cope with being divorced. She quit her job with the electronics chain, seeing as she associated it with the influence Mitch had exerted over her. Instead, she took a new position as an accounts manager at the Desert Valley Credit Union… mostly owing to its compatibility with a single parent lifestyle. She eagerly departed one venue of employment as the person known to have been recently divorced, and entered the next only as the person described on her résumé. For her daughter's sake, she maintained the surname they held in common… despite her now regretting having ever taken it as her own.

Bridget did not know what to make of it, but the divorce produced little outward effect on Blaire. The girl never cried or raged. Everyday was largely as the one before. Bridget poured through books on the subject, hunting for some insight into her daughter's apathy. The grim statistics on the fate of children-of-divorce worried her greatly, yet Blaire showed no signs of depression, overly deviant behavior, loss of motivation, or any self-destructive tendency. It was 'Blaire as usual,' with the girl consistently displaying a callous boredom anytime the conversation veered in the direction of her father. In initially being consumed by her own grief, Bridget had let the issue slide, but with encouragement from her support group, was more frequently pressing the subject of the divorce upon Blaire… with little success to show for the effort.

"Mother, there's really nothing to discuss. Like I've said dozens of times before – he made his choice, you made yours… and now I'm making mine."

"I just thought we… I mean, you and me… could benefit from talking it over. Maybe even go see a counselor. I'm sure I could find someone you approve of. It could really help you cope with…"

"Go if it suits you. I'm good on my own."

"What about a friend… have you tried talking it over with one of your…"

"Mother, you know full well what I think about 'friends'… so are we going to waste time discussing that too?!"

Something about her daughter was not right… at least not compared with how children typically responded to a broken home. Blaire remained completely untouched.

10

MEN IN HER LIFE

Despite the liberal trend to these modern times, the golf course remains a place where men can freely exert their opposition to the presence of women. Well… not all women. Not those vivacious young ones who prance about in skirts and tight shirts with their ponytails bobbing over a visor strap. Such females are a more-than-welcome enhancement to many a man's golfing experience. But the aggressive, competitive, complaining ones… they always end up disrupting the proper order of things. Those should stay home with their children because the golf course is the legitimate domain of men. After all, men design and build the courses… as well as pay most of the dues… so men should have the right to grant or deny access.

Some women just refuse to accept how things are. They regularly contend for the prime tee times during the men's Saturday and Sunday morning scramblers. They annoyingly lobby for equal access to the 19th hole, as well as larger locker rooms and a presence in the leadership of the club. They show themselves to be nothing more than irritants when they claim cabinet space in the trophy room and more of their clothing to be sold in the pro shop. They might have their Women's Golfing Association, but it is nothing more than a poor replica of what the men have perfected in their own professional league. While all those unreasonable women vie for control of the snack shop's TV in order to air their WGA tournaments, the men allow it only as long as the 'competitors' remain attractive… and nothing else of interest happens to be on.

Advancements were sure to continue in equipment, training and technique, but the heart of the sport would never change... because golf is a man's game.

Blaire was always amused by the way men thought they owned the course. Most were fairly pathetic at the game. She was only a teenager... and not nearly as strong... but could still best most country club men... forward tee boxes or not. Sure, the capable ones could out-drive her, but the majority of those spent so much time in the rough as the price for their bravado. Very few of them understood the subtleties of control the way she did. Stay in the fairway, master the irons and short game, and she would get to the green in fewer strokes. Once there, she was second to none. There was nothing compared to beating a man... and then rubbing it in with a smile and a soft touch to his shoulder.

Such idiots...

As much as she hated to admit it, she needed men. Men to train her, and men, as stepping stones, to get her where she wanted to go. She would also eventually need men to sponsor her. So she would tolerate their condescension... for now... because her eyes were set on her future. She was going to be a professional... the best of them all. Then the men would be watching her, adoring her, and fantasizing over her.

In her remaining years of high school, she would outwardly adhere to the way things were done yet without compromising her plans. She would get out of them everything she wanted... and then get even in her own time. After all, her whole life had been that way.

Her first exposure to the male world of golf beyond the game had been nothing more than a simple business arrangement. At age eight, while walking along with her father, she discovered the value of being out on the course at dusk. Duffers tethered to their golf carts and lacking in sufficient night vision would invest little effort toward locating their errant shots, particularly on the last few holes of either the front or back nine. Not only did it please her to find and keep what others thought lost, but she was also able to exchange these balls for cash at the pro shop. She got a good price too, as the men working there could not resist her charm.

As she came to spend more time about the course, Blaire found other ways of exploiting the lazier side of male golfers. Unbeknownst to her father, she began cleaning clubs after school. Most of her clients were old men who sat by as she worked, often boring her with stupid stories from their youth... but sometimes showing her golf techniques she had not yet picked up on. They usually overpaid… simply for the pleasure of her company.

On those occasions when she encountered a worn-out grip or a faulty shaft seal, Blaire would take these to the country club's equipment managers who were reimbursed directly by members. She got good at flirting with these men, who showed her everything she needed to know about regripping and remounting of club heads… all for free. They never realized that everything she learned ended up taking business away from them. Every little bit of knowledge, no matter how it was obtained, went another step toward increasing her sense of destiny.

On becoming thirteen, she was already completely comfortable within the male world of golf, but found herself with a problem. Her mother sat her down a month after her father left to explain that because finances were extremely tight, some unfortunate changes must be made. Blubbering on in a long-winded speech, her mother said over and over how much she regretted the way things had turned out, how unfair life sometimes was, and… *blah, blah, blah.* The woman just could not keep from bemoaning over how it pained her to make difficult decisions. After what seemed like forever, she finally got around to saying the thing Blaire had been expecting all along – that the family membership at the country club would have to be terminated as a cost-cutting inevitability of the divorce. This included all golf lessons… something her mother could never comprehend was an on-going need for any golfer serious about the game.

Then, for an inexplicable reason, the woman ventured off into a sobbed-filled account of how no one at the country club had bothered to console with her about either the divorce or the loss of membership. No cards had come to offer sympathy or appreciation for her many years of service… just silence more painful than the insult of a slap.

Jeezz… get a grip!

So what to do? Blaire could come right out with suggestions on ways she could continue on in golf… just a few seeds planted in her mother's rather slow mind… especially since the woman was totally lacking in the creativity needed for seeing a path forward.

Nah.

Blaire much more preferred the planting of splinters.

She had it all figured out. She would mope about the house looking depressed… alternatively sitting alone in her room for hours on end. (*Even though that'll be pretty boring.*) Add in a bit of crying in the middle of the night… along with some breaking of stuff about the house in a fit of rage… and then her mother's conscience would be pricked to it's breaking point. In the meantime, Blaire would sneak onto the course and play whenever she wanted to… like nothing had ever changed.

Let them try to keep me away! I know everything that goes on down there!

To her surprise… and disappointment… Blaire ended up being denied this particular pleasure of needling at her mother. The woman cleared the tears out of her eyes and informed her that she had arranged for a meeting at the club manager's office in order to seek a solution.

The whole way on the short drive to the clubhouse, her mother took on that sickeningly lofty tone she got whenever explaining how some supposed sacrifice of hers was sure to work out for Blaire's good. If golf was so important, she said, and if it could be a diversion capable of driving away the pain of a father's rejection, then she would act decisively on behalf of her daughter. She would do that which was most difficult to do. She would boldly stride into the very business office that had employed the woman who broke her heart, and negotiate there with the men who knew fully the dreadfulness of her family's shame… all for her daughter.

Whatever…

They came in together through the main entrance to the club manager's office suite, her mother holding her head up high in what so obviously was her way of putting on a brave front. As they passed by where that woman once sat, Blaire made a point of asking… all innocent-like… if that was her desk, just to see how the question affected her mother. She got the expected reaction – her mother looked away and pretended not to have heard. Blaire was on the verge of repeating the question… to double the fun… when Claude Beesinger called them into his office. Timmons was already there, and though he went first to shake hands with her mother, Blaire did not miss that his eyes and smile were for her alone. Beesinger, on the other hand, was an old tub of lard totally incapable of caring about anything other than where he would eat that night and how his gout was keeping him from playing up to his near-scratch proficiency.

As if…

This was all sure to be a waste of time, so Blaire took a seat as far away from the adults as possible and began looking around the office for something of interest. It was all the typical meaningless stuff – old furniture, junk adults liked scattering about to make themselves look busy, and walls of pictures showing the man posing with people only he knew. Despite how boring their conversation was, Blaire easily picked up on the gist of it.

Mother: Mitch ran off with Dot.

Kurt and Claude: We heard. That's terrible.

Mother: I can't afford membership.

Claude: That's a shame.

Mother: I still have the house.

Claude and Kurt: That's great.

Mother: My daughter loves golf.

Kurt: We know.

Mother: Maybe we can work something out so she can still play on your course.

At the word 'your,' Blaire let out a snort of laughter… which unfortunately went unnoticed by the adults.

Claude and Kurt: We're listening.

Blaire already knew all the stuff they were discussing – the club's policy prohibiting minors from being on the course without a member and California's labor laws regarding minors. Those were things Blaire could not care less about. Timmons said something about golf lessons, then Beesinger launched into a dreadfully boring explanation of the liability clauses to their insurance policy. Throughout, her mother could not keep from piping up about things she had learned during 'all of her extensive committee work'… occasionally glancing over as if desperate for support from a thirteen year old. Blaire made a point of yawning each time. The men were soon proposing odd jobs that could be done around the pro shop to compensate for advanced instruction from Timmons.

All of a sudden, they got quiet and looked together toward her, the lot of them so obviously proud of themselves for having worked out a legitimate reason for her being out on the course. Blaire shrugged her shoulders, smiled sweetly, and nodded her agreement to the plan they had come up with. She tuned them out after that, for she had gotten exactly what she wanted from them… what she fully considered to be hers already.

The combination to the bank and the keys to the candy store.

From the very beginning, Blaire consented to work for Kurt Timmons with an appearance of the eagerness and diligence needed for gaining the man's trust. Her schedule, agreed upon in the office meeting, was originally limited to Friday afternoons and a few hours on the weekend, but since the golf course was the only place she cared to be, Timmons soon found himself having to deal with her seven days a week.

His first task for her… one she knew few within the greenskeeper's cadre cared for... was the cleaning of golf carts. In preparation for the course's busiest time – the weekend – she would take soap, bucket, sponge and hose to the course's eighty five carts each Friday afternoon, then repeat the job on Saturday and Sunday. She found the chore to be beyond irritating, especially when it came to dealing with the debris left behind by morons who knew nothing about the inner workings of a trash can. Still... the job presented her with three unexpected benefits, the most obvious being that she got to drive a cart... something her parents had repeatedly denied her the pleasure of doing. She also got to see more of the day-to-day operations of the greenskeeper's shop... particularly where they kept the keys to the various storage sheds. Her final motivation for cleaning carts might strike someone of lesser mind as odd, but Blaire found great value in the collecting of scorecards abandoned on steering wheel clipboards. These, she would study in private, sometimes as a curiosity of different scoring methods and sometimes to amuse herself with how poorly certain members played. On occasion, she would even subtly inquire about how someone's round had gone... just to see if the person might lie.

Once she had shown herself to be responsible at cleaning carts, Timmons began treating her like his own personal assistant. He soon gave her access to his own private golf cart in order to run errands for him. She cheerfully performed all tasks given to her with the intent of becoming indispensible in the pro shop. Though she considered it degrading to be treated like a servant, she nonetheless found many benefits that compensated. For one, she learned which golf equipment was most effective and which was promoted only as a money-maker. Soon, she was restocking shelves and assisting customers... which allowed her to better eavesdrop on their conversations. Before the year was out, Timmons was comfortable enough with her manning the till when things got hectic. This was the moment she had been waiting for – the turning point in her relationship with the male employees of the country club. Her presence was a given.

She had been taking things from the pro shop almost from her first day working there. Initially, it was little things nobody would miss – a ball or two from the discount barrel, a bag of tees from the shelf, gloves from the lost-and-found, and a spike key someone left laying around. It was not that she needed any of those things, nor did the concept of someone else's ownership over such things ever enter her mind. She stole because she could. After all, the course... and everything on it... was already hers.

Taking things soon became far too easy. She stole a hundred dollars from the cash register on one occasion... just to prove to herself that she could...

yet never repeated the act. It was more important to stay on the good side of Timmons... as she had plans that involved him. She sought, instead, more creative ways of amusing herself around the pro shop. She would erase a person's tee time from the log book if they had hassled her in any way. She would give out confusing information on pro shop products to mess with the more naive shoppers. She would even secretly switch clubs between unattended golf bags... anything to relieve the immense boredom she often felt with a world that was so painfully slow. She once had the rare opportunity of personally returning a wallet she found in a golf cart. Without touching the cash, credit cards or driver's ID, she removed and destroyed all of the pictures, insurance information and other non-essential items, and then sweetly returned it to the owner as if that was the way she had found it. For days afterward, she delighted in the memory of the man's bewildered expression.

The only place in the pro shop that she never found boring was the full-length mirror set aside in one corner. Whatever shoppers saw as they disgustingly ogled themselves was nothing compared to the magic of what that glass revealed to her. Beyond its surface was a realm in which her true self ruled without the slightest interference from the mundane or tiresome. Whenever she could, Blaire would pass by this mirror in order to share a secret moment with the person within... for only that girl understood. This mirror did not exist to provide her with any kind of affirmation. It was there for only one reason – so she and it could revel together in how truly pathetic the rest of this world was.

On reaching sixteen, more significant changes took place in her life than anything she had experienced in going through puberty. She could now legally drive a car, which finally allowed her to break free from her mother's hold and get out on her own. The little bit more of the world she saw in no way swayed the confidence she had in herself. More important than having the freedom of the road, by club policy and California labor law, Blaire was finally able to be hired on officially by the pro shop. Timmons pushed it through clubhouse management surprisingly fast... as he should given all that he owed her. By then, she had taken nearly all that there was to be had from him. She had also exceeded the limits of her high school coach's instruction. It was now time for some serious training from a true guru of the sport. She went first to her mother, but not for permission... only to mess with her.

"Blaire, I'm sorry, but we can't afford to lay down hundreds of dollars for you to attend a golf clinic. I really wish we could... you know I'd do anything for you. But honestly... I don't understand why you still need golf lessons. Your coach says you're already good enough to win a full scholarship."

Even with so many years of being *her* mother, the woman still did not get it.

"Mother, it's not your problem. I'm taking care of it myself. I have over four grand saved up."

Blaire could almost see the little gears in her mother's head revving up and down, trying to figure out how she could have amassed even a tenth of that amount. If the woman ever got up the nerve to ask, Blaire was prepared with her most innocuous 'here and there' accounts of her financial dealings at the club. For weeks following that exchange, as Blaire went about using her influence at the club to get into the golf clinic of her choosing, she silently took pleasure in seeing her mother struggle with the burden of not knowing where the money had come from. Although she earned a good portion through legitimate means, none of that was her mother's business. From time to time, the woman would elude to the topic, but never pressed it simply because she lacked the courage to risk doing damage to their relationship.

By seventeen, Blaire already had numerous sexual encounters through which she explored her ability to exploit men. Her first, with a greenskeeper, affirmed to her what she had always suspected – that most men were pathetic little creatures desperate for fleeting pleasures and oblivious to their insignificance in the greater world. This insight, she was sure, could be used to her advantage. She soon found it easy to lure a man in, get what she wanted out of him, and then drop him like he was nothing.

Making it with Timmons was no different – she got from him exactly what she was after… even though he turned out to be a bit of a disappointment. Not in the deed itself. That was okay… as sex goes… but he fell without putting up much of a challenge. Playing him was like playing par-three golf.

Way too easy.

Still… because it was important… she carefully planned out every stroke. For weeks beforehand, she sought opportunities to brush up against him… or linger in exchanging some item… or come face-to-face long enough to hold his eyes… all innocent acts that hid her real intent. Relentlessly, she went about pushing back the boundaries on his personal space, knowing that the time was right when he started giving her furtive looks about the pro shop. Maybe he actually had feelings for her… or maybe he was not getting enough at home from his pregnant wife. Either way mattered not to her. Blaire chose the end of a slow day, breezed right into his office, locking the door behind her, and then quickly straddled him in his desk chair before he knew what hit him. He was completely helpless from the moment she started kissing him. The whole thing lasted all of ten minutes… fifteen tops… and from then on, Blaire had him right where she wanted him – totally terrified of her. To drive the point home in the days to follow, she maintained a constant string of sweet little gestures that kept him on edge. Simple stuff like touching him when he was not expecting it, slyly smiling at him in public, going out of the way to chat with his wife whenever the woman happened to stop by, or calling him at home in the evening to ask some stupid question about the next day at the pro shop. Within two weeks, it was clear that he would do whatever she asked simply out of fear of being exposed.

Love… or being in love… never really registered in her way of thinking. Regardless of what pop music peddled, she concluded that no one could truly love another. Everyone was in it for themselves… and only she had the advantage because only she knew that love was an illusion. Still… having to hear others talk about love always irritated her… especially when some idiot used the term to express admiration for golf equipment.

As if they had any idea what they were talking about! They're all hacks. Only I know that kind of love.

I love him because he's strong and powerful. Everyone takes notice when we're together because he's flash and flare… and everything that's male. When he does his thing, it drives me crazy like a ravenous animal.

I love those others too. They're not as strong as him, but they're like iron for me. Not as loud as him. They don't need the attention or praise. It's their ruggedness that excites me. They get me out of whatever trouble he gets me into. They can cut through anything. They're my beloved workmen. They make me feel indestructible.

The little men, I have deep love for them too. Not as strong or as handsome, but so very dependable. They never stray far or fall short for me. They're like… househusbands. I can always count on them to get me over whatever's in my way. They make me feel secure.

Then there's my buddy. He goes with me into the tall grass and into the sand. He'll even play in the water if that's what I want. He can do the most amazing tricks – flips and spins – and then like a puppy he'll set it right down where I want him to. He makes me laugh.

But none of those others can please me like the last one. He is oh so subtle and smooth. Those imbecilic girls at school who go on and on about sex… they can't possibly understand what ecstasy really is. Like when I gently stroke my lover, and he, from a great distance, puts it right into the… hole. There's no one more passionate than him. He makes me feel alive.

I love them. I love them all.

Timmons, through intense lobbying, finally got her accepted into a two week workshop at the Kensington Center in Long Beach, one of the top golf clinics in Southern California. The progress she made in those few days was remarkable… sufficient for the Piper Mountain Country Club trustees to retroactively sponsor her for the clinic. She ended up not having to spend a dime of her own money. Through the recommendation of the Kensington, she earned a slot at the WGA's qualifying school in Orlando, better known as 'Q-school.' Blaire knew full well that this was actually no school, but a six day competition for one of a dozen tour cards the WGA granted yearly giving newcomers the right to go pro. She withheld that information from her mother, opting instead to depict Q-school as some sort of advanced academy for golf. It took near on a month to persuade the woman to allow her to miss out on a week of high school in order to attend. But since Piper Mountain had rightly granted Blaire a second scholarship to cover the cost, her mother finally conceded… not that Blaire cared in the least for her approval.

She went to Q-school in November of her senior year, competed with the world's best and brightest young women golfers, finished fourth, and returned home with her tour card… something she kept as a complete secret from her mother.

CHAPTER

11

THREE BECAME TWO, BECOMES ONE

"You know, Mother… it occurs to me that I've never mentioned this really important thing I learned recently."

The previous month of living with Blaire had been uncharacteristically easy. Bridget might even go so far as to say that her daughter had somehow turned pleasant since coming back from that Q thing in Florida. She did have a bit of a tussle in getting her to take the SAT exam the week following Thanksgiving… though that was expected. Blaire absolutely hated being tested. But with that requisite step in the college application process out of the way, and her having personally pushed through the admission paperwork, Bridget was hopeful that their last holiday season together in the golf course house would be their best… especially since Blaire already had several scholarship offers in her pocket. In retrospect, she had been wise in allowing her daughter to continue on in golf. The game was going to pay for four years of college, something that she could not otherwise have afforded on her own. With so many exciting prospects on the horizon, Bridget was now convinced that Blaire was about to turn a corner in life.

All of this put Bridget into a festive mood for the holidays… even if Blaire was less so. The spirit of Christmas… sad to say… could never quite mesh with her daughter's way of thinking. Still… they shared a simple gift exchange that morning, a modest holiday meal at noon, and were now seated together sipping spiced cider in the shadows about the glow of their dimly lit tree. Throughout the day, she had tried to engage Blaire in conversation about her hopes for the coming year, as well as what stood out from the past one… all without success. Blaire offered little more than a word here or there… even when Bridget ventured off into golf-related topics in hopes of drawing her out. As they sat in that evening's silence, she was startled when Blaire suddenly perked up with the prospect of something personal… maybe even something regarding her aspirations for college and beyond.

"Really? What's that?"

"The key to a successful recovery. It's all about envisioning a window in space that's your only way out. So… try to follow me in this… you've gotten yourself into trouble doing too much… or maybe it was just bad luck and not your fault at all. It doesn't matter. The only thing that really matters is the way out. There's a window of recovery there. Sometimes high and sometimes low… but it's always there. Most can't find it because they're too busy stuck in the past… you know, dwelling on the shot that got them there."

Like air escaping from a punctured tire, the reality of Blaire never sharing anything of substance suddenly hit Bridget, completely deflating her anticipation of the moment.

"Are we talking about golf again?"

"No, Mother – *I'm* talking about golf. What I'm *trying* to do is teach you something about the philosophy of the recovery shot. So how's about you let me finish?!"

"By all means… go ahead."

"Here's the deal. You can't go back and fix the last shot. Where you are is where you've ended up. All you can do is prepare yourself for the next one. And that one will never work if you don't believe there's a window of recovery available to you. That's the hard part."

"You make it sound easy."

"It's not… for *normal* players."

Bridget slumped back into the living room corner where she sat. Although she could no longer make out whatever expression was on Blaire's face, the tone to her words was plain enough. As always, the girl's contemptuous attitude made it so very clear that she did not consider herself to be a normal player.

"It's a given, Mother, that every window has its cost… usually in distance and direction. You've got to be willing to pay that price because ultimately it's all about the score. Get through or lose. So… once you're over that, then you…"

"Over what?"

"Mother – do I have to explain everything to you? Try paying attention."

"Fine. I won't interrupt again."

"Once you're over the fact that you've just made a lousy shot… the golfer has to look to their feet. They've got to accept where they've landed and decide… No – be *decided*! They've got to be fully reconciled on what it's going to take, right where they stand, to get through that window of recovery. There'll be a myriad of things to make it difficult… maybe even impossible for some. It might be the risk… or the strength needed… or the fear of more failure. The golfer has to figure it all out quickly… and then get over those distractions. But the last thing is really critical… you have to concentrate on the window and picture yourself going through it. Not just the ball, but you, as the golfer. You shut everything else out, because nothing else matters. It's only you and that window. And then… you take the shot.'

"And what if it doesn't work out?"

"Then forget the past, and look for that window… the next one… the only one that matters."

Blaire went quiet after that, and though Bridget was tempted to kindle a conversation toward the subject of her daughter's future, she had already been treated rudely enough. For a brief moment, her thoughts went to what it might be like to have Blaire off at college. Bridget was sure to be lonely… that was a given… but maybe in that loneliness she might also find relief from having to constantly tiptoe about on eggshells. Living with Blaire had stolen so much enjoyment out of life. Maybe… with her gone… there might actually be a window through which she could recover something approximating a normal life.

Blaire went to bed without offering a goodnight… or a Merry Christmas… leaving her alone to consider the conversation differently. Blaire had spoken confidently about a game, but Bridget sat in the darkness considering an extension of the concept to her own life. It had been years since the divorce, yet in many ways her pain felt as if it were yesterday She had actually lost Mitch twice – once to a game and then ultimately to another woman. She had never found anything in the way of a window of recovery from that.

For her, the years since he left were like the endless flow of freeway traffic, always moving yet constantly displaying a sameness in its opposing directions of travel – what she longed for out of life and the reality of what she was actually stuck in. Although mile marker and exit sign provided her with some measure of the time being traveled, such small indicators on the shoulder of her journey were too often obscured by a bumper-to-bumper sadness that clogged up her awareness. Like a complex cloverleaf interchange, her mind seemed to loop about the same memories, occasionally venturing off for a brief side trip into some distraction, but invariably forcing her to re-enter and cover the same stretch of struggles all over again. None of the roads available to her ever led to the desired destination of her heart – a loving and harmonious family. She had lost a husband along the way, and perhaps… in a different way… a daughter too.

Entering the new year, with Blaire set to graduate from high school in June, Bridget listed the house on the real estate market, as per the terms of the divorce settlement. It ended up selling within a few weeks owing to the long list of club members eager to live on the course. Ironically, the very transaction that marked the last remaining detail of her failed marriage was also the only thing in her association with Mitch to have a return on investment. When the sale eventually closed in June, they would split the profit evenly… as per the mediated agreement… with Bridget having enough to cover a down payment on a place of her own. A small comfort for beginning life again… alone. She nonetheless took the prospect of change fully to heart. While somewhat fearful of her soon-to-be empty-nester life, she undertook house hunting as a significant step toward moving on. Perhaps it was a window of recovery after all, not unlike that which Blaire had once talked about regarding golf.

Bridget spent months in pondering over what she desired in the way of a new home. It had to be a place of refuge, a place of reflection and tranquility, and ultimately a place where she could find the margin needed for coping with life on her own. Finally being shed of the golf course… it always lurking off the back edge of the property… as well as the fringe of her thinking… would surely bring her a step closer toward experiencing the freedom of coming home to a home rather than to a collection of horrible associations to Mitch. Of course, she made compulsory efforts toward including Blaire in the house hunting process, though she was secretly relieved to find her daughter completely disinterested. That was fine… actually, more than fine. Bridget was immensely gratified to know that whatever she chose as her next home, Blaire's influence would be limited to holidays and the occasional weekend away from college.

In narrowing down the real estate possibilities, Bridget began by focusing her attention on regions north of the San Gabriel Mountains. Even though it meant a longer commute, rational or not, she drew a strange pleasure from the thought that a wall of rock would serve as a separation between her new home and the rest of Los Angeles County… though in actuality, she was unlikely to find anything affordable closer in to the city. After extensive research, she came to place an offer on property in a gated community of Palmdale. The house was on the smallish side… just two bedrooms, one bath, a contiguous kitchen/dining/living area, and a one-car garage, all set back from the street by a narrow rock-covered patch of a front yard. None of that really mattered. Ironically, the selling point for her was not unlike that of the golf course house for Mitch. The backyard, encompassing an area slightly larger in size than that of the house itself, was fully enclosed on all sides by a six foot high redwood fence. The previous owners had outfitted this space with a variety of ornamental trees and shrubs, put in an immaculate stretch of lawn that weaved between bark-covered flower beds, and installed a covered porch rimmed by lattice work intertwined with flowering vines. There was even a small fountain peacefully gurgling its recirculated water. She fell in love with the space the moment she stepped through the porch's sliding glass door. Free to spend money on herself, she would purchase new furniture for both the house and the patio, pick out a grill, and hang hummingbird feeders. This would be a place of solitude where she could set aside all of her self-sacrificing ways and escape from the intrusion of the world.

Blaire, having accepted a golf scholarship to Pepperdine University, insisted on starting out in the summer semester as it would afford her immediate access to a higher level of training and competition. Though a bit odd… seeing as most freshman opted to begin in the fall… Bridget nonetheless considered the timing to be perfect. The golf course house was set to close in the week following Blaire's graduation… as would the new place… which meant that Bridget could immediately settle into an empty-nester's lifestyle without her daughter's prickly presence ruining the summer.

Blaire's last month of high school did not turn out as meaningful as Bridget had hoped, what with the girl remaining involved in a constant stream of golfing activities. At least Blaire acquiesced time for a few shopping trips to get college supplies, things to outfit her dorm room, and new school clothes. Their final night together in the golf course house presented one last opportunity for Bridget to make a connection with Blaire… something that might help them both start out well on their own. They had separated out those things each wanted saved, some for campus and some to be shifted by movers to Bridget's new residence in the morning. Everything else had either been sold off at a yard sale, given away to thrift stores, or was destined to be hauled away by garbage trucks. The house had to be emptied by the weekend in order for the cleaners to prepare it for the new occupant. All that remained after were the goodbyes. So, as they sat about in their box-filled living room eating take-out after a day of packing, Bridget made one last attempt at discovering Blaire's feelings regarding the divorce. Her opening words, unfortunately, got cut off.

"You know… this would be a really good time to clear the air about how your father…"

"Mother – seriously?! How many times have I got to tell you?! I'm not interested in discussing him! That's in the past!"

"I really don't understand you, Blaire. Your father walks out, and you don't hear from him in years… he doesn't even acknowledge your graduation from high school or the fact that you got a scholarship to Pepperdine… and you're telling me it has no effect on you?! That doesn't make any sense! You should be angry. You have every right to be angry! But to you… it's some sort of… inconsequential thing."

She waited, yet Blaire would not respond.

"Fine. Then we're going to try something I learned about in recovery. We're going to relive the whole thing… but in a way I think you'll feel comfortable with. We're going to treat it like a history lesson… like something that happened to other people long ago. Would you be up for that?"

By way of an answer, Blaire rolled her eyes and fell back on the couch.

"Trust me, Sweetheart – this will help. You need to work through what your father did. You might even learn something new that could…"

With a display of sudden force, Blaire sprang to the edge of the couch and pointed a finger directly at her.

"No. It's *you* who'll learn something new!"

"What're you talking about?"

A self-assured expression slowly crept over Blaire's face… one that Bridget knew well to be a harbinger of something ugly lying just beneath the thin layer of prettiness that all-too-often was her daughter's false-front.

"I knew about Dad and that woman for months before he left."

Momentarily taken aback, a maternal reflex within her brought forth a shaky recovery.

"I'm… sorry you had to find that out on your own. It must have been… a terrible burden for you to bear."

"It wasn't. It clarified things. Told me who he was, who you were… and who I am."

"What do you mean by that?"

She posed the question with all the sincerity of a caring mother, inwardly relieved that Blaire was finally sharing something of what she had gone through.

Whatever variant of 'abandoned,' 'victimized,' or 'unloved' came forth, Bridget would be there for her daughter. Yet what she got was not what she expected.

"Not someone to be lied to."

Their eyes locked for several seconds as a new reality of her husband's departure slowly crept over her. The watch on her wrist ticked off its intervals as the only sound, faint as it was, to compete with the rage growing within her. Through that fierceness, Bridget spoke as seldom she ever had, propelled on by the wicked smile of self-satisfaction spreading all over her daughter's face.

"Damn you, Blaire! How could you be so coldhearted?! It was you, all along, wasn't it?!"

"Yes, Mother. It was me."

CHAPTER

12

VENGEANCE

Prior to that day, golf had been just another thing Blaire was good at... another thing others were envious of... another way in which she demonstrated her superiority. But on that day... the day her father emerged from a cluster of trees and peeked up to a third floor balcony... golf became something much more to her. It would be her only friend. The path ahead would be walked together with golf, and through it, she would reek all of her fierce vengeance on this pitifully boring world... with the first terrible blow falling upon him.

She alone had uncovered her father's secret, and though it was not her personally that he was cheating on, she nonetheless took it as an insult directed at her. He had lied about what he was doing out on the course alone... and lying to her was unforgivable.

Blaire now understood the private means by which some woman on that porch communicated with him, but still wanted to be absolutely certain before carrying out her plan. She would need to position herself directly across from the condos to know for sure. She selected a knot of acacia bushes located on the rough between the 15th and 17th fairways as her best means of concealment... although getting there without being noticed would be tricky. She managed to reach those bushes on the next day well ahead of his arrival at the 15th, but was disappointed to find the drapes on the porch closed. Her father, when he came to the tee, played the hole with a driver as one might expect. As he approached where his shot landed, she noticed him glance toward that porch. With amused delight, she watched him not bother to set his feet properly before swinging… he just walked up to the spot, threw down his bag, and whacked his ball… a terribly thin seven iron that overshot the green. Blaire silently smirked to herself as he snatched up his bag and trudged off toward the clubhouse, not even bothering to retrieve the errant shot.

Poor Daddy didn't get what he wanted today…

At the next opportunity, she again headed to the acacias with confidence that today would be the day, but was intercepted on the way there by Mrs. Fletcher and her foursome of batty old ladies. Blaire got yelled at for 'not knowing her place' because she, as a minor, was out on the course without an adult. Quickly reacting, she turned on a teary-eyed performance over a lost dog… despite her family having never owned a pet… and implored them to allow her to continue searching the course for 'Scruffy.' Her act proved too good. Mrs. Fletcher, an avid dog lover, offered to leave her party behind and help scour the course for this fictitious pet. With a grandiose display of gratitude, Blaire declined the woman's offer… but decided it best to leave for home rather than risk running into them again.

The third attempt at those bushes brought success. From her hiding place, she saw both the open drapes and her father moving into the trees. Then, for the first time, Blaire got a good look at the woman as she briefly came out onto her porch… right before reentering and closing the drapes. Blaire recognized her immediately. Had it not been but a few weeks ago when this woman tried to make small talk with her in the clubhouse? She had complimented Blaire on her outfit… or her hair… or something stupid like that. At the time, Blaire considered the encounter to be nothing more than the typical nonsense of an adult trying to be friendly with a kid… but now she knew different. The woman had been patronizing the daughter of her secret lover… and Blaire would make her pay.

She lay in those bushes the entire time her father was inside, lingering even after he left. She was not lost in sadness over the discovery of her father's betrayal… or what it would mean to her mother… but instead was fully engaged in estimating angles and distances… and in deciding how best to carry out her plan. She only vaguely registered the presence of golfers passing by. She was angry, and her anger, under control, would be used to beat him. It would beat them both.

In the weeks to follow, Blaire practiced like nothing else mattered… for nothing else did.

There was an old tree, rotted to its core, leaning against the outer edge of the driving range's protective screen. This tree happened to give way in a wind storm the week prior to Blaire's discovery, falling across the netting and tearing a sizable slit in it. As this opening in the barrier posed no immediate danger, it being located behind the pitching range and near the greenskeeper's equipment shed, the staff were in no hurry to patch what had not yet become a problem. Blaire made it their problem. She set her designs on that hole. Experimenting with several different clubs, she settled on the five iron as the one providing her with the best combination of loft and distance. At first, she was only able to get one in a dozen range balls through from thirty yards out. One such fortunate shot ricocheted off the shed and smashed the headlight on an ATV. The next day, she discovered that the hole had been covered over with a blue tarp awkwardly sown into the mesh. This makeshift solution was cheap and effective, though in time the clubhouse would receive so many complaints about its second-rate appearance that the entire forty by hundred foot section of netting would be replaced. In the meantime, the tarp proved to be the perfect target for Blaire.

She was at the driving range every day after school and on the weekends laboring over her swing, completely losing track of how many buckets of balls she ended up sending into that screen. All she could think about, day and night, was hitting that tarp. Her accuracy gradually increased to a point where half of her shots hit home. An excellent rate by most golfing standards, but all those failures just infuriated her. She began working into the evenings, with her hands blistering even though she wore golfing gloves. The greenskeepers had seen her at it day after day and told Timmons, who eventually came out to investigate. His arrival initially suggested to her that someone had caught on to her plan, but she relaxed on discovering that he was there to offer his expertise… for free.

"I see you're working on your recovery shot. Well, Blaire… you're trying to hit it too hard. The objective is to put your ball through that window in space… not knock a hole in the hole that's already there. Why don't you move up a club face, shift the ball up a bit in your stance, and take something off the swing. That should help with your mechanics. More importantly… you need to work on your mindset. Concentrate on that window and shut everything else out. You don't even have to worry about what happens to your ball once it's on the other side, because it's live or die getting through."

His advice proved to be a breakthrough. In another week's time, she was close to four hits out of five, with the misses not straying far from the target.

She soon found that it was not necessary to aim at the tarp each time. She could concentrate instead on quickly getting the correct stance and reproducing the swing. The window would remain in the same place in her mind.

The next step in her plan was more challenging – she needed to do it in the dark. This meant sneaking onto the course at night, an action that could derail everything if she were caught. She was especially concerned about the noise of contact being registered by the afterhours greenskeeper charged with maintaining a watch over the course. To minimize the odds of being heard by him, she chose what she thought to be the safest practice times… during *Saturday Night Live* and *Monday Night Football*… two television events she knew most men would not dare skip. It took fifteen minutes by moonlight to collect enough range balls for the first test. The outline of the tarp against the transparent netting was marginal at best, but fortunately she could at least hear the difference between a hit and a miss. Her accuracy dropped considerably the first night, but rose back up on the second. She was ready.

During all those days of practice, her mind was also occupied in refining the details of her plan. As with most crime, she knew that failure was frequently encountered during the escape. Preparing, getting there, and doing the deed were of no value if she ended up being caught on the way out… whereas being suspected was an entirely different matter. That would gnaw an even deeper wound than the deed itself. She toyed with several exit strategies before finally settling on the best one.

She selected the day – a Wednesday – as this almost always was an 'open-drape' day owing to the woman having work off. The previous weekend, Blaire managed to ferret away two baskets of range balls and hide them in the bushes near the greenskeeper's shack. At midnight, she snuck out after being convince that her parents were asleep. Based on previous late-night visits to the chosen spot, she also knew that the woman would be in bed.

Clothed completely in black, Blaire lugged the two buckets, sixty balls in all, through the darkness of the course. The walk had to be done without the aid of a flashlight… though she carried a small one in her pocket just in case. She was especially wary about alerting some of the old duffers who lived in the same condo complex. They were always complaining to her about their baby bladders… or insomnia… or some other old person problem. One crotchety man, in particular, often bragged about sitting out on his porch in the middle of the night scanning the golf course for intruders like he was some kind of home-front defense.

Fortunately, she arrived at the spot without a problem. The moon had set, but the city's ambient night lighting was more than sufficient for her to neatly array the balls into four parallel lines, spaced a yard apart from each other. As she worked, a memory came of having watched a war movie with her father in which a phalanx of riflemen fought off thousands of invaders. The similarity to what she was planning to do with her lines greatly amused her.

Once finished, she lay back in the grass. She had been sweating and needed to cool off. She was also surprised to find that her heart was racing... she needed that to cool off too if she was to be steady for the deed. Resting there in the dark, she listened attentively to the night sounds, caressed the cut of the fairway, and marveled at stars that even the Southern California city lights could not pollute away. She was at perfect ease with what was about to happen.

For no obvious reason, she jumped up and approached the first ball. Her swing topped it badly, sending it trickling through the rough to the out-of-bounds marker ten yards away. That failure angered her... which was good, as it brought her a determined intensity to do better. The next shot, however, hit off the facing above the first floor, causing her to freeze with fear. As she listened, the yelp of someone's lap dog faintly came to her, but the overall silence of the condo complex soon brought her relief.

She reprimanded herself once more, this time for forgetting to concentrate fully on the target as she had done at the driving range. For the next minute or so, she stood there picturing in her mind the tarp draped over the dim outline of the porch. She then envisioned the swing needed to put a ball into the center of that imaginary tarp. Lastly, she took on the imperative – that it was life or death whether she put each shot through that window in space.

She drew in a deep breath and approached the third ball in line. This one she sent sailing over the railing of the third floor porch, dramatically shattering its sliding glass door. She did not stop to take in the effect. The next twelve shots either ricocheted within the confines of that same porch, broke new glass in what remained of the door and the transparent panels that bordered the porch, or found their way through newly-made openings into the interior of the condo. Her mind registered the occupant's screams, as well as that porch lights up and down the complex were coming on... yet she did not stop. Quickly moving to the second line of balls, she made brief note of the many dogs barking within the complex. Screams were now turning into curses, as the voices of the woman's neighbors were also shouting out hysterically into the night, each adding their own particular version of panic. She went on to the third line. A man on the second floor was yelling out to others that someone was on the 15th fairway… which Blaire thought should be obvious. He was demanding that the person out in the dark should stop or he would get his gun. She silenced him with a single shot into his porch. Her rockets were now flaring out into adjacent balconies as adrenaline took command of her swing, yet she would not stop until there was nothing left of the fourth line. In all, she was sure that at least thirty golf balls had made their way into the condominium of Dorothy Sutherland.

The siren was both her cue to leave and the ultimate test of her escape plan. Initially, she headed deeper into the fairway darkness, but then moved laterally in order to cut back toward the cluster of trees. Her bike, left in the drainage ditch at dusk, was waiting there. After climbing down in, she pivoted about to find that several residents had moved out onto the fairway with flashlights. Some were appraising her work site, and others were searching the darkness for the culprit. After a minute through which she caught her breath, Blaire put the four iron across the grips of her bike and rolled it out onto the edge of the condo's parking lot. The police, she knew, would arrive through the main entrance, so she took the prearranged path through a hedge, across a vacant lot, and onto barren streets leading her home.

As she rode on, the siren's whine slowly faded, being replaced in her ears by the grinding of bike gears and the sound of herself panting. It occurred to her then that such effort was unnecessary. She could relax and take the remainder of the ride at a leisurely pace. Her plan had been carried out to perfection. She leaned back a bit and let up on the pedals in making the final turn onto her street. There, her feeling of invulnerability instantly evaporated on seeing a familiar set of headlights coming her way. She immediately lurched forward over the handlebars in a desperate attempt to bring her bike about and head in the opposite direction. As her front wheel warbled at the grip of the breaks, a completely different option occurred to her. She had already slowed to a near halt, but now picked up her peddling to the previous easy pace. Rather than fleeing, she would give ample opportunity for the driver to make her out. In coming abreast of the passing car, its dashboard illumination provided her with all the means she needed for seeing the driver's head crane about in bewilderment. That look was exactly what she wanted to see. He had recognized her, and probably also noticed the four iron bridging her handlebars. In that moment, she hoped that the street lighting was sufficient for her father to fully comprehend the satisfaction spread all over her face. She wanted that smile burned into his memory for a lifetime.

It was now a simple matter of stowing her bike in the side yard where always kept, and then climbing back through her bedroom window. Once inside, she peeled off her sweats to reveal her typical pajamas beneath. The last task before getting in bed was to check that the small wad of paper she had inserted between door and jam remained wedged there. Neither parent had peeked in, though one now knew… or would soon know… the fullness of what she had accomplished this night.

Blaire threw herself down in bed with the full intent of replaying the night's adventure in her mind. Her revelry, however, was interrupted because not all in the house was silent. Off toward the master bedroom, she detected something faint coming to her as if wind whining its way through a poorly sealed door frame… except the pitch was much raspier. She pondered on it for several seconds before finally recognizing the source. Blaire reached up to a wall switch beside her bed and activated the overhead fan whose squeaky revolutions would more than effectively mask the sound of her mother crying. Her hand then came down on the golf ball she had placed in a saucer on her bedside table a month before. Picking it up, she brought it close to her face. Faint street light provided sufficient means for her to gloat on her father's ball.

One day, I'll probably chuck you into the ocean… but for now, I'll keep you as a little souvenir.

She put the ball back, then folded her hands behind her head and stared up into the rotating blades. It had been a brilliant addition to her plan, and she dearly hoped that both her father and the woman noticed. She had carefully penned his mark – O'C – on every single range ball. An added insult just for him.

Now Blaire's vengeance would begin. Everyday that he looked into her eyes, he would see the truth. He would know, but be incapable of doing anything about it. He would deign to live with the terrible secret rather than dare tell anyone… especially either of the two women. That would be doubly humiliating for him. He would not have the courage to confront her either. So he would pretend not to have seen her on the bicycle, and instead imagine it all away as a trick of the darkness. That thought, more than anything that had transpired that night, brought a broad grin to Blaire's face.

CHAPTER

13

SEPARATION

Expectation is the smallest of seeds capable of nestling within any crack to wisdom, common sense, or the natural order of things… wherever it can take hold. There, it lays dormant, coexisting in wholesome symbiosis with other thought until an inkling of imprecise perspective leads to its germination. Expectation then rapidly grows, sending out shoot and root that draw energy from conscious light and nutrient from uncertain dark. In order for it to survive, expectation must now claim all space as its own. The struggle for irrational control of the rational is intense, so much so that expectation sends out invasive runners keenly adept at seeking out and strangling all contrary concern. It then takes full command of the bed with assurances that act as toxic preemergents against second-thought. Water and feed are now reserved exclusively for its own cultivation. Soon, expectation has grown so strong that the host becomes the epiphyte… nothing more than a measly clump of starving lichen clinging to the surface of its persuasion. The tragic end to it all is that this genus of conviction is destined to unwittingly destroy itself… and its owner. Expectation flowers without fruit, then wilts away in poisoning its own soil with bitter disappointment.

For months following the attack on Dot's condo, the Piper Mountain Country Club's gossip network extensively debated a myriad of possible explanations, with two ultimately rising above all others. Either a spurned admirer had acted out in malice, or Dot's ex-husband had gotten his revenge. When it became known that Mitch O'Connor ran off with Dot, adherents to the various theories quickly wove in the emerging details of the affair to support their version of events. The police never caught the culprit… never even had a serious suspect… though the use of range balls and the curious O'C marking on each accounted for why they had concentrated inquiries on several employees at the club and on the O'Connors. Nothing definitive was ever confirmed or refuted well enough to the gossiper's satisfaction, particularly as the principle parties never returned to Piper Mountain following the incident.

From Bridget's perspective, the abuse inflicted upon Dot's condo could never compare to the magnitude of Mitch's offense toward her. Glass could be replaced, dents repaired, and mars repainted, but her heart would forever remain devastated. She nonetheless respectfully answered each question put to her by the police regarding her husband's relationship with the victim, managing not to fall apart until after the squad car had departed from her curb. She, like those wicked two, was determined to never again set foot within the walls of the very place responsible for her husband rejecting her for the comfort of another woman's arms. Instead, she hid herself from everyone she knew, purposefully arranging for her soon-to-be ex-husband to pick up his things while she was away at work.

In all the years since then, no one ever put the pieces together sufficiently to suspect the twelve-year-old girl who had practiced so diligently on a driving range at hitting a piece of plastic sheeting the size of a sliding glass door. For her part, Bridget had childishly fantasized far too many times about a white knight defending her honor when she should have considered the person residing in her own home. That oversight was yet another example of her failing to see things as they truly were.

During those weeks following Mitch's departure, Blaire would frequently come home to recount some little tidbit of gossip she picked up while out on the course. Having to hear what people were saying behind her back tore open the wounds in Bridget's fragile self-worth on nearly a daily basis. Yet she would never have forbidden Blaire from sharing such things. To do so, Bridget feared, might close off the lines of communication between them. She chose, instead, to tolerate the seemingly callous way in which Blaire went about relating news only because she believed that her daughter had also suffered a great loss.

Bridget now knew differently. Blaire, with her sick twisted sense of humor, had been torturing her all along. As her daughter slouched back on the couch at the conclusion of her story, Bridget realized for the first time that she had absolutely no ability to comprehend the dark depths of the girl's mind. She had considered her daughter to be misunderstood, troubled, distant, extremely difficult, and all too often inclined toward not considering the feelings of others. But there she sat, completely bored with how deeply hurtful this revelation was to her own mother. Minutes before, Blaire had been so animated in recounting what had been hidden for six years. Now, all her previous enthusiasm was gone, replaced by a droopy-eyed self-satiation that hung there on her face… almost as if a tryptophan-ish effect had taken hold from having gorged herself on the recollection of a triumph. Blaire's final words, that everything had gone according to plan, struck Bridget as the cruelest finish to it all. She wanted no part of that warped thinking, but must confront this complete lack of decency… or burst out into tears.

"No, Blaire… it didn't turn out like you thought. Or maybe you just didn't care about the consequences." She caught a hint of perplexity on Blaire's face, which nonetheless quickly morphed back into her usual indifference. "You must have known that your father never slept in this house again after that night."

"Yeah… so what?!"

"I don't know what might have happened otherwise… Maybe I never would have found out about the affair, or maybe I would have by some other means… and then divorced him on my own terms. And who knows… maybe he would have eventually ended it with me… or with her. Regardless… what you did drove him irrevocably to her. Blaire… you had no right to put an end to our marriage."

"Your marriage?!"

The response came far too quickly, making it impossible for Bridget not to pick up on the derisive tone through which it was delivered.

"You know, Blaire… you're not so smart as you think… and not because the outcome inconvenienced you in any way. It's evident that you think something as sacred as someone's marriage is… beneath you. But in so doing… you've displayed your limits. You never ask yourself 'what if'… you just do whatever comes into your mind. But it's evident you can't see into the future well enough to predict the outcomes of your own actions. You really have no idea what it's done to you, do you?"

She waited for the words to settle in, hoping that they might somehow reach a nerve of introspection… but the girl's self-assured smile never budged.

"I think I've had enough of you for one night."

Without permitting a response, Bridget departed the living room for the evening… her last one in that house. Lying awake in bed well after having turned out the lights, she could help but replay in her mind, for the thousandth time, the events of that night years ago. They had been awoken sometime well after midnight by Dot's phone call. As Mitch had been groggy-headed in answering, he did not immediately register the voice and depart the bedroom. He stayed, and Bridget ended up hearing both sides of the conversation. Dot was in hysterics, screaming about having been attacked and that someone was trying to kill her. Over and over, she could hear the young woman insisting that he come without delay. Then came the word that was still burnt into Bridget's memory – choose. As a brief silence took over, Mitch made eye contact with her for the first time since picking up the phone. Maybe Dot's voice had finally come under control or maybe she was simply waiting for a response. Either way, Bridget knew that the course of her life hung in the balance of that silence.

Mitch then spoke with unusual calm before ending the call.

"I'll be right over."

He rose and dressed, purposefully keeping his back turned away as she flung out a torrent of questions and accusations. He said nothing to any of them, coming about to face her only after he was ready.

"I've got to go, Bridget. Goodbye."

She had never been alone with him since.

The revelation that her own daughter had been the one to vandalize Dot's condo kept Bridget flailing about in bed all night. She was unable to arrange her pillow or coverings in any way capable of inducing thought-free sleep, as images of Blaire kept intertwining themselves into the memory of Mitch's rejection. Her humiliation bore a new burden, one that might permanently damage another relationship – hers with her daughter. Blaire offered no apology, nor any degree of sympathy, and in no way acknowledged her part in catalyzing the end of a family. In truth, Bridget now saw herself as a failure twice over. She was just as powerless toward influencing her daughter as she had been toward preserving her marriage.

She rose the next morning determined not to allow the hurt and anger she was feeling toward Blaire to interfere with what needed being done this day. Delivering Blaire to college was actually a big step for the both of them… maybe even more so for Bridget. She would finally have some relief from being treated horribly by Blaire… and relief from having to keep a constant guard on herself so as not to fall into the girl's traps. No longer would she have to put work into rehearsing every interaction… or laboring over whether saying 'yes' or 'no' at any particular moment was the right thing to do. Not that she was cutting Blaire out of her life… she could never see herself doing that… but at least a much needed separation would finally go up between them.

This should have been a proud and exciting day. She had endured the many ordeals of being a single parent. Her daughter was finally heading off to college, a dream Bridget had fostered from the girl's youth onward. All she could do now was hope that Blaire took to her new responsibilities, maturing in the process… just as Bridget had once done herself. Perhaps, after that, there would be no end to the good things Blaire might accomplish in graduating, starting out on a career, and one day building a family of her own.

As most of Blaire's things had already been loaded into the car the day before, they were off in short order that morning to the campus of Pepperdine University, little more than an hour away. Through the drive, she did not engage Blaire in conversation, who seemed more than content to remain affixed to her iPod. That was fine enough with Bridget. After unloading the car at Blaire's dorm, she lingered there in helping the girl get situated into her room… again, without any of the enthusiasm she had once envisioned for that moment. Fortunately, the stay had to be kept short, as the movers were coming in a few hours. By the time she pulled away from campus, Bridget settled into a tired-out acceptance over having been crushed the night before. At least she could console herself that through many years of pain she had finally delivered her daughter over to the next stage of life. Her expectation was that someone else… a roommate, professors, coaches or fellow students… would pick up where she had not succeeded with Blaire.

Four days of silence transpired through which Bridget heard nothing from Blaire. Although immensely curious as to how things were going, she kept to herself, concentrating instead on settling into her new home. Waking up in the morning to a different set of walls, she was excited to get at boxes begging to be opened so their contents could get sorted into new places… to start decorating those new spaces… to begin exploring her neighborhood… to find the best shopping… and to finally be free from the presence of Blaire.

All her enjoyment at being on her own evaporated the moment she received a phone call from the university's athletics department informing her that Blaire had not attended the mandatory orientation meeting for all new scholarship grantees. Bridget's irritation rapidly turned to concern as call after call to Blaire's cell went unanswered. Only after reaching Blaire's coach… and finding out that Blaire had not shown up for any of the practices… did Bridget decide to leave work and drive to the university. There, she stood outside Blaire's locked dorm room waiting for someone to show up. No one passing by on the hall had seen or knew anything of the new girl. As the afternoon wore away, the roommate finally arrived from class to say that Blaire had not slept a single night there, with Blaire's side of the room being exactly as Bridget had left it.

Panic took hold of her as no one in campus security had any idea of what had become of the freshman. Bridget took off more work in an effort to reconstruct her daughter's movements, repeatedly making detours to personally contact hospitals and checkup with law enforcement on her missing-person report. She was desperate… even on the verge of contacting Mitch… when a single line of text appeared on her cell phone in response to the dozens of messages she already sent out in fear.

busy txt u l8r

Relief was a short-term tenant in Bridget's mind, as irritation and anger quickly moved in as truculent squatters to take up full residence even before she finished typing a response.

Please call me right now!

I've been terribly worried.

How could you disappear like this?

She followed these strings of text up with variations on the theme… along with a few more phone calls… all of which went unanswered. Still fearing the worst, she crafted one more desperate message.

How do I know this is Blaire?

I want proof or I'm calling the FBI.

A reply came back almost at once, even though nothing else followed despite Bridget's many additional attempts.

dropped out gone pro tell u 2moro

No amount of tomorrow could quench the fire burning within Bridget.

Cleaning up Blaire's mess at Pepperdine was a day of humiliation Bridget was sure she would never forget. Aside from the very frustrating call with Blaire… which lasted all of two minutes and yielded nothing good… Bridget was on the phone all morning with campus housing, the registrar and the athletic department, then spent the afternoon clearing out Blaire's dorm room under the watchful eye of a roommate that never was. Bridget hurriedly emptied the closet and dresser, gathered up books and school supplies, and pulled down wall decorations… all things that she had not a week before brought into that room. She then met with the women's golf coach to personally apologize to him for having wasted a scholarship on Blaire. In that meeting, she spent considerable energy trying to smooth things over… only to be shown a clause in Blaire's scholarship agreement that indicated the University was to be compensated for tuition, room and meal plan if a student athlete left the team for any reason.

On finally being able to depart campus, the thin veil of control Bridget held over her shock fell away… and she completely broke down into tears. Those things she considered as important in life… those things which guided her hopes and expectations… those had once more been trampled under foot by Blaire… who had deceived and betrayed her… and then ran off leaving her mother to face the consequences.

Despite periodic attempts to reconnect, Bridget heard nothing from her daughter over the course of a full year. No phone calls, no texts, no cards and no visits. A gradual realization crept over her… sometimes in fits and starts, yet always building toward an inescapable conclusion… that Blaire was more than content to shut her out. For Bridget, it was not so much that near-on two decades of sacrifice had slipped away… even though acceptance of that fact had been pounding away at the front door of her mind ever since Blaire abandoned Pepperdine. Instead, it was that nothing she could do… no amount of care or involvement… could alter the trajectory of their relationship.

In the place of direct contact, she maintained a connection of sorts with Blaire through the sporting news. She took up the practice of watching women's golf nearly every weekend, and would daily comb through her paper's sports section for tidbits about her daughter. Bridget maintained this level of effort throughout the year as a means of keeping current with Blaire's life… in the off chance that the girl called. Of course, she was elated to see that Blaire regularly finished near to the top in her tournaments… though had not yet won one.

After the WGA tour ended in November, she lost touch with her daughter except for occasional mentions in the golf magazines she subscribed to. Her first Christmas alone came and went without word from Blaire. With the New Year, she was relieved to see her daughter's name reappear in the list of players competing in WGA tournaments. After a few weeks into the season, her local paper was referring to Blaire as a native success story. Then, a month into the spring, she happened to catch a segment on an LA-based morning talk show in which her daughter was one of the guests. Blaire looked much as she had during any of her tournaments… lovely and full of life… but especially beautiful now owing to how make-up and a mulberry dress brought a sparkle to her eyes. The host made a point of referring to Blaire as a rising star in the world of women's golf, and then queried her about life before becoming a professional. Bridget sat expectantly through the interview, waiting for something from Blaire regarding her family… though no such comment came.

She absolutely wanted Blaire to be a strongly independent woman, capable of making her own way in the world. That was something for a mother to be proud of. So she told herself not to be too hard on her daughter, as the girl's head must be awhirl with all her new experiences. Competing on a national stage must be overwhelming, so it was perfectly understandable that Blaire should be caught up in the excitement of it all. Perhaps Bridget should make allowances for the… unusual… manner in which Blaire went about turning pro. Maybe she felt she had no choice… seize the once-in-a-lifetime opportunity or see it slip away. Still… the girl could have handled it more considerately. Even now, Bridget was willing to overlook the offense of dropping out of college… had not Blaire completely shut her out.

On a day like any other day, Bridget came home from work to an empty house. As was her habit, she collected the mail from the box and dumped the entire pile on the kitchen counter in lieu of sorting the useful from the junk. Setting her mind toward preparation of dinner, she casually noted how the half dozen or so envelopes on top slid across the glossy surface of a magazine beneath. Before turning away, she happened to note her daughter's name on the cover. Sweeping the other items to the side, she recognized the magazine to be the *Women's Sporting World*. This particular one was far from her favorite seeing as it often catered to men who kept track of women's athletics… for less than wholesome reasons. Its cover photo was almost always distasteful, but this one made Bridget's jaw drop, for it was of her daughter… more precisely, a side of her daughter that Bridget had never seen before. The way some photographer had captured Blaire leaning with arched back against the pin on a green immediately gave off the feel of a pole dancer. With bare midriff and ultra clingy top, Blaire had one arm seductively intertwined about that portion of the metal rod above her head, with the heel of the gloved hand on the other arm casually resting against the hem of her short skirt… inadvertently lifting it so that a shockingly inappropriate amount of her upper thigh was on display. The image was too painful to look at, causing Bridget instead to seek out the lead-in title for the feature article.

Half fumbling and half ripping, Bridget rifled her way through the magazine until she came across the article. At the head of it was another photograph of Blaire, except this one was quite different. Dressed modestly, Blaire stood beside a golf cart extracting a club from her bag. With a slight downturn of the head, Blaire's eyes ventured off to the right in providing a modest smile for the camera... almost as if she were embarrassed to find a photographer capturing the moment. This representation was altogether wholesome, yet somehow struck Bridget as more deviant than the one on the front cover.

She pulled her eyes away from the picture to the opening sentences of the article. The writer was describing his initial impressions upon meeting 'the beautiful and talented Blaire O'Connor' at a Long Island country club Bridget had never heard of. She compelled her eyes onward, scanning rather than reading in the simple hope of evading words that might be unpleasant and tripping upon those that were good. However, it was one unexpected word, prominently italicized, that drew all of her attention to the middle of the page.

> 'We asked the young star if she had ever considered posing in the nude.
> "Yes. In fact, I happen to have an invitation from *Playboy* to do just that once the tournament season's over." '

Revulsion more intense than surging anger caused Bridget to hurl the magazine to the floor.

I can't believe this! I didn't raise her to be a slut.

Gripping the edge of the countertop, she closed her eyes in an attempt to steady herself, but a noiseless sorrow rose up instead, convulsing her into tears. A decision to pose in the nude would surely haunt Blaire for the rest of her life, making it more than difficult to develop any kind of a meaningful relationship with a man. Blaire was on a path toward self-destruction.

Through the tears, Bridget looked down to the floor and found the magazine lying in disarray at her feet. Without a moment of hesitation, she kicked it, sending the thing flailing across the kitchen floor. On colliding with a cabinet door, the pages somehow righted themselves in such a way that the magazine lay flat with its cover facing upward. Even from across the room, she could easily make out Blaire's seductive smile, mocking her frustration.

'See, Mother... like I always say... everything turns up right for me.'

Bridget moved to stand over the magazine, yet without wanting to pick it up. From five feet up, the image of Blaire on the cover seemed rather small... not nearly as one capable of doing the terrible thing the article suggested. Yet Blaire was not a child with a lifetime of possibilities ahead of her. She had already chosen her path. In ways new and old, Bridget felt the insult of having Blaire as a daughter. Nothing of what she personally valued... responsibility, genuine concern and healthy relationships... had ever been held in regard by the girl. Not yet twenty years old... with hardly any time out on her own... and Blaire was already exposing herself to the world.

Without another look, Bridget scooped the magazine off the floor and deposited it in the trash container beneath her sink. Leaving the kitchen for her back porch, she fell to crying on the floral upholstery of her indoor-outdoor couch... though its scotchgarded surface refused to receive her tears, pooling them in every spot where she sought to bury her face.

This porch was supposed to be her haven from the cares of the world. Not more than a year ago... when she first moved in... she had meticulously fashioned it to be her escape. In laboring over its decoration, she had firmly determined that this space, amongst all sites in her new house, would never see sadness of any kind. Here, all of the tension from a day's labor and the battle of a freeway's commute would be set aside on passing through the sliding glass door. She had even put effort into arranging the furniture within her small living room such that passage into the wide-openness of this backyard would not be impeded in any way. Here, she could enter a realm completely set apart from the hectic lifestyle of Southern California, easing herself into a mindset of calm.

It had never turned out to be so. Frequent sadness over her daughter found its way in, sometimes quietly and sometimes... like today... with many tears. Here, she had found rest for her body and escape from the outside... but not peace for her heart or mind.

After her weariness had decided how much crying was to be done over the magazine, Bridget sat up on the couch and stared out vacantly into the yard. The grass obviously needed cutting... and there were weeds popping up in the beds. Her eyes shifted up to the ferns hanging from a crossbeam off to one side – their wilt was another reminder of the many things that laid claim on her. Such had always been the case. The redwood boundary all about her yard might keep out the rest of the world, but not the burdens of her heart… for she always brought them with her into this place of seclusion.

As she sat there regaining a normal pace of breath, Bridget began to think more clearly. Blaire's decision to pose nude was in no way the fault of a mother. No lapse in parenting… willful or not… could have precipitated such a thing. She could continue to mull over in her heart the indebtedness she felt over how her daughter had turned out, but it would make no difference. Blaire would do what Blaire chose to do… so why go on bearing that guilt? Why blame herself over and over for what she had no power to change? This back porch may not be free of sadness… but here she could at least remind herself not to carry the burden of self-incrimination. Maybe, instead, she could sit here each day with a conscious effort aimed at putting that behind her. She had made plenty of mistakes in raising Blaire… but maybe it was time that she forgive herself for those.

That's it! I've… passed the expiration date on blaming myself. All those guilty feelings have been stuck in my head for so long… they've gone sour and moldy. I can't trust any of them. All my hurt and fear… it's made them rotten to the core.

So… I'm going to make this back porch a place of neutrality… with absolutely no extradition treaty into shame. Whenever I think of her, I'll… just… remind myself that there's a statute of limitation on punishing myself. That way, I can finally be free.

Without really trying, she began rehearsing the most horrible things Blaire had done to her as a means of cementing in her mind the right she had to forgive herself. Blaire had lied, and Blaire had deceived. She had stolen a mother's joy and replaced it with daily tension. She demanded and never gave in return… and instead tramped on every good thing a mother could give… without ever once saying thank you. Dwelling on these things would certainly be enough to make her forgive herself.

In the days to follow, as Bridget ventured out onto her back porch, she would come to see in the winding lanes of her lawn a reminder of Blaire's crooked ways. She would hear in the gentle gurgling of her fountain an irritating sarcasm to her daughter's every response. She would behold the wonder within her flowering beds and come to resent anew how false Blaire's beauty was… and how much work it had been to live with her. And always that six foot fence would be a reminder of how impenetrable Blaire's wall of resistance had been.

Despite her best efforts to forgive herself, Bridget still remained dreadfully sad and disappointed.

CHAPTER

14

THERAPY

Blaire wanted the call out of the way as quickly as possible. Normally, torqueing with her mother's feelings through a drawn out silence amounted to an amusing distraction, but she had better things to do with her time. There was lots to get done before her first WGA event next month. For one, she was seriously anxious to get the grips redone on her tournament clubs by a specialist in Ventura. That opportunity finally came now that she was past all the college bullshit. She had pulled off the big joke on her mother with perfection… even though it took months of tedious preparation in enduring all the woman's nonsense about applications, class selections, shopping, and all those idiotic ramblings about sorority rush. As enjoyable as the culmination of her plan had been, that moment was in the past. It was now time to put her mother in the rearview mirror and concentrate on the road ahead.

Blaire brought the top down on her new convertible, got up to cruising speed on the One-O-One, and felt the thrill of air rushing through her hair. Only then did she place the call, fully expecting the noise to muffle out the worst of her mother's whining. She would not bother trying to explain her decision to drop out… neither would she get embroiled in her mother's many emotional issues.

The call went as expected – totally unsatisfying. Blaire hung up after the second demand that she give up professional golf and return to Pepperdine.

Collegiate competition was for losers, whereas she was destined to compete at the highest level… and win. That was precisely why she had chosen to seek representation with someone who specialized in the promotion of female athletes.

Well… to be accurate… it was Bernie who first contacted me. But what difference does that make?! Just shows how much better I am than anyone else on tour.

She had heard the name 'Bernie Pearl' spoken of by high school girls who wistfully aspired toward professional representation in other sports. Blaire had always planned on going pro on her own. That was the way it was done in golf. She nonetheless consented to be interviewed by this so-called 'famous sports agent' in the month prior to her graduation out of curiosity… and because he could personally attest to having watched her compete in the State Golf Championship. He immediately went about asking her all sorts of stupid questions about herself… idiotic things like did she consider herself to be charming… and was she clever enough to accomplish the sorts of things normal people hesitated to try… and did she have any regrets about the past… a whole long list of such tedious questions… all of which she reluctantly tolerated in order to find out what he was offering.

When he finally got around to stating his real objective – the identification of an exceptional individual who did not fit into the WGA's mold of the female golfer – Blaire instantly knew he was the agent for her. But she agreed to take him on only after getting him to pay her a substantial signing bonus. For him, it was a no-brainer. He could easily tell that she was destined for greatness. So she would tolerate him as long as she found him to be useful. His only request was that she get on tour immediately… something she was planning to do anyway… after royally messing with her mother's mind by ditching college.

From the get-go, Blaire turned her alluring looks and over-the-top charm into instant popularity on tour. At eighteen, she had started out a year or two later than most girls did, yet the fans were feeding off her as if she were a veteran. None of them were real to her. The weight of their presence bulging the gallery ropelines did not change in the least how hollow-looking each and every one of them appeared. Blaire was now doing combat with the best golfers in the world, yet even they were mere shadows to her. Simple obstacles to be overcome on her path toward greatness. She was being treated with respect by the fans, the press and tournament officials, as they fondled over her growing success as if it were their own. She soaked it in… but was not softened by one moment of their attentions. Not even the steady flow of cash coming in chunks from her weekly winnings made much of an impression on her. She gave Bernie his small cut, then spent as the moment suited her, sometimes using her newfound riches as a means of showing herself off to the 'less fortunate.' Most of it, though, was left to pile up in her bank account. Money was nothing compared to winning. Yet after four fairly profitable months on tour, Blaire was angry. For one fated reason or another, she had not yet won a tournament.

Despite being denied that first victory, she had to admit, there were many upsides to her growing popularity on tour… not the least of which was that she got what she wanted, when she wanted it, just by snapping her fingers in Bernie's face. Yet the most pleasant surprise was the camera. Odd… she always hated how her mother would stick one in her face and squeak out a feeble plea for a smile. Blaire fully expected the same irritation toward every cameraman who dared to draw near. At her first tournament, not a month out of high school, she discovered that their cameras were larger than her mother's… so much so that she could often see her own reflection in their lenses. She did not care about what the camera saw in her – it was discovering herself in there that surprised her. To every lens she smiled warmly at that small glimpse of her own reflection… and that place she longed to be part of… where her other self dwelt supreme without the slightest hint of an irksome world.

But not every encounter with a reporter ended up being enjoyable. All too often, the subject of her family would come up from idiotic media members hell-bent on getting details about her private life… apparently because she was one of the few golfers who travelled alone. She wanted to tell them all to fuck off, but bit her lip in biding her time. For some reason, Bernie thought that her having a well-scripted response for such occasions was necessary. Of course, she already knew that 'family' was nauseatingly important to the league's wholesome image of the female golfer. Parents, siblings, boyfriends and husbands often accompanied players around the circuit, offering their constant support.

Oh my god… I'd be embarrassed as hell to have my pathetic excuse of a mother following me around!

Still… she understood well the value of playing the game within the game, so Blaire got the routine down rather easily. Whenever asked about her family, she would offer a hint of pain in her voice, and then, with downturned eyes, choke out words about having experienced the estrangement of a broken home. She would let that stand for a moment before throwing out a well-timed chin-up grin in expressing her desire for making good in life… for herself and for so many other girls with similar struggles. And if she was in a particularly good mood, she would end with hopeful expectations of one day having a family of her own… once her playing days were over.

Such bullshit.

The fans and the media ate it up, but Blaire never told anyone… Bernie especially… how terribly tiresome this game was to play.

On the anniversary of Blaire having dropped out of college, and not more than a week after that *Women's Sporting World* article, Bridget received a phone call that was yet another reminder of how poorly her daughter had treated her.

"Hello… this is Bridget speaking."

"Mrs. O'Connor… hope you're day's going well…"

"It is… How can I help you?"

"My name's Alexia Melendez… I'm the one who's now managing your daughter's account with Mr. Pearl. I just called to introduce myself and ask if you could…"

"I'm sorry… I… don't know a Mr. Pearl. And what account are you referring to?"

"Mr. Pearl's your daughter's agent, of course. You know… the one representing her to sponsors and the like."

"Ahh… this is actually the first I've ever heard that Blaire had an agent."

"Really?! So… Blaire's never mentioned Mr. Pearl?'

"No… never."

"Well… umm… maybe I should have you discuss this with her first."

Not likely, seeing as she never returns my calls…

"Did you say your name was Alexia?"

"Yes…"

"Unfortunately, Alexia… Blaire and I are not exactly on speaking terms at present."

"Oh, that explains it all! I'm so relieved."

"Excuse me?"

"I'm sorry… I didn't mean anything personal by that. It's just… well… the reason I'm calling is because Blaire asked me to set up a counseling session for the two of you."

"She did what?!"

"I know this must be catching you off guard. I mean… she said you would know. Maybe I should talk to her again and…"

"No. You're okay. It's… actually true… we've not been speaking lately.

Not since she… well, I really don't want to get into it. Tell me about this… counseling session."

"Mr. Pearl… he's very conscientious about such things… he's arranged for the two of you to spend some time talking with Dr. William Fletcher. He's a highly respected sports psychologist who specializes in family counseling… you know… for helping athletes deal with their lives as professionals."

"So you think Blaire's actually willing to do this?"

"She's the one who had me call you. You know… she's not yet won her first tournament… and I rather think Mr. Pearl believes this will help her get over the hump."

"Wow… this is… umm… well… really unexpected."

Bridget's mind was racing. For Blaire to have explored such a thing… a year after dropping out of college… made no sense. Why would she now care about their relationship? Perhaps the stresses of competition… and not winning… somehow brought about a change in her outlook on…

"Mrs. O'Connor?"

"I'm here… Sorry. I was just thinking. Umm… Mr. Pearl… your boss… he believes this is a good idea?"

"Definitely. As a matter of fact, he's agreed to cover the cost of as many sessions as you two need. It so happens that Dr. Fletcher can squeeze you in for the first of these next Monday at noon. His office is in the Pricewater Building. That's downtown… not far from where Blaire said you work."

"And she's definitely going to be there?"

"Absolutely. She's on the West Coast next week for a tournament… so it's perfect timing for her."

Well… what do I have to lose… other than wasting a lunchtime? Actually… it would be nice to see her again… in person. And who knows… maybe things'll be… different between us.

"Okay… I'll be there. Please extend my appreciation to Mr. Pearl… and tell him I look forward to meeting him one day soon."

Bridget hung up the phone in total confusion… with a good measure of leeriness added on. She was familiar enough with women's professional golf to know that a sports agent was not only unusual… it was totally unnecessary. Only the cream of the crop… the top tenth of a percent… could garner any sort of name recognition worthy of the types of endorsements that required an agent's consideration. The sport was just not that popular. In fact, the league was managed in such a way as to make the involvement of agents unwanted. She knew well that the WGA desired their athletes to maintain a wholesome image… and agents tended to mess that up. She also knew that most women in the league bought into this premise… or at least appeared to.

So why does Blaire need an agent… and what's in it for this Mr. Pearl?

And how in the world am I to prepare myself for a counseling session with Blaire?!

CHAPTER

15

UP AND DOWN

Bridget briskly covered the half dozen blocks to the Pricewater Building, rode one of its elevators to the 25th floor, and entered the reception area of Dr. Fletcher five minutes early, not convinced of why she had agreed to be there. Given that Blaire had chosen not to speak with her over the past year, to hope that something miraculously had changed in the girl was nothing but foolhardy. Yet Bridget would never deny the possibility… however remote… of repairing the breech between them. Otherwise, she would surely end up blaming herself for failing to try. So she would listen patiently to whatever Blaire had to say… and be ready to speak her own peace.

That morning, particularly onward from the hour prior to lunch, Bridget arranged and rearranged her arguments regarding how Blaire had treated her. She finally decided that it would not be necessary to venture too far back into the past in order to convince the therapist. She would focus on the way Blaire deceived her regarding college, for that as much as anything demonstrated the cruelty underlying nearly every one of her daughter's actions. Bridget would relate the shame she had experienced in front of the Pepperdine recruiters, coaches and academic advisors. They took out their anger over Blaire on her… with that humiliation coming on the heels of her thinking Blaire kidnapped. Dr. Fletcher, as a seasoned counselor, would surely come to sympathize with her, and then expertly communicate to Blaire how inconsiderate she had been.

Perhaps if Blaire could see the shock in an impartial authority such as this Dr. Fletcher, then maybe there was still hope for the two of them.

Now… if their discussion happened to flow into Blaire's career decision of golf over college, then Bridget would handle this subject more delicately. Although she could not see how playing a game would ever amount to a livelihood, she knew that plenty of professional athletes made a go of it. So… she would keep her feelings on the subject of sports to herself.

In some ways, she actually admired Blaire for knowing what she wanted out of life and pursuing it vigorously. After all, that was what Bridget valued too. The thing that hit her hard was the completely callus, ungrateful and supremely disrespectful manner in which the girl deceived her. Had Bridget not proven herself to be more than an open-minded parent?! Had she not always been there for Blaire?! Surely the girl could have bothered to sit down with her during the college application process and share her misgivings. She could have asked Bridget for advice, and they, as mother and daughter would have worked it out together. Even if Blaire had been genuinely wavering on the subject of college right up until the last moment, all she really needed to do was confide in her… and Bridget would have understood. But to disappear… and thoughtlessly put a mother through the trauma of a manhunt… that was unpardonable.

While waiting, Bridget ran through in her mind several times what she hoped to convey, being interrupted only once – when Dr. Fletcher stepped out from his office to introduce himself and request of his receptionist that they be shown in as soon as Blaire arrived. With many furtive glances between that receptionist and a clock on the wall, Bridget's unease over the appointment gradually heightened as the minutes wore on. By the time Blaire showed up… nearly twenty minutes late… Bridget was in a complete wad of frustration. Without so much as a hello after a year of not seeing each other, Blaire waltzed right past into the doctor's office as if she lived there. With a grimaced apology to the receptionist, Bridget quickly trailed in behind… entering just as Blaire was commanding Dr. Fletcher to 'get this going. Quietly taking a seat, she resisted the temptation to apologize on behalf of her daughter.

Let him understand for himself what I've been up against.

Dr. Fletcher began by giving them a brief overview of his years of counseling. Through this, she paid close attention to his experience. He seemed to have worked with all sorts, and in the process developed approaches for helping athletes and their families cope with the pressures of professional sports. He even made a point of saying that many of his fondest success stories were clients of Mr. Pearl's. Bridget was in the throws of asking if any of those had been female golfers when Blaire rudely interrupted.

"Mother – will you focus! I don't have time for nonsense. I want this over as soon as possible."

Though embarrassed, Bridget was somewhat relieved on receiving a sympathetic smile from Dr. Fletcher.

"Well then, let's do get started. How about an opening exercise… just to get things rolling. This might seem a bit awkward, but I'd like both of you to close your eyes and imagine… Ms. O'Connor, you may roll your eyes if you wish, but Mr. Pearl assured me that you would cooperate."

Bridget had straightway complied, but could not help from peering over to Blaire… whose head was lulled back in a mocking display of boredom.

"Now, I'd like you both to imagine you're the only person in the room, and you're speaking out loud to yourself. It may seem silly, but I'd like you to describe yourself to yourself, and then briefly explain to yourself what you hope to gain from these sessions. Mrs. O'Connor…"

"Please call me Bridget."

"Okay… Bridget, would you be willing to go first?"

"Sure…" She closed her eyes again, requiring only a few seconds of thought before being prepared to speak. "I'd say I'm a fair-minded person… and believe that life is about building positive relationships. When things aren't working out, then I think both parties should sit down and sort through their issues together… you know… to find common ground. I'm not saying people can't be their own people. I'm just saying that the two individuals should look into the future together and decide what kind of relationship they want… then move in that direction. That's what I want from these sessions."

"Excellent. I think we'll make rapid progress with that attitude. Ms. O'Connor, now it's your turn."

Bridget opened her eyes to notice Blaire lazily glancing up from her cell phone.

"What's the question?"

"Please describe yourself to yourself, as well as tell yourself what you want from these sessions."

Before responding, Blaire sent a nasty scowl his way. "Why would I want to do that?"

"Well… it's an exercise in communication. So if you could…"

"You want communication?! Fine – I'll communicate! I'm a competitor. What I want I go after without being bothered by stupid, idiotic distractions. Describing myself to myself is a total waste of time."

"Oh… okay. Is there anything else you care to say?"

"What else is there?"

"What about your mother?"

"What about her?"

"What about what she said?"

"I wasn't paying attention."

Dr. Fletcher paused there, turning slowly her way.

"How does that make you feel, Bridget?"

"About the same as always – disrespected. She couldn't care less about me."

"Ms. O'Connor, how does what your mother just said make you feel?"

Blaire had her eyes back on her cell phone.

"I'm good."

Bridget had reserved a miniscule hope that this appointment might lead to reconciliation, but now knew for certain that her daughter was not interested.

Then why in the world did she arrange this?

"Well, I see that our time is almost up for today…"

"Wait… aren't we going to get into the root causes of our disagreement? I should at least be given the opportunity to tell you my side of how Blaire dropped out of college."

"Hold it right there, Mrs. O'Connor… Bridget. I want to assure you that we'll get into the details during the next session, but I'm terribly sorry… I do have another appointment scheduled for now. Unfortunately, we got off to a late start today, but rest assured… we've made some progress… though there's clearly plenty of work to be done. I can see straight off that the two of you have lost the essence of the mother-daughter connection. Maybe you've forgotten all of the wonderful moments in your lives together. Tell you what… let's have an assignment for next week. Bridget… do you have any family photo albums?"

"Yes, of course."

"Would you be willing to share those with us? Not just individual photos… What I'd like to do is have you two sitting side-by-side and flipping through an album together. I've found that to be a remarkably effective way of refocusing the parent-child relationship… and getting at some of those hidden resentments. What's say we start with some of your daughter as… a toddler… and then… maybe when she was first learning to play golf?"

"You want me to bring them… here?"

"Yes. If that's not too much trouble."

Bridget shot a quick look over at Blaire, whose eyes were no longer on her cell phone.

"I'm willing, Mother… if you are. That is… assuming you really want a healthy 'parent-child' relationship."

From that response, Bridget immediately came to understand the sad meaning behind this charade.

It'll work. Maybe it wasn't as fun as I'd expected, but good enough to get what I want out of her… and good enough to produce that hilarious deer-caught-in-the-headlights expression on her face. Priceless! As always, she's totally clueless. Now if I can get the hell out of here without being dragged into any of her ridiculous drama…

With the session finally ended, Blaire found the perfect moment to bolt for the door – just as her mother was reaching out to shake hands with Fletcher. The woman would probably stand there forever exchanging sappy reassurances with the guy, giving her time to reach the elevators alone.

She got by the two of them, through the reception area, and into the lobby of the 25th floor… only to have her mother come trotting along behind her.

Shit! Just great!

"Blaire! Please wait. We need to talk. Tell me this whole thing wasn't concocted so you could get a hold of your childhood photos!"

Not so clueless after all…

Blaire jabbed a forefinger at the 'down' button, intending the gesture to serve as her response.

"So I'll take that as a yes. Blaire… couldn't you just ask for them like a normal person? Why go to all this trouble? Can't you see how warped this is?"

Sensing the coming of another long, boring lecture, Blaire turned her back on her mother and concentrated her attention on the elevator indicator lights. As there were four sets of doors, each as likely as the next to respond to her bidding, she found herself rapidly shifting her eyes from one to the other. This would not do. In no way should she show even the slightest hint of desperation before her mother. She should do something to put things back on her own terms.

"Well, what do you expect from the child of a broken home?!"

Look at her flinch. She's got absolutely no control over herself. That one flattens her every time.

"Blaire, that was uncalled for… and not an excuse for deceiving me."

"I don't need an excuse… and I shouldn't have to ask for what's already mine either."

"What are you talking about?"

Well beyond the point of subtlety, Blaire turned sharply on her, wanting to make her meaning perfectly clear.

"Those photos are of *me*! They're of my childhood – not yours! But if I had to come out and ask for what's mine, then you'd just hold it over my head. Make me go to lunch or something stupid like that. I shouldn't be put through the hassle."

She went back to jabbing at the down button… this time with much more force than was needed.

Come on! Hurry the hell up!

"Oh, so this makes more sense to you?! Here we are, actually wasting our lunch hour, all on the pretense of a counseling session so you could… Wait… that's it, isn't it?! Not only did you try using Dr. Fletcher to get what you want, but he was your protection from me, right?! Just another opportunity to get what you want on your own terms. Another conquest of mother. Another game within the game. I'm so sick of all your nonsense…"

Fortunately, a 'ding' interrupted the woman's rant. Blaire took a quick step toward the doors of the arriving elevator, standing near enough to close out the sight of her mother and see only her own reflection within that polished metal surface. Blaire was in the process of exchanging a private moment of irritation over the situation with her other self in there when she was completely caught off guard.

"Blaire, this is far from over!"

The hissed voice came from behind, but it was the appearance of her mother's image beside her own that shocked Blaire. A shudder ran up and down her spine as that woman's reflection looked directly back at her. As the doors opened, Blaire quickly made for a back corner, hoping that she was mistaken over what she had just seen. It could not possibly be that there was a mother such as hers within that other world.

The elevator is an invention going back millennia to Archimedes' screw, designed for the raising of water. Not until Elisha Otis conceived of his 'vertical railway' in the 1850's did someone venture to employ such a device exclusively for the lifting of people. Before the end of that century, Otis's company, as well as other elevator pioneers, had abandoned screw-driven mechanisms in favor of the pulley, and similarly began replacing hydraulics with electric motors. With these new elevators, the functionalities of buildings quickly moved beyond the limitations of five or fewer floors. City growth patterns radically changed from 'out' to 'up,' as faster, more powerful, and more dependable systems ushered in the age of the skyscraper.

Unfortunately, the logistics of elevator operation remained primitive, derived as they were from the decision-making ability of a single individual. The elevator operator was entrusted with assessing load sizes, prioritizing the direction of motion, optimizing the positioning of cars, and ensuring passenger safety. That profession, however, dealt itself a death blow in the 1940s when the New York City elevator operators' union went on strike. The Otis Elevator Company, sensing opportunity, unveiled a new mechanism by which an elevator's doors opened only after the car was flush with the level of the arriving floor... all without human oversight. Within two decades, such innovations completely supplanted the need for elevator operators, with the phrase 'watch your step' falling to the wayside of the American vernacular... being replaced by canned music.

Further advances in efficiency came in the 1960's with the advent of the 'elevator algorithm.' As first conceived, its decision-making processes were essentially a mechanically derived 'yes/no' flow chart optimizing an elevator's response to multiple requests. Algorithms soon became more sophisticated as banks of cars were coupled into a system. Utilizing computers and software, elevator algorithms greatly increased in sophistication, becoming capable of minimizing wait and delivery times, conserving energy, balancing air flow within shafts, providing security, and optimizing complex usage patterns. A dominant 'upward' trend at the beginning of a work day could easily be transitioned into a uniform 'up-and-down' pattern at lunch, and then a 'downward' flow as the workday ended... with 'floor-to-floor' traffic managed throughout.

Ironically, the decision-making processes employed in the elevator algorithm became the first model for how hard drives managed the many 'read/write' processes routinely carried out in nearly every early computer. The two technologies soon became tied together in co-dependent operation, with every elevator being managed by a computer. Although one's existence flowed from the other, that one eventually became the controller of its originator.

Blaire, as the daughter, had come forth from Bridget, the mother, deriving an existence from her. Yet even before she was a teenager, the daughter had flipped the order of things, gaining control over the mother. Their relationship had seen very few 'ups'... and many more 'downs'... as a result of Blaire having decided the direction of flow. Finally out on her own, the daughter was choosing to exit at the ground floor.

When Blaire first pushed the 'down' button, the elevator control algorithm alerted the building's operational control room of a request for descent from the

25th floor. As the lunch hour was on-going, the algorithm was currently managing the building's four cars in a balanced approach. One car had been dispatched to the first floor to retrieve a group having recently finished their lunch in the lobby's cafe, whereas another car was already on an upward path returning a half dozen well-fed employees to the accounting firm on the 19th floor.

Blaire's summons initiated a new factor into the protocol. A nearly full car was descending from the 30th floor bearing consultants heading out for a late lunch. The algorithm chose, for energy conservation reasons, not to interrupt this car's downward progression, allowing it to proceed unimpeded to the ground floor. The elevator in shaft two flowed by without recognition on the part of either woman. Instead, the algorithm opted for sending car four in response to the request on the 25th floor. This car, currently on an upward trajectory, was soon to reach the top with an inter-floor traveller from the 22nd. It would then begin a descent for pick-ups on the 27th, 16th and 12th, as well as the two women waiting on the 25th floor. Car four had made the turn and was on its way to the 27th when Blaire began repeatedly jabbing at the 'down' button. The algorithm, unfortunately, possessed no programming capable of responding to impatience.

Had the O'Connor women arrived at the elevator bank on the 25th floor a few minutes earlier, or had they presented themselves thirty seconds later, the algorithm would have placed them on a different car with different passengers. As it were, the doors on number four opened to reveal a single occupant, the pick-up from the 27th floor. A middle-aged man within held a finger on the panel's 'open' button while using his somewhat pumice-colored cowboy hat to restrain one of the elevator's double doors. Bridget politely nodded her thanks to the man, whereas Blaire ignored him altogether as if he were a throwback to that bygone era of the elevator operator. The women quickly retreated to a far corner, one to escape and the other deciding it impractical to continue her argument while in the elevator. As a courtesy, the man moved in closer to the control panel and fixed his eyes upon its digital floor indicator.

The car resumed its descent, covering eight floors before initiating a routine deceleration for the pick-up on the 16th. At that very moment, the algorithm failed, throwing the entire operating system into complete disarray… along with the lives of those in elevator four. In an instant, everything changed.

California happened.

CHAPTER

16

SHAKEN

Hollywood and the Golden Gate are renowned worldwide, as are the region's beaches, palm trees, redwoods, deserts, mountains, and cities of angels and saints. California is America's gateway to the Pacific, the nation's trend-setter, and bountifully both a winery and grocery. Yet long before the Anglo sought gold within its interior, or the Spaniard laid claim to its shores... even prior to the first human inhabitants that migrated down from the Bering Strait... what is seen today has dwelt for eons in conflict. In all its beauty, California is not at peace. To the north, subduction drives the Juan de Fuca plate beneath the continent, undermining stability with volcanic repercussions. Along the southern and central coastlines, the North American plate slides southeast past the fragmented edges of its larger Pacific neighbor, resulting in friction on an unimaginable scale – the infamous San Andres fault.

The geophysics responsible for the state's topography is normally of little concern to those who dwell upon its surface. Yet at distinct times, these subterranean conflicts, budging along at a mere inch per year, are more than capable of driving away all the petty turmoil above. On such occasions, no one finds it interesting that Robert Mallet discovered plate tectonics in the mid-1800's by mapping the world's earthquake zones. Similarly, knowledge of the isostasy of floating continental crusts, as detailed by Wegener and Taylor, can not possibly be of aid to the person in peril. All such things are trivial at best...

simple factoids of no greater import than learning that Charles Richter, the father of the earthquake scale, happened to grow up in LA.

When things begin to shake, shear propagation has infinitesimally small relevance in comparison to that of sheer terror. In that petrifying moment, nobody cares about fault lines... or slip-stick motion... or the intricacies of seismometry... and most certainly the names San Gabriel, Carrizo, or Newport-Inglewood carry little significance in comparison to the identity of the person in distress. Liquefaction and S-wave sonication do not adequately describe how that individual's courage dissolves away in a heartbeat. It is the ride upon a ten mile thin crust, floating atop a molten core eight hundred times thicker, that is as paper-thin ice over a red-hot fireball. Within its deep places, the earth is searching for peace... and the tormented souls above with their many hidden burdens must wait out its release.

As with anyone who claimed Southern California as home, Bridget would later recount to friends and coworkers where she was and what she was doing when the 5.2 magnitude earthquake struck. She, like nearly everyone she spoke with, readily brought forth tales of having experienced far greater earthquakes in the past. This, she privately accepted, was simply another way in which the citizens of LA dealt with their fears. After nearly two decades of living in the region, she had come to accept that nobody... herself included... dared to speak openly about what actually went on in their minds during an earthquake.

She would later learn from the evening news that the total duration was about eight seconds... though it seemed much longer at the time. Her immediate impulse was to clutch a handrail and ride out the quake. The power in the Pricewater Building lasted through the first few seconds, with low-level emergency lighting kicking on only after the turbulence had completely ceased. The elevator was pitch black when everything suddenly became cloaked in a reddish glow. Remarkably, she did not find herself overcome with distress... that is, until she became aware of Blaire crouched down in a corner trembling uncontrollably. In getting down on her knees, Bridget... with hands held firmly on the girl's shoulders... was finally able to calm Blaire down with assurances that they were safe. Throughout the turmoil, she lost track of what the man was doing, but soon found him working away at the panel.

"Phone's dead. Either of you two got a cell?"

Happy to be of practical use, Bridget eagerly sought hers... only to find that it lacked signal. She was in the process of persuading Blaire to check hers when a metallic shrill filled the elevator, seemingly coming at them from all sides at once. Blaire instantly had her hands to her ears and was shouting out disjointed words Bridget was barely able to piece together over the alarm.

"OH… MY… GOD… BUILDING… ON… FIRE…"

Bridget froze in fear of the possibility… when she felt the man gently tap her on the shoulder. Turning to face him, she found him shaking his head in a reassuring sort of way. Still processing the odd contradiction between his smile and the unnerving circumstances, she suddenly was jolted to the side by Blaire, who unexpectedly sprung up and began beating on the doors… alternately trying to wedge her fingers into their gap. The man, in helping Bridget off the elevator floor, gestured to the control panel.

"NOT FIRE!"

She followed where he was pointing… to an orange 'emergency' button… just as he pushed it in. The volume level of the same high-pitched ring more than doubled within their small space, forcing Bridget to cover her ears. He then deactivated the alarm, at which point she realized that the other one was coming from an adjacent shaft. Fortunately, that one soon ceased… just as the normal lighting flickered back on. As a burnt-in echo slowly wore off… along with the need for blinking away the comparative brightness of the restored lighting… she was surprised to find Blaire still working away at the door.

"Miss… there's no need for that. We're going to be fine."

"Really?! Who the hell are you to say?! You want to stay in this… this… death trap… then fine by me… but I'm getting the hell out… before a cable breaks."

"That won't happen. There're safety devices on…"

"Shit! Now look what you made me do!"

Blaire, reeling back from the man, began vigorously shaking a hand about in the air… only to give that up in exchange for sucking on a single fingertip. Bridget immediately moved in to offer her assistance, but withdrew on seeing a look of sinister proportions on her daughter's face. Without another word to either of them, Blaire plopped herself down in a corner.

"I'm terribly sorry… she didn't mean anything by that. She's just… in a bad mood."

"Not a problem, ma'am. But she's got the right idea now. Might as well get comfortable. Who knows how long it'll be."

He took up the corner away from Blaire's… who was mumbling far too loudly.

"Not a bad mood… just don't like… elevators. 'Get comfortable'… what a fucking idiot."

The all-too-familiar wave of embarrassment hit Bridget, but before she could muster an apology, the man waved it off and casually leaned back in his corner as if considering its suitability for a nap. Still… she should whisper a correction to Blaire… if only to prevent a reoccurrence. The girl, however, had crammed sunglasses on her face and was fiddling with a set of earbuds. In a matter of seconds, Bridget picked up on the strains of beat-intensive music. Perhaps Blaire would no longer be a problem.

She felt awkward being the only one left standing. She had no desire to be anywhere near to her daughter, but felt that sitting too close to the stranger would be inappropriate. So she positioned herself on the floor between them… only a tad closer to Blaire than to the man. Putting a shoulder to the wall, she rotated partway toward the stranger in order to face him while speaking… at the same time taking a small pleasure in having turned her back on her daughter.

"So… what do you think's going on? Why aren't the elevators working?"

"Probably a computer problem."

"Elevators have computers?"

"Just about everything these days does, Darlin.'"

The word instantly made her blush.

In all her preoccupation with Blaire, Bridget managed only a discrete look at this man on first entering the elevator. She now took greater note of him, particularly his cowboy hat, boots and western-looking clothing, as well as the slight twang to his accent… not Southern or Texan… but something altogether different. Perhaps it was in keeping with wherever he was from to refer to her, a perfect stranger, in such a familiar manner. She would overlook it, despite how it added to her unease. Far worse was her discomfort over her daughter… who just then uttered a very audible 'sheesh.' Bridget turned about to find that Blaire was not listening to her music after all. Looped over each ear, her earbuds dangled beside her earrings, flopping about as she made a show out of wagging her head in disgust. Determined not to be bothered again by Blaire, she came back to the man as he went on speaking.

"What bothers me… mind you, only a hair… is that the system should have restarted by now. It's first duty in an emergency should be to deliver all the cars to the ground floor. Of course… backup generators don't have the power to move more than one car at a time…"

She was surprised to feel Blaire lean into her back.

"Mother… you do realize he's making this shit up…"

"…so the controls are designed to get them down one-by-one. I've been listening… when I can… haven't heard any of the other cars moving. I reckon they're stuck too. We obviously have power…." Her eyes followed his up toward the lights. "So… I'm figuring it's got something to do with computers. We're just going to have to wait until someone sorts out the problem."

In one of those strange coincidences to life, the elevator phone buzzed at that very moment. The man was already on the way up to answer it when Blaire jumped up to race him there. Owing to the shorter distance, Bridget was relieved that he got there first.

"Hello?"

"Give it to me! I want a piece of whoever the hell that is."

Blaire had a hand out, fingers flapping back and forth in a rudely insistent manner. Fortunately, the man casually pivoted away while continuing to speak on the phone.

"That's right, just the three of us… me and the two ladies."

She noticed him glance up to where a small camera lens was recessed into the top of the control panel.

"I understand… How long before it's up and running?"

Blaire was not giving up, bouncing about in trying to reach around the man. Bridget discretely touched her thigh with a hand… which Blaire swatted away. Everything about the day suddenly came back to her. Against all of her best efforts at parenting, her only child had proven… once again… to be a supremely offensive and manipulative person. More than anything at that moment, Bridget longed for the emergency lights to come back on so there would be no way for this stranger to see in the reddish glow how utterly embarrassed she was because of her daughter.

"Okay… I'll let the ladies know."

No system of safeguards is without shortcomings, particularly when extraordinary circumstances come into play. For the Pricewater Building manager, a moderate earthquake was the least of his problems. Dealing with incompetent employees was a whole different matter. He had been over and over the procedures with the maintenance crew in preparation for initiating the refurbishing work on the basement's service spaces. Electrical lines had already been strung through the newly installed conduit, with the switchover supposedly only requiring a few minutes. Rerouting of the control room's backup power had been scheduled for that night, but somehow his building engineer got it into his mind to do the work during the lunchtime lull. The quake just had to happen at that very moment. When the main power temporarily blipped, there was no backup power for the control room's computers. With emergency lighting on everywhere else in the building except the control room, the electrician scrambled about by flashlight trying to connect the backup lines. The job was barely finished when the main power was restored, throwing the computer systems into a mandatory diagnostic rebooting process. Fortunately, this was a minor problem, soon to be rectified. None of it needed to be communicated to the fifteen individuals stranded in the four Pricewater elevators. The calls to each car were only to make sure that there were no medical emergencies.

"That was the building manager. He said for us not to worry – it's only a minor quake. No apparent damage to the building. Unfortunately... they're having some computer problems... nothing they can't handle. Should only take a few minutes before the elevators are back working."

Blaire snatched up the phone as he put it away... and then slammed it back into its place on finding no one there. An uncomfortable silence then filled the car, with both Blaire and the man reclaiming their previous spots on the floor. Bridget had not risen, but nonetheless inched a bit away from Blaire. For the first time since entering the elevator, the reason for being there came back to her. Blaire had tried to trick her into handing over the photo albums. Mr. Pearl's office was obviously in on it too – they were the ones who set up the appointment. She could understand Blaire being deceptive... that was her way... but why should this Mr. Pearl be so? She would gladly have shared the albums with him... if he had but asked. Perhaps he was trusting Blaire... and perhaps the appointment was a genuine attempt to reconcile their relationship... and Blaire used it to accomplish her deceit.

But then how did Dr. Fletcher know to ask for the albums?

No... the doctor was in on it too. Everyone of them trying to make a fool out of her. Well... she would have none of their games. The photo albums were special to her. They were her work and her memories, and they would stay put on the shelves where they belonged. She would remain above it all, not showing the least bit of hurt she was feeling on the inside. Besides, nothing had changed. In no way would Blaire concede to having done something wrong. The moment the elevator doors opened on the ground floor, the girl would be gone.

At least the earthquake revealed her true colors. She's not in control like she thinks she is. She can be rattled just like the rest of us. I so wish I had that moment on video to prove to her how frail she really is!

"By the way, my name's Lowell... Lowell Paxton."

Bridget had not been thinking about the man seated beside her now that the moment of getting out of this elevator was so near. But there he was, extending his right hand out toward her… so she accepted it. His grip started out gentle and progressed to a measure that Bridget thought marked his assessment of her strength – a polite firmness.

"Hi… Pleased to meet you, Mr. Paxton… well, sort of, if you know what I mean."

She laughed along with him in that superficial way meant to smooth over an uncomfortable situation.

"I'm Bridget… and this is my…"

Perhaps Blaire had been anticipating the moment, as the promptness with which she interrupted surprised her.

"Mother – stop!"

"What?"

"We don't know anything about this guy."

A mischievousness suddenly came over her. Bridget turned back to Mr. Paxton, trying not to show any of the private amusement she was anticipating.

"So… do you happen to know who she is?"

She jabbed a thumb back over her shoulder in the direction of Blaire's corner, not bothering to turn about. The man bent forward to take a closer look… and Bridget caught the faint scent of Old Spice.

"Well… I did hear you refer to her as 'Blaire,' but other than that… can't say that I do. Never laid eyes on either of you… though I'd say you're both quite handsome women."

Bridget, caught off guard by the compliment, paused a bit longer than she would have preferred. During the brief silence, a very audible intake of air… as over clinched teeth… came at her from behind. That settled it for her.

"Actually… she's becoming fairly well-known in the world of women's athletics. I don't suppose you watch golf on TV?"

"Not really. Got one of those D-V-D players from my daughter a few years back. Been putting it to good use. Mostly westerns. Don't much care for anything else." He leaned forward for another look at Blaire. "So… she's one of those golf players, huh? There any money in that?"

Unable to restrain herself, Bridget suddenly burst out into laughter. Fortunately, in smiling back, he did not at all seem bothered by her enjoyment of his response. Yet the one thing capable of ruining the moment for Bridget did – Blaire, whispering into her ear.

"Mother, I'll handle it from here."

To say that she was annoyed would amount to an understatement of colossal proportions. The entire situation sucked.

Somewhere in the basement of this building are a bunch of morons with their heads up their asses blindly trying to find the fucking 'go' button. If it was up to me, they'd all be fired.

Everything from Fletcher's office on had not gone according to script. Of all the times for her wretched mother to grow a backbone!

Okay... so what?! Lightning struck... and the woman miraculously saw through one of my ruses. Big deal!

Of course, in no way did Blaire actually feel it necessary to reassure herself as to where she stood relative to her mother. She hardly put any effort into the Fletcher thing. Some idiot in Bernie's office must have tipped her off, as the woman was not that clever enough on her own. Next time would be different. Next time, Blaire would unleash all of her cunning to make sure she got exactly what she wanted.

Because I'm sure as hell not sucking up to her by asking like the pretty little girl she's always wanted!

But what an incredibly stupendous hassle!

Blaire hazarded a quick look toward her mother and that old fart of a cowboy she was cozying up to. How could the woman not see that this fossil was right off the bus? Yet what bothered Blaire more was that neither of them seemed put out by the earthquake... or being stuck in a dinky box suspended who knows how many floors up in the air. Of course... that could easily be explained. Neither of them had much of a brain in their heads to see how over-the-top dangerous the situation was. No... she was the only one who really had it all together. Her mother might look calm on the outside... as did the stranger... but Blaire bet her clubs they were freaking out on the inside. So all she needed to do was keep cool.

Damn earthquake... made me look bad.

She tried listening to music, hoping to drown out a bizarrely disturbing sensation... but that had not helped. She was not weak. Such things were not her. She was strong and in complete control. It was just that she deserved better than this. To be stuck in an elevator during an earthquake... That was it... the earthquake knocked her off balance a bit... somehow putting things on her mother's terms. All she needed to do was take a moment to get her stance right... ensure a good grip... regain her swing... and then everything would clear up in her mind. This elevator was the real problem. It was stuffy and too cramped for her liking. The wide open golf course... that was the place for her. That was where she could put distance between herself and everyone else.

Nothing the two of them gabbed about was all that interesting, but Blaire still found herself listening in. The urge had nothing to do with some latent desire to be connected to another human being during a moment of peril. Such frailties were for weaker beings. And neither was she in the least bit paranoid that they might be discussing how she had cracked up under pressure. No… she was only following their conversation as a way of amusing herself with the brainless prattle of her mother. Trying to get comfort from a stranger… that was almost as sickeningly feeble as a lost puppy clinging to the first person it came across.

Good god… now she's talking about me!

Who knows what was waiting for them once the elevator finally reached the ground floor? Maybe a reporter… or a blogger… or someone in the business. The less this hick had to say about his experiences in being stuck in an elevator with Blaire O'Connor, the better. So it was well past time to put an end to this nonsense with a clear message to the stranger: *back off!*

Blaire dumped her cell into her bag, whispered into her mother's ear, then rose and stepped over into the narrow space before the man. In the process, she delivered a little heel jab into her mother's hip, fully expecting her wordless message of 'move into the corner' to be heeded.

Even before rising, Blaire had already decided on what version of herself she would call upon to accomplish the task. In standing before him, she brought her legs together so as to present the greatest height difference. Throwing her shoulders back a bit, she lifted her chin slightly in order to achieve something approximating an air of detached nobility. That would surely be read by him as unintended disdain… even though she meant every bit of it. Now with her hands… she allowed the fingers on her right to gently seek out contact with the railing that ran about the elevator's walls. This would surely send a soothing message that she was willing to make a reluctant connection to him via their surroundings. Slowly then, she lifted her left hand up in a graceful arc, elegantly pulling the sunglasses from off her face with a delicate fingertip grip… right before rolling her eyes downward upon him. The rest of her displayed a kindly demeanor, but the piercing glare would deliver her real message.

"Mr. Patton, you said?"

"Paxton."

She curtly nodded an acknowledgement to him, knowing his actual name all along. She then exhaled out just enough air to convey to him the great price it required in lowering herself to his level.

"You are so kind to offer us reassurances for our safety. I am sure my mother agrees – we are most grateful. As you can imagine, this has been a trying experience. Would you be so kind as to grant us privacy for the remainder of our time together? It would be most appreciated. In exchange, perhaps I could arrange for some small favor to come your way... something such as... prime tickets to the sporting event of your choice?"

She made sure that her act was so very over-the-top, rich in false graciousness... though she sprinkled every word with her hidden contempt. The performance would be impossible to refuse... irrespective of whether or not he took her up on the offer of tickets.

Which there's no way in hell I'd ever bother fulfilling...

"I understand, ma'am. No offense intended... and none taken."

The man dipped his head in a shallow nod, and Blaire was satisfied.

Bridget leaned back against the wall in order to gain a view of Mr. Paxton around Blaire. His expression through her daughter's ridiculous speech was wholly unexpected. He seemed not at all phased by it. There was not a hint of him having been insulted. He simply smiled and gave what she considered to be the most gracious reply possible. She looked up toward Blaire, but could not make out anything from behind as to how his response was received.

Well... she certainly had some thoughts on the matter. There was no way she was going to sit by idly while Blaire insulted this man... and neither would she allow him to wonder what kind of a mother she was. She would put Blaire in her place... and was on the verge of opening her mouth to do so when the floor began to shudder... almost as if... in contradiction to her wishes... thousands leapt to their feet in unison to offer praise for Blaire's masterful performance. The spontaneous effect continued up the elevator walls to vibrate the entire ceiling, enveloping this small stage in thunderous applause. Although the entire audience consisted of two, the actor nonetheless fell upon the handrail, clutching it in a humble bow. Her encore, so very different from that of the main event, was to transform this aspiring celebrity golfer into a frightened little girl screaming into the reflective surface of the elevator wall. As the spot lights flickered, Bridget sought out the stranger beneath the narrow archway formed by Blaire's prone posture... and unknowingly received back a small measure of calm from the compassion he seemed to be showing toward her terrified child. The shaking ceased as the power went out once more, briefly casting the theater into a complete darkness through which only the wailing of the show's young star could be heard.

When the emergency lighting came on for a second time, Bridget found Blaire on the floor beside her, whimpering there in a crumpled heap.

CHAPTER

17

CUP AND TEE

Prior to the aftershock, the building engineer's full attention had been on the progression of his computer reboots. When the aftershock hit, once more disrupting the main power, the engineer was startled out of his wits by a loud electrical bang and a shower of sparks… followed by complete darkness. His electrician's hasty patchwork wiring on the backup lines had failed. Fumbling about for a flashlight, the building manager… whose next door office was also in the dark… scampered to make a 9-1-1 call, only to find that he could not get through owing to the emergency center being flooded with requests. As the manager repeatedly redialed, he kept up a heated debate with his engineer as to whether the building should be evacuated. His eventual connection to a 9-1-1 operator did not settle the issue. The city's fire stations were overwhelmed with tripped alarms, so if there was no obvious indication of danger to the Pricewater Building, then they should expect low priority. At this point, the building engineer prevailed, convincing his boss that they could handle the problem on their own. The upshot of their hasty inspection was that the only things significantly damaged in the control room were the computers. Their surge protectors and motherboards were all fried. No amount of rebooting or debugging would reconstitute them. Though the engineer firmly asserted that the elevators could be lowered through manual operation, the manager would have none of that. He trusted only the computers. After the main power was eventually restored to the control room, it took the engineer over an hour to bring a replacement computer online.

When the elevator phone buzzed a second time, Bridget was relieved that Blaire made no attempt to answer. Mr. Paxton came off the call with news that it would be a bit longer, as the building manager said they were still having computer trouble. With Blaire back in her corner, earbuds firmly in place, Bridget hoped to spend the remainder of the wait without further incident. Rather than sit there twiddling her thumbs… or mulling over her daughter's abominable behavior… she decided to engage this man in casual conversation. As he previously mentioned his DVD player, she started out by asking him what westerns he enjoyed most. From there, they chatted aimlessly as he named off movie after movie… most from long ago. For her part, she was able to contribute by recalling her father's preferences. She had seen most of Mr. Paxton's favorites: *The Searchers*, *My Darling Clementine*, *High Noon*, *The Shootist*, and *Destry Rides Again*, but could not remember the plotlines or characters to any nearly as well as he could. He immediately included her suggestion of *The Magnificent Seven* to his list… though she chose not to disclose that she only cared for its music.

Finally at ease, she ventured into something mildly personal by telling him that her father had named his children after movie stars. He seemed overly fascinated by the association of her to her namesake, which caused her another moment of trepidation over whether he might renew his comment about her being a handsome woman. To her relief, he steered the conversation toward how Brigitte Bardot was an open advocate for the abolishment of the rodeo… and how he knew this because he, in his youth, had competed as a rider. Bridget found this to be a captivating topic… and a safer one too. As he began to relate his experiences at breaking in wild horses, she struggled with what could be said of herself that might seem even half as interesting.

Divorced, employed at a credit union, and mother to an embarrassment of a daughter. Not much to go on.

She was thankful when he sprinkled in questions that she, as a resident of Southern California, could easily address. Things like what she thought about the various parts of the city, what were the things a visitor should see, and how one could best get around freeway traffic. Their conversation flowed effortlessly, with her soon losing track of the minutes… and that she so happened to be trapped in a tight space suspended high off the ground.

As he began telling her about his travels around the country as a rodeo rider, starting with a story about doing an event in Alaska, the elevator motor jolted into action. All three of them scrambled to their feet as the descent to the ground floor began. She was not surprised when Blaire positioned herself directly before the doors and was the first off, uttering a single-syllabled farewell to her... and nothing to the stranger. Bridget was on the verge of calling after her, since they had matters to resolve, when she became distracted by how Mr. Paxton was holding open the doors for her with his cowboy hat... just as before.

Not really intending to linger, she nonetheless found herself meandering out with him toward a man who was sheepishly beckoning other passengers forward. This man, who identified himself as the building engineer, made apologies for the inconvenience, and then briefly answered questions regarding the earthquake and the stalled elevators. In short course, most everyone dispersed, leaving her standing with the stranger she had spent nearly two hours with.

"Well... Mr. Paxton..."

"Lowell... remember..."

"Yes.... Lowell... it was nice meeting you. Thank you for the kindness you showed in there. It may not seem like much, but it really helped."

She was about to turn away, yet hesitated in feeling that she had not quite said enough.

"I should probably apologize for my daughter. She's just..."

"Begging your pardon, ma'am, but no one should have to apologize for the actions of another adult... daughter or not. She's who she is and... you and I... we're who we are."

It made no sense, but the way he grouped her with him... rather than with Blaire... straightway became the deciding factor. She was fascinated by him... by his calm in the face of danger and by his matter-of-fact attitude toward Blaire's terrible behavior. Since she had taken the afternoon off... and had nothing better to do... the words were out of her mouth before any thought to prevent them.

"Would you be interested in getting a cup of coffee... if there's no where you need to be? There's a place right here in the lobby... assuming it's still open."

She was more surprised at his response than she was with her own boldness. His face reddened all about his snow-white moustache... a feature she had not paid much attention to before that moment... giving him something of a jovial Santa Claus feel... despite how the rest of him was as thin as a rail.

"That'd be a pleasure. As it turns out, I'm free."

Even though the idea was hers, she waited for him to make the first move toward the small eatery she noticed on arriving at the building. He held out one arm as if to direct her, with the other coming around her back. Neither made contact, though she was still fully aware of his gentlemanly conduct as they crossed the lobby together. It struck her with a rather indescribable sensation… neither good nor bad… of being completely unfamiliar with such a simple attentiveness from another person. Only as a waitress seated them in a booth did she suddenly come face-to-face with the realization that this was not just a person… but a man of her own age. She felt a wave of second-guessing come over her as they ordered – her, a coffee, and him, a cup of green tea.

Now that's interesting…

"You know… you kind of strike me as more of a… straight-up-black coffee drinker."

"I used to be… but my daughter got me into tea… for my health."

"She sounds like a persuasive person."

"You don't know the half of it. In fact… she's the reason we're in Los Angeles in the first place. Can't wait to hear whether she felt anything. Say… out of curiosity… how often do you get earthquakes around here?"

"Not that often… if you don't count tremors. I've been through a few major ones, but nothing nearly so severe as to knock down buildings. How about you… was that your first?"

"Yes, ma'am… and pretty exciting too."

Bridget could not help herself, poorly managing to rub her nose in a discrete effort at hiding the smile coming to her face.

"Did I… say something off?"

"No. It's just the way you keep calling me ma'am. It's been a long time since anyone showed me such… regard. Ma'am is nice… but please call me Bridget instead."

"Yes, ma-… I mean… Bridget."

He did that quaint little thing again that he had done in the elevator… the hand gesture at his forehead signifying the tipping of an imaginary cowboy hat, the alter-ego of which she knew to be lying beside him in the booth.

"You've probably figured out by now that I'm not from around here. Originally from Rapid City… that's in South Dakota… near the Presidents…"

She came very close to doing the typically rude Southern California thing of asking why anyone would live there, when it occurred to her that she would gladly live anywhere that did not require a freeway for getting around.

"So… you're here on vacation with your daughter?"

"Here for work. Helping her out with her business… but thinking about staying for a bit. Never got to know this part of the country."

"I hope the earthquake hasn't made you nervous about being here. Like I said, it really doesn't happen all that often."

"Guess the earth's going to do what the earth's going to do."

The waitress brought their orders. Bridget, trying not to look like she was watching, could not help but follow how he went about preparing his tea. He took a moment to read the tea bag's packaging before carefully unwrapping it. He then gingerly dipped the bag in the hot water… almost as if he was allowing it to get acclimated to its new environment… just before releasing the string over the side of the cup. He added a small amount of sugar, lightly stirred the spoon so as not to entangle the tea bag, and then sat back as it brewed.

It struck her all of a sudden, for reasons she could not quite articulate to herself, that it might have been wiser to part ways in the lobby rather than to extend an acquaintance with someone she would never see again. Sure… she could be proud of herself for having done something spontaneous and out of her usual norm of 'safety first'… but whatever credit that brought to her had disappeared. She should have stuck with what was familiar. Right now, she could be comfortably seated in her own car… maybe even already on the freeway heading out of the downtown area… though it likely was a tangled mess of traffic after the earthquake. Still… something had gotten mixed up in her thinking, making it seem like a good idea to stretch out her time with this strange man.

"To tell you the truth, Bridget… I'm glad to be here. It's not every day you get a shot at experiencing an earthquake. Some things only come 'round once in life… and you have to greet them with open arms when they do. Wouldn't you agree?"

Such talk was not what she needed to hear. Not that she was disposed toward disagreeing with him… only that it was easier not to consider whether she already had her shot at life… and failed. This man, in contrast, made a point of saying in the elevator that he had traveled to all fifty states during the course of his adventures as a rodeo competitor. Whether it was the fact that his life had been much more exciting than hers or that he seemed to have a healthy relationship with a daughter, she could not quite say. Either was enough to make her envious of him… and sad for herself.

The cup and tee, together, form the well-understood finishing and starting places to any hole of golf. In the very beginning, the ball is held aloft as if newborn upon its tee, cradled within a tee box. With a sudden metallic cry, it is sent out on a torturous path toward its final resting place – a green pinned as a monument. There, the ball ends its course, being destined to fall into the earth. From the tee to the cup is as a lifetime.

Such symbolism is not often considered during a run-of-the-mill round of golf. Yet every stroke along the way decides how well the finish is made. The golfer is afforded a scorecard from which to look back at choices made… some bearing remarkable outcomes and some resulting in lingering regrets. A lapse of skill, coupled as it were with impatience, imprudence, bravado, or some other excess, can always be overcome in starting out on the next hole. That is the way of the game. Whereas the cat is fabled as having nine lives, the golfer is granted twice that number from which to benefit. Eighteen opportunities to consider the course.

Such is not the case in life.

Her mind strayed to the all-too familiar longing for things she had been denied. For one, ever since childhood, she had wanted to behold the wonder of Mount Rushmore… but her father could never be made to take the family on vacations… and Mitch had always been preoccupied with his career and golf. The sad truth was… she had never done anything truly amazing in her life… never visited interesting places beyond where she happened to be living. Not Hawaii, not New York City, and definitely not anywhere abroad. Even closer to home, there were experiences she had not taken time to enjoy… not in a very long while… while there were others she never would. The warmth of a dinner table packed with children of her own… festive holiday and birthday celebrations… and someone to grow old with. Those things would forever remain foreign to her. Life had not turned out the way she expected.

"Is something the matter?"

"What?"

"You… went silent there for a minute."

"Oh… sorry. I was just thinking about… well… about what the words 'cup' and 'tee' mean to a golfer. Just a silly side thought. Never mind me… You were saying?"

"That I'm glad to be in Los Angeles."

"Yes… LA can get interesting at times… I suppose you're also pretty happy about working with your daughter…"

"That's for sure. But strictly speaking, I work *for* her… not *with* her. She's a bit of a troubleshooter. She and her stepfather…"

Stepfather? Now that's odd…

"…have a consulting business that focuses on helping nursing homes and retirement communities improve their operations. He wins the contracts and she does the leg work."

"So where do you fit in?"

"Mostly I travel around with her… more-or-less as her assistant. She'll come into a place for a week or so, get a feel for it, then figure out what's working and what's not. It doesn't pay much… most of their contracts are rather small… but I'm not in it for the money. I'm in it to spend time with her."

"So you two must get along fairly well…"

"Emmeline's incredible. She has this way about her… knows how to win people over. When she makes a recommendation, facility managers end up claiming it as their own. She doesn't care about the credit… only helping people. I'd say I'm lucky to have her as a daughter."

Whereas being the mother of Blaire O'Connor is no cup of tea.

Bridget did not need to hear any more of his words to know that his relationship with his daughter was very different from hers. The soft smile on his face told her enough about how he cared for this Emmeline of his… and that he was genuinely grateful for the opportunity to be working for her. How he got there was a different matter. He clearly said 'stepfather,' which meant there had been a divorce… likely coming with at least some pain and estrangement.

All of a sudden, she wanted to know more about how he came through the heartache, what it might have cost him, and how he handled seeing his ex-wife marry someone else. How could he be around that person… and how did he keep it all from affecting his relationship with his daughter? His circumstances were undoubtedly different from her own, yet the feelings would likely be the same… grief, hurt, anger and loneliness. To know that someone else had experienced what she had… and come out sane on the other side… was more than worth the risk of inquiring.

"Mind if I… ask you something… personal?"

"Not at all."

"I gather you're divorced…"

"Yes… that's true."

"Yet you and your daughter remained close…"

"It wasn't always so. But yes… we're fairly close now."

"How'd you do it? How'd you come through the trauma of a divorce… and still manage to have your relationship with your daughter intact?"

CHAPTER
18

A SOLDIER'S BURDEN

The twentieth century, a century of unprecedented world war, closed out with the most lopsided of conflicts. No historian will ever doubt that the thirty-four nation coalition assembled in the aftermath of Iraq's 1990 surprise invasion of Kuwait was anything other than an American-led effort. After months of preparation, 'The Lucky War'... as some in the U.S. military would come to call it... lasted all of forty days. Yet the war's most distinctive characteristic was neither its short duration or its extraordinary degree of multinational cooperation. Unlike all previous conflicts, the First Gulf War amounted to the most well-orchestrated and media-friendly engagement ever fought. Daily press conferences held audiences mesmerized with videos of laser-guided precision bombing, embedded reporters participating in rapid tank deployments, and on-the-spot accounts of SCUD missile attacks. It was a media's war, with virtually every aspect openly displayed for all to see. In the end, the coalition's generals... many of whom experienced defeat twenty years earlier as junior officers in Viet Nam... were now depicted with historic redemption. Even the vanquished, already war-weary from a decade-long conflict with Iran that claimed a million lives, were not spared from the media's scrutiny in being humiliated by the West. Only the individuals who bore the unseen scars of that war were left in obscurity.

At the time, Lowell Paxton had a young wife and a child to support. He supplemented his meager rodeo rider's income by hauling freight and enlisting for a stint in the National Guard. There, he picked up new skills in a mechanized infantry brigade. With his commitment soon to be completed… coincident with his unit's scheduled deactivation in the fall of 1990… Lowell had begun exploring the possibility of a community college education. Those plans, unfortunately, were put on hold when Iraq invaded Kuwait in early August of that year. Within a week, his unit was called up and dispatched to Fort Lewis for training in preparation for deployment to Saudi Arabia.

His part in Desert Storm was marginal at best. He would later describe himself as nothing more than the Bedouin's version of a gas station attendant, having been trained to operate a tanker truck destined to trail far behind the advancing armor. Much of his time was spent in boredom or in rushed refueling cycles carried out beneath the dusty downdrafts of guardian AH-1 Cobra gunships. His unit's support role presented him with no combat exposure, as they were there only to replenish the tanks, to provide the men with needed supplies, and to hear their accounts of war.

His journeys through barren desert were nonetheless punctuated by frequent sites of destruction. Though following in the tank tracks afforded safety, the aftermath of their battles was impossible to avoid. Much was seen that he would later wish to forget. Highways littered with the vehicle wreckage of fleeing civilians, many having been caught in the carnage of relentless air-to-surface missile attacks. He was often made to behold up close Iraqi personnel carriers of Cold War vintage turned into twisted and smoldering tombs, appallingly displaying their contents. The smells made the sights twice as disturbing in memory – burning rubber… and flesh. Occasionally, he came across lines of fly-covered bodies decorating the roadside where some fastidious armored cavalry officer had demanded an accurate count of enemy KIA. Worst of all were the infrequent instances in which some tank commander chose to leave his mark of conquest upon the desert – a gruesome display of bravado in the form of an appallingly mangled corpse shredded by a tank's tread. Everything that once identified this as a person was gone. Such images were destined to haunt him for the rest of his life.

Army Specialist Second Class Lowell Paxton returned stateside in early May of 1991, forever changed. It was not so much having witnessed war… or the continued memory of it. To be sure, he was kept awake many a night by visions of hollow-eyed Iraqi soldiers. He also carried with him the putridly acrid smell of an oil field set ablaze and the grinding feeling of sand stuck deep within his sinuses. Mostly, he struggled with his manhood… with questions of futility, sanity, and his inability to move beyond the past. The lasting legacy of those few months of his life amounted to a lingering ailment birthed by that war. For years, the condition would go underappreciated in VA hospitals, meriting a medical description no better than that of a syndrome. Later, it would be linked in rumor to WMDs or some mysterious airborne toxin emitted from plumes of burning crude. The combined acronyms GWS and PTSD left veterans like Lowell with years of unshakable depression and a complete loss of purpose in life.

His initial months back were marked by a self-denial that packaged his growing lethargy within a framework of 'adjustment.' Yet no matter how hard he tried, the energy to compete... or even to work... was not there. He broke his left wrist in an awkward fall from a horse... something that never would have happened before the war. The break was set improperly, healing in such a way that he could no longer grip anything firmly enough to continue on as a rough stock rider. He turned to a combination of pain killers and alcohol to cope with the wrist, as well as to deal with back spasms brought about because of the cooperative impact of desert terrain and inadequate Army vehicle suspension. The drugs, his conscience would often remind him, were obtained illegally... though he refused to care. The Army was guiltier in having stolen his livelihood.

His wife began applying pressure on him to seek professional help, something his cowboy pride would never allow. Arguments grew heated, then violent. She took their child and left him in early 1992 after he struck her in a drunken rage. His daughter was twelve at the time. He would not see her again for fifteen years.

Lowell spent months without awareness, all of which too easily accumulated into wasted years. He flitted between homeless shelters in Denver, spending his days engaged in either panhandling or petty theft. Periodically, he made efforts to sober up by means of some VA-sponsored detox program, and then ply his hand at work. Always, the memories of what he witnessed... and what he lost... would drive him back to bottle and pill. In the midst of his umpteenth relapse, through circumstances he was never quite clear on, he somehow found himself in the care of a Vietnam vet who operated a government-sponsored rehab facility outside Fort Collins. The day Lowell passed beneath its archway would always be remembered, for carved there were the words he came to live by.

What becomes of you is up to you.

Although dedicated to the care of veterans, this center was also a fully-operational cattle ranch delivering meat to local grocers. By compulsion,

Lowell and others adhered to a strict regiment of labor six days a week, along with time spent in individual counseling, job training, and solitary devotional reading. More than these things, two activities eventually helped him turn a corner.

The first was the center's mandatory group therapy sessions. These weekly meetings were initially approached by Lowell with extreme skepticism. For the month after his arrival, he remained withdrawn, unwilling to make connections with either the person who shared or with what they related. But in time, he began to see how the group's stories convoluted the normal experiences of life with the horrors of substance abuse, failed relationships, disabilities, lost dreams, and intense recollections of war. He soon found that these men did not consider him to be someone whose prideful silence constituted a small notch carved out of their close-knit circle, nor did they view him as a pathetic victim whose concealed fears warranted him being shifted to the very center of their ring. Instead, he began to see himself as a single link connecting this tragically assembled collection of lives. These were wounded souls, just like himself… brothers in arms. For most, the years of service were far in the past, yet each man eventually came to accept that his very existence was that service. It was then that Lowell's stories poured forth, and in each, he found himself accepted by them… and after a long while, by himself too.

Now fully committed to the difficult path of healing, Lowell's dreams of war surprisingly became more frequent and more chilling. One reoccurring nightmare was of him in a non-descript VA detox facility being dumped out of his bed by marauding Iraqi soldiers… something he knew for a fact actually occurred in Kuwaiti hospitals. He was often ashamed of himself for this irrational dream, but eventually worked up the courage to share it with the group. He was shocked to be greeted with laughter, but relieved to discover it was only because such dreams were common… not unlike those of college students who imagined themselves arriving naked for a final exam. On such occasions of breakthrough, a brother would invariably repeat that war's ridiculous motto of taunt toward enemy forces in hiding… 'use it or lose it'… except all heads would nod in agreement, as the statement was an encouragement for each person to seek out the group's support.

The second miracle was no miracle at all, though the way it came about seemed miraculous enough. He discovered a new sense of worth. The ranch, as a core tenet to its rehabilitation methods, immersed each veteran within the culture and habits of a cowboy lifestyle. Livestock management, horseback riding, western wear, and bunkhouse life were all part of the daily routine.

Of course, Lowell recognized that the center's presentation of such things was a mere facsimile of true western life, yet he felt no contempt toward the simplicity of the approach. He took in each moment as if it were new, because to the wretched man he had become, all was new.

The staff put on a semiannual mock rodeo as something to stir the veterans' competitive spirits. As Lowell had been a rider, he found an immediate place in which his experiences brought value. Nothing of this rehab rodeo was as serious as the ones he had known. Participants threw ropes over wooden steers, navigated trotting horses around traffic cones, and fought to stay astride a mechanical bull. He nonetheless discovered that his stories of actual rodeo life were sought after. He spoke freely about the joy of competing against his best friends, about the fearful thrill in that moment before a chute opened, about the many tedious hours of highway travel in the bed of a truck, and all the cheap motels and excellent BBQ. But mostly he remembered how wonderful it was to be around cowboys with their ridiculous stories… and the feeling of freedom he found in riding a horse.

This miracle of his happened at one of these mock rodeos. While waiting his turn to rope, a car horn somewhere happened to spook the horse ahead of him, sending it into an uncontrolled prance about the riding corral. It was no big deal for Lowell to come alongside and drag its helpless passenger onto his own saddle. As a bronc buster, he had been on the other side of such transactions countless times in both practice and competition. He retained a deep appreciation for those who rode nearby to retrieve and protect. Many a round of beers had been bought for the pickup men who pulled him from a tangle of hooves, inserted themselves between him and an arena's railing, or drove off a crazed horse that just deposited him semi-conscious into the dirt. Yet he had never done the task himself in competition where a rider was most vulnerable. That day, when he rescued a terrified vet from a not-so-dangerous situation, a light clicked on for Lowell.

Within a month, he had gotten discharged from the facility and presented himself for work as a pickup rider at a regional competition in Topeka. His previous credentials, far from distinguished, were nonetheless recognized and accepted. Lowell then began a life of true recovery, moving about the country in developing and peddling his skills as a pickup rider. For the next twelve years, he lived simply and soberly, owning little beyond a cowboy's gear, borrowing stock as was commonly done, and constantly improving. He would eventually become the first three-time winner of the International Rodeo Rider Association's Pickup Man of the Year award, given in recognition of service and expertise. He would also receive countless bruises, lacerations and broken bones in the pursuit of cowboy safety, these going even further toward earning him the respect and admiration of three generations of riders.

Yet he walked away from it all one September Sunday after being summoned to the coordinator's trailer at the Pendleton Round-up. There, he had a visitor. A young woman wished to meet him. Her name was Emmeline Paxton… his daughter.

CHAPTER
19

DESERT STORM

Now he was the one staring into his tea, obviously searching for some means of answering her question. In taking his cup around in slow rotations on its saucer, she gathered that he was struggling to condense down a lifetime of experiences into as few words as possible… which only made her feel insensitive for having asked.

"It's a long story. You see… I was a soldier in the First Gulf War…"

"Lowell… I'm terribly sorry… I really didn't mean to pry."

"No, it's not that. It's just… that's a war nobody took seriously."

She was definitely part of that 'nobody,' but would never be so thoughtless as to admit it. She recalled that news coverage ran almost 24-7 during those winter months back in 1991, but she had paid little attention to any of it owing to their move from Seattle to LA. To her, the media's fascination over bombs being dropped on the other side of the globe hardly seemed as important as the need for getting her young family situated into a new apartment.

"It must have been horrible for you."

"Yeah… it was rugged. Suffice it to say, there's one thing I learned from the Army – war's hell on marriage."

Peacetime certainly wasn't very kind to mine.

"I was only over there a short time… six months or so… but when I got back… everything fell apart. I couldn't sleep… I had no appetite… and I definitely couldn't bring myself to work. Truth is… I completely disconnected. Call it pride. It took me hitting rock-bottom… and getting a good look at myself… before things got turned around."

"You mean with your daughter?"

"Among other things… yes. She eventually forgave me… and is now really enjoying giving me orders!"

He laughed in an awkward way that seemed to suggest he hoped the subject to be done. So was she. Discussing things that had to do with war… even in its aftermath… was far from a favorite topic. In the silence, she offered a smile as a natural transition toward opening her purse and dropping a few dollars on the table.

"I should probably get going. It's been really nice chatting with you, Lowell."

"For me too."

They parted in the lobby with simple goodbyes. Bridget then went to the directory, found the appropriate room, and descended a set of stairs to the basement level. There, she encountered a buzz of activity from maintenance workers. She asked one for help, and was led to the building engineer's office where she found the same harried-looking young man she met in the lobby. After re-introducing herself as one of those who had been stuck in an elevator, she sheepishly made a request he initially objected to… citing liability issues… but eventually caved in when her steady cajoling made it clear to him that she would not otherwise leave his office. He worked his keyboard for a few seconds and then beckoned for her to view the computer screen over his shoulder.

As the footage played through the events occurring in elevator four during the aftershock… right up to the point when the surveillance feed was interrupted… Bridget slyly captured as much of it as she could on her cell phone. When the desired video portion was done, she pocketed her phone, thanked the man, and quickly headed from the building.

In the days following the earthquake, Bridget would repeatedly revisit this short video clip, each time suppressing an awareness that a caring mother should never have preserved such a thing. Blaire, already severely unnerved by the initial quake, became scared out of her mind when the aftershock hit. Witnessing her daughter in distress should have broken Bridget's heart… or at least made her feel guilty. She nonetheless pushed herself past those feelings… simply because she wanted a record of Blaire in a moment of weakness. In time, she began to concentrate on herself sitting in the background of the scene… almost as one indifferent to Blaire's distress. That self did not seem to contend with the camera's perspective over how Blaire was being depicted so inhumanly out-of-control. The video's grainy quality somehow added to the feel, enhancing an unsubstantiated claim in Bridget that this actually was not her child flailing about on a handrail… not really a person at all… only a poor representation of something vaguely inanimate brought to life by the shaking of an elevator. In the end, the power always went out and the screen became blank, leaving Bridget without a hope for her daughter's future.

After a week of saturating herself with each second to this short video, Bridget transferred it over to her laptop and deleted it from her phone… wanting now to put it out of her mind. She longed to be close to her daughter… hoped for anything that might bring about a change in the girl. But in retrospect, expecting such a thing to be a counseling session now seemed ridiculously naïve. Even before leaving Dr. Fletcher's office, she resolved never to go back. Such seemed to be the case for Blaire too, seeing as no call for a follow-up session ever came.

In the aftermath of the failed therapy session, Bridget once more took up her practice of following Blaire in the sporting news… being incapable of ignoring the fact that she had a daughter. From the newspaper, she learned that Blaire was at the Desert Classic in Phoenix. After the first three rounds of play, she and Christy Tompkin, the previous year's winner, had so separated themselves from the rest of the field that the tournament was essentially a two-woman contest. Bridget had a feeling… the kind that required action. Her daughter was on the brink of her first victory, and she wanted to be there to show support. Perhaps with a taste of such success, Blaire might finally acknowledge the sacrifices made on her behalf.

The six hour drive to Phoenix necessitated waking well before sunrise in order to arrive at the start. From the morning's front nine all the way through the afternoon's back, Bridget kept to the rear of the gallery, in no way allowing her presence to be known to Blaire. This, she did both as a surprise for when the tournament was over and as a precaution against becoming a distraction. While she delighted in following along as part of the small 'Blaire the Flair' throng of fans, she repeatedly resisted the temptation to identify herself to those around as the golfer's mother… even when the back-and-forth battle with Christy Tompkin finally tilted in Blaire's favor.

Entering the final hole, with Blaire a stroke in the lead, Bridget worked her way to the rope line for the first time, with her caution giving in to the anticipation of seeing Blaire sink the winning putt

This is my day and my moment. I'm in complete control. Nothing can stand between me and my prize.

That morning, Blaire fought through the more difficult front nine, clawing her way to within a stroke of Tompkin. Now on the back, where she had excelled throughout the tournament, Blaire was closing in for the kill. To her amusement, her extraordinary play made the fans and reporters have to scurry back and forth between her party and Tompkin's, one back of hers. Blaire put an end to all that on the 16th, draining a thirty foot putt for a birdie and the lead. As the gallery erupted, she bestowed on them a morsel of what it would be like to have her as their champion. Skirting along the rope line, she liberally gave out high-fives to the fans… and smiles to the cameras… knowing that everyone would be fixated on her for the remaining two holes.

She kept that precious one stroke lead arriving at the par five 18th. Her tee and second shots could not have been more perfect, leaving her a pitch and birdie putt away from her first victory. The four months in her rookie season, along with the first five in this one, had been a grueling ordeal, what with her repeatedly being denied a victory. That frustration was finally over. Today, her dominance would begin.

Moving up to where her ball came to rest, she looked ahead to plan her next shot. The rope line restraining the gallery's sea of senseless faces was bulging all about the 18th green, with only a sandy-white bunker eclipsing the emerald carpet that led to her success. She would chip over that without a problem… getting close enough for that decent chance at a birdie. That would certainly seal it.

No way that Tompkin bitch can come back from two down.

Blaire left her caddie standing at her ball and went up to study the green, knowing that it was not really necessary for her to do so. She had been over and over its contours in the days leading up to the tournament, and knew every break of it, as well as precisely where to place her next shot. Still… this was her show on her stage, and she was determined to make the most of it. Her slow walk there and back would hold everyone spellbound. She was not savoring the moment, but allowing them to savor her… for her own enjoyment. As she turned away from the green to head back along the fairway to her ball, a young girl… maybe in her preteens… shouted out from the gallery the very words that Blaire happened to be thinking at that moment.

"I love you, Blaire!"

Perfect!

She turned toward that section of rope line and blew a kiss… with appreciative cheers breaking out all along the gallery. She put them out of her mind in a mere second.

Taking her pitching wedge… her buddy… from the caddie, she focused her attention fully on the shot. Adjusting her grip, she felt a surge of pleasure in the control it brought her. Settling her feet into their accustomed stance, she looked up once more to take in the measure of her target.

Beyond the spot where she intended the first bounce to occur, across the remainder of the green to the gallery bordering its far side, Blaire recognized a face she had not expected to be there. A pulse of irritation hit her… one that quickly transitioned into anger as she came back down to her ball. She should take the shot quickly before thinking any further on the discovery. Indecision surged within. No… she should look again… just to make sure… to know for certain that she had been mistaken. A tremor ran down her arms to her wrists, reverberating a warning that it would be better not to know. Blaire drew back the club without further delay and swung into the ball.

In that hushed moment of free-fall… as everyone in the gallery all about the 18th green was held captive in anticipation of gravity's outcome… Blaire already knew that something had gone terribly wrong. What she always adored about golf – that rush of certainty as to where her shot was heading – was completely absent. As she tracked its flight up and down, a mass groan erupted from all around as the ball deflected backward off the upper lip of the green's forward trap, rolling down its steep slope and settling into its sand.

On that excruciating walk, Blaire… the professional… fought to keep all else out of her mind. This failure… with its humiliation and her anger as to the cause… she put aside for the moment in order to focus on the next shot. She took to the sand without a word to her caddie, intending to use the same pitching wedge that had just failed her. The sensation of her feet sinking and sliding was familiar… though she nonetheless had to steady herself against a more unsettling feeling deep within. She was not free… not yet. She twisted that thought about in her mind, grinding her feet deeper into the sand. With the wedge held an inch off the surface, its angled face rotated so as to give maximum loft, she drew back with violent intent and swung hard at the earth. Her ball launched upward, becoming liberated fully from its confinement. Out along with it came a spray of fine-grained sand, which… like a protective cloud of dust… completely shrouded Blaire's sight of that face.

A beautiful recovery totally wasted on that miserable mother of hers.

Heartbreaking… that was the only way to describe it. For Blaire's approach shot to hit the lip and land in the trap… after all her excellent play to gain the lead… it was simply unfair. Bridget would have given anything for that shot to have cleared. In tense apprehension, she watched as Blaire two-putted for a bogey, and then took to a remote quadrant of the rope line with less-than-enthusiastic applause. That was unfair too. Her daughter deserved better than what these fair-weather fans were giving her. From there, everybody waited nervously for Christi Tompkin's party to play through the 18th green. When it came time, Bridget groaned in disbelief as Christi birdied the 18th hole to take the Desert Classic from her daughter.

Blaire was devastated, that much was evident from the stone-faced look she was giving off as Christi celebrated the victory. Bridget longed to skip the rope line, dash across the green, and hug her daughter. She would console with her over the loss… let her know how proud she was of her… and reassure her that there would be other tournaments to come. None of that would be expressed here… in front of others… for Bridget knew it would embarrass her daughter. Besides, Blaire had interviews to do, autographs to sign, and perhaps other business to attend to before the two of them could talk.

She made an effort to push through the crowd… just to let Blaire know that she was there… but lost sight of her in the post-tournament bustle. Moving away from the 18th green, Bridget latched onto a lone golfer and followed her toward the ladies' locker room. Not having a pass, she was compelled to wait outside with a small cluster of reporters and fans. She listened attentively to the things being said with regard to Blaire's performance… most of the talk rather flattering… though interspersed was a tone of disappointment over Blaire's performance on the last hole. In ten minutes or so, she caught sight of Blaire approaching alone, still clutching her pitching wedge… which seemed a rather odd thing to be carrying. She did not look happy, but that was to be expected given the heartbreaking loss.

"Blaire, I'm so proud of you for…"

Without a word, Blaire seized her by the wrist, waived off the security guard posted before the doors, and dragged her inside the locker room. The place was far from empty, as numerous golfers were still engaged in their preparations for leaving. Bridget was about to renew her words of encouragement when Blaire cut her off.

"Shut up and listen! You've got nothing to say that I want to hear! Nothing! How dare you show up at *my* tournament without my say so!"

"But… I thought you might…"

"What?! That I might want you here?! You just don't get it – I don't need you at all. In fact, I never want to see your face again as long as I live! Do you understand me?! Stay the hell out of my life!"

The shock of these words tore their way into Bridget's comprehension… made all the more startling by the sudden silence enveloping the locker room. She need not look around to know that all eyes were on them… yet the only ones she was aware of at that moment were the steel gray pair narrowing their anger upon her.

Before Bridget could utter a syllable of apology, Blaire turned away to a nearby locker. The quiet in the room now reverted into hushed whispers, which somehow roused Bridget from her paralysis. This was all just Blaire's disappointment and frustration speaking. So… Bridget took a bold step forward to offer whatever might smooth over the moment, but fell right back on catching sight of Blaire in the heavily glossed surface of her locker door. Blaire's eyes were forward, staring with intensity at her own likeness, but shifted as Bridget moved in closer… with clear loathing in the reflection. Blaire raised her pitching wedge, hesitating for a second, and began savagely beating her locker door. Dent after dent was deposited into its polished surface, sending dislodged wood fragments cartwheeling off in all directions. The full intensity of her daughter's rage was present in the violence of each stroke… as well as the accompanying stream of profanities… and both shook Bridget to her core. Blaire did not stop until the club head gave way, arcing over her shoulder in a tumble to the floor. An unnatural quiet then overtook the locker room as Blaire stood for an unreal moment glaring in wonder at the bare shaft in her hands… almost as if stunned that the club had failed her a second time.

Despite a brief opportunity in which to speak Bridget could find nothing to say. She stood there as a prisoner, bound in silence by her daughter's fury and completely unable to forestall whatever came next. And as if half expecting it, she watched in horror as Blaire turned about to face her, saying nothing other than to hiss air across her clinched teeth and glare in a way that echoed the obvious message: 'That, Mother, was for you!'

Somehow, Bridget found strength to make her feeble voice heard.

"I'm… so sorry, Blaire… really, really sorry."

Her apology was not received, but immediately answered. Blaire flung the shaft of the club directly at her, but fortunately with such reckless awkwardness that its ragged metal end clipped an overhead vent and deflected to the floor where its club head already lay. Having flinched in the expectation of being hit, Bridget recovered quickly enough to flee the locker room before Blaire's spear had clattered to a rest.

As per league rules, the sanctuary that is the women's tournament locker room could never be breached by reporters. Outside its doors, those who had seen the intensity of Blaire's arrival, as well as heard the sounds of conflict within, were all packed about waiting to discover what had happened. As Bridget emerged, digital recorders were thrust in her face with questions flying at her from all directions. Everyone seemed to know that the tantrum within had come from Blaire O'Connor, with Bridget… the golfer's mother… available to account for her daughter's unprofessional behavior. She could produce no words for them, and instead pushed her way through while waging an even greater battle against the humiliation threatening to crumble her from within. She held back what could not be restrained for long, barely reaching the parking lot before bursting into tears.

As never before, she faced the terrible realization that she was despised by her own daughter. Bridget wanted nothing more than to be back at home… in bed… where she could forever cry alone. But there was a six hour drive… and her car would surely need gas… and there was no way she was going to make it back in one piece.

Two hours of tearful driving finally brought her out of Arizona. Crossing the Colorado River and coming through the city of Blythe, the interstate suddenly became inundated with dust, choking away any recognition that the place she was passing through had been named after joy. Fine particles filtered through every seam in her car, permeating the interior and causing her eyes… already swollen from crying… to be stung anew. Within her nasal passages grew a sharp, burning sensation akin to breathing the vapors from grinded metal. The resulting congestion, supplemented by a gritty sort of cough to her throat, compounded the discomfort she was already experiencing as an outcome of her sorrow. With visibility cut, she was forced to reduce her speed in order to minimize the danger of a pile-up. Willing her eyes forward, she managed a weak inward gratefulness for the distracting imperative of safety.

But then this desert storm added to her pain. The ethereal effect of her headlights in the swirling sand produced apparitions from which her wounded mind brought forth unwelcomed shapes from memory – a young woman cradling her pregnant midsection, a beautiful newborn, and flashes of three figures pressed together in an illusionary semblance of family. She would have none of those lies, and made the rash decision to spray away these phantoms with windshield wiper fluid. To her insult, the wet glass collected more of the desert into a chalky sludge all about the fringes of her wipers' reach. Like everything she had ever tried, it only made matters worse. Streaks and stains could not be removed with a more vigorous adjustment to the blades. The mess simply compounded.

Bridget pulled off the interstate at a rest stop, unable to see past the thin glassy layer before her… as tears continued to stream down from her eyes.

CHAPTER

20

RESIGNATION

Bridget moved through the following week as a body devoid of spirit. The meaning she derived from motherhood had abandoned her… just as that of marriage had done long ago. All that remained was the tiresome plight of a worker… and in this, the clock was her only friend.

Hands pointing down – time to eat.

Hands pointing up – time to eat.

Hands pointing back down again – time once more to eat.

Those hands then swung round in the darkness to senselessly repeat, with all the space in between becoming as nothingness. The ticking or clicking or flipping of numbers was the heartbeat that so poorly substituted as a sign of life. Time woke her in the morning, sent her into the day, and in its limited kindliness put her to bed at night.

Daily tasks were her only breath.

In box, out box.

In box, out box.

In box, out box. Over and over, and over again.

She could not fathom how there was enough oxygen in the sky or paper in the world to sustain her through this suffocating grief. Coworkers, she was sure, had lives of their own, but to her they were as the computer, copier or coffee maker – fully functioning office machinery offering no relief. She drove to work without the enjoyment of music, without awareness of anything other than the road. She returned in the same manner. The city let her be, sensing little life there left to steal. Once home, she did not read the mail or the newspaper, as their language had become foreign. Her social sphere had collapsed years before from cocktail parties and country club functions to lonely dinners before the TV, where the ghost of her mother haunted her. But after Phoenix, she passed her evenings on a back porch. There, she sat in silence tracking the lengthening shadows that foretold of growing darkness… and a gloom taking hold within.

All her life, she had consistently considered herself to be a forward-thinking person. Yet in the days following Phoenix, all of Bridget's thoughts were sadly bent toward second-guessing.

What if I had been firmer with her and not put up with so much disrespect?

What if I'd not gone back to work… and stayed home rather than putting her into daycare?

What if I'd forbidden her from pursuing golf… or at least restricted her time in it?

And what if Mitch and I had stayed together… and there had been a second child?

Would anything have made a difference?

Every relationship she ever touched had fallen apart. Her father, her mother, her brothers and sisters, Mitch… and now her own daughter would have nothing to do with her. She sacrificed so much for Blaire, yet there had never been anything resembling a relationship between them. Always, it was Blaire manipulating her, Blaire abusing her, and Blaire ignoring her… and Bridget, with her head in the sand, tolerating it all. Phoenix showed her how foolish she had been. Blaire neither needed nor wanted her friendship. The girl desired only to be free of her.

Despite a warning in her head to distance herself, Bridget nonetheless sent out a multitude of texts and voicemails to Blaire's cell phone… most of the apologetic variety… yet with a good number pointing out that Blaire also owed her an apology for the locker room behavior. She even left messages with Mr. Pearl's office. Not one was ever returned.

After a week of wandering about in despair, Bridget sought for a means of closing the door on her relationship with Blaire. She would strive to become… indifferent… laying claim only to having once raised a daughter. She purposed to test this shaky resolve in an unorthodox manner. She would watch the final round of the Plinkerton Open on TV. According to the paper, Blaire had opened up a wide lead. If that held out, she was sure to win her first major tournament. So Bridget would watch without investing any emotional capital in the outcome... for she had none left.

I'll be totally indifferent. I'll take it in without an ounce of caring... I won't be effected in the least... and then I'll just... casually change channels when it's over.

As the network commenced their broadcast, Bridget discoverd that Blaire had just finished the front nine with a five stroke lead. With her party taking a short break before starting the back nine, the television coverage bounced from group to group, and hole to hole, yet always with the announcers returning their discussion to 'the O'Connor outburst' of the previous week... and how this particular tournament was turning out so very different for the golfer. At each reference to Phoenix, Bridget blanched in fear that she might be mentioned... but the narrative had already changed, cloaking Blaire in the guise of a winner. Phoenix, an announcer said, was just one of those amusing eccentricities of the professional golfer. Another chimed in to suggest that a fit of rage was sometimes exactly what a fierce competitor needed to get out of a slump... just another fascinating aspect of the incredible game of golf. Bridget's desire to remain unaffected immediately dissolved away. The terrible abuse she received from Blaire was being reframed as a good thing... for Blaire.

Already hurt, Bridget nonetheless hung on for that first significant look at her daughter... which came as she was preparing to start the back nine. From the camera's perspective, Blaire teed off on ten with such ease... such gracefulness and athletic beauty... as if golf was second nature to her. Yet what Bridget saw was not a highly skilled golfer, but a person who had completely shut out her own mother.

The network broke away from the tournament too soon... before Bridget could process the hurt and turn it into something approximating numbness. In the first few seconds before the commercial break... as the announcers cajoled their television audience to stay tuned... resentment swelled within her. Everything about living with Blaire had been a battle. Every interaction had Bridget getting sucked into her daughter's mind games. So she should turn the TV off and in no way subject herself to another second of this horrid person.

Bridget snatched the remote off the coffee table and put her finger to the appropriate button... but somehow could not summon the meager amount of energy required to push it. No matter how damaging, she was powerless against the craving for one last sight of her daughter. Her arm flopped down to her side as she slumped back against the couch. From there, she stared vacantly through a lawn fertilizer commercial that asserted its product's ability to make all things green, then another on a deodorant that left no stain, and finally a sports drink with its promise to quench all thirst. By the time the network coverage resumed, Bridget had no feeling left in her. She neither willed the camera back onto her daughter nor did she cringe at the anticipation of seeing her. She felt only emptiness.

The broadcast returned with the lead announcer whispering of an amazing development on ten. As he spoke, camera footage showed Blaire striding along alone, her caddie several paces behind. It was then that Bridget recognized how she was dressed – completely in pale yellow – her daughter's 'success' color. She also saw the fire in Blaire's eyes… a determination that nothing was to get in her way.

The announcer had said something about Blaire's performance on the 10th, though Bridget completely missed it. Soon a replay provided her with a visual. Blaire, with a wedge from fifty yards out, struck the stick at its base, with the ball instantly disappearing from view – an eagle that extended her lead to seven strokes. Bridget knew then, as did the announcers, the galleries, and every golfer on the course, that today was Blaire O'Connor's day. By the time her group reached the 18th green, Blaire was eight strokes in the lead on the way to winning her first major tournament.

Far from being bittersweet, Bridget wiped away painfully hollow tears as the broadcast broke to a post-tournament interview with the champion.

"Blaire, tell us what this win means to you."

"I can hardly breathe, I'm so amped… my first major…"

"We're sure it won't be your last."

"You're so kind."

"Share with us your thoughts from that moment when the final putt fell."

"Well… I really want to start by thanking the Plinkerton organizers for putting on a fantastic tournament… and also to the Compton Country Club for being such a great host. I've loved this whole week in Jacksonville – what a wonderful city! I also want to thank my agent Bernie Pearl… Hello, Bernie – I know you're watching. And my caddie Robbie Wine… he was incredible out there today. And to all the other players… you girls were an amazing group to compete against. Thank you… Thank you so much."

Bridget longed to rejoice along with this TV version of Blaire… but it was all lies. Blaire had never shown genuine gratitude about anything… especially not for a mother's many years of sacrifice. This should have been one of her proudest moments, yet all Bridget felt was resentment… for this empty climax and for a lifetime of loss.

Blaire was now being asked to give a blow-by-blow account of the happenings on the 10th hole, so Bridget put the TV on mute and studied the girl in silence. Such a lovely young woman to behold... bright eyes, perfectly clear complexion, and such animated expressions... moving fluidly from smiles and nods to a look of concentration when responding... and then to wholesome laughter at some joke Bridget could not bear hearing. For all of her daughter came with that false front and the briefest glimpse of the fierce heart within that only Bridget recognized. Blaire O'Connor... beauty and the ugly beast.

With that unsettling realization accepted in her heart, Bridget felt the TV slowly pull away... even though its actual distance from her remained unchanged. Blaire's part in her life was shrinking with her own growing feeling of separation. Bridget took the remote in hand and turned off the TV, with the last image being of her daughter blinking from off the screen.

Then she waited... not in the least bit delusional. She simply needed to know for certain. Repeatedly referring to herself as pathetic... like a middle school girl's angst for a call from a secret crush... she sat in silence on her couch staring at her cell phone. Her relationship with Blaire was clearly dead... with no breathing life into it... yet maybe... just maybe... now that Blaire had reached this goal... there might be a bit of room in her life for someone else. The phone might yet ring.

Hope and denial... my only friends.

She pictured in her mind Blaire finishing the interview and then receiving off-camera congratulations from tournament officials. They would probably spend a few minutes admonishing her about her new role as their champion. Next would come the trophy presentation, with Blaire holding it aloft for all of her fans to see. Bridget envisioned Blaire slowly shedding herself of admirers in order to accommodate more interviews... or perhaps quick meetings with her caddie and a WGA representative.

Blaire's first phone call would probably be to her agent. As Bridget's own phone sat silent upon the coffee table, she imagined Blaire making her way to the ladies' locker room, being stopped several times to receive adoration from fans who hung around in hopes of that special moment. Within the locker room, she would encounter a few players offering their congratulations. Bridget could almost see Blaire at her locker placing a second call, this to confirm her travel arrangements. Blaire would then shower and dress before heading to the airport... and still Bridget received no word from her.

Having sat crying on her couch for hours after the tournament's end, Bridget finally rose and made her way to the kitchen. She managed to construct something vaguely resembling a chicken salad sandwich from a glob of mayonnaise, some shredded lettuce, and a couple of microwaved chicken nuggets… all mushed together between two end pieces of bread. Returning with the sandwich and a fresh box of tissue, she sat before the TV for the remainder of the evening while flipping through the major sports channels with the sound on low. She caught a few stills of her daughter's face, a brief clip of the victory moment, and several replays of the eagle on the 10th.

At 11 PM, with the box of tissue half emptied, Bridget switched off the TV, deposited the plate with its uneaten sandwich into the kitchen sink, and headed for bed. She undressed, donned a night gown, and attended to the bathroom routine as usual, no longer on alert for a call from Blaire.

On her bedside table lay the novel she had been engrossed in prior to Phoenix. The pages of the front half were well-worn, while the back half remained pristine, signifying her progress through the book. She vaguely recalled that the heroine was in the midst of some formulaic tragedy through which the character would undoubtedly persevere. With sudden revulsion for the falseness of the storyline, Bridget swept the paperback into her bedside trash basket where its fall was cushioned by a mat of spent tissue, amassed there from a week of tearful moments wholly unrelated to the novel. Once more, Bridget began to cry, extracting tissue after tissue from the box at her bedside. In a matter of minutes, as she struggled with the realization that her life would be spent entirely alone, a new layer came to bury the book from view.

She slept fitfully that night, dreading the appearance of another day. When Monday morning came, she rose lifelessly to the sound of her alarm. She showered, dressed, made coffee, ate oatmeal, and then drove into the city for work… feeling that there remained absolutely nothing of value left in life.

CHAPTER

21

AWAKENING

On the Thursday evening following Blaire's first victory, Bridget, for no particular reason, aimlessly took an indirect route from her back porch to the kitchen. Passing before the TV, which had not been turned on since Sunday, she happened to notice that her cell phone was left lying on the coffee table. She could not remember how it had gotten there or when it was last used.

What good is it anyway? No one ever calls me...

Intending to pass it by, she nonetheless paused in indecision over a vague obligation. Picking it up, she continued to the kitchen, depositing the phone there in its charging dock. The screen momentarily lit up to reveal that she had a message. Though the battery was down to a few percent, she ignored its need over hers, quickly snatching up the phone. Sadly, the caller's number was blocked... which likely meant a telemarketer. She played the three-day-old message without an ounce of anticipation over its possibilities.

"Mrs. O'Connor? This is Alexia Melendez... you know... Mr. Pearl's assistant handling your daughter's account. We spoke before... You probably already know this from your daughter, but Mr. Pearl would like to extend to you a personal invitation to attend the celebration he's hosting in honor of Blaire's victory at the Plinkerton. Mr. Pearl would appreciate it if you could come to his house this Friday night at nine."

Bridget quickly rooted around in a kitchen drawer for pen and paper to write down the address of Mr. Pearl's home in Malibu, along with an RSVP number. She listened to the message a second time to make sure she had the details down correctly... and then once again, just in case there was some deeper meaning to be had from a more careful consideration. On the third replay... as the battery gave out... the obvious hit her. Blaire had not made the call herself... because her mother was not welcome. Bridget dropped the phone back onto its charger, turned out the lights, and went to bed, falling asleep with the same feeling of resentful hopelessness she had dwelt in all week.

She was in a bright grassy meadow, cool air flowing across her face and bare arms. On three sides about her towered massive, snow-capped mountains, their barren faces giving way to fingers of evergreen forest climbing up narrow valleys to touch above the purest of white. Below, the mountain contours rose and fell in the wavy patterns that constituted their skirts. The alpine realms merged there into a single massive domain of pine and aspen stretching from all around toward her, encompassing and forming this, her meadow. Somehow, she found the confinement to be far from constricting. It offered comfort and clarity to the secluded place in which she sat.

On her fourth side, the meadow fell away in a gentle slope devoid of trees, yet punctuated in places by rocky outcrops that decorated the development of a valley below. That valley was bright green in the sun's rays, though many trickles of reflected blue led away, downward, converging on a single river whose graceful curves cut narrow gaps into the forested landscape. Farther on, all definition gradually gave way to the soft purplish haze of great distance.

Bridget knew instinctively that she was the only being within everything she surveyed. There were no signs of birdlife or insects anywhere, and neither were there roads, structures, or forest cuts. Even the sky was clear of contrails, adorned only by wisps of horsetail clouds. She was the only creature, and she was at peace.

In the dream, her focus turned to herself. She was a young girl, no more than eight, clothed in a pretty pink dress, the skirt of which spread out about where she sat. She held up a hand, and the sight of its nimble little fingers made her laugh. She moved that hand up the smooth skin of her other arm, across the sleeve of the cotton dress and then down to its hem, oddly fascinated with her own ability to feel.

It was then that she noticed, starting at the fringe of her dress and spreading out uninterrupted throughout the meadow, a sea of wild flowers. Most were circled about by petals, but others took on the forms of umbels, tubules, spikes or panicle clusters. All about her were pale yellows and bright blues, purples, multi-toned reds, pinks and whites, many decorating contrasting centers.

She casually reached out to pluck the nearest one, to bring it up close for examination, when the air grew painfully still. Immediately drawing back from contact, she suddenly knew for certain it was terribly important that none of the flowers be disturbed.

The breeze returned to the meadow, yielding gentle undulations to its colors. It was a sign to Bridget of the flowers' appreciation that she understood. They had such a short time to exist, to enjoy warmth and rain, and each other. In their dance, they spoke to her, explaining that all too soon the snows would move down into the meadow… then their time would be over. But for now, it was their moment to be.

The young Bridget nodded in agreement. She was sure of it. No one had sat where she sat. No one in the history of the world had ever seen these flowers. Both bud and bloom were there for only her enjoyment.

Now there was urgency in her to savor the flowers, for they were beginning to wilt. The first petals unexpectedly dropped off as the sun's path became eclipsed by a mountain peak. The air instantly chilled. It was happening too fast. She had barely taken time to appreciate their presence, and yet all around her the flowers were losing their color. As they aged, so did she. Her dress too began to pale, fading through shades of gray into a deepening dullness. With it, an unseen force bent her over as if she were suddenly weighed down by the accumulation of many years… all brought on in an instant. The grasses all about her became brown and matted down by that same invisible burden of time. Her once bright meadow was now shrouded in shadow by a darkness moving in from the forest with a frigidity that shook her limbs. Snowflakes fell. Not the small delicate ones, but heavy globules of cold wetness. She stretched out a withered hand to the last remaining flower, a columbine… but not to pick it… only to comfort it. Her feeble reach came up short as its last petal fell.

Bridget awoke in a startle to the midnight of her room. For minutes afterward, she lay in bed as the course of the dream repeated itself in her disturbed mind. The meaning was almost too painful to acknowledge. The years in which she had felt young, able to take on any challenge, were gone… and it was far too late for her to start over. Being made to face that… to consciously accept that a wilt had already set in… that was so terribly unfair of her subconscious self.

She threw off the covers with a shudder on being confronted with the coolness of the room's air… reliving again the dream's very last moment of despair. Quickly rising from bed, she went to the bathroom in the dark, then came back in the same darkness to resume her previous position beneath comforter and sheet.

But as dreams often do, the substance of this one was already beginning to fade… even though the feel of it lingered. In that brief wakeful span of time, she lost the record of the dream… just as if it had slipped away with a rush of water down her sink's drain. Before sleep could creep back in to cleanse away concern, she sought once more to reconstruct the dream, coming away with only one small fragment for her memory.

Wild flowers… in a mountain meadow.

On rising to her alarm's summons, Bridget greeted the Friday morning sunlight without preoccupation on the night's dream, yet with thoughts oddly bent toward an inexplicable purpose. A new day… and it was time for her to live. She took pleasure in feeling the shower's stream course through her hair, in drying herself with a terry cloth towel, in having options with which to dress, in tasting sweetness spread over toast, in being out her door on time, and in feeling mechanized power move her car across the most magnificent highway system on the planet.

Work – what a poor word to describe the opportunity set before her, for she suddenly saw her job in a new light – to be richly paid to do small acts of service on behalf of others! This day, she was reviewing a stack of loan applications, mostly for new home purchases, but a few for refinancing. These were people's hopes and dreams. In most cases, the credit union could make those loans possible, but in others, Bridget would help the applicants understand why they had been denied and what avenues might be pursued. She willingly… even joyfully… dispensed out real hope.

For lunch, she invited several coworkers to a taco truck, and ate a spicy chicken burrito while they exchanged ridiculous stories about their wildest of food truck adventures… interspersed as those were with silly office gossip. She smiled and laughed like she had not done in weeks… in years. The afternoon presented more forms to process and more calls to make, and in each Bridget sought life over despair. She made a customer laugh with the lame joke about the banker, the plumber and the duck, and consoled another over his financial woes. For each person, she shared of herself without partiality. Not once during the course of that day did she stop to think about Phoenix. From that moment onward, whatever her future might turn out to be, she was determined to embrace it purposefully… for she had come to see that it was still her time to bloom.

PEACE PARTY

To Bridget, Fridays in LA were unpredictable. Always, there was the constant, ever-present motion of the freeway, but added to or subtracted from this was whatever trend the approaching weekend presented. On some occasions, a significant percentage of commuters started in early on the rush, with traffic petering out sooner than normal, whereas on others it seemed as if all Southern California had set its designs on spending the entire weekend on wheels. Either way, Bridget was in no hurry on this particular Friday. She could ride the wave of whatever flow the city had to offer, and eventually it would lead her home.

She left work with her mind turned toward that night's celebration for Blaire. The commute was not spent in planning how she would dress, or what things she would say, but in how best to position her state of mind. For one thing, she would not approach this party with the same deference she had been compelled to show at her ex-husband's social events. In no way would she give herself sacrificially toward being overly impressed by whomever she met. She would strive instead to see beyond the façade to the core. And most importantly, she would not be ashamed of being herself.

If it had not been for the subterfuge behind the ridiculous therapy session with that Dr. Fletcher, Bridget might well have been taken in by Mr. Pearl's invitation to a party at his home. She had been burned once by a hopeful naiveté… she would not be burned again. Too many times Blaire had lifted up her anticipation, only to bring it crashing down in dramatic fashion. So she would not expect anything from her daughter other than deceit. She would not give a moment's thought to the possibility that she had been invited to share in the celebration, because her daughter never did anything for anyone unless something was in it for her. And to hope that Blaire was having second thoughts about Phoenix… that the invitation was some unspoken admission of her abominable behavior… that was even more ludicrous. Getting the girl to apologize for anything would require a miracle akin to making the sun stand still in the sky. Blaire did what she wanted, when she wanted, and how she wanted, with absolutely no regard for others. No… guilt was as foreign to Blaire as was speaking Chinese.

Something else was up.

Mr. Pearl was a different matter. Though captivated… and concerned… by this agent's influence in Blaire's life, Bridget had not yet been given the opportunity to meet the man.

I suppose it's only natural that he invite me since I'm the mother of his client… but somehow the timing seems off. He's been representing her for over a year now without a single word to me. Maybe he's really trying to help smooth over… But no – that's the same foolish optimism I had regarding the counseling session. Face it, it's unrealistic to expect such a man to care about my issues with Blaire.

Once home, she replayed the phone message to confirm the address and time. For some reason, it had not occurred to her until then to find out something about where Mr. Pearl lived. She plugged the address into a browser's map function to reveal that he owned a large piece of ocean-front property. He had to be very rich to afford that… and equally influential to edge out all the other incredibly rich people in Southern California vying for the same status. She would be so very outclassed by everyone there. That was fine with her. She was not attending this party to gain anyone's acceptance. She was going in order to lose something… and come away freer for it.

She opted for one of her more conservative party dresses, with hem just below the knee, a closed back, and a modest neckline. She put effort into her make-up and hair so as not to appear too plain-looking… otherwise Blaire would surely take the opportunity to embarrass her. At that thought, she reminded herself once more not to evaluate herself based on anything Blaire might say or do. She would no longer live off of the expectations of others… especially those who refused to be close to her. She would forgive herself of that burden too… and in no way be ashamed of having once cared so much about Blaire's opinion of her.

She left home ninety minutes before the start so as not to be in a rush, arriving at Mr. Pearl's mansion on time… including the fifteen minutes spent cruising back-and-forth along a stretch of the Pacific Coast Highway to relax herself. She pulled up before a terraced walkway, stepping out of her car as casually as could be done while holding an evening clutch in one hand and accepting a small piece of paper from a valet with the other. That young man directed her up three sections of bricked steps toward a columned front porch. She could easily hear the music that indicated a party was in progress. To her surprise, a young woman on the porch stepped forward to intercept her.

"Are you Mrs. O'Connor?"

"Yes."

"Welcome to Mr. Pearl's celebration for your daughter. He's asked me to escort you inside."

"Thank you. I didn't catch your name."

"It's Mandi. I work for Aces Events. We specialize in catering private parties… especially for prominent personalities such as Mr. Pearl."

This description of Blaire's agent caught Bridget off guard, though she quickly recovered by reminding herself… once more… not to be affected by anything that evening.

"Do you know if my daughter's arrived yet?"

The young woman paused on opening the door, perhaps in need of adjusting to the intense noise level now coming at them.

"SORRY… WHAT'D YOU SAY?"

"IS BLAIRE HERE?"

"I THINK… SHE'S WITH… MR. PEARL."

The pounding of a bass-heavy beat made all further communication between them painfully difficult. Mandi led her over the threshold into a rather large oval foyer. There was no other way for Bridget to put it – the decor here was terribly overdone and conflicted. Above, a frieze of a seashell-like pattern encircled a domed ceiling filled with a dendritic crystal chandelier. Like an oddly lit Christmas tree anchored by its top, its branches stretched to the dome's boundary in delivering dimly asynchronous pulses toward the floor. There, the dark hues of irregularly shaped marble slabs sucked up the light without reflection. All around this foyer were alcoved plinths manned by statues of what looked like Greek gods… except their forms seemed distorted as if the stone had somehow been melted. Part way through, she did an uncomfortable double-take at a post-modern painting hanging on one section of the curved wall. Irrespective of the artist's intentions, the warped geometrics bent Bridget's perception of space, pricking at her natural appreciation for orderliness and harmony.

As it was, not much else of the artwork could be seen owing to the clusters of partiers standing along the walls. On first stepping inside, it struck her as odd that nobody stood in the wide-open middle of this foyer. Yet in the brief time required for Mandi to lead her across the dark tiling, Bridget came to understand that the center was left vacant for a purpose – to better observe those arriving. As faces turned her way… and then quickly back again in dismissing what they beheld… she could not help but think less of them for it. These people were there to notice and to be noticed.

Mandi continued through an archway into a large room jam-packed with strobe-lit dancers. The sound in this ballroom-like space was nearly unbearable… though its intensity did not keep her from wondering how it was that Blaire could possibly know this many people. That aside, all of their fashion was so far beyond Bridget's means. Not wishing to be lost in this throng of gyrating bodies, Bridget turned her full attention toward remaining within arm's reach of Mandi. As she fixed her eyes on the young woman's three-inch-wide designer belt, it occurred to her that there was more style encompassing that size zero mini dress than Bridget possessed in the entirety of her own wardrobe.

Finally emerging through to the other side, Bridget followed Mandi as she made directly for the center of three sets of French doors, all of which opened onto an enclosed colonnade of sorts. This too was packed with young people, though the music thankfully lessened as they made their way to the mansion's back patio… it equally crowded. A tuxedo offered her a glass of some sparkling beverage, which Bridget declined seeing as she required a clear head. Besides, in this crowd, the drink would likely be spilt long before she reached Mr. Pearl. She was momentarily distracted by splashes, boisterous laughter, and the sight of much bikinied flesh… but in glancing up from the pool she was unexpectedly overwhelmed by the fading embers of a Pacific Ocean sunset view from Mr. Pearl's cliff top vista.

Now that's something worth being impressed by.

The pause allowed her a brief moment to relax, but then she had to hastily catch up with Mandi, who was heading to the far end of the pool where stood the heart of the party – its host.

"Excuse me, Mr. Pearl… allow me to introduce you to Blaire's mother, Mrs. O'Connor."

Bridget extended her hand to a man of contrasts on par with the house she had just passed through… maybe even greater. Her first thought of him, she would later admit to herself, was not altogether flattering. Stripped of pretense, Mr. Pearl was a short, over-tanned, already balding, middle-aged man… perhaps no more than a decade younger than herself. She might even go so far as to describe him as frumpy, though the way he carried himself in his riches clearly hid all obvious signs of that. He, as a businessman first and foremost, made a powerful distinction between himself and the rest of the party. Before her was a classically tailored suit, fine weave cotton shirt of pale blue, and red power tie. She noticed the heavy gold watch that adorned the hand he offered. Most everyone on the premises could probably identify its maker, as well as that of his shoes and apparel, but to her, the collection spoke only of wealth.

"Mrs. O'Connor, what a pleasure to finally meet you. Thank you for coming to this celebration party for Blaire."

As she shook his hand, she noticed that the cluster of people about him abruptly dispersed. Maybe that had been prearranged, or maybe they were avoiding an uncomfortable interaction. Sort of like finding oneself in the presence of an amputee and wishing to discover how the deformity had occurred… yet knowing it supremely insensitive to ask. Bridget had not lost her sense of style in some tragic fashion accident. It had been slowly withered away by duty. At least Mr. Pearl showed no discomfort in her presence, displaying what she silently accepted to be his core competency – a keen understanding of the bottom line. She was connected to Blaire, and Blaire was the object of his investment.

"Thank you for inviting me. Your house is very impressive, and all these people… they're all friends of Blaire's?"

Her tone might have come across as from a mother overwhelmed at the discovery of her daughter's popularity, but she put forth the question as a simple test – to see if Mr. Pearl might exploit her impressionability. She was pleasantly surprised by his response.

"No, I don't think Blaire knows more than a dozen people here. But they all know her… and that's the truly important thing. That's my job, Mrs. O'Connor – to make sure she's well-known. And I intend to do that job well."

He paused in anticipation of a response… but she purposefully composed herself into a pleasant smile. This party, with all its glitz, was not her world, and she would not succumb to the temptation of becoming part of it… not for some foolhardy hope of reaching Blaire. The true nature of their relationship had been revealed in Phoenix. Theirs was a one-way street in which her daughter's lack of appreciation traveled alongside her own obligation. Normally, she might thank him for his effort on behalf of her child, and then launch into her own aspirations for Blaire's future. Instead, an unaccustomed determination compelled her to remain silent.

"Look around you, Mrs. O'Connor... what you see is the future of this city. These young partiers are the energy that keeps LA in the world's spotlight... drawing all eyes to us. Of course, many you see here are important in the industry, but I want to point out a few who are equally influential in the world of sports. Now see that man over there?"

He pointed, discretely from waist-level, at a rather large individual dressed entirely in black... except for the mass of gold chains about his neck, each of which sparkled in the pool's rippled lighting.

"He's the third-most profitable fight promoter ever to come out of the state. And that man over there by the bar... the one in the pink tie... he's the most sought-after basketball talent scout in the country. And that woman there, she owns... oh, never mind... just went inside. But that gentleman there by the palms is the agent of several prominent MLB players. And that man there with a young lady on each arm, he's the..."

Back and forth his hand went, almost as if rocking the imaginary cradle of her daughter's infant golf career. As impressive as all his connections seemed, her mind was occupied elsewhere.

Does he expect me to find any of this important? Perhaps Blaire's not told him that I don't care for sports... assuming she's talked about me at all. Besides, what difference does it make if someone's third or thirty-third in their career?! Come to think of it, why isn't he mentioning any names?

"You're probably wondering why all these people are here. What does any of this have to do with your daughter? Simply put, they're here because I invited them."

He paused again, this time with a self-satisfied grin that allowed his claim of influence to settle in. She was impressed... anyone would be... yet none of it changed in any way how she was feeling regarding her daughter. Blaire might have the greatest sports agent in all the world, but that fact altered nothing regarding how she treated her mother. These people, highly successful or not, might drop everything to attend one of Mr. Pearl's events, but Blaire would remain unchanged.

Mr. Pearl unexpectedly leaned in close to her as if to whisper... even though he had to maintain a raised voice in order to be heard.

"They appear to be partying… but they're actually hard at work."

Bridget immediately made a point of seeking out the nearest bikini.

"Well… most of them… if you understand my meaning. Some people… the fans… might think all this to be a product of celebrity… a constant display of success and privilege… but that couldn't be further from the truth. Don't misunderstand me, your daughter's going to be a star… no doubt in my mind or I wouldn't be investing in her. But this party has a different purpose. I guarantee you that everyone here of substance is here for business. You don't see it, but deals are going down all around us. A few may have to do with Blaire and my promotion of her, but many others don't. I just so happen to attend events such as this quite regularly… often without the slightest interest in any of the frivolity. You might say that I'm…"

All of a sudden, her confusion over why she had been invited to this party was cleared away. Mr. Pearl wanted her there for only one reason – to reach a deal regarding Blaire. This was about turf.

All because I showed up unannounced at one of her tournaments…

Now that she understood with perfect clarity that the conversation was a negotiation between 'agent' and 'mother,' Bridget was ready to get down to business.

"Excuse me for interrupting, Mr. Pearl, but where's my daughter?"

Her question left him with mouth open midstream, though he quickly collected himself into a sly smile.

"Have a drink, Mrs. O'Connor."

He motioned toward someone behind her, and an attendant immediately arrived at her side. At that moment, she did not actually care for anything, but thought it more of a distraction to refuse. On reaching out to take a glass from the tray held out to her, she found Mandi standing there… almost if she too had been summoned by Mr. Pearl.

"Ahh, yes… Mandi… would you be so kind as to locate Ms. O'Connor for me? Please let her know that her mother has arrived at the party and wishes to see her."

"Certainly, Mr. Pearl."

Mandi turned on her heels and made a beeline back toward the house. Bridget would never go so far as to describe herself as a particularly observant person, yet she could not help but notice that Mandi made no effort to search the crowded patio. The young woman already knew exactly were Blaire was. With that understanding, Bridget also came to realize that this whole interaction with Mr. Pearl had been staged. Even the arrival time seemed more like an appointment rather than anything to do with an invitation to a party. Perhaps some of this may have struck her as odd prior to Phoenix, but now everything to do with Blaire definitely put her on alert.

Turning back to Mr. Pearl, she caught the faintest of smiles on his face, hastily covered up by his glass of Champaign.

"Mr. Pearl... you're not concerned about me getting in the way of your plans for Blaire, are you?"

He continued a slow sip on his drink, concluding with a bit of a frown.

"Should I be?"

"So far, your involvement with Blaire has cost you what... maybe a few minor expenditures and a party? But you've yet to invest anything close to the level of care that I have. I wager that'll change soon enough... and then you'll get a taste of what I've been experiencing for years. When your sacrifices tip the scale against mine, then it'll be me who's concerned for you. In the meantime... I'll answer your question. You have nothing to worry about from me. Blaire and I have parted ways... and at the moment, she's completely incapable of understanding how that will impact her future."

"This is most unfortunate."

"Why? I would have thought... as her agent... that it made your job easier not having a meddling parent in the picture. Or perhaps you mean it removes some angle you might want to play in your promotions?"

"Mrs. O'Connor... really! You do me a disservice."

"Perhaps... Time will tell. I'm sure you've worked with all sorts, but let's you and me have an understanding – Blaire is now your problem. Don't expect me to..."

Unfortunately, Blaire chose that moment to appear at Mr. Pearl's side, interrupting the negotiations. Two weeks prior, Bridget would have been ecstatic to see her daughter, but now wished Blaire would go back to wherever she came from so the one-on-one with Mr. Pearl could continue.

"Mother, I'm so excited to see you. Isn't it wonderful – my first major tournament." Blaire paused then, her expression becoming slightly amused in looking back and forth between them. "What's going on? Am I interrupting something special?"

Bridget responded at the same time as did Mr. Pearl.

"Yes, you are."

"Of course not."

The contradiction had no effect on Bridget. She turned back to Mr. Pearl, while directing her clarification toward Blaire.

"You might have interrupted our conversation, but it's really not something for you to be concerned about. After all, this is a party… not a business meeting. Am I not correct, Mr. Pearl?"

She was pleased with his reaction. Once more, he was forced to rescue himself with his liquid lifesaver. She still noticed a slight flick of his eyebrows over the rim of his glass. That look, more than any finality she might have derived from their interaction, told her it was time to leave.

"Mr. Pearl… it certainly has been a pleasure meeting you and hearing all about your wonderful plans for Blaire. I'm so relieved that she has you in her life. Thank you also for the conversation. It was… most illuminating. I'm sorry, though… I really should be going seeing as I have work in the morning. We can't all party hearty, can we?" She ended it with a bit of a false laugh… just for his benefit… and then turned to Blaire. "Would you mind escorting me to the front door?"

Without waiting for a response, she took hold of her daughter's arm and swung her in the direction of the house. Once out of earshot of Mr. Pearl, a more familiar version of Blaire chimed in.

"What the hell was that all about?"

"Nothing for you to worry about, Blaire. You're the master of your own destiny."

"Oh, I know that tone. You're pissed because…"

Fortunately, Bridget lost track of her words due to the noise coming from within the house. She nonetheless kept a firm lock on her daughter's arm while retracing her steps through the various rooms. Not until they emerged onto the front porch, with the party a dim distraction, did Bridget address her again.

"Blaire, it's obvious that you no longer want me in your life, but you should know that I also no longer want…"

"Mother, really! This isn't the place for…"

"Don't interrupt. I'm really not interested in anything you have to say. My world has revolved around you… and your father… for far too long. Not anymore! These past few weeks have been a real eye opener. Suffice it to say, I'm not interested in sharing my life with anyone who behaves like you do."

She paused there for a second to confirm her own feelings, as well as to search for any sign of softness in Blaire's face. Nothing was there other than the usual arrogance.

"You're on your own. Go back to your party."

"Mother…"

"Goodbye, Blaire."

Without another word, Bridget turned down the stone steps to the valet station at the bottom. She suddenly became aware of the ticket given to her upon arrival. Instead of transferring it to her purse, she had held it in her hand the whole time. Opening her fingers, she found that the thing had become a crumpled wad. After rendering it over to the valet, who took a moment to unfold and examine it, Bridget was tempted to turn about to see if her daughter had returned to the party… or perhaps was still standing outside the front door watching her leave. As the young man took off to retrieve her car, she told herself not to look back, knowing that no satisfaction would come from discovering whether or not her daughter was there. For Blaire had rejected the third possibility… the only one offering a glimmer of hope for their relationship. She had chosen not to follow her mother down the steps.

The valet soon pulled up in her car, hopped out, and held open the door for her. She was vaguely aware of his hesitation in assessing the possibility of a tip, but promptly closed the car door once she was seated inside. She put the car in gear and moved cautiously through Mr. Pearl's extensive driveway while pondering the significance of the valet tab wadded up in her hand. She had come to the party prepared to leave. She had left even before arriving.

CHAPTER

23

BITTER RESOLVE

In nearly every moderately-sized city, the owner of a filthy car has options. There are always those ubiquitous stalls of coin-operated sprayers situated along some thoroughfare lined with fast-food joints. Within the privacy of two walls, the driver gets to decide exactly how clean is clean… as is usually defined by a cupholder's limited stash of quarters.

Conversely, while munching on fries, the driver becomes a passenger as their vehicle is slowly drawn through an automated facility that pelts the exterior with water jets, slapping polymer brushes, and forceful blowers… all as entertainment diverting attention away from the mess accumulated within. Such establishments excel at the quick and efficient 'hands-free' approach – a superficial cleaning that gets at what is seen.

Then there are the bouncy, bikini-clad armies of sign-wielding teenagers intent on raising funds for prom or the senior trip. These car washers are especially adept at luring in the male driver with something of a false promise. Though a five dollar donation achieves a two minute rapture of dish detergent vigorously smeared about the exterior of the man's car, such care by these young souls is never meant to address the loneliness seated within.

With deeper pockets, any driver can obtain a detailing company's deluxe package. From top to bottom, both inside and out, a professional will carefully attend to every issue of concern, finishing off with wax and water repellent – a holistic automotive cleansing experience complete with underbody scrub and that new car scent. Yet no amount of money can alter the universal rule of the road – the clean car never stays that way.

At one time or another, most everyone has tried a little of everything… or done nothing at all.

Such is the modern mindset – a self-help book, a podcast, a therapist, group counseling, communing with Nature, or perhaps some timely TV advice from a renowned personality… all of which have benefits adaptable to one's liking. Yet in life, it is only the driveway do-it-all-by-yourself approach that achieves lasting results. To be truly clean, a person must pull themselves up by their garden hoses, take bucket and sponge in hand, and come face-to-face with their own mess. Such realizations are conceived in solitude, embraced by a force of willingness, and then brought to fruition through much hard work.

That evening, finally back in Palmdale and finally calm, Bridget set herself to accomplish all that she had conceived in the somber drive back from Blaire's party… the first step of which was to accept what she had been denying for years. Always, she had found a way of convincing herself that things with Blaire were not as bad as they seemed, and that something good would eventually happen to turn everything around. It was high time that she stopped being a slave to such foolish expectations. What she was planning to do, she would not cave in halfway through, for even before crossing out of Mr. Pearl's property, Bridget had decided once and for all to forgive herself for Blaire having not turned out as a decent human being.

Pulling into her narrow driveway, she called upon the determined resolve she had built up on the way home. Coming inside, she immediately took her laptop to the back porch and went online, canceling one-by-one all of her magazine subscriptions pertaining to sports. She did likewise with her daily delivery of a newspaper. Next, she put in a call to her cable provider's twenty-four-hour number and terminated her contract. A very nice customer service representative with an Indian accent tried to persuade her to accept a discount offer for two more years, but Bridget politely declined. Her mind was fully made up that she should never again put herself through the pain of watching Blaire on TV.

Once those tasks were accomplished, she set aside her laptop and phone to undertake a more difficult and costly next step.

Don't think… just do.

Heading down her hallway to a set of folding doors that hid a small utility closet, she drew out an empty laundry basket and quickly reversed direction toward her house's second bedroom. For a brief time, after first moving in, this spare room had contained a bed, a dresser and a desk... all the meager trappings necessary for appeasing a college student while home on break. When that purpose no longer ended up being necessary, she briefly considered leaving everything as-is... in case an occasion somehow presented itself in which a guest room was needed. That plan lasted all of six months worth of silence from Blaire. Bridget then had the room cleared out and refitted as her hobby space. She put a folding table in the center, and on its surface piled periodicals from which she extracted clippings regarding Blaire's exploits.

Ignoring the table with its mess for the moment, she concentrated first on two sections of shelving that lined one wall. Placing the laundry basket on the floor, she removed a photo album from a shelf and laid it neatly inside. From this first one onward, Bridget fought off an urge to open the next and peak in at its contents one final time. To be fair, she fully expected this feeling to come over her from the very first moment of resolving to remove the influence of these albums from her life. In fact, she knew exactly where she was on the One-O-One coming back from the party when she swore to herself that these photos must go... seeing as every image was taken within a false expectation for the future.

Now, with a second album in her hands, she found herself fighting an intense battle with second thoughts. As a meager defense, she established a rhythm in her motions to keep from opening a cover.

Left hand... take one from the shelf... shift it to the right... careful... keep your eyes straight ahead... place it in the basket... quickly reach for the next.

With each successive transfer, the craving within grew such that she could no longer fight off the temptation. After a brief pause in which she accepted the price to be paid, she opened at random the fifth album off the shelf. The first photo she laid eyes on was of Mitch hanging out in the Piper Mountain Country Club's bar with his golfing buddies. He had that so-very-satisfied-with-himself look on his face as he held up a mug of beer to the camera. She slammed the cover shut and dropped that album into the basket. She should have expected this... to be confronted with the sight of him would instantly bring back the disgust she had thought to be long gone.

Pulling the next off the shelf, she fully hoped her previous resolve to come back... but instead, she found herself cradling this particular one in her arms... remembering. There were those miserable months following the divorce in which she had turned to these albums as an opiate for the dulling of her pain. Night after night, as Blaire lay securely asleep in bed, she would flip through page after page, languishing over what once was and imagining what could have been. It had worked… for a time… until she began to get sicker on the sadness. Only when she finally forgave herself for a failed marriage did going to these albums become less about the supposed joys of family and more about her trying to hold onto Blaire. That had not made her feel better either. Now, after so many years, the memory of how she repeatedly relapsed on these pictures only brought her shame. These albums had been nothing more than a drug to her. They were her false fortress, built brick by brick… photo after photo… on the shaky foundation of Mitch and Blaire.

The albums needed to go – that fact remained obvious to her. Looking down at the one in her arms, she decided to try one more time… but only because she wanted something other than Mitch to be her last memory of these albums. Delicately, Bridget plied along the pages using the same kind of finger-and-thumb action a dealer might employ in carefully shuffling a deck… stopping only when she was convinced of the card to be drawn. Catching a glimpse of Blaire's youthful face, Bridget immediately opened the album to a half-dozen pictures taken at a birthday party. Her own captions indicated that this was Blaire's thirteenth. She remembered it well. This was supposed to have been a special occasion, what with Blaire becoming a teenager. Mitch was obviously no longer on the scene… which was another reason why she had worked so hard to make this particular birthday an incredible experience for Blaire. She mailed-out invitations, ordered a three-layer cake, bought party favors, hung elaborate decorations, and came up with a variety of fun games. It had all been lost on Blaire. Bridget did not need to study the sulky expressions on her daughter's face to recall how terrible that party had turned out. Blaire found fault with everyone and everything, even bringing one of her guests to tears by throwing that girl's gift in the trash… right before the giver's eyes.

So much effort had been invested in helping Blaire develop meaningful relationships… any kind of relationship. No matter what Bridget tried, one way or another, everything went wrong. Sleepovers, play dates, trips to the mall, outings with other junior golfers, and even carpooling classmates after school… in each case, Blaire would end up insulting the prospective friend so severely that the relationship blew up before it even got started. Bridget would back off… give it some time… and try again with a different prospective friend in a new setting. The result was always the same. Blaire's obstinacy always hit Bridget hard… so much so that she eventually gave up trying, having burnt through relationships of her own with coworkers, neighbors and country club acquaintances in search of a child who could tolerate her daughter. The irony of it all was that Blaire could not have cared less about friends.

Bridget slowly closed the album and placed it in the basket with those already there. Grabbing the handle, she dragged the basket down the hall to the garage and slowly began relocating the albums one-by-one to a vacant shelf on a metal rack. Tomorrow, she would find boxes big enough and strong enough for their long-term storage.

With empty basket in hand, she returned to the spare room for three additional trips. In the last of these, she loaded down the basket with various mementos from the room, as well as framed photographs stripped from both wall and shelf. These were almost exclusively of Blaire from her middle and high school years, ranging in significance from graduation day to victory poses after various tournaments. A thin layer of dust that had collected on these since the last cleaning was a reminder to her of that miserable car drive back from Phoenix, not more than three weeks before. The thought hit her that these framed reminders of Blaire's childhood were no more substantive than those of the desert mirages of swirling sand she had endured after getting her heart broken. Both were deceptions.

Wiping away her tears, she purposed to go about the remainder of her task with the same callus indifference Blaire had always shown toward her. Turning her attention to the table she used as a work surface, Bridget swept into the trash the piles of articles she had cut out, each waiting to be mounted in one of the scrapbook she used for tracking Blaire's accomplishments. To this bin, she also dumped a sizeable stack of newspaper sport sections awaiting her attention, as well as an accumulation of golf magazines. Pens, tape and other scrapbooking tools, she collected up in a shoe box until the table was perfectly clean.

She turned next to the only set of bookshelves in the room still bearing items. The lower levels of this held paper and hard backs collected over the years for her personal enjoyment. She left those in place. Instead, she drew down from the upper shelf the half dozen scrapbooks that were the fruit of her newspaper chronicling efforts. She had always viewed these as a trump card of sorts. One day… when Blaire finally grew out of her selfish ways… Bridget envisioned presenting these as a gift… a memorial to her daughter's golfing days that might be passed on to the grandchildren. The gratitude that Blaire might show in that moment had long been a dream of Bridget's. All such fantasies had vanished from her thinking in the wake of Phoenix.

She placed the scrapbooks on the table, one atop the other, until the pile was complete. She then slid the whole mass off in her arms in the way a librarian might go about moving a huge stack of books. The laundry basket would have made this task easier, but she intended the fate of the scrapbooks to be entirely different than that of the photo albums. In this particular facet of removing Blaire from her life, Bridget decided to bear the full load… hoping it to be the very last time she must do so.

Hefting the pile down the hall to the garage, she unceremoniously dumped each scrapbook… one at a time… into her thirty gallon rollout waste container. As this bin had recently been emptied by her weekly trash pickup, the resounding thud of the first scrapbook hitting the bottom startled her with the finality of what she was doing. From there, the job got easier, as subsequent scrapbooks produced more muted slaps on impacting another. She made one more trip from the spare room to the garage, dragging along the plastic trash bag with all its paper. This, she tied off and dropped into the bin on top of the scrapbooks.

From start to finish, the entire chore took fifteen minutes… a mere quarter of an hour to dispose of a lifetime's worth of devotion to the cause of family. Bridget returned to survey the spare room, having absolutely no idea with what to fill its emptiness.

Somehow, she expected to feel differently than she did. She had just relieved herself of an immense burden… self-imposed though it might have been. She should feel free, maybe even exhilarated… or at least expectant that some good thing would come rushing into her life, filling the void left behind by Blaire. Truth was… her heart had always been empty. Although she continually held open the door, Blaire never entered in. Worse than that, Blaire repeatedly belittled and scorned her invitations, compelling her to plead or placate for a part of her daughter that was a mother's right to share.

She had been such a fool in trusting her heart to someone like Blaire. Never would she allow that to happen again. From now on, she would steel her mind toward keeping herself safe. Her feeling of outrage… of anger over how she had been treated all of Blaire's life… this, she would not put out on the curb with the rest of the trash, nor would she box it up and hide it away on some dark and dusty shelf. She would mull upon the injustice of it all, turning over and over every instance in which Blaire had treated her with disdain. In fact, she would start a new album of sorts… a mental one that chronicled the true history of their relationship. In this, she would display every hurt and every offense, there at the ready for her slightest need of protection or validation… all to ensure that she never again played the fool. Only when the richness to every nuance of her resentment had been explored… only then would she finally be free.

CHAPTER

24

REALITY

With time, Blaire began to see the whole ordeal of Phoenix as a milestone in her career. Yeah… she lost that particular tournament by a single stroke, but a much greater victory had been won in finally putting an end to her mother's meddling. Not that Blaire had any intention of refraining from doing likewise toward her. That woman was… and always would be… her most convenient target of amusement.

So Phoenix would be remembered fondly, Blaire cut out newspaper headlines from after that day and posted them inside her private locker at her home course.

'Conclusion of WGA Event Marred by Player Outburst'
'Tompkin Takes Desert, O'Connor Makes Storm'
'O'Connor Facing Fines, Suspension'
'Blaire the Scare'

The most impressive… and her favorite… was from a small piece in the *Woman's Sporting World.*

'A Bitch is Born'

Anyone who happened to see these ended up thinking that they were there as a motivation for her to do better, but Blaire had them on display as a tribute to one of her finest moments in golf.

Despite a week of bad press… as Bernie insisted on putting it… the media was soon back to calling her Blaire 'the Flair' O'Connor. Her popularity on tour skyrocketed after the Plinkerton, as she won more majors… including her first WGA Open.

Through Bernie's introductions, she was now regularly partying with some of the biggest names in the sporting world. She easily got herself in front of as many cameras as she wanted in dating the cream of the crop. Never seriously though. She would leave an MVP big leaguer in the on-deck circle to take up with a Super Bowl star… only to sideline that quarterback for some up-and-coming movie exec with the means of getting her an invite to the Academy Awards ceremony. She skipped out of that man's dinner plans on the next weekend to go windsurfing off Cape Hatteras with the heir to a line of designer clothing. She spent a couple of days with that guy before becoming totally bored with him. Pretty men, after all, were a dime-a-dozen, and she found more pleasure in using one to make another jealous.

Always, Bernie's attentiveness to everything she did was near on stifling. He had other clients… several she begrudgingly admitted brought in more notoriety than her… but she was clearly his favorite. His big plans to revolutionize the WGA meant nothing to her. He was only a means to an end. She would allow him to look over her shoulder at the script of her life… for a time… but only she would write it. So she permitted him to get her endorsements, spots in ads on TV, and appearances on talk shows… but that was it. She would not respond to his text messages unless it suited her… nor would she return any of those ridiculous phone calls from his fleet of brainless twits pestering her about showing up on time for some godforsaken photo op. She would do what she wanted, when she wanted, and wherever it suited her fancy.

To make her point perfectly clear to him in the month following the Plinkerton, she downed a good portion of a six pack in the parking lot prior to a community college's annual awards banquet, and then slurred her way through a motivational talk on her experiences in golf… while some idiot assistant of his sweated it out in the front row.

Totally hilarious!

She would get drunk any time she damn well pleased… underage or not… and no one would dare tell her what to do on the stage of her life.

From the very first occurrence onward, seeing her daughter on the cover of a tabloid always came to Bridget as a shock. She should be numb to it… seeing as she had invested significant effort into untethering herself from Blaire's poor choices… but was not really. To her credit, she had made considerable progress in the year since Phoenix toward freeing herself from wrong thinking. For one, she was no longer chained like an addict to her daughter's golfing career. She still cared… could still be made sad over what Blaire was doing to herself… yet everything changed after Phoenix. She had become… a realist. What Blaire did in her life was Blaire's business, and there was nothing a loving mother could do to turn that around. Nevertheless, every time she went grocery shopping, Bridget braced herself against what she might see in the checkout line.

On a day like any other, she left work planning to make a brief stop at the store. After trudging up and down aisles getting needed items, she lazily went about unloading her shopping cart at the register, venturing a quick peek at the nearby magazines… just as nearly every shopper does. She almost dropped a carton of eggs off the conveyer belt on seeing a cover photo of Blaire, all blurry-eyed, holding a cocktail at some nightclub. Snatching the top copy off the rack, she hastily read the caption to herself (*Drunken celebrity golfer craves daddy's love),* and then thrust the magazine back from where it came… except facing in the other direction. For reasons she did not stop to comprehend, Bridget fled the store for the parking lot, abandoning her partially unloaded shopping cart in the checkout line. A feeling of humiliation followed her on the remainder of the trip home… tinged as it was with the absurd notion that every driver she passed somehow recognized her as being the mother of the spectacle that was Blaire O'Connor. Once home, she microwaved a box dinner and took refuge on her back porch. As evening came on, she lingered there, completely incapable of enjoying the development of a pleasant twilight.

It is a scientific certainty that sound does not travel in a vacuum. The modulated expansion and compression of a medium is the very means by which acoustical vibrations propagate. Remove the medium, and there is no sound. Laugh, cry or scream in terror… within a vacuum, nothing is ever heard… no matter how sincere the hope.

Such is always the case whenever one tries to defy the laws of physics. No determined act of will, no youthful sense of indestructability, no surety of one's uniqueness can ever alter the consequences for when frictional forces give way at excessive lateral velocities. Things will slide… all too often out of control. At such moments, every proud soul faces the lie of its own making. Either by daring, faulty reason or simple neglect, a belief has somehow crept in that the certainty of how things work in this universe simply does not apply. But in striking at the most fragile and precious of things, reality – the cruel teacher – painfully instructs otherwise.

That very night, just before midnight, Bridget was startled awake by her cell phone. Scrambling to get her bedside light on, she finally managed to locate the thing and get it answered before the call went to voicemail.

"Hello?"

"May I speak with Bridget O'Connor, the mother of Blaire O'Connor."

"Ahh… this is she."

"Mrs. O'Connor, my name is Sgt. Nieves with the California State Patrol based in Pasadena. I'm terribly sorry, ma'am… but your daughter's been in a serious car accident."

In an instant, every bit of Bridget was sucked away into that phone, leaving nothing behind but a vacuous fear through which every phonetic quality to the trooper's words resonated within her ears.

Minutes from ending the call, Bridget was in her car speeding to the Hamilton Memorial Trauma Center. The drive there was a blur of trepidation. All she knew was that it was dark when she left and dark when she arrived. Pulling her car into the first available spot, she sprinted across the parking lot, only vaguely aware of a commotion at the emergency entrance where several stenciled vans were posing an inconvenience to those trying to enter. She ignored these, not thinking much about their presence until a man stepped in front and proclaimed to all that this was the mother of Blaire O'Connor. Within a camera flash's span of time, she was jostled into the center of a mass of bodies. They were piranha, and each of their questions was a bite, ripping away at her terrified soul.

"I don't know! I don't know! Please let me through to my daughter!"

Beyond the point of tears, she forced her way out of the cluster of reporters, entered the ER, and then dodged across a waiting area clogged with many others burdened by the fears of their own emergencies. Spotting a set of double doors labeled Trauma Center, she pushed through into a smaller waiting room. Beyond this were treatment alcoves arrayed in a semicircle about a central station. After quickly scanning what she could see of the occupied ones… none of which had her daughter… a nurse informed her that Blaire had been transferred to a stabilization unit.

"What's that mean? Is she going to be okay?"

"You'll have to speak with the doctor on duty."

Bridget backtracked according to the new directions, halting at an intersection she had not expected to be there. Confused over which way to go… and far too worked up on the inside to look for signage… she chose at random and ended up at another nurse's station. The pathway from there to

Blaire's room was equally unclear, as she simply followed behind some kindly intern who knew the way. Every room she passed had a view to an occupant laying motionless in a hospital bed, which only intensified her feeling of dread.

Her initial shock on entering Blaire's room was not at the sight of her daughter… but of her ex-husband standing just inside the open door.

"Mitch… I didn't… How'd you… How's she…?"

"She's unconscious."

Bridget made to move around him, but froze on first sight of Blaire. She had not prepared herself for seeing her daughter in any particular state other than that of someone in need of emergency care. As she sped along the freeway and then dashed through corridors, her distress only managed to picture Blaire as lying on an operating table on the verge of death… yet oddly with the sort of placid expression of a sleeping child. She had not expected to see Blaire's face covered by a breathing mask… or that most of her head would be bandaged… or that her neck would be tightly encompassed by a brace. In fact, the only parts of Blaire's face that could be seen were her right eye, brow, cheek and part of the jawline. Even in these, Bridget had not anticipated all the bruising and abrasions. In her shock, she looked briefly to the tubes and monitors connected to Blaire, and then… in being sufficiently steeled… came back once more to Blaire's face. That beautiful face… now terribly damaged.

"Oh my god… is she… is she going to be okay?"

"The doctor was just in here. He said it looks far worse than it really is. She's got some hairline fractures… probably a concussion… and all this bruising. The good news is… he said she'll recover… "

"How'd this happen? All I know is that she was in a car accident…"

"Bridget… she was drunk. Completely lost control of her car and caromed off a retaining wall… then hit a tree… head-on. She's lucky to be alive. Must have been going seventy according to Bernie…"

Bridget was about to move around him again, but once more abruptly stopped.

"You know Bernie Pearl?"

The way he looked down briefly before answering… it was like being back with him all over again. She could almost see his thought pattern searching for some way to bend the truth to his liking. Even though terribly distraught over Blaire, she still had space left in her to loath this once love of her life.

"We've spoken… a time or two. He called my home in Seattle, and Dot… well… it was she who told him that I was in town on business… a company retreat. That's where he got ahold of me… and of course, I dropped everything and immediately sped over here as fast as I could."

So Bernie calls the father who abandoned his client at a young age rather than the mother who raised her!

"You might still catch him."

"Catch who?"

"Her doctor… He just went down the hall."

"Mitch… I'm the parent who stays and you're the one who leaves, remember?"

"Bridget… please. I know we've had our differences, but it's important that we're both here for her now."

He suddenly made to hug her, but she, with all the determination of a running back turning the outside corner seeking open space, stiff-armed him in the chest and continued on around to the other side of the bed.

"Your corporate retreat awaits you, Mitch… I've got it from here."

It was not worth the effort to engage this man any further. She was vaguely aware of him constructing some kind of a response, but easily tuned him out in being overwhelmed with the harm done to her daughter.

In pulling a chair up to bedside, Bridget brought her face in close to Blaire's… and to the many abrasions cutting across her right cheek. Without realizing it, she found herself drawn to these over any of the more serious injuries, for interspersed in their midst were small patches of perfectly smooth skin. She kept staring back and forth between these… the hurt and the unhurt… willing herself to recall how beautiful her daughter had once been… and telling herself in a reassuring sort of way that Blaire would be so again. Mitch was still there blabbering on about himself, so Bridget held back her tears… saving them for when he was finally gone.

Remaining fixed on Blaire's face, she fumbled about for a part of her to hold. She touched first the cold plastic of an admittance bracelet, and then moved beyond to Blaire's hand. The warmth she found there, above the empty assurances coming from her ex-husband, gave her real hope. She gripped that hand lovingly, envisioning that her presence could somehow flow into Blaire… to all of the damaged parts of her… healing wounds, diminishing abnormal hues, and soothing away all pain.

Owing to how the scratches seemed to slant upward across Blaire's face, Bridget soon came to concentrate most of her sympathy upon the bruising all about the exposed portions of her brow and upper cheek. The lid was swollen and dark, but that soon became the definitive sign of life, for beneath twitched what Bridget knew to be the steel gray fire of Blaire's eye. The effect, however, was equally unsettling… almost as if Blaire was fighting to open that eye… to wake… to come back to life… yet lacked the simple strength to do so. Irrational panic would grip Bridget whenever that hidden eye went still, compelling her to search all the more diligently for even the slightest hint of movement within. In time, she came to rely on the beeping of the nearby machinery… along with the strangely soothing sound of air flowing through tubing… to convince herself that Blaire was alive… as that eyelid stubbornly refused to open.

The young woman before her, fully responsible for herself, was still her child… and completely helpless. Memory after memory began flooding in to darken Bridget's own eyes with tears.

Not like this… not before she understands.

She needs more time… we need more time… together.

When she next looked up, it was not to see her ex-husband standing there, but instead a man in green scrubs signaling for her attention. She quickly wiped her eyes before speaking.

"I'm… sorry… were you saying something to me?"

"No worries… I just need to take the patient out for some tests."

"Is she okay? Has something happened?"

Bridget looked toward Blaire's swollen lid, and then to a rapid scan of the medical monitors for anything that might inform her untrained eye as to a problem.

"No, everything's fine. We're just doing some routine diagnostics… a CT scan to check for cranial swelling. I'm sure the on-call doctor'll be along shortly to explain it all."

Moving out into the hall, Bridget maintained a watchful eye on the orderly as he wheeled Blaire's hospital bed out of the room, down the corridor, and through a set of double doors. Only after those had swung themselves into stillness did she feel anything in the way of weariness brought on by her fears. She needed to find the ladies' room… get something to drink… and then get right back so as not to miss Blaire's doctor. Instead… she found herself collapsing against a wall.

None of this should be happening. It's all so wrong.

On being eyed by a passing nurse, Bridget rallied herself enough to ask for directions to the nearest vending machines. Back with a granola bar and a bottle of water, she took up her previous seat and waited. Struggling to sit still, she repeatedly rose to stick her head out the door and then returned to her seat more tense than before… only to pop back up minutes later at the next hallway noise.

When Blaire was eventually wheeled back, she seemed completely unchanged. Taking up a hand as before, Bridget once more lost track of time within her state of anxious concern, except that a part of her remained attentive to anyone arriving in the room. A doctor eventually appeared… after how long she could not say… but his news was not what she had been praying for. Slight cranial swelling had him concerned, as did a hairline fracture to Blaire's brow. The contusions and lacerations to her face would heal… but likely with some visible scarring. The answer to Bridget's question regarding how long it would be before Blaire awoke was more so unsettling.

"There's really no way of knowing. We'll keep monitoring her, of course, but a coma's a tricky thing… very unpredictable. Your daughter's fortunate… the airbag saved her life."

There was nothing more to be done that night, he said, so she should go home. Bridget did not bother to explain that she purposed to remain. It might make more sense to be well-rested, as tomorrow may require even more from her… but no mother would leave at such a time as this.

Bridget dozed on and off through the night, periodically rising to stretch her legs in walking about Blaire's bedside. Nurses would occasionally ferry her out of the room in order to perform some duty of theirs, leaving Bridget to pace circles in the hallway. The staff turned over in the early morning, with the new shift nurse finally persuading her to go home for a few hours of sleep. She left before the sun peeked into the sky, moved unhindered across scarcely-occupied freeways, and arrived at her house as the new day dawned. After a brief shower, she threw herself into bed, slept surprisingly well, and rose at noon terribly late for work… with no intention of showing up. After two quick calls… one to checkup on Blaire's condition and one to explain her absence at the credit union… Bridget packed a shoulder bag with comfort items for passing a long day at the hospital.

As before, she fought her way through a gathering of reporters, smaller in size than before, yet equally bent on pestering her for comments about Blaire's condition. Unlike the previous night, she was surprised to also see a cluster of fans bearing signs expressing their wishes for Blaire's speedy recovery. Whether out of genuine concern or to play to the cameras, it was nonetheless upsetting to have these strangers hanging on for news about her daughter.

She cringed on entering Blaire's room, as Mr. Pearl and his assistant were there ahead of her. He, busy on his cell, raised a finger to her in a way that might pass as a greeting… or maybe 'I'll be with you in a minute.' At least the young woman who introduced herself as Alexia displayed sincere sympathy in hugging her. They were exchanging what they knew about Blaire's condition when Mr. Pearl came off his phone in a manner very inconsistent with the situation.

"Mrs. O'Connor... I'm glad you could be here. I'm sorry this has happened. It couldn't have come at a worse time."

"I'm not sure what you mean by that... I can't imagine a good time for her to have been in a car accident."

"Of course not. That's not what I meant. It's just that... everything was working out perfectly. She was playing so well... winning or placing high in nearly every tournament she competed in. Did you know that WGA viewership is up twelve point two percent over this time last year?"

"I... don't see how that makes a difference. Look at her... she's terribly hurt. I don't think she's going to be playing golf anytime soon..."

"That's exactly what I'm saying."

Bridget was about to point out the craziness to his words when his cell went off – a ringtone of Wagner's the *Ride of the Valkyries*. She wanted him gone... or at least for him to have the decency of stepping out into the hall... but immediately changed her mind on overhearing the instructions he was having Alexia feverishly scribble down. When the call ended, Bridget was all over him.

"What do you think you're doing?! You can't possibly be suggesting that she should be moved!?"

"Mrs. O'Connor... this place is subpar for someone of Blaire's status. I've arranged for..."

"This is one of the premier hospitals in all of Southern California."

"It's not the care. I'm sure they're quite good. It's the... atmosphere. We can do better for Blaire elsewhere."

Bridget, in wonder over how anyone could be so deluded, suddenly realized that Mr. Pearl was actually not concerned about either the gaggle of reporters or the small mob of crazed fans. He actually wanted more of those things, for they were the means of transforming Blaire's disaster into an opportunity. What evidently bothered him about this hospital was the same thing behind why he had invited her to Blaire's party – he wanted to be in control.

"Well, I won't allow it!"

"You've got no say in the matter."

"What do you mean? I'm her mother!"

"Mrs. O'Connor... Bridget... I have power of attorney. Blaire's given me the authority to act on her behalf."

In disbelief, Bridget's eyes darted to Alexia, fully expecting to see some kind of discomfort there at having witnessed her boss tell an obvious lie. Instead, the young woman lowered her head to the floor… confirming Bridget's fear. Mr. Pearl was still babbling on about how he had Blaire's best interests at heart… when he reached out consolingly to touch her shoulder. Acting on impulse, Bridget jerked away from contact, then did her best to glare fire back at him. He just shrugged his shoulders before beckoning for his assistant to follow him out of the room.

After waiting long enough to be sure that he was not coming back anytime soon, she turned to the room's windows, looking for something to face other than the unfathomable… that Blaire trusted a sports agent more than she did her own mother. Bridget took hold of the nearest draw string and yanked open a set of blinds… perhaps with more force than was necessary, as a tiny sprinkle of dust came down on her.

After Phoenix, she had convinced herself that the days of Blaire hurting her were finally over. She had put aside her meek nature and become impervious to the cruel things Blaire enjoyed doing. In reality, she had only deceived herself. Even from a coma, Blaire could still reach out to hurt her. Maybe that was the way it would always be. No matter what she might try in the way of a renewed mindset, the incalculable ability of one cruel person to hurt her would always be there. Forever, she would be at the mercy of Blaire… to be wounded by her, and left to pass alone through denial, anger, grief and resentment… all before she finding the resiliency to be whole once more… just as the cycle was started again.

She wiped her eyes and sought for something outside the window with which to distract herself. By happenstance, the view from Blaire's room was of the area outside the ER entrance. There, a group of photographers was lulling about a media van. Farther off, on the edge of the parking lot, a small knot of fans sat in lawn chairs, also waiting for something to happen. A broken stream of people nonetheless came and went from the hospital, each eyeing the reporters and fans with what Bridget interpreted to be a mixture of curiosity and apprehension.

Just as she was about to turn back to Blaire, she noticed a young man in hospital scrubs emerge from the ER and walk directly up to the reporters. He spoke animatedly to them, gesturing a hand back toward the hospital. Suddenly, the group bolted for the entrance and disappeared within. More reporters materialized from the periphery of her view, crossing quickly to the sheltered overhang and also entering. The fans then perked up, with one young woman breaking off to follow the reporters inside. Unnoticed by all except Bridget, the man in scrubs turned his back and made directly for the parking lot… with a smile on his face. She was following this man's departure when more activity at the entrance distracted her. The reporters and photographers abruptly emerged as a group in being herded out by a hospital security guard. While one man lingered on the entrance's sensor pad, forcing its doors to remain open, the rest dashed in the direction of their vehicles.

Because the happenings outside were so engaging, Bridget did not immediately notice that Mr. Pearl had re-entered the room. As he appeared beside her at the window, she could not miss the glow of satisfaction on his face… which she at first interpreted as some juvenile delight in having startled her. But as his focus was outside, she came to realize something different.

"Are you in any way responsible for all that?"

"You might say so."

"What'd you do?"

His smile slowly broadened. The effect on her was not unlike that of a moviegoer suddenly confronted with one of those clowns whose jovially painted face only superficially covered over some great evil beneath. Bridget repulsively stepped back, and then turned to where Alexia stood in the doorway. Unlike Mr. Pearl, only shame was written there.

"What'd he do?"

The young woman's eyes darted toward her boss, and perhaps in receiving some form of non-verbal permission, haltingly answered her question.

"He… ahh… hired an actor to… impersonate a hospital employee. That guy just told the press that Blaire's… dying."

CHAPTER

25

SENSELESS ACTS OF COURAGE

Arriving in the morning for her third day at the hospital, Bridget found that news of the impending death of Blaire 'the Flair' O'Connor had circulated so widely that the ER entrance was now a media circus. In no way did she attempt to address the throng. With a scarf thrown over her head... just as she had seen scandalized individuals do on TV... she pushed her way through to the inside. On the previous day, when the rumor first got started, she chewed out Mr. Pearl up and down the hospital hallway to no avail. He emphatically refused to correct the story. She then did her best to thwart him, speaking first with Blaire's doctor and then with a hospital administrator. Both were completely indifferent to her pleas. The latter, on hearing her account of how Mr. Pearl was intent on moving Blaire, openly expressed his relief that a nuisance to his hospital might soon be removed. On her own initiative, she then went outside the ER to inform the gathering of the deception... but in becoming overwhelmed with the callus manner in which the paparazzi pressed upon her, none of her words were able to counteract the apparent confirmation provided by her tears.

On arriving to Blaire's room, she found her still unconscious... though perhaps with diminished facial swelling. As on the day before, Mr. Pearl had beaten her there. He was on his cell phone again, keeping up a string of 'good,' 'excellent' and 'perfect' with whomever he was speaking. Initially wishing to ignore him, she immediately honed in instead on hearing him discuss plans for moving Blaire. As soon as he was off, she launched into him, insisting that no piece of paper with Blaire's signature on it meant that he knew what was best for her daughter. The legal issue of who had the authority to make decisions on behalf of a comatose Blaire could not be nearly as important as who had the rightful place. He, nonetheless, held firm to his stubborn insistence on relocation. She demanded to know where, which he waved off with a vague promise of informing her when it was time. That got her really angry, as it was clear that he wanted the new location kept a secret from her. In confronting him, she was trying hard not to exceed the bounds of hospital decorum… keeping it to a whisper-shouting match… but became incensed at his refusal to acknowledge her role in Blaire's life. She had just begun to raise her voice when a nurse appeared at the door… though fortunately not to scold her.

"Sorry to interrupt… but you really should take a look at what's going on outside."

As the woman pointed to the window, Bridget dodged about Mr. Pearl in the assumption that he, once again, was responsible for putting the media into an uproar. Raising a single slat with her finger, a small glimpse was enough to make her hastily lift the entire set of blinds.

Outside was pandemonium. Reporters and camera crews were in full retreat from the hospital's ER entrance. Even though she could not adequately hear them, their angry expressions suggested that many were shouting out curses. Similarly, the fans, more numerous than the day before, were scattering pall-mall into the parking lot. As Bridget began seeking for the cause of this mayhem, the panes of glass to Blaire's room became blasted with a jet of water, causing both her and Mr. Pearl to jolt backward. A high powered stream, from source unknown, then moved up the building's side to the floor above. Aware that Mr. Pearl had broke away from the window, she remained there, completely mesmerized by the water's flow and the anticipation of discovering its source. For a few seconds, as the sheets continued to cascade down across the window, she beheld only the rippled reflection of Blaire lying lifeless in a hospital bed behind her. The effect was entirely unsettling… as if the essence of her daughter had somehow gone shapeless.

The current soon abated, allowing her to see back outside. People were still darting about, mostly away from a central figure who stood almost directly before Blaire's window. That person… a man… was dousing down the media throng with a fire hose. His spray then came around and hit the building above Blaire's window again, with everything going as fuzzy as before. By the time this second deluge diminished, she found that most everything outside had calmed. The scene, however, was an utter mess, with banners, signs and flowers smeared out into the parking lot. Nearby, reporters were picking their drenched selves up from off the pavement. Where the man had stood was now only the fire hose lying static in the grass, water dribbling from its nozzle. She quickly looked toward the ER entrance and caught a hint of him being hustled inside by hospital security.

Having seen enough from this angle, Bridget turned about toward the hallway, intending to follow in behind Mr. Pearl. Halfway to the door, she was unexpectedly brought up short by a faint voice muffling out a single word.

"Mother…"

For the remainder of that morning, Bridget reserved little thought for what had occurred outside the hospital, as her attention was fully upon her daughter. With Blaire finally awake… and in obvious need… Bridget spooned ice chips, fluffed pillows, added or removed blankets, and did whatever else could be done to ease her daughter's discomfort. The breathing mask immediately came off, and then near on noon, some of the heavy wrappings about her head were replaced with isolated bandages. Bridget now beheld what the car accident had done to the left side of Blaire's face. Along with more bruising and small cuts, she was shocked to discover that a significant portion of Blaire's hair above the left ear had been shaved in order to stitch up a long gash that ran to the middle of her forehead. Rather than think about how horrible that cut appeared, she concentrated her concern on Blaire's blackened eyes, both of which stood out painfully.

Mr. Pearl eventually came back from the spectacle outside the ER to get in the way. Though he expressed relief that Blaire was awake, he seemed more preoccupied with jabbering at her about his plans. Bridget bit her lip through it all, marveling that a man as busy as him could find the time to remain for long at an invalid's bedside. He was finally gone by lunch.

In the afternoon, Blaire was sharp enough for conversation, but made it clear that she had no interest in discussing the accident. Mr. Pearl showed up again just before the evening news. Together, he and Blaire began flipping through the local news broadcasts, whispering their thoughts to each other on the quality of the coverage filmed from outside the hospital. One report claimed that Blaire had made a miraculous recovery from her near-death condition, whereas another offered skepticism that the accident… along with the related hysteria outside the hospital… had all been staged as a publicity stunt. Yet each report agreed on two points: doctors asserted that Blaire 'the Flair' O'Connor would fully recuperate… and a man by the name of Lowell Paxton was charged with several counts of misdemeanor assault, destruction of personal property, and unauthorized use of a municipal fire hydrant.

Bridget withdrew to a corner during the news broadcasts, cringing her way through it all. Although she kept it to herself, she instantly recognized the man in the video clips as being the same one with whom she and Blaire had shared a Pricewater Building elevator during the earthquake in the previous year. One account clearly showed him, fire hose in hand, dousing a group of Blaire's fans. At least the drenching of the hospital windows now made sense, as Mr. Paxton had diverted the stream so as not to hit a mother and child approaching the ER.

As soon as the local news stations finished with their pieces on Blaire, Mr. Pearl went outside to address the assembled reporters. Through the window, Bridget watched him speak expressively before the cameras. He returned to Blaire's room with a report that he had just given an impassioned plea to the press that they respect Blaire's need for privacy. For the first time since meeting him, Bridget was genuinely moved… until Blaire started choking out a gurgled laugh… which produced a broken smile from Mr. Pearl.

"Take it easy, Babe, or you'll bust a stitch."

"I don't understand… what's so funny?"

"Seriously, Mother… wise up. That's… nothing but agent talk… for… getting more attention… from them."

Bridget pulled completely away after that, as the two began discussing their plans for manipulating the press. She should interrupt… seeing as Blaire was clearly scratchy-throated and needed her rest… but the calculated way the two of them went at it made up her mind. She would leave… especially since Blaire was no longer demanding her help. While gathering up her things, she froze on hearing Mr. Pearl relate his thoughts for exploiting 'that lunatic's fanaticism.' Looking up, she found him holding a tablet out before Blaire, showing her again the news clips of Lowell dosing the press with his fire hose. She could not help herself – no matter how odd Lowell's actions were, she would not allow them to include him in their schemes. Flying from her corner, she snatched the tablet out of Mr. Pearl's hands.

"Hey! What gives?!"

"Is there no limit to the depths you'll go to for an angle?!"

"Mother… give the iPad back to Bernie."

"No! Not if he's going to use it to besmirch the reputation of a decent man."

"You've got to be kidding, lady! That guy's a certifiable nutcase!"

Of a sudden, the fear and anxiety she had been experiencing over the past few days got reshaped into an anger directed at Mr. Pearl. Bridget gave into the transformation, hesitating for only a second in order for the feeling to adequately swell before releasing it on him.

"Wanna talk about a nutcase – it's you! What a fraud! You're the one who lied to reporters about Blaire dying! You're the one who's exploiting her accident! And you're the one who's hell-bent on moving her... irrespective of her condition. You don't care in the least about her as long as you can exploit her for your..."

"Stop it, you two!"

Her anger instantly evaporated on recognizing the effort it took for Blaire to make her scratchy voice heard. As Blaire fell back against the pillows, Bridget thrust the tablet into Mr. Pearl's hands and snatched up a cup of water... which Blaire shook off.

"Bernie... let's not... make anything out of this. Okay?"

"Sure thing, Babe... but you do realize we're missing out on a golden opportunity here. The guy's done us an incredible favor with all this extra media play. You know... in retrospect... I should have Sanchez get one of his PI's to look into him. We don't want another crackpot stalker pestering you."

Bridget was about to ask who this Sanchez was when the word 'another' distracted her. It had never occurred to her before then that Blaire had actually become popular enough to attract the attention of unstable individuals... with this Mr. Paxton perhaps being just such a person.

"Bernie... forget the PI. The guy's not a problem. Instead... get Sanchez to... help him. Clear him of charges... or... whatever. And Bernie..."

"Yeah, Babe?"

"No exploitation. I don't want to hear you've milked this guy."

"Whatever you say, Babe... but I don't get it. I mean, it's not like you owe him anything. After all, he did wreck your coverage..."

Looking back and forth between the two as they interacted, Bridget changed her mind. She would wait out Mr. Pearl's interest in being there in order to speak privately with her daughter. As Blaire offered him no response, Bridget thought the moment was at hand for him to leave... but he piped up again with greater intensity than before.

"You do realize you've got a court date of your own? Drunk driving charges, remember? I should have Sanchez working on your defense... not that wacko's. Hey... that gives me an idea. How's about we play the 'reformed alcoholic' card? That ought to work with the press. I'll get Sanchez to go over the..."

"Bernie... enough. I'm really tired... and... I want to speak with my mother before sleeping."

Despite her frustration over Blaire's power of attorney preference... something Bridget had decided not to bring up... she still found herself touched. That is, until she remembered that Blaire often said something sweet... build up her expectations... and then turned it horrid for some devious reason. So she would not make too much out of Blaire's moment of softness. Mr. Pearl certainly was not. He stood there fussing with his cell phone, ignoring that his client was dismissing him.

"Bernie... tomorrow, okay?"

Mr. Pearl lifted his head, yet not toward Blaire... as Bridget expected... but at her. Something in his eyes... a quizzical sort of expression... seemed to be weighing the implication of her being there. She tensed up, convinced that he was on the verge of saying something offensive. But in completely misunderstanding his intentions, she was stunned when he leaned over and lightly kissed Blaire on the lips before heading out the door. In shock, she turned toward Blaire, expecting to see intense displeasure over Mr. Pearl's audacity. Bruises or not, she found Blaire to be as she always was – completely indifferent to a sign of affection being shown to her. Recovering as best she could, Bridget latched on to an odd piece of comfort – that this was Southern California, a place where disgusting agents kissing their young female clients actually meant nothing. She discarded the unsettling event and opened the conversation to where she wanted it to be.

"So, Blaire... did you recognize him?"

"Yeah... I recognized him. Can't figure that guy out. Fire hose... that makes no sense."

Despite the happenings of that day, Bridget had been afforded a few opportunities to think... usually while Blaire napped. There had been an hour in which Blaire was wheeled off for tests that she debated over whether to mention that Mitch had come by. But seeing as he had not returned... or called... she decided not to bother. Besides, it was the first time since the divorce that she realized how little impact the man still had on her.

Wow... now at least that's some progress in life.

Instead, she spent more time considering what she knew about Lowell to account for his odd behavior with the fire hose. He had been in a war... lived a cowboy's life... and currently worked with the elderly. That scant knowledge still left her far short of understanding him.

"Blaire… I think he was being… protective. Sort of like he wanted to… Now don't make that face at me! Even with all those bruises and bandages, I can still tell when you're belittling me."

"Mother, what you're saying… it's pure nonsense. Nobody does shit like that for no reason…"

"I didn't say it was for no reason. You know, Blaire… you've never been able to see things from beyond your own perspective."

"Good god, Mother! I'm far too tired for a lecture. Besides… I'm not so self-absorbed as you might think. I'm just… surprised he would do that for me. We didn't… really… hit it off, you know."

"Tell me… what was your impression of him. . in the elevator?"

Before responding, Blaire came up on her elbows to make a performance out of adjusting the incline to the bed. From all that effort, Bridget understood that her daughter was not actually struggling with physical discomfort, but with a thing completely beyond herself.

"Of course… I was annoyed as hell that he was there. Who wants one of the public stuck with you in a box during an earthquake?!"

"First off… he wasn't 'one of the public' because he didn't even know who you were… which I think really annoyed you. And second… you're not answering my question. What did you think of him?"

"I don't know… he was just there! Listen… my head's killing me… and I'm totally worn out. Can you just get to the point?"

"Forget it, Blaire. It's nothing. You obviously need your rest. Goodnight. Maybe I'll see you in the morning…"

With a mind toward gathering up her things, Bridget moved away from Blaire's hospital bed. She was totally worn out from all she had experienced over the past few days, and now that her daughter seemed out of danger, nothing remained in her for playing the sorts of games Blaire enjoyed.

"Don't go, Mother. It's okay. Seriously… I… really want to know what you mean."

She turned back to see an odd sort of softness on her daughter's face… though maybe it was only the bruising. Bridget inhaled deeply for the means of pushing herself through an explanation… half expecting the old Blaire to pipe in well before she was finished.

"He was a gentleman. He treated us with respect. He was a… calming influence… at least for me. Blaire… we made fools of ourselves in that elevator… you have to admit it… but there wasn't a hint of ridicule in him. It was like… he was outside of himself… even though I know he was probably as scared as we were. You might not have noticed it, but I remember that he kept tipping an imaginary cowboy hat at us. How ridiculous is that? It was almost as if the earthquake hadn't happened… and he was carrying on a normal conversation. I'm not trying to make too much of it… other than… that's who he is. The fact of the matter is… the person who hosed down the paparazzi and your crazy fans… he was the only sane one out there today. You saw those video clips… he just walked right up and turned himself over to hospital security. He could've made a run for it… or better yet, why even bother? I'm sure we'll both end up one day thinking the whole thing was funny… but to be honest with you… I have absolutely no idea why he did what he did. And until I do…"

She left it hanging there, for to go any further was to risk too much with Blaire. Despite whatever good might come out of the car accident, their relationship was far from whole.

"What're you saying, Mother?"

"Nothing… nothing at all. You need your rest… and I need to find a way out of this hospital without having to run into that freak show outside. If you're up for it, I'll stop by briefly in the morning… otherwise… I've already missed two days of work…"

Without comment, Blaire slumped back down in her bed. Bridget waited for a response… not expecting one… and got nothing other than Blaire groping about for the corded TV remote. Perhaps that settled it – she would not bother stopping by tomorrow. So… she offered a goodbye, then leaned over to kiss an undamaged portion of the girl's forehead. An unintended association to Mr. Pearl's kiss popped into her thinking. She was no closer to her daughter than was that agent. Probably never would be. In no time, Blaire would recover from her injuries and be ready to put the car accident out of her mind… along with everything that had been done for her.

Moving out into a barren hospital hallway, Bridget once more came to accept the familiar ache of a solitary life on her own.

TWENTY THREE HUNDRED HOUR LIVING

Having found out from a hospital security guard where the man worked, Bridget already made the call there… and now… with half a Saturday morning's worth of perspective worn away… she was beginning to doubt the sanity of what she was purposing to do. So… she would keep the appointment brief.

Find out what you need to know… and then leave. No big deal.

Despite repeated self-assurances, her unease gradually grew as the last hour of the morning turned into noon. Too nervous to eat lunch, she retreated to her back porch to wage anew the battle going on within.

This is all so stupid! I mean… what do I really hope to accomplish?! And what in the world am I going to ask… other than the obvious… 'Why'd you do it?'

Settling back into the cushions of her indoor-outdoor couch, she wished very much that she could remain there all day. Always it was the same with her… trying to make connections with other people… trying to build bridges that no one wanted built. The way her mother use to call out her name… in commanding fashion… and how her brothers and sisters made fun of her for it… it was no different than now… except that she was the one calling on herself… and ridiculing herself at the same time.

Bridge it, Bridget… here I go again!

The gaps in her life had always proved to be far too wide to span. Those things she longed for in the deepest part of herself could never be reached… whereas those things putting demands on her from the outside always won out. In a few hours, she would try again to build a bridge, not altogether sure of exactly what she was hoping to accomplish. Perhaps only a connection of sorts with a man she scarcely knew… simply to discover the reason behind why he acted the way he had. His reckless behavior at the hospital was not all that different from countless exhibitions she had witnessed on the part of Blaire. Maybe she would find him to be just like her daughter… or maybe he would be as kind and considerate as he had been in that elevator.

By the time she needed to leave, Bridget managed to work herself out of a state of second-guessing and back to where she had been on first making the appointment to visit him at his workplace. She sincerely wanted to understand what made this man tick, and was more than willing to pay the price of a long freeway trip to find out… as long as she could leave whenever she felt like it.

With all her contemplation on the person of Lowell Paxton, Bridget had not put any thought into the nature of the place she was now heading. In pulling into the parking lot of the Brookline Care Center, it suddenly occurred to her that she had never been to a nursing home before… though knew them by reputation not to be particularly nice places to end up in one's old age.

On entering, the first thing she encountered was the smell – an unpleasant heaviness she often associated with very old buildings… except this odor carried along with it traces of cleaning products and urine. She ignored the implication and moved straight through a small seating area to a receptionist.

"Hello… I'm here to see Lowell Paxton. I called this morning…"

"Are you with the press?"

"Umm… no. I'm Bridget O'Connor…" On voicing her own name, it instantly occurred to her as to why this woman would ask such a thing… and the realization made her even more nervous. "…the mother of… Blaire O'Connor… you know, the one Mr. Paxton… visited at the hospital."

'Visited'… that's got to be the lamest thing I could've said…

A knowing smile then crept over the woman's face.

"Yes… he mentioned you'd be stopping by."

Bridget was about to explain herself further… with what she was not sure… when she became distracted by a small, gruff voice.

"Virginia… is that you?"

Her eyes went to the side… to an old man seated in an armchair with his walker directly before him. Along with his question, he had a hand up as if offering her a shaky wave of greeting. He must have gotten a better look at her then, for he dropped his hand back down to his walker as a sour frown came over his face.

"Don't mind him… he's probably just disappointed you're not his daughter. Sad... he sits there most days waiting for her to return. We've told him he should engage himself in some of the center's activities... but there he sits. So... you'll find Lowell in the first office on your left down this hall. It's at the back of the facility, so you'll go a ways before getting there."

Bridget thanked the woman and moved off, passing by the old man. She wished there was some word of comfort she could offer him... especially since she understood the feeling of being abandoned by a daughter. As nothing of significance came to mind, she went past into a long hallway with doors to the right and windows to the left. A short ways down, she came upon a wide opening to a community room of sorts. Pausing there... initially to get a better feel of the place... it occurred to her that she was not yet ready to meet him. She knew what she was going to ask, but suddenly found herself dreading to find out the answer.

Glancing within the room, she noted a listless group of wheelchair-bound residents staring blankly at a flat screen TV. Most were women, and nearly all were clothed in what looked to be institutionalized bathrobes. The whiteness to the sparse hair on their heads struck her as an especially cruel touch to old age.

As if going gray wasn't bad enough...

Without considering why, she lingered simply to see if any of these people might move or speak... but each seemed locked in silence by the confinement of a wheelchair... or maybe it was just the TV. Still... to be so near to others without much ability to interact... that was the worst sort of loneliness a person could endure. Standing there, she wished to envision something else in these people... anything other than what they had become. Rationally, she knew that each had once been young. Some of the women might even have been considered rare beauties, fervently courted by men who themselves had been quite handsome. None of them now showed any signs of having ever been so. All of their splendor was spent... forever gone.

Enough, Bridget! They're just normal people at the end of normal lives. They came from families and likely built families of their own... though still somehow ended up in a place like this.

That was the difficult part to accept. Maybe they once had grand dreams of living out a full life of independence... being loved to the very end. Surely they also had made noteworthy accomplishments in their lives, yet right now... in looking at the half dozen spent bodies mesmerized before some 1950's rerun... all Bridget saw was sadness. Life's one chance at something special was gone... and their end was to wither away alone.

She turned from the community room, wishing she had continued on without venturing a look inside. She had come to accept that Blaire would not be there for her in her old age, yet it had never occurred to her that she might end up in a place like this because of it. She swallowed that little stone of a feeling, and resolved once again to make this visit a short one.

Moving on, with the sound of the TV diminishing behind her, she picked up a faint squeaking noise from ahead. Another old man, also dressed in a bathrobe, was coming out of a doorway to the right and turning toward her at a creep, powered in his wheelchair only by the baby-stepped locomotion of his feet. Thinking his purpose being to make for the community room, she shifted to the opposite wall so as to allot him as much space as possible for passing. In so doing, she was startled to find him change course directly for her. She backed up a few steps past the entry to the community room… and still he came on. The whole time, the old man said nothing… nor did he actually pose her much of an obstacle… yet an indistinct feeling warned her that he meant her harm. With as polite an 'excuse me' as could be managed, she dodged about his wheelchair and hurried on down the hall.

I don't understand how anyone could bear working here.

She passed other doorways to the right, determinedly keeping her eyes forward so as not to expose herself to another unpleasant encounter. The hallway took a slight jog through a small lounge where a vacant-eyed woman sat before a partially completed puzzle. Bridget quickly moved past this woman and set her sights on the other side. Beyond the bend was an office, and there she found Mr. Paxton at a small desk.

"Hello… I'm here…"

He immediately looked up with a wide smile on his face.

"Mrs. O'Connor… Bridget… glad you could come by. Please… have a seat. Any trouble finding the place?"

"None. It was easy."

"Great. I was hoping to speak with you at the hospital, but that didn't work out. And I forgot where you said you worked…"

"At the Desert Valley Credit Union… downtown branch."

"That's right. How's your daughter?"

"She's recovering pretty well. Should be back on tour in no time."

"That's great news. So… I should… get right to it. About the hospital… I owe you an apology. What I did there was down-right crazy. Because of me… a trying time was made even more difficult for you and your daughter. I stuck my nose in where it didn't belong…. and for that, I'm ashamed of myself."

His apology seemed genuine enough, though he had not yet explained the reason behind his actions.

"Thank you… but don't be. It's… okay."

Still feeling awkward, she broke off eye contact to scan his office walls. She was not really interested in the elderly care posters or the western artwork hanging there, as her mind was searching for some way to get directly at why she had come. Fortunately, he picked up on where she was looking… and not what she was thinking.

"Remember last year in that elevator? I mentioned I was in LA with my daughter's consulting business. Well… this is where we were working. The company that owns this place… and a half dozen others like it… offered me a part time position after the contract expired. I've been here ever since."

She opened her mouth to respond, but found that the only thing she could manage was a terribly artificial 'that's wonderful.'

"I guess after what I did at the hospital… the facility manager is wondering whether it was such a good idea keeping me on. They've been flooded with calls about my… stunt."

"I'm sorry to hear that. You're probably really good for this place."

The way he smiled at her, dropping his head and shoulders a bit… it was as if a part of him had softened with relief. It had not occurred to her until then that he might also be nervous.

"I'm curious, Lowell… why'd you do it… the fire hose and all?"

"Yeah… well… I guess it has something to do with a news clip I saw on TV about your daughter's accident. They showed some footage of the site… and the wreck… it looked horrible. You must have been terrified…"

"It was… difficult… to say the least."

"They also… showed a bit of you…"

"Me?! Really? When?"

"It was a brief bit of you trying to pass through a flock of reporters at the hospital. They didn't mention you by name, but I recognized you immediately. Seeing them shove you about… it angered me. My mind went back to the three of us stuck in that elevator, and how you were struggling with your daughter. And there you were on TV, trying to break through to her. The news anchor… he made it sound as if she was dying. I could only imagine what you were going through. So… I overreacted. Like I said… it wasn't any of my business."

"Don't worry about it. What you did… it really wasn't an inconvenience to me… I mean, to us… to my daughter and me. Actually… it was quite chivalrous."

Chivalrous?! Who says chivalrous?! Now I'm just babbling! I should shut up and let him do the talking.

But he was doing it again… smiling in the same kind and patient way he had in that elevator. It made her want to smile back… and put some effort into coming across as more intelligent than she actually felt.

"You know… Blaire wasn't really dying. That was just something her agent concocted to get more publicity. I had nothing to do with that…"

"Of course not. No caring mother would."

"Well… if it's any consolation… Blaire's done far crazier things than what you did at the hospital." *And for much more selfish reasons too.*

"Sad to say… so have I…. that is, in my youth as a rough stock rider. Those fellas tend to cause all sorts of trouble in their off time. Kind of goes with the territory."

"What's a… rough stock rider?"

"Oh… that's a type of rodeo competitor. Bull and bronc busting. Remember I mentioned having been in the rodeo?"

"Oh… that's right."

"Ever been to one?"

"A rodeo? No… I mean… I've seen bits of them on TV… but never in person."

"Suffice it to say, if a man's crazy enough to sit on a deranged animal, then he's liable to do anything."

"Like take a fire hose to a crowd of reporters?"

"Yeah… especially when a gal's honor's at stake."

She instantly felt a blush come over her, and tried to laugh it away. No one had ever made a fuss over her… and what was she to do with that? Perhaps she should admit to herself that this was the reason she was there – to find out if he had made a scene on account of her. With a shiver of embarrassment, it then occurred to her that she might owe him an explanation as to why *she* was there… and she found herself blurting out the first thing that came to mind.

"You know… Blaire didn't make me come… I wanted to know for myself."

"That's good, because I didn't do it for her… I did it for you. So those reporters would think twice next time they tried harassing a lady."

Again… what in the world was she to say to that? She gave an awkward thanks, once more fighting back the feeling of a blush, and asked him as a diversion what kinds of things he did around the nursing home. As he went into an explanation of his efforts at coordinating activities to keep the elderly engaged in life, she was only half listening. More so, she was racing through a myriad of feelings over what he had said. She had those words of his to account for his actions, but not enough of the measure of him to feel confident regarding the intentions behind them. Flattered that he would consider her to be worth getting in trouble over, she was equally ill-at-ease that he would do so. She was not sure whether she should admire such a person… or avoid him. But here she was, enjoying his company once again. In no way did she think it wise to savor such misguided pleasures, as there was still too much confusion in her mind regarding his flagrant actions at the hospital… especially compared to his gentlemanly behavior during the earthquake. For that matter… how was it that a former rodeo rider should be working in a nursing home?

"…and then there's bingo night or beanbag baseball… they love those… or when volunteer musicians come in… that's always a big hit… especially when they play show tunes. Of course, most of my time's spent one-on-one… listening to their stories and lifting their spirits."

"You know… I can really see the need for that. This place is so… dreary and depressing. Plus… I don't know… there's a strong sense of… fear and foreboding."

"Now that's interesting… This'll sound strange… but I've never really thought of it that way. I know they're afraid of all sorts of things… everyone is… but I rather think most are struggling with the past. Some are brokenhearted because they've outlived spouses… and sometimes a child… and some are angry and hurt over being rejected by their families. Just about all of them are lonely. So you see, for them, life's far from over… they're still working through things."

Which pretty much summed up how she was feeling about her own life. Up until the car accident, she had managed to put a barrier up between herself and Blaire… and felt good about it… but still had so many wounds from the past left unhealed… not to mention the regrets. She could hide all day on her back porch and still Blaire would be there in her mind, tormenting her with the person she had become.

Now… finally with an explanation… she was ready to leave this place, as what it suggested about her own life was not something she was interested in exploring. In seeking a natural way of parting, she suddenly realized that she had no idea what to do with the knowledge that this man seemed to like her. He, a stranger, had acted outrageously on her behalf. Was this a one-time thing… or would he do it again… in an even more embarrassing setting? She had been stupid on so many levels to come here.

"Well… thanks for clarifying things for me. I should probably be going…

and let you get back to your work."

"Of course. Allow me to walk you out."

She was relieved to be departing, but as they stepped from the office, he motioned in the opposite direction from which she had come.

"Mind if I take you back a different way? Only take a minute. I'd like to introduce you to my favorite resident… and show you it's not all bad here."

How could she say no to such a thing? So she followed him down a hallway much like the one she had already been on. On the way, they passed residents ambling along in their wheelchairs or walkers, and in each instance, Lowell stopped to make contact with the person. He shook a hand, patted a shoulder, or gently gripped a forearm. For one woman, he bent over to give her a prolonged hug, whispering words that Bridget could not make out. She did not quite know what to do with all this show of affection. It seemed… out of place… particularly for someone who had been a rodeo rider. He was gentle with these people… just as he had been kind to her in the elevator… yet still went crazy in blasting a pack of reporters and fans with a jet of water.

…all because of me.

They entered another hallway, this one populated on both sides with resident rooms. Most of these were closed off, but here and there an open door allowed a TV within to blare out its programming. He had not said where they were going, and it seemed too late for her to ask… even though she was becoming increasingly nervous over the possibility of another unpleasant encounter with an old person.

They came to an awkward stop before a door where it seemed that the resident had dumped their trash out into the hallway. Lowell, by the way he apologized, was clearly embarrassed, and quickly got down on a knee to clean up the mess. Not wishing to make out anything in the clutter, Bridget kept her eyes fixed on the occupant's nameplate – a Cecil Wojnaski.

"Sorry… this gentleman's family put him in here last year… but he's still having a hard time making the adjustment. By the way… that's her room there…" He pointed across the hall to another door. "…the person I wanted you to meet. Hang on while I throw this stuff away."

As he scurried down the hall with both hands filled with Cecil Wojnaski's garbage, Bridget moved to the door of Ellie Baker. On it was a poster, taped by its corners, depicting the branches of a tree suspended over the edge of a violently churning waterfall. Nestled within a crook was a nest where a mother bird was feeding her chicks. Underscoring the whole scene were a string of words.

'Peace that passes understanding.'

She stared back and forth between those words and the birds in the nest, trying to figure out what it all meant. The mother bird had obviously chosen a very dangerous place to build her nest… yet seemed to be doing well despite that. Bridget would even go so far as to say that the birds seemed oblivious to the torrent raging all about them.

"I'm back. Sorry about that. I promise this'll only take a minute…."

Lowell knocked gently, then lifted his eyebrows at her as if suggesting she was in for a treat. After a second knock, the door was eventually opened by a small woman, stooped over by age such that the crown of her head did not even come to Bridget's shoulders. She was in the same type of bathrobe as the other residents, with a distinction being that her feet were stuck into a pair of fluffy pink slippers.

"Ellie, hope you're feeling well on this Saturday afternoon…"

"Feeling fine."

"Sorry to bother you, but I wanted to introduce someone to you… a friend of mine. This is Bridget… we met during the earthquake last year."

"Oh, that was a good one! Gave me goose bumps all over. Very pleased to meet you, Bridget. Any friend of my boy is a friend of mine…"

"Ellie here's one of my favorite people. Everywhere she goes, there's this… aura about her. Always has a kind word to brighten someone's day."

"That's awfully nice of you to say…"

"All true."

"So… are you two young ones a couple?"

Bridget immediately blanched, having not in the least expected either that question or the bluntness through which it came.

"Oh, no! We've only known each other for a very short while. I'm just visiting because… ahh… to say hi."

Lowell went on to offer his own explanations to Ellie, though Bridget was more mindful of the sidelong glances he occasionally gave her… again making her uncertain as to his intentions. He was now laughing with Ellie… so Bridget laughed right along… yet could not shake an uncomfortable feeling that she was being sized up by the both of them.

"You'll have to forgive me… I'm a great grandmother twice over, so in being old I often say whatever comes to mind… and usually get away with it. Do you have any children?"

"Umm… yes, I have a daughter. She's twenty two."

"Studying in school?"

"Ahh, no… she's a professional golfer."

"That the game with sticks and balls?"

"That's right."

"Never was any good at that. Hated trying to get the thing to roll through those… those bendy things…" With shaky hands, Ellie seemed to be tracing out an arch. "You know… those loopy things..."

"Oh, I'm sorry – that's croquet. She plays an entirely different game. The one where you hit the ball into a hole."

Ellie suddenly burst out giggling. "Now you know I'm old *and* crazy. Silly me… I've seen that game on TV. Everybody's whispering. Puts me to sleep. So… do you see much of her… your daughter?"

"No… she… travels a lot… so we don't talk much."

"Me too… I don't see mine either. I have four… and a bushel load of grandchildren. They're all so very busy with work and school. Let's see… one lives in Florida… She's married with three kids… they're dentists… not the kids… her and her husband. Their oldest has two babies. Then I've got two sons in… I forget the place. One of those tiny states back east. And then there's my youngest… she's the reason I moved here way back when. But she doesn't live here anymore. Her husband got a job that took them away. I miss them… terribly… and I'm sure they miss me too… just can't get out here to show it."

If this was what he was after… making her feel depressed at how cruel life was… then he had accomplished the goal. Being as discrete as possible… without wishing to hurt the old woman's feelings… Bridget leaned over and whispered so only he could hear.

"I need to get going."

He nodded, and then turned back to the old woman.

"I'm sorry to cut this short, Ellie, but Bridget needs to head out. What's say I come by later for a visit?"

"That would be wonderful. It was nice meeting you, young lady."

She shook Ellie's hand when it was offered, but found it cold and bony. From there, he took her on down another hallway and then through a door back into the lobby.

"It was nice seeing you again, Lowell. I… ahh… appreciate what you did for me at the hospital."

"My pleasure on both counts."

He put out his hand, so she accepted it… perhaps a bit too eagerly in her anxiousness to leave.

"Goodbye, Lowell."

"Goodbye, Bridget."

CHAPTER

27

THE FEAR OF WOO

It started with flowers and a note, both awaiting her return from lunch. The dozen red roses in a porcelain vase, positioned in the very center of her desk, had filled her small niche of an office space with a subtle sweetness. She took to the note with a measure of cautiousness, assuming the arrangement to be a gesture from Blaire… brimming with hidden motives.

> *Bridget,*
> *Please accept these flowers as a token of my admiration for*
> *all you went through during your daughter's hospital stay. You are*
> *an amazingly courageous and beautiful woman.*
> *Sincerely,*
> *Lowell Paxton*

She would not deny being surprised… touched… even flattered… that someone should bring her flowers at work. More so, she was relieved at having not been here, seeing as the arrangement showed signs of being personally delivered. She sat down at her desk and began slowly rotating the vase about in order to take in the flowers from every angle. The arrangement was exceedingly lovely, and clearly expensive given the number of blooms. She looked to the note once more. He referred to her as being both courageous and beautiful…

in the same sentence. She was pretty sure no one had ever done that before, and since he did not strike her as one prone to exaggeration, it must be true.

Him thinking it, that is.

How was she to process such a compliment without it turning into something more? After all, she was decidedly not interested in being interested.

She read the note again.

What I 'went through' at the hospital… Well… he certainly played a part in that! Maybe this is just another apology… him showing that he was still feeling guilty about the fire hose thing.

No… can't be that. He used the word 'admiration.' That's way too personal.

Now, more so than the flowers, the note became the focus of her attention. It was just ordinary cardstock… nothing special… with his message printed in bold block letters… so typical of what a man might do. She reread the note slowly another time, coming away with a conclusion. Nothing in it obligated her to reciprocate. No open-ended invitation that they get together. No subtle suggestion that he would appreciate hearing back from her. Still… she should think about some way of sending him a gracious reply that put an end to all such attentions in the future… before things got really awkward. She could call the nursing home… like before… but maybe that might give him the wrong impression. No way was she going back there. She had barely cleared its parking lot the other day before swearing to herself that she would never set foot in the place again… and then spent the whole drive home brow-beating herself for having been so vulnerable.

Shifting the vase to a far corner of her desk, she set about completing the tasks left undone from before lunch. In short course, coworkers began filtering into her office. First one… then two together… then her supervisor… and then a group of tellers on break… all of them stopping by to inquire about her flowers. Some came with hesitant smiles, and some with probing questions. To all, Bridget offered only that the flowers were a pick-me-up of sorts for what she experienced after her daughter's car accident. The identity of the giver, she kept to herself.

All through the afternoon, the scent kept drawing her eyes back to the flowers. In no way would she allow her enjoyment of them to soften her determination. She refused to become involved with this man… even though the nature of her exact feelings toward him remained unclear. Of course it was a lie that she was not interested in him. She was… and not just from some remote, academic standpoint. He was cute… and quirky… and mysterious… all things that made a man interesting enough… under normal circumstances.

The rodeo stuff was a great example. Through his adventures, he had come to see so much more of the world than she had, and also experienced things she probably never would. Clearly he followed his own compass. That alone made him interesting... especially since she had no idea where she was pointing in life. Odd, he seemed not to hold that deficiency against her... which made him even more interesting. As to his nursing home job, that was more than a bit strange, but at least he was doing something important for others... an enviable trait she always admired in a person. Still... it was more than that. In her memory of him in that elevator... and recently in how he conducted himself around those old people... it was his kindly spirit that she found most intriguing. None of that was enough to change her mind. She would remain... aloof. Besides... she still had much to do in sorting out her feelings regarding Blaire, which hardly left room in her life for a man.

But why me? I'm not that interesting...

In thinking back over their limited time together, she could not identify one thing she had said or done to cause this man... or any man... to find her interesting. As far as he was concerned, everything about her had revolved around Blaire. She needed to do more thinking about that... about whether or not her life had become separated enough from that of her daughter's.

As the work day drew to an end, she settled herself comfortably into an imposed indifference toward the person of Lowell Paxton. Up until this point, his appearances in her life had been purely circumstantial, but if he were to make any further attempts at getting close to her... well... she would tell him... for his own good... and hers... that she was not interested.

She purposefully drove home without the flowers or the note, leaving them in her office with an understanding that they were not meaningful enough to her. She binged on movies all night, doing her unarticulated best at keeping her mind on anything other than him. On arriving at work the next morning, she found that several of the petals had fallen off, with most of the stems bent over. She had forgotten to put water in the vase before leaving. Without considering what vitality might remain in the blooms, she took the arrangement to the break room and disposed of it in the trash, then rinsed out the vase and placed it in a cabinet for anyone else's future use. With the lid of the trash securely in place... and the cabinet door closed off... she was finally convinced of having no further temptation toward getting to know Lowell Paxton better.

That resolve was tested before the day was old. Just as she was getting ready for her morning coffee break, he unexpectedly showed up with espresso… exactly the way she liked it. Seeing him come walking through the credit union lobby toward her produced an instant skip in her heart… and an indescribable annoyance… of which had greater import, she could not say. His smile somehow left her with no ability to think. She managed to thank him for the drink… and the flowers… and was on the verge of asking him how she knew her coffee preference, when he promptly excused himself with an assurance that he was not there to interfere with her work. His goodbye left her feeling confused… and strangely disappointed.

Almost immediately, the doorway to her office where he had stood became filled with the credit union's receptionist. The woman, in rapid fire, began quizzing Bridget as to who that 'hunk of a cowboy' was… and could he be the one responsible for the flowers… and was the coffee done correctly, seeing as she was the one who told him what to order. Through all the woman's fervor, Bridget endeavored to stoically sip on her drink as a simple distraction from all the questions. Her mind, however, was flying off elsewhere.

Why didn't he stay longer?

They could easily have chatted for a couple of minutes about something safe… maybe their shared memory of the elevator or the hospital… before she took it upon herself to politely get back to work.

Now, everyone at the credit union knew that there was a man showing interest in her. Through the remainder of that day… and the next… Bridget unsuccessfully tried to sit quietly at her desk processing loan applications, but was repeatedly interrupted by coworkers asking her to recount how she and that cowboy had met during last year's earthquake… and was he the one with the fire hose… and had he, in fact, once been a rodeo rider as the receptionist claimed. His two visits to the credit union had her talking openly about him… yet ironically she had hardly been given an opportunity to talk with him.

But what would I say anyway? It's not like we have anything in common.

His intentions seemed clear enough… to pursue her… which made her feel both complimented and conflicted.

But what if he's planning to do something weird again… like stalking me?

That seemed highly unlikely given what little she knew of him so far. But even if he turned out to be a perfect gentleman in the future… just as handsome and just as charming as when he showed up with a smile and a perfect double-shot cappuccino, extra foam, with a sprinkle of cinnamon on top… why should she give in simply because he got her coffee right? Why should she risk lowering the guard on her tormented heart for a stranger? There was no way he was going to stick around for long anyway… not once he discovered what a total mess she really was. Surely he already had a glimpse of what her complicated life was like based on the time they spent together in that elevator. He had been so cool and calm in the face of Blaire's abuse… which was so much worse than the earthquake itself. Even all that western ruggedness aside, he was clearly so very different from anyone she had ever met. Surely such a person was worth getting to know. But no… not if it meant she might get hurt again. Nothing was worth that. Besides, it was too late for a redo on life. At most, they could be friends… acquaintances with a few odd adventures in common. But then he would surely want to know why… and the only legitimate reason she had in her mind was fear… and fear might not be enough to make him go away. Truth was, she liked him, yet would never be able to look at him without being reminded of the things she had seen at that nursing home. Through him, she had come face-to-face with her own end… and just like how terrifying it had been during that earthquake… and while Blaire lay unconscious in a hospital bed… such were hardly experiences worth building a relationship on.

Once more, Bridget put thoughts of Lowell Paxton out of the front regions of her mind in order to concentrate on doing her job.

On the Friday of that week, Bridget's reserve was tested again. She returned to her desk after an especially long planning session in the conference room to find an envelope sitting atop a note written on her legal pad.

Bridget,

I'm sorry to have missed you. They tell me you're in a meeting. I'm leaving you this note instead, seeing as I'll be tied up at the nursing home for the rest of the day and all through the weekend. Call me if you can. I was hoping you'd accompany me and my daughter to a concert next Saturday at the Hollywood Bowl – Beethoven in the style of the Boston Pops. If you're available, I'd be happy to pick you up, or we could meet there if you prefer. The envelope has your ticket.

Looking forward to seeing your lovely smile once again,
Lowell

Aside from the minor gaffe of mentioning the Boston Pops in reference to the Hollywood Bowl Orchestra… something no one in the latter would appreciate… she had to credit the man – he was clever. She really enjoyed

Beethoven's music… a thing she vaguely recalled telling him during that long wait in the elevator last year… and the way he dangled out the presence of his daughter… that made going it a safer bet… and harder to turn down. Plus, someone who went so far out of her way to restore a broken relationship was probably worth meeting. So… having his daughter at the concert might make it a bit awkward… but nothing as bad as being alone with him on a date.

Which I've not had in over a decade…

She would definitely phone him, whether to accept or decline she had not yet decided.

Despite the effort she invested that day in trying to convince herself that she was not interested in the man, she nonetheless kept his note handy so her eyes could occasionally stray back to its last line.

My smile's not really that lovely… is it? Is that what he really thinks?

Without being able to resist the urge, she had a compact out of her purse and… after a furtive look out her office door… went about recreating a variety of smiles, wondering which it was that he had been referring to. Try as she might, she was unable to find one worthy of being labeled lovely.

As the workday wore on, Bridget found herself doing a lot more smiling than her Friday afternoon anticipation of a weekend typically produced. At closing time, she left the credit union purposing to sleep on the invitation before calling… even though in the back of her mind the issue had already been decided. After putting a few hours into her Saturday morning… so as not to seem overly eager… she called him at the nursing home. Accepting right off, she told him that she would drive herself there seeing as she had work that day… which would be another thing that helped keep this from feeling like a date. They arranged to meet outside the Bowl, then chatted pleasantly about what the weather would be like… right before he raised the stakes.

"I've told Emmeline all about you… and she's really anxious to meet you."

"She is?"

"Of course… I mentioned how you handled all that stress at the hospital. Very impressive… if you ask me."

Now that was real pressure… intended or not. She should have anticipated something like this… being put on the spot. Was she to be evaluated by his daughter… or worse… shown off?! With the call ended, Bridget drifted out to her back porch on a wave of doubt, having left herself absolutely no room for bailing out.

From afar, her first impression of Emmeline was simply as a daughter attached to the arm of her father. As Bridget closed the distance to where the two of them stood in the Hollywood Bowl plaza, she could not help but notice that his daughter was not nearly as attractive as her own. Emmeline's rounded shoulders, wide-framed glasses, and page-boy haircut all contributed to what Bridget reluctantly considered to be a rather mousy look… perhaps more so because of the walnut brown color to her dress. With Lowell actively scanning the passing crowd, it was Emmeline who first noticed her making directly for them, and gently tugged on her father's sleeve. In an instant, Bridget's opinion completely changed. As Lowell looked down to his daughter, her face lit up with an immense smile… so warm and confident.

"Bridget… glad you could come. Let me introduce you to my daughter Emmeline."

"Very pleased to meet you… your father's spoken quite highly of you."

"And he of you too… And since Dad never exaggerates…" Emmeline paused here to give an affectionate little nuzzle into his side. "…then I guess we must both take him at his word."

Everyone laughed and smiled together, with Bridget's revised impression deepened. Already, she could tell that Emmeline, like her father, was sensitive, perceptive, and kindhearted… all attributes Blaire sorely lacked. Even as their brief handshake was completed, Bridget decided two things – that she liked what she saw in Lowell Paxton's daughter, and that she needed to be extra careful not to make any further comparisons to her own.

They moved together to the entrance, with Bridget hesitating for a moment as to which place she should take up in the order of things… in front or behind the two of them. Lowell settled that for her by motioning both of them ahead in line. They produced their respective tickets… her after awkwardly fumbling about in her purse while the others waited… then moved through as a group. After another uncertain moment in which they got their bearings as to the direction they should head, she was surprised when Emmeline stepped out slightly in front. Not being sure what to make of this, Bridget put effort into drawing the young woman back into the casual conversation she had started regarding her previous visits to the Bowl. When they finally reached their row within the amphitheater, Emmeline slid in first, then Lowell moved in so he could sit between them.

They spent the ten minutes or so prior to the beginning of the concert talking about the earthquake and the hospital. In relating her side of those events to Emmeline, Bridget naturally found herself leaning forward in her seat… with Emmeline doing likewise… so the two of them could make eye contact around Lowell. As her accounts evolved, she found him gradually sinking back on finding himself the target of their lighthearted teasing. He was not altogether defenseless, stammering out a word or two of clarification every time Bridget went out of her way to embellish on some point of amusement. She knew he was actually enjoying the attention, especially when Emmeline was brought to tears in laughing so hard over her slow-motion account of a reporter getting plastered square in the face with a jet of water from her father's fire hose. Through it all, what struck Bridget as most noteworthy was how Emmeline had a hold on her father's arm and was playfully shaking it… and then how Lowell took that arm and wrapped it about his daughter's shoulder in a gentle embrace as the girl struggled to come out of her hysterics. The sight of two people expressing affection toward each other should not have seemed so distinct, yet their open display… free of pretense or unease… caught Bridget by surprise. Of course, it was only natural for a parent and child to feel close to each other. There were likely other such examples going on all about her in the amphitheater. Yet it painfully struck her how long it had been… ten years at least… since someone last touched her like that.

"Your daughter, Bridget… what's her name again… Dad's told me, but I forgot…"

"It's Blaire…"

"That's right… So what did she make of all this?"

"Well… umm… she was… still in a coma at the time…"

"Oh, I'm terribly sorry! Of course… how stupid of me. That must have been a horrible experience for you. Forgive me… I'm sure it wasn't a laughing matter."

Just to have something to say… and perhaps to experience a bit more sympathy… Bridget gave a brief account of Blaire's accident, leaving out the drunk driving part. She got up to her own overnight stay in the hospital when the concert suddenly began with the opening notes to the *Consecration of the House Overture*. In a matter of minutes, as the orchestra's tempo built, all of her unease at being reminded of Blaire wondrously dissipated within the joyousness of Beethoven's music. Nothing else was expected of her… so she need not perform. She could relax and enjoy. From time to time, as she ventured a look over at the other two, she took unexpected pause from seeing them leaning against each other, totally wrapped up together in the music.

At intermission, she and Emmeline excused themselves for the purpose of visiting the ladies' room. A long line snaking its way from the entrance gave Bridget the opportunity she had been hoping for.

"Your father said you often travel together as part of your business."

"We used to… before he took a job here."

"So what was it like working with a father?"

"Actually... I've worked with both of them... my father and my stepfather. In both cases, it was a delight. They're fairly different from each other... one's a businessman and the other's... well... still a cowboy at heart. But they're also a lot alike in that they both really care about people."

Emmeline paused here, so Bridget took the opportunity to craft better words for getting where she wanted to go. As they inched forward in line, she took a backdoor approach to discovering the circumstances as to how Lowell, the rodeo rider, became Lowell, the nursing home worker.

"So... how was it that the two of you ended up working together... if you don't mind me asking?"

"Not at all. Well, first off... believe it or not... Dad's a natural with the elderly."

"I know... I've seen him at it."

The way she nodded her head... more as confirmation than in agreement... suggested to Bridget that her visit to Lowell's workplace had already been a topic of conversation between the two of them. Fortunately, as Emmeline quickly continued on, Bridget did not have to think back on how terrible that experience had gone.

"You know... maybe it has something to do with all his years in the rodeo... he feels deeply for those who've come out on the short end of life. You know he doesn't have any kind of a formal education... other than the training he received from Russell. That's my stepdad."

"And they... do they... you know... get along okay?"

"Surprisingly well... though I know what you're getting at. I sometimes think it's strange too, having one's father working for one's stepfather... with me in the middle. Actually... according to Mom... Dad's a completely different person than he was back then."

"Back when?"

"So... he's not told you much about his past?"

"A little. I mean... I've heard about his time travelling about in the rodeo... and I know he was in the army... and that somehow led to... to the divorce. Is that what you mean?"

"For the most part... but he should probably be the one to fill in the gaps."

Her words, themselves, might have come across as a mild rebuff, but the way Emmeline smiled... right before dipping her head... suggested that she expected the story to be more meaningful coming from her father.

"He did tell me a little bit about your role in reconnecting with him. That must have been... really difficult."

As they had just reached the bathroom entrance... with the noise of automated hand driers making it impossible to be heard... they delayed the conversation until after they had left. As they finally made their way back, weaving through the promenade's crowd, Emmeline pointed to a vacant bench off to one side and suggested that they sit there for a few minutes before returning to their seats.

"So... you were asking about how I reconnected with Dad?"

"Yes... I was kind of curious... but only if you're comfortable saying."

"It's fine. I don't think he'd mind either. He might have told you that he left us when I was young... even though it was really we who left him. I only remember a little bit about that... the rest I learned from Mom. Anyway... I... umm... grew up more-or-less hating him for... his problems. When Mom met Russell... that was when I was in high school... he became the father I never knew. It was not until I graduated from college that Russell started encouraging me to reconnect with Dad. According to Mom... he had changed... but for some reason had not reached out to me. Of course, I thought it was because he didn't care about me... but I learned later that he was ashamed of himself. Long story short... when I started working for him... Russell, that is... my very first assignment was to do workforce assessment at a local nursing home. I can still remember it like it was yesterday. Bridget... I'm ashamed to tell you... I didn't handle it very well. It was a dreadfully miserable experience. I'd never been around old people before."

"Neither have I... so I know what you're talking about."

Emmeline nodded... more sympathetically than Bridget had expected... or deserved.

"They were so slow... and irritating... and difficult to talk to. I couldn't wait to get out of that place. In fact, I was ready to quit, thinking I wasn't cracked up for the job. But I'll never forget what Russell said to me. 'One day, I'm probably going to end up in a place like that, and when I do, I don't want to be forgotten.' That's why he started his business – to help the forgotten ones. And that's why I finally decided to hunt down Dad. No matter how angry I was at him for leaving me without a father, I just... couldn't stand the thought of him ending up alone. So... I made calls to some rodeo folks Mom knew, found out where he was going to be... someplace in Oregon... and then I went there to meet him."

"Wow. That's... that's the most amazing thing I've ever heard..."

"Don't be impressed. It doesn't mean I forgave him right off. That didn't happen for awhile."

"So… how did you come to forgive him?"

"I don't really know… I just did. I guess I had to. A week or so later, Dad showed up in St. Louis… that's where we were living at the time… and apologized to Mom in person. I could hardly hold the past against him after that. And then Russell up and offered him a job. So it was either forgive him… or be estranged from both of them."

"You know… your father's right… you are an amazing young woman."

"Thanks… You… ahh… do realize that this invitation was all about him trying to forge an introduction between us?"

"Yes… I sort of gathered that."

"You should really watch out for Dad. He puts on this folksy cowboy front, but he's terribly sneaky when he wants to be. But you know… I see what he likes in you… you're so… centered."

She had no idea how to respond to that. 'Scattered' was more like it. For Emmeline to have come to such a conclusion… in so short of a time… could only mean that Lowell had given her the wrong impression… or that this young woman was not so sharp after all.

Best not to find out which…

"Maybe… but maybe your folksy father's gotten to you too… especially if he's given you the impression that I have it all together. So… what say we go see what he's been up to…"

They found him waiting for their return with Spanish fried chicken, fries, bottled water, and plenty of napkins. For Bridget, something so simple as sharing food from a common basket while chatting over rather inconsequential things… the level of spiciness to the flavoring, their thoughts on the concert thus far, the mountains all about their view, and their mutual enjoyment to the emergence of the night sky above the Bowl… became the very means needed to help her forget herself in the moment.

The second half of the concert was as enjoyable as the first. All the way through, she found herself basking in the music as if it were the soft afterglow of a pleasant camp fire… even though she had never been camping in her whole life.

At the conclusion, they lingered in their seats chatting about the concert while a mass exodus from the amphitheater went on all about them. Somehow, as the place emptied, she found herself reminded that she should not be so comfortable in being with this man… daughter or not. She liked him… and she liked Emmeline… but she could not see how the idea of liking should become something more.

They walked together from the Bowl, with Lowell insisting that he escort her all the way to her car. Once there, she thanked them both again for inviting her… and suddenly found herself being hugged by Emmeline. For no other reason than it was the polite thing to do in parting, she inquired casually as to the duration of Emmeline's stay in LA… and was mildly relieved to learn that the young woman would be departing for the East Coast in the morning. That was good – no pressure to meet with her again.

Then, before she knew what was happening, Lowell swept in and gently kissed her on the lips. He then said goodbye… amongst other things she did not quite register… as all circuits were suddenly overloaded with the sensation of him being so near. How she got in her car… and got it started… was beyond her. Her mind would not snap back… even after the last sight of them had faded from her rearview mirror.

Hopping onto the One-O-One, she was still freaking out from having been kissed. Her thoughts should be filled with the music… or with having met Emmeline… but her emotions, in a whirlwind, would not allow her to relive any part of the concert other than the very end. She was stuck trying to convince herself that she had not enjoyed the kiss. The argument became so engrossing that she nearly missed the exchange that kept her on the Hollywood Freeway. This would not do.

Get a hold of yourself! The kiss meant nothing.

She obviously knew otherwise. It was tender… and not in the least bit forced. Actually… she had never been kissed by a man with a moustache. It sort of… tickled… in a good way. He had been so kind throughout the entire concert… such a gentleman… and a pleasure to be with. He laughed at her jokes… and truly seemed to enjoy being with her… as she did with him. She could easily see herself getting kissed by him again… perhaps a bit longer… and closer.

Completely unaware that she had successfully navigated onto the Five, Bridget realized too late that she had blown past her exit to Palmdale. In having to backtrack through Santa Clarita… her previous city of residence… to regain Highway 14, she suddenly took up a different version of the evening. She was not going to make the same mistake she had made with Mitch. She was not going to get sucked in by a handsome man… and find herself turning down the wrong road in life… yet again… only to expend so much time and energy in rerouting herself.

He called later that night to make sure she had arrived home safely, and then again the next day to say how much he appreciated her coming to the concert. Neither call would have an effect on her. She was firmly resolved to remain as she had purposed to do from the very beginning – with a guard placed firmly over her heart.

In the week following the concert, Bridget began using her lunch hour to take short walks alone rather than eat with her coworkers. It was easy for her to justify this change in routine, as she made clear to them that there was a dress size to lose. In truth, she went about the downtown area trying to find herself. She spent most of those walks in an ongoing debate with herself over the person of Lowell. He had gone silent since the phone call on Monday… perhaps waiting for her to initiate the next contact .. and that put her into a quandary as to her true feelings.

On the fourth day out, a sunny Thursday, she headed from the credit union in a new direction, and found herself at the Pricewater Building. On recognizing its entrance, an odd idea came to her, and she immediately went inside to its bank of elevators. In what she knew to be an awkwardly girlish whim, she declined opportunities to ride up in elevators one, two and three, opting instead to wait for the very one they had met in. For some reason, she hoped that the two persons most on her mind… Blaire and the man… might somehow sort themselves out by her being there once more.

Through a fortuitous circumstance, she ended up in elevator four all by herself. Once inside, she hesitated for a moment in deciding what to do next. Her first impulse was to push the button for the 25th floor, as that was where Dr. Fletcher's office was, but to be there again… in that lobby where Blaire had revealed her deceit… that would never provide her with clear answers.

So what floor had he come from?

She vaguely remembered him saying it. A number popped into her mind, and she pushed the corresponding button. The two halves of the doors met, the elevator's mechanism kicked into operation, and she found herself remarkably at ease within the same small space where she had once been in terror. The uninterrupted ride up was brief, though plenty long enough for her to become completely immersed in memory.

He sat there… and she sat there… and I was in the middle.

A part of her was tempted to drop to the floor… to put herself exactly where she had been in order to fully explore the feeling… but then the elevator's chime dismissed the thought. The doors opened, and she stepped out into a space that was somewhat smaller than the corresponding lobby two floors below.

I wonder why he was here…

As there was no harm in exploring, she took off in one direction of what turned out to be a looped hallway about the 27th floor, not really expecting anything to amount from this circuitous rabbit trail. She passed doors labeled with the names of various businesses – an investment firm, a law office, consultants of various kinds, and another therapist… any of which could have been his reason for being there. Some bore company names and some of individuals, with nothing striking her as significant. On the last leg, with the lobby in view ahead, she came upon a door bearing the label 'Wojnaski and Son,' and stood there pondering it.

You know… I think that's derived from the word for war… or strife… or something like that.

Of course, identifying the root meaning from the little bit of Polish she retained from childhood was not the reason she had stopped there. The name was familiar for an entirely different reason… and it hung right at the edge of her comprehension.

It's got something to do with Blaire's stay in the hospital. No – the nursing home.

It then hit her – she previously stood before a door bearing this odd name… just as Lowell went about picking up its occupant's trash. It immediately struck her that he had come to this place on the 27th floor of the Pricewater Building in order to meet with the son on behalf of the father… the father who was having a hard time adjusting to being alone.

She continued down the hall to the lobby and rode elevator one to the ground floor, all the while contemplating what he might have said to Wojnaski Jr., and if his message had reached sympathetic ears. Regardless of the outcome, Lowell had gone out of his way to intercede on behalf of the forgotten one.

Exiting the building and turning toward the credit union, Bridget made up her mind. She would put aside her fears from the past… even though she had no assurances against something similar happening in the future. She would allow the day to speak for itself… and enjoy the moment while it was hers. Now, she was no longer afraid of falling for Lowell Paxton… for she knew for certain that he cared.

Of course… it was much more than that… for she had just decided to be the one who pursued him.

CHAPTER

28

COUNTRY CLUB FARE

'Indestructa-Blaire!'

That was the byline to the *Tribune's* piece on her return to play three weeks after leaving the hospital. During a brief trip up to Chicago to scout out the course of the Great Lakes Open, her first tournament in getting back, Blaire squeezed in a series of interviews that set the groundwork for how she wanted the media to frame her car accident. She then had to get right back to LA... at Bernie's insistence... for some idiotic pro-am he was hosting. She would have blown off that circus, and stayed in Chicago, had it not been for the personal matter that must be addressed.

For the most part, she was pleased with the attention she was getting from the press. It went a long way toward refocusing her on where she wanted to be. Not that she actually needed anything... or anybody... to affirm for her the obvious. She was unique. Who else could have wrapped their sports car around a tree and practically walked away from it laughing?! Nobody! No one could have brushed the whole thing off as effortlessly as she had... and in such a short period of time. Even Bernie was amazed... though that did not keep him from badgering her about taking it easy. Him, she could handle, as his attempts at controlling her were always amusing... even when he transitioned into that disgusting sagely tone of his.

"After all, Blaire, you're only human..."

225

Such bullshit! Nobody patronizes me!

She would put a stop to his ceaseless pestering over plans for how she should handle the press. Over and over, he insisted that she should downplay the recklessness of the accident and claim it was not her fault. He even concocted some lame tale about her having to swerve because of a dog in the road.

I'd have plowed that mutt right over…

Above all, he stressed that she should deflect all questions regarding her drunk driving charges.

Even more bullshit!

The press was putty in her hands. So instead of doing it Bernie's way, she would do the exact opposite. She would milk the accident for all it was worth, smearing her superiority into everyone's face. To anyone who would listen *(…and who could resist me?!)*, she would make an elaborate show out of recounting how exhilarating the crash had been. Everywhere she went, people would end up thinking her cooler for it. Soon, her stunt would become legendary. Even that ridiculously unnecessary stay in the hospital would be forgotten. Of course, she would still make sure everyone was reminded of how badly she had been banged up. Those scars only accentuated her remarkable recovery. She would show them all just how extraordinary Blaire O'Connor was.

As to how she was handling her near-death experience on the inside… whether the whole ordeal had given her a new perspective on life… Blaire categorically refused such questions to be given serious consideration during interviews. If someone dared ask, she casually brushed them aside. All of her outward efforts were bent toward propping up the notion of her invincibility, so that it, like a virus, would spread widely among her fans, the media and her competitors alike. In time, everyone would become infected with the image of Blaire O'Connor.

Somehow, though, each exposure of her version of the events to someone new strangely sickened her, as patient zero, more than it did any of her victims. Despite her presumptions, the accident repeatedly challenged her sense of invulnerability. She was not untouchable after all. Headaches like no human ever experienced came on her without warning, forcing her to flee whatever she was doing and make for the nearest toilet before she threw up.

Fucking idiot of a doctor… of course there's something odd about my MRI! My head's killing me!

Because of the migraines, she had to have at the ready a purse-full of prescription meds Bernie scrounged up for her from who knows where. She hated taking pills. They made her feel needy.

On top of the headaches, a nagging little click had developed in her left wrist as a result of the accident. There was no pain to it… it had absolutely no effect on her swing… but every time she bent or moved her hand, there was that annoying sound as a reminder. As if she needed another one…

All of her waking thoughts would be dealt with, but those coming to her at night were beyond her control. She could not shake a reoccurring dream… a nightmare… that always plagued her into daylight. In its various forms, it lasted for only a few seconds, but always the dream caused her to scream herself awake, panting in a sweat at the vision of an iridescently glowing tree racing out of an eerie darkness directly at her. Never was she in a car, as always the dream had her hovering in midair as that tree propelled itself toward her at an indescribable speed. She might turn to one side or the other, but always it hit her head on.

Refusing to allow the weakness of her subconscious to pollute her mind, Blaire began taking sleeping pills at night, sometimes washing them down with a shot or two of bourbon. Gradually, as the weeks went by, the dreams became less frequent… and then stopped altogether… though she kept up the pills and the booze… just in case.

The first time she drove a car after the accident… it was totally ridiculous… she was actually nervous. She could not keep from scanning her mirrors with a jittery sort of rapidity that was inconsistent with her usual carefree style of driving. It was almost as if she was actually afraid of being at the mercy of other drivers. The whole time out, she told herself all sorts of lies to deal with her anxiousness. That she was still suffering from the lingering side effects of her pain meds. That she was not yet accustomed to her new sports car. Or that she had lost her favorite set of shades in the accident… and the replacement pair needed getting used to. Such a natural at bullshitting the media, and now she was having to do the same thing with herself. So… in a determined act to rid herself of uncertainty, she forced her foot down on the accelerator, once more intending to go faster than was safe… all to blur her senses with a rush of speed. She barely got to seventy before becoming so nauseated that she had to pull off the freeway.

She had not been remade new… not like a brand new car. She had mistakenly embraced the false assurance that everything would run as smoothly as before. Instead, she found herself to be more like a car that had been restored after a fender-bender. To be recovered physically… more than well enough to reenter the tour… but to have something still going on inside of her... an irritating little vibration not there before the accident... a nagging little voice that rattled away at her with a message so contrary to her previous self-assurances. The faster she drove her life, the louder it became. Even the roaring revs of her anger could not drown out this new fear.

None of this was her. Frailty was a lie of somebody else's making. She would show them. She would shock the world, and so shock herself right out of this malaise of mediocrity... before it ate away at her confidence. Even if it took making an exhibition of herself, she would turn the tables on fate... and scatter those silly concerns across the delicious distraction of torturing others. She could easily hide herself... no – find herself... within someone else's discomfort. Soon, the whole incident would become nothing more than a momentary blip on her road toward perfection.

Something simple needed to be done as a first step toward setting all things right... and Blaire knew just the thing. There was that one voice with its intolerably out-of-balance tone... like the irregular knock to a poorly tuned engine. Catching even a wisp of that irritating voice would surely be enough to bolster her sense of superiority back to its rightful place. She needed to hear again that which was truly ordinary in order to appreciate how extraordinary she was.

Before setting off to Chicago for those interviews and a practice round at the site of the upcoming Great Lakes Open, Blaire put in motion her plans to meet with her mother. Talking to that woman on the phone would not be enough to accomplish what she was after. Blaire had to see her in person, and watch her feeble mind dither about. With only five minutes of torquing on that woman's emotions, Blaire would be fully restored to her true self.

Man, I really need this...

No... actually I don't 'need' it. I don't need anything from her. I could easily go for the rest of my life without ever laying eyes on her again. I choose to do this... for my own amusement.

Besides, in the weeks since leaving the hospital, Blaire had not yet dangled out any of those lame expressions of appreciation her mother sold her soul for. The prospect of a 'thank you' had always come in handy throughout childhood, so Blaire was assured it would work now too.

I'll convey a morsel of gratitude to her, and she'll end up dancing about for more.

As she detested the possibility of a long drawn-out conversation with her mother, Blaire sought for a venue that she could control. Something completely on her own turf, with a definitive beginning and ending that her mother could do nothing to alter. Realizing just the thing, she made a call to Bernie's office.

The phone was still clutched in her hand even though the call had ended several minutes before. The invitation from Blaire, delivered as it was through Alexia, had caught her by surprise. She naturally accepted it… straight off… without pausing to question why it was that Blaire had not extended it herself. As the immediate shock wore off, she began to struggle through questions she should have asked before hanging up. Simple things like… why Sunday brunch? Why not meet for coffee someplace casual? As a former country club member, Bridget knew that inviting someone to your club's Sunday brunch was a big deal. The meal was expensive, and it was often difficult to get a table as most members chose to make that a prime time for socializing and showing off their connections.

There's no way Blaire's intending to show me off to anyone.

She should probably call back for more information. Perhaps Alexia forgot to relay some minor aspect regarding the invitation. Or maybe she could call back about something more innocent sounding. Something like… asking about the dress code. Surely the Butera Country Club had specific standards pertaining to their Sunday brunch. Piper Mountain certainly had… She would never forget having spent weeks of tedious committee work revising their dress code. All they ended up doing was wrangling over miniscule details about skirt lengths and jacket styles. As country clubs were concerned, she knew that Butera was in a league well above that of Piper Mountain, so appropriate attire for this Sunday brunch would be just as specific. Bridget then realized that calling back to ask about what to wear would make her seem silly… especially since she could easily inquire of the club herself.

Wait… did Alexia actually say it would be just the two of us?

A shutter ran down her spine at the thought that Mr. Pearl might be there too. She hated the thought of being cornered by the two of them. Or maybe there would be someone else. Maybe Blaire was intending to introduce her to a friend… a boyfriend?

Bridget practically snorted out her amusement at the thought.

Right after hell freezes over!

Blaire needed no one in her life, and in no way would stoop to share even the most trivial of relationships with her mother. Whatever devious trick was up her sleeve, Blaire would most definitely not rely on someone else's help to pull it off. Bridget knew it almost for certain – it would only be the two of them.

Realizing this tendency in Blaire did it for her. Bridget would not fall prey to the same old ploy – being a sucker for a false relationship. In no way would she play Blaire's games anymore. They were tiresome, beyond frustrating, and so full of hazards. Her daughter knew no shame. Always, she worked Bridget up into a hopeful enthusiasm by holding out the prospect of something genuine. Then came the twist, and before Bridget knew it, she found herself in Blaire's trap once more. Years ago… even before that horrible experience in Phoenix… she swore to herself that a wall would stay in place between them for her own protection. And just because Blaire survived an accident… of her own making… did not mean that anything had changed between them.

Maybe *she* should bring someone with her… someone capable of shielding her from Blaire.

Lowell!

Instantly, she knew he would agree. He would gladly do anything for her. Even though they had only been dating for a few weeks, he was essentially her boyfriend… and already knew something of what Blaire was like.

Bridget had the phone up ready to call Alexia about bringing a guest when it occurred to her that the only way to protect herself was not to inquire.

For once, let Blaire be the one caught off guard.

The small amount of confidence she gained from briefing Lowell on the drive over was completely lost the moment he turned his car into the winding, palm-lined lane leading up to the Butera clubhouse. She had not been this close to a golf course since Phoenix. The sight of golfers ambling across manicured lawns, oddly accentuated by the subtle freshness of newly cut grass, brought an instant flood of association to her… no part of which was good. Not that the pristine grounds all about her lacked anything in their display of beauty. Everything was exceedingly lush… exactly what she sought from her own backyard haven. It was more the grating feeling she remembered all too well… of being at odds with such a place.

Anticipating this uneasiness all weekend had her now in a state of high anxiety that not even Lowell's encouraging presence could abate. At least seeing how amazingly handsome he looked in a suit and tie did much to cheer her up. The way he took her by the arm and led her through the parking lot's array of luxury cars made her feel special. Still… this was not a well-meaning get-together, so it would not do for her to openly display any affection toward him in Blaire's presence.

Coming through ornate glass doors into the entrance of the dining area, Bridget was instantly filled with new apprehension as they passed by a dozen or so well-dressed couples waiting for tables. Without a note of nervousness, Lowell led her right up to the maître d', but she… already in hyper-sensitive mode… could not help but imagine the worst from this man's momentary scrutiny of their attire before turning to his registry.

"Ah yes… the O'Connor party. I believe Ms. O'Connor has already arrived. Carl here will show you to her table"

A tuxedoed young man, barely out of his teens by the look of him, stepped forward to lead them through the nearly full dining area. With Lowell gesturing her forward, Bridget fell in behind Carl, immediately noting the linen-covered tables arrayed with crystal and fine china. An even stronger association to the past now crept into her expectations of how this brunch would go. Mitch had always overshadowed her at country club functions, making her feel completely forgettable. Her daughter… with that twisted sixth sense attune to the frailties of others… would surely know this, and be quick to hone in on the slightest sign of discomfort.

Their escort led them to an intersection in the walkway, with a stretch of tables running off in either direction before the dining room's rear wall of glass. Outside was an expansive panorama of the golf course. Thinking that this young man was to turn down one side aisle or the other, Bridget came to an abrupt stop, waiting for him to choose. He, instead, motioned them forward to a prominent table where sat an odd looking character whose facial features were somewhat shrouded by sunlight pouring in from behind. At first glance, she was sure that the host had made a mistake, as the outline of this individual seemed foreign to her. With shadows cutting across the face, Bridget was taken in more by the upturned collar to the person's silver blazer. It… in being buttoned up to the neck… clashed terribly with the paleness of their entire head. The whole outfit oddly struck her with the feel of a cheaply conceived sci-fi get-up. As the person was speaking on a cell phone, it was not until they glanced up that Bridget recognized the wicked smile. It was Blaire… and she was completely bald.

With the recognition came overwhelming shock. For Bridget, it was more than that Blaire had shaved her head. Mothers of daughters such as hers were sadly conditioned to rebellious behaviors. Blaire had done so many astonishingly outlandish things with her appearance in the past that being caught off guard… being severely unnerved… even being saddened to see all those lovely strawberry blond waves cut away… was actually standard fare for her. If only it had been just the hair… for running from above Blaire's left ear to her forehead was the remnant of the gash she received from the accident. It stood out so grotesquely amidst the paleness of her shaved skin. Surely Blaire knew this. Knew that the scar was still puffy and purple, and that its jagged bulges would nauseate anyone forced to behold it up close. And as if to confirm that thought, Blaire turned her head slightly to better show off the scar.

Riveted to the appalling sight, Bridget was completely unaware of herself standing in the middle of the main walkway. She might be able to feel things… the shoes on her feet… or Lowell's hand ever-so-gently urging her on… yet was incapable of moving. Against her will, she gave way to a pain rising up from within her chest that shook her arms and shoulders. This was an ache only a mother could experience in beholding a harm done to her child. Blaire surely understood this… and knew that her mother would be overwhelmed with sadness at the sight of that scar. So Blaire was more than flaunting it. She was collecting up Bridget's pain and smearing it back into her face… ridiculing as a weakness the empathy she naturally felt as a mother. Of all things her daughter had ever done, this was the darkest and most disturbing… for it revealed something ugly that went far beyond skin-deep.

Bridget could not help but look away… though not for relief. Her eyes convulsively shot about to the neighboring tables. From the occupants' expressions as they looked up from their plates, it was clear that these diners had already been made to witness Blaire's spectacle from the moment of her arrival… for they too were having their faces rubbed in it. Blaire was challenging them all with the indecency of her scar and bald head.

Bridget felt Lowell's hand pat her once more, sending a pulse of recognition into her mind. Surely he too had recognized Blaire by now… and seen that horribly unhealthy-looking scar.

What must he be thinking?! How could anyone have raised such a warped and disturbed person… bent on offending everyone in this club… her mother included… and now he's being made to experience it too!

An unexpected surge of anger arose within her. It was one thing for Blaire to humiliate her… it was another thing altogether for Blaire to take the lid off her disdain and unleash it so openly. At least in the past, Blaire's contempt had been concealed behind her perverse pleasure for deception. As difficult as that had been for Bridget to endure, she consistently counted on her daughter's secretiveness as a sort of self-restraint. But now, the openly raw look to Blaire's disfigured scalp betrayed for all to see the viciousness inside. The false charm was gone, uncloaking a savage lust for affronting the whole world. Blaire had crossed over to a much more dangerous place.

"Oh… I see the problem. We need another setting."

At Carl's voice, Bridget snapped out of her thoughts to look down at the table for the first time. It was rectangular, seating six, but currently having only two settings. Blaire, seated at the head, had not expected her to bring a guest. As Carl went off to gather up the necessary items, Bridget felt once more Lowell's hand gently touch her back as his voice came in a whisper to her ear.

"It'll be okay, Darlin.'"

Carl was back promptly with all that was needed for the third setting. Blaire, still on the phone, gave an insistent finger jab for this to be set up on her other side. As Carl went about it, Bridget, still in shock, slowly registered that Blaire intended for her to be separated from Lowell. He would only be across from her, but it might as well have been on the far side of the moon, for what she needed most in order to muscle her way through this brunch was to be holding his hand beneath the table.

Sadly reconciled to the arrangement, she was about to seat herself when Lowell unexpectedly stepped around her. In a series of rapid movements, he reached across the table and shifted the pieces of the third place setting – the bread plate, the ceremonial dinner plate, the silverware, the water and wine glasses, the napkin – all of it – so that he could be seated beside her. As he went about putting the final touches on the new arrangement, Bridget ventured a hesitant look up. Blaire was narrowing her eyes in a clear message of displeasure at Lowell's presence… and what he was doing to her plans for brunch.

Once he was done with the new setting, she reluctantly moved to take up the seat beside Blaire… only to feel a gentle tug on her arm. Without a word, Lowell steered her to the new place setting… even pulled out the chair for her, smoothly pushing it in after… right before he plopped himself down in the seat beside Blaire. An overwhelming sense of relief came over her… that Lowell would be insulating her from the worst of Blaire's disgrace by directly facing that horrid scar… and the person who owned it. With him between her and Blaire, she might actually have a chance of keeping in place the separation she had worked so hard to foster in her heart. Now, she was no longer worrying about what he might be thinking, because he was thinking of her.

Once seated, he nodded sweetly, and then turned with a pleasant smile toward Blaire. Touched beyond measure, Bridget felt the tension slide off her shoulders as she took up his example to relax until Blaire had finished her call.

"Bernie, I don't have time for this bullsh:t. Just do your job. I want everything sorted out before I leave this afternoon."

Without so much as a goodbye, Blaire terminated the call and immediately gave off the fabricated warmth of her typical false smile… distorted as it was by the bald scalp and scar. In that brief moment of silence before her daughter spoke, Bridget purposed to say as little in response as possible… irrespective of what baited barbs ended up being cast her way. It might make her appear weak and clueless, but she would not give in. She would not fall for the same old tricks leading to shallow hopes and deep resentments. Lowell could do the talking for the both of them. She would distance herself completely… and against her nature, deny her longing for a relationship.

"Mr. Paxton… so good of you to accompany my mother to brunch."

"Pleased to be here."

Blaire gave a flick of her wrist in a direction over Bridget's head, with a server instantly appearing at the table.

"I've taken the liberty of ordering for us. I hope you approve of what I've selected – grilled salmon, pilaf and… something-or-other."

She followed Blaire's casual look up toward the server.

"Umm, yes, ma'am… it's fresh asparagus with our special hollandaise… and to start, we have a delightful potato bisque or a very lovely spinach sal…"

"That's enough. Bring three of those."

"Can I interest anyone in a beverage? The chef has an excellent list of recommended wines and cocktails for…"

"We're all having water… so you can leave."

To delay looking directly at Blaire… and because the server seemed crestfallen at having been treated so brusquely… Bridget followed that woman's progression away from their table. Salmon was not something she typically ordered as an entrée for herself. Despite having lived in the Pacific Northwest for a time, she had never developed a taste for that particular fish. Blaire probably knew this, and even now was taking a pompous satisfaction out of giving them no choice over their meals.

"So, Mr. Paxton…"

"Please call me Lowell."

"…why exactly are you here? Are you my mother's escort or…?"

"Sorry to interrupt… but you seem to have forgotten something. Aren't you going to greet her?"

In apprehension, Bridget watched Blaire's eyes flash with anger… just before she turned them sweetly toward her.

"Yes, of course. I wouldn't want her to feel left out. Hello, Mother… so wonderful to see you this morning. Such a pity you're having trouble speaking for yourself…"

Don't respond to that. Don't appear in the least bit riled. And don't justify why Lowell's here. You asked him, and that should be enough. Remember – no small talk of any kind… she'll turn it around on you. And whatever you do, don't say anything about her head… or that disgusting-looking scar. Don't even glance at it. That's what she wants – to shock you into making a fool out of yourself.

Bridget, already reaching for her glass, purposefully took a long, drawn-out sip, aware that Blaire was waiting with a smirk on her face. The delay in answering, she knew, would betray the nervousness inside… but at least the cool water would steady her voice.

"Not at all. And you… you seem… better."

"I'm absolutely fine, of course. More than good enough to be back on tour. But I actually don't have time for silly chitchat. I invited you to brunch for the sole purpose of acknowledging you're… small contribution… to my recovery. Bernie's mentioned that you managed a couple visits early in my hospital stay. That was good of you. And since you're here, Mr. Paxton…"

"Lowell."

"…I should also extend a small measure of appreciation to you. I was… impressed… by that show of passion toward me outside the hospital."

"I think you might be reading a bit too much into it."

"There's no need for false modesty. What you did with that fire hose to disperse an annoying crowd of paparazzi… it was quite touching. I know for a fact that few golfers have fans as devoted as that."

"I'm not what you'd call a fan."

"Really? Such a shame. Well… either way… it took courage to do what you did for me… and I admire courage above all things. "

"I suppose… but I didn't do it for you."

Without a hitch, Blaire instantly morphed from a charming smile into an ugly sneer… made more startling by the abnormally round look to her face.

"Aha! I never actually thought you did. It's pretty obvious you were taking advantage of my popularity… and my situation… to give yourself a moment in the spotlight. I can't tell you how many nameless parasites have tried to photobomb me."

"Maybe I did it for a different reason. Say… for your mother?"

"For her?! Don't be ridiculous. That'd be even more pathetic than… Wait… you're actually serious? You made a complete fool out of yourself… for her?!"

Blaire gawked directly at her… even though she was clearly speaking to him.

"It's true, Blaire… He told me himself the day after… when I went to the nursing home where he works."

Instantly, Bridget knew she had made a mistake. In her desire to answer sincerely, she provided Blaire with too much information. With a slight pause meant to accentuate her theatrical show of disbelief, Blaire turned back to Lowell with what could not be mistaken as anything other than unbridled glee.

"Really?! You... work at a nursing home?! Now that's rich! I bet you're wicked with bedpan and walker. So what's that pay... a couple of dollars an hour over minimum?"

"I get by."

She could not see the full extent of his face, turned as he was toward Blaire, yet Lowell's voice remained easygoing. Blaire had not come close to ruffling him. For her part, Bridget was on the verge of boiling over, and in no way would tolerate him being treated rudely. In coming forward in her seat to confront Blaire, she was surprised to find a hand placed lightly on her knee. Biting back a temptation to ignore his meaning, she instead turned away to stare out over the heads of the nearby diners until she could bring herself to look upon Blaire again. Fortunately, the arrival of their salads at that moment went a long way toward quelling her anger... especially as she felt compelled to put on a grateful demeanor for the benefit of their server.

Without hesitation as a salad was placed before her, Blaire took up a fork and speared a clump of leaves. In lifting it to her mouth, she briefly provided them with a little wave of her wrist, obviously meant as her way of giving them permission to eat.

She's always got to be the one in control...

Once more, Bridget purposed to say nothing, and instead went about raking the greens around on the china plate before her. This salad was beautifully done... sprinkled with caramelized walnut pieces and lightly tossed in a reddish vinaigrette dressing. By the feel of it when poked with her fork, she could tell that the spinach was especially fresh. On any other occasion, she would already be enjoying it, but the sight of Blaire's scar had taken away her appetite. Lowell, on the other hand, was moving through his salad at a slow pace, intermittently looking up at the golf course scenery out the window.

Blaire was the first to finish, and in pushing aside the remnants, leaned within an uncomfortably close proximity to him.

"So let me get this straight... you just happened to be passing by the hospital where I was brought... saw the crowd there expressing their concern for me... and then up and decided to hose them all down... just for her?!"

"That's not exactly how it went... but close enough."

"Well... *Lowell*... now that I know it wasn't out of consideration for me, tell me what actually inspired this daring act of yours on behalf of my mother?"

"I'm sure you remember being stuck in that elevator some time back?" He probably failed to notice it, and most likely would not have understood what it revealed, but Bridget picked up on a slight twitch at the corner of Blaire's mouth on being reminded of that earthquake. "Suffice it to say... situations like that don't come along very often. They tend to... focus a person. I saw something special in your mother that day... a calm strength I like very much. What I did at the hospital... I did it out of respect for her."

"Really?! Out of respect... for her?! I find *that* incredibly hard to believe. Here's a more plausible explanation... By all outward appearances, what you did looks more like a personal attack on me. After all, it was *my* fans and *my* media. But I actually don't care why *you* think you did it. All that matters to me is why *she* asked you to do it..."

"Blaire! I would never..."

"...because that's the only thing that makes sense."

"Actually, I heard about your accident on the news and acted on my own. Your mother had nothing to do with it. But seeing as I've offended you... please accept my apology for..."

"You're apology?! Wow! Now that's incredibly generous of you! Out of curiosity, what exactly do you think that's worth to me? Will it repair the shambles you made out of my media coverage at the hospital? Will it make my fans feel any better about being humiliated on TV? Or how will it compensate for all the time and effort my agent had to put into cleaning up the mess you made of my image? But you know what... maybe it'll be enough to cover the cost of this brunch... because I'm not signing for any of it."

Without another word, Blaire threw her napkin on the table and rose to leave. At a former time in life, Bridget would have jumped up in pursuit with whatever manner of appeasement might bring Blaire back. Instead, she lay her fork across her salad plate and slumped down with her face toward her lap. Everyone about them, she knew, was looking their way, but the person she was most embarrassed before was sitting right beside her.

"Bridget... I'm terribly sorry... I've made a mess out of your time with her. I should've kept my mouth shut."

"Don't be sorry, Lowell. As Blaire goes... her leaving like that was rather mild. To be honest, I don't think the brunch went the way she hoped... all because you were here to protect me."

"You do realize you're more than a match for her."

"You don't understand... and I don't think I did until now either. I've never really needed protection from her... what I've needed was protection from myself. I've spent so much time thinking about this brunch, rehearsing over and over in my mind all of Blaire's tendencies in order to prepare myself... but I completely neglected to focus on my own... weaknesses. Time after time, I've yielded to a longing for a sincere relationship with her... and she knows it... and knows how to play me because of it."

Bridget hesitated for a few seconds, then decided to bring forth into speech what was already obvious to him.

"Lowell... if it had not been for that scar... seeing all of its... raw ugliness... and realizing what it said about her true nature... well... I might have fallen into playing the same old game with her. But now I know for certain... there's nothing in her that cares for me."

"Out of curiosity... have you told her about how you were treated outside the hospital?"

"You're forgetting... we don't talk."

"Oh... that's right. Still think she should know... You've given her the best you have... and she should be lavishing you with appreciation. Instead... she pushes you away... all to protect herself."

"Why do you say that?"

"I don't know... maybe to prevent her choices in life from becoming the subject of a conversation. I'm not saying it'll make a difference... there's only so many chances in a person's life to hear what they need to hear before they close themselves off. Maybe she has and maybe she hasn't... not my place to say. But one thing's for certain – when I'm around, I'm not letting her treat you with disrespect."

She suddenly felt very close to him, and leaned over to make it so. In kissing him on the cheek, his color immediately reddened. He went from pit-bull to puppy-dog in a second. She liked very much having that effect on him.

Their server arrived with only two entrées, hesitating for a moment in looking at Blaire's empty seat. By that, Bridget recognized that most everyone in the club probably knew that Blaire had stormed out and would not be returning.

"Might as well enjoy this. What say you let me cover the tab... seeing as she walked out because of me."

"Thanks... but I think I should be the one to pay seeing as she's my daughter. Besides, you've just earned yourself a new enemy... and a very dangerous one at that. There's no telling what Blaire's going to do to you... or me for that matter."

At the conclusion of brunch, as they left the club, Bridget turned sideways in order to wrap herself about Lowell's arm, so thankful that he had come into her life. All the way to his car, and on the drive from the club, he tried valiantly to distract her with talk about other things… how lovely she looked and what grand plans he had for them together in the coming weeks… but soon fell silent in sensing that she had no real desire for conversation. She was certainly relieved that the brunch was over, but also still overwhelmed with dread for Blaire's future. That familiar sense of hopelessness had already set in – that her only child was self-destructing, with nothing that could be done to prevent it. Perhaps there never had been.

In looking out at the things they were passing along the freeway… especially the cars going in the opposite direction… it occurred to her that she was only responsible for going her own way in life. Just as it was silly for her to become tangled in the sights along the road… or get twisted up in wondering about the destinations of other motorists… it would be equally senseless for her to unduly dwell on the course Blaire had set for herself.

Her entire life, Bridget had been afraid of facing a future without family. Afraid that all of her desperate efforts… all of her sacrifices… might not be enough to keep that grim future from becoming a reality. Yet her worst fears had come true. Even before Blaire bolted up from the table, she knew in her heart that her daughter was dead to her. So it was finally time that she stopped fearing that future… for that future was now firmly in the past.

CHAPTER

29

SNAKE

From lesser to greater, competitor bestowed upon competitor a nickname reflective of the golfer's persona on the course. Some were derived from the way the player carried herself around the locker room, some came about in reference to a humorous incident or an odd habit, and some simply meant that the golfer could whack the shit out of a ball. Blaire was well aware of this league tradition going back before her time in Q-school. She knew that sooner or later every girl on tour ended up with a label that followed her throughout her playing days.

Even though most golfers clung affectionately to their nicknames, Blaire considered herself to be above such idiotic conventions. To her, a nickname was a meaningless sentimentality... a crutch meant for propping up a damaged self-esteem. Embracing a nickname... even desiring one... was a feebleness fit for only normal people. The true competitor... such as herself... would never stoop to an illusion of camaraderie. She was in it for total domination. So on or off tour, Blaire used someone's nickname only when she found it a useful means of manipulating a weak mind. Otherwise, she addressed each golfer by their last name... or nothing at all.

Shortly after going pro, someone in the press made a passing reference to her flair in the short game, and Bernie pounced on it. 'The Flair' soon became her nickname all around the league. From then on, he wore her out with all his inane schemes for exploiting 'Blaire the Flair,' putting up with him and his office of twits only when it suited her greater goal. She readily acknowledged his reputation as a highly successful promoter, but could not see why everyone considered him to be so clever.

He's nothing compared to me!

A year or so after her first win… well after she was firmly established on tour… Blaire began responding randomly to Bernie's promotional efforts. Sometimes it was in wholehearted compliance… in which case she would conveniently forget to do whatever he was asking… and sometimes in adamant resistance. The essence of his plans never mattered, for what she really sought was to control him.

Besides… what the hell could he possibly know about my flair?

Her enthusiasm for the game went so far beyond his feeble comprehension… and equally well above that of anyone else on tour. Golf was life… her private battle for ultimate perfection. Nobody could possibly understand the depth of her devotion to the game because nobody came even remotely close to her uniqueness. So the press and her competitors could call her whatever the hell they liked, and it would make no difference to her.

Now that's real strength!

In short time… and in no way owing to Bernie's obsessiveness… she saw her growing fan base adopt 'Blaire's Flair' as an emblem of their enthusiasm for her. Outwardly, she gave off the impression of embracing their attentions… just as an adored star would… yet inwardly she harbored contempt for anyone so shallow as to call themselves a fan. She always found a crowd of such persons to be amazingly predictable. With a single tear of appreciation, shed as it was without an ounce of feeling, she could easily throw the whole lot of them into a frenzy… and then leave them hanging there in abject disappointment after handing out only a single autograph.

And still they'd fall all over themselves to follow me. Such idiots…

Of course, it was only natural that she should be idolized… anyone with half a brain would be drawn to her. She craved none of it… none of their admiration or affection… yet savored every opportunity of control it brought her. The only thing she really cared about was her own greatness.

Which was why being reminded of that outburst of hers following the Desert Classic always rankled her. She had easily corralled the press and her fans into interpreting that fit the way she wanted them to, yet her competition about the league had not been so malleable. Although it was years since Phoenix, older players still whispered at the new girls on tour to 'watch out for Blaire O'Connor's tantrums'… as if what she had done to her locker with a pitching wedge was all that special. She did shit like that all the time… especially whenever anyone dared to get in her way. At least none of them were clever enough to recognize the difference between a true fit and one of her cunning charades.

Sometime after Phoenix, she became aware that her competition was referring to her in private by a different nickname. 'The Flair' was still spoken of her on the course and before the press, but in the ladies' locker room Blaire had become Snake. Not 'the Snake' – just 'Snake.' Their implied meaning was obvious – they considered her antics to be a terrible influence on their league. She had entered their peaceful paradise in much the same way that fabled serpent had snuck into the Garden to deceive Eve. Any other woman might be insulted, but Blaire found their association to be fascinating. After all, every golf course garden belonged to her, and every Eve out there was her competition. So to be called Snake, the enemy of all women, was something more significant than a nickname. None of them intended it as such, but Blaire took Snake to be the ultimate compliment.

Not that what others thought of her meant anything. She was at the top of her game, and none of them could touch her. Anything she wanted, she would have. Bernie and his army of PR chimps leapt into action at her slightest beckon… or she could ignore them completely if it so happened to amuse her. Everywhere she went, the fans and media flocked to her. And best of all… she had her mother exactly where she wanted her – at arm's length begging for attention.

Then came the accident to ruin it all.

Now, a week out of the hospital, Blaire was forced to accept that she had a shit-load of work to do in getting things back to the way they should be. Standing in her way were all those annoying follow-up doctor appointments and a stint of rehab to restore lost muscle tone.

If only those were the worst things she had to deal with.

Above all other annoyances, she hated most that small voice not present in her head prior to the accident. That little thing tormented her with a tickle of thought. Always at the edge of her awareness, it whispered that she was not so almighty as she had presumed. She could make mistakes. She could be hurt… permanently… maybe even killed. No matter what mind games she played on herself, she could not get that voice to stop nagging her. She dreaded every syllable of its message, for not a word of it could be altered, controlled or muzzled… only muffled with pain killers, alcohol and noise… lots and lots of noise. She kept her television on day and night, and never went anywhere without people around to drum out that voice. Her thoughts were obviously safe from others... no reporter's microphone could venture inside her mind… though she still feared that something of these inner struggles might show through.

So wherever she went during the weeks following the accident, Blaire kept a steady stream of music blasting away through her earbuds, just so the only thing anyone ever saw was her head bobbing to the beat. Against her habit, she took her music along on her first trip back to the practice range, and was relieved to find that she could work her swing into form without the interference of that small voice. She had finally beaten it.

Or so she thought.

Her feeling of triumph lasted right up until her first practice round a week before the Great Lakes Open. In that tranquil setting where she had always been able to rise above all things mundane, Blaire was appalled to discover that the voice had not actually gone away. It laid dormant in her mind, waiting patiently for that special moment within the peaceful atmosphere of a golf course. As she stood on the first tee, that voice came roaring back into her head, imploring her with a disgusting earnestness that she heed its message. From the first swing on, it would not stop tormenting her. She had her caddie maintain a constant stream of chatter about whatever he could think of… even if it meant enduring him drone on about his insignificant family and meaningless interests… simply so she would not register that voice. Yet on every stroke and every putt, there it was, plaguing her with its gentle insistence that she consider a different reality… that she was not so special after all.

By the end of that practice round, Blaire was so infuriated with her inability to turn off that voice that she hurled her putter into the drink rimming the front of the eighteenth green. She had played her worst round of golf since high school. There was absolutely no way she was going to make it in competition with that voice going off in her head. Everyone would see that her game had slipped, and they would all come to believe that she was like them… sadly normal.

Blaire caught the first available flight back to LA with the intent of spending a night in her own bed before attending Bernie's pro-am. Once home, she found herself to be far too agitated for sleep. Though well past midnight, Blaire raged about her condo cursing herself for her weakness. She had the will to deal with this intruder to her thoughts… but somehow not the means. It must be quenched. It had to be… or that voice would drive her crazy. But nothing she did to herself… no pill, no drink, no distraction… seemed capable of dealing with that voice. Even music had now become ineffective… which did not much matter since it was forbidden in tournament play. She screamed and pounded away at her skull all night until a migraine came on, and even that pain would not bring her relief. After tossing about in bed gripping the hair on her head, something marginally resembling sleep finally crept over her.

In the morning, with a few hours before the start of Bernie's pro-am... and a day before the anticipated brunch with her mother... Blaire stood before her bathroom mirror, having hardly slept at all that night. She was a total wreck – pale as dirty cotton, blurry-eyed, and hair in complete disarray. All her tossing about in bed rubbed off the concealer some imbecilic makeup artist in Chicago had layered over her scar. She could easily make out in the mirror where the gash started on her forehead and progressed in a slight arc around to above her ear. At least the wound was no longer tender to the touch. Bernie assured her... repeatedly... that plastic surgery would have her looking good as new. He even made an appointment for her to see a specialist, though she was determined to wait until the off-season. She had already missed too much golf.

Lifting a tuft, she followed the jagged line around her head to that narrow patch of bare scalp where someone at the hospital shaved her in order for a doctor to stitch her up. Reddish blond stubble was growing in to partly obscure the scar. She had already come to accept that this disfigurement was part of her. It might get covered over by the trickery of hair style, makeup or surgery, but it would always be there... just like the voice.

While alternately raising and lowering her hair to compare the difference, an odd thought popped into her mind, growing with credibility the longer she considered it. It could not possibly be true... that was evident... but in considering the ugliness to her forehead, a convenient association to her problem with the voice took hold. This gash was more than a wound received from an accident – it was the very means by which that small voice had entered her head.

A sense of relief instantly came over her... that she was not weak after all. That perverse voice of conscience was actually not hers. It had come from somewhere else. It had entered into her thinking through the gash... and having that wound healed over... and covered up by hair... it had somehow trapped that voice inside her head. If the scar could be reopened... if it were exposed for the lie it was... then maybe that voice would finally leave her be.

Suddenly, Blaire became gripped with a wild desire to cut herself... to reopen her scalp and rid her precious mind of the vileness inside. She would bleed that voice right out of her thoughts and send it back to wherever the hell it came from. Only then would she be free.

She tore through the drawers of her vanity, wildly searching for anything sharp enough to mar the mar in her flesh. Something like… the hard plastic tip of a styling comb… or a safety pin's needle… or a metal nail file… and then…

Scissors!

With one hand awkwardly restraining her hair and the other gripping the opened blades, she carefully brought a shiny edge up to the side of her head… and then wavered at the look in her own eyes.

This is lunacy…

Angry at herself for once again showing weakness, she slammed the scissors down on the counter… but in so doing, snagged a bit of her hair between its blades. The twinge of pain smarted for only a second, but more so cleared her mind. Looking down at the strands caught in the scissors' mechanism, a splendid alternative came to her.

Why cover it up like I'm ashamed of it?! Embrace it! Display it for all to see! Smear their faces in it! Be the scar… and be free.

Her immediate inclination was to phone her salon and have the cut done professionally. Of course, they would drop everything to fit her in. A twinge of second thought then hit her. Someone there would surely see her, snap a picture, and post it all over the web before she was ready to reveal it in her own way. No… she could never allow that. She had to be the one to unveil the height of her own boldness in her own timing… which obviously meant doing the job herself. Cutting her own hair, she knew from childhood experience, was never as easy as it sounded. It would take forever… and she would make a total mess of it… though that did not matter given her plan.

Following a quick trip to a nearby drugstore, cloaked in sunglasses and a ball cap as was her norm when shopping, Blaire was back at her bathroom mirror with the necessary items. Starting with a brand new pair of scissors… and being careful not to cut her fingers… she began hacking away at fistfuls of her hair. With a trash can propped up in the sink, she threw down the first few wads with a fabricated disgust… something she felt to be necessary in getting over the hump of what she was doing. To further take her mind off the development of her raggedy appearance, she concentrated on manipulating the scissors in much the same way she adjusted her grip on a club… by feel rather than by sight. And to keep her eyes from straying… for they were a poor judge of the proper orientation to the blades… she locked them upon themselves in the mirror. As clump after clump got severed from her head, the eyes in there showed her more than their acceptance… more than their satisfaction. The woman in that other world was deeply proud of her.

Content that she had done all she could with the scissors, Blaire switched to electric shears… the kind with a built-in adjustment for trimming to various heights. As before, she held her eyes in place and cut by feel. This part of the remake ended up being more tedious than she had expected, for it required her to awkwardly reach around her head in aligning the corded implement's clipping guide even with her scalp. Many a time she cursed in frustration at the difficulty of working on the back, and repeatedly fought the impulse to hurl the shears against the wall. The whole way through, her reflection was there to calm her, encouraging her to be just as methodical… and just as determined… as when golfing.

After what seemed like forever, she finally reached the lowest height setting on the shears, and was convinced that no more could be cut with them. In pausing to study herself in the mirror, she felt a sudden wave of anticipation come over her. The renegade look would surely shock the hell out of her mother… it would shock the world. She could stop here and get something of the value she was shooting for… though that part of the scar on the side of her head… it would not be as prominent as it deserved to be. Her reflection told her to go on. With an electric razor, in stroke after stroke, she shaved her entire head bare… even around the sensitive skin of the scar.

When the job was completely done, and she came eye-to-eye with herself in the glass, what Blaire beheld took her breath away. The woman in there… her true self previously covered from plain sight… was finally liberated. The smile in the mirror came back to her with a sense of deep relief… yet that was not its truest essence. There was an altogether new intensity to those steel gray eyes… a brightness… as if a fire had been lit there to burn back into her mind, scorching away all remnants of that small voice. With its cleansing purge, Blaire no longer beheld the same person as before. The Flair was gone… forever replaced by Snake.

I will be beautiful beyond the wildest trappings of female allurement.
I will become so much more than woman.
I will rise above all such mundane descriptions.
I will be known as the one who cheated death.
And I will make myself untouchable!

She showed up at Bernie's pro-am in a snake-skin golfing outfit she picked up some time back. From the first moment on, she took delight in the shocked expressions on all the faces… especially Bernie's. As he scanned her up and down without a word as to her appearance, she knew he was freaking out on the inside. Throughout the pre-golf preparations, she relished the many sidelong stares and hesitant comments, especially from the celebrities who forked over thousands for the rare opportunity of playing alongside her.

Then Bernie, as master of ceremonies, spoiled it all by introducing her over the loudspeaker as "Blaire 'the Flair' O'Connor... with a new look." The sponsors laughed, the fans laughed, the other pros laughed... even Bernie chuckled his way through it... and Blaire laughed right along with them all. Inwardly, she was seething at their total lack of respect, and purposed to fully unleash the reptile within. From the first tee on, she laced every sentence with F-bombs, lavished her ridicule on the other members of her group for their shitty play, and made a shambles out of every photo op by pointing a finger up at her scar. That, at least, got Bernie's attention. He tried his best to chew her out privately during the break, but she ignored him and repeated the whole act on the back nine. She left at the conclusion of that pro-am reasonably convinced that everyone had gotten the message.

Nobody tells Snake what to do!

No longer would she put up with Bernie's bullshit... or anyone else's for that matter. She would take what she wanted out of life and leave a trail of wreckage behind... if that so happened to please her.

She went into the Sunday brunch on the following day with the supreme confidence that she would deliver the same message to her mother... and shock the shit out of her in the process. The brunch, however, did not go as she planned. Sure, her mother practically wet her pants at first sight, but somehow recovered too quickly... and without a word about the new look. There were none of those hollow compliments that showed how uncomfortable she was. None of her lame advice or endless prattle of small talk to poorly cover over the fact that she was shaken to the core. No idiotic questions delicately worded as her pathetic means of trying to understand. Not even her usual plea that they do better at staying in touch.

It was all the cowboy's fault. She would not have thought it possible, but her mother actually showed a modicum of cleverness in bringing someone with her.

Why him though?

Contrary to his own words, Blaire could not see how anyone could be interested in her mother. He must have an angle, and not knowing it gnawed at her... almost as badly as had that voice. She had been unable to rattle him... as he just sat there smiling back with that nasty moustache of his. Well... she would get even. The last laugh was sure to be hers. In her own perfect timing, Snake would make them both pay.

Blaire took her general feeling of dissatisfaction over the brunch along with her into the Great Lakes Open. From the first moment she strolled into the tournament venue for the opening ceremony, every spotlight would be on her. She would steal the moment away from the other players.

Not steal – win!

However, from the get-go, the press, the league officials, the tournament organizers, and her opponents seemed not to take her seriously enough. She could tell that they were genuinely shocked… just as her mother had been… just as everyone at the pro-am had been… but they all got over her too quickly. None of them grasped that this was no stunt. She was serious. How could they have the nerve to express their cheap admiration at her daring, while at the same time spouting off stupid questions about what message she was trying to send?! Though she smiled her way through each encounter with a camera in the same charming way the Flair had always done, inwardly Snake doubted any were capable of capturing her true self. Soon enough, they would all see.

Blaire entered the first round without the slightest concern as to whether that little voice might come back, for she knew it was gone for good. In its place was an insatiable craving to offend. She unleashed the same vile mouth she had shown at Bernie's pro-am, cursing out anyone who dared approach her. The growing rage within her over their disrespect could not be restrained. Even before taking a single swing, fury had taken hold of her game. She shanked the opening drive into the rough, and from there the round only got worse. After three-putting the second green, she let loose her anger by flipping off a network camera that ventured too close, and from then on at her caddie whenever he dared remind her to keep cool. The calm center that had always allowed her to tune everything out was inexplicably gone. All through the front and back nine, she found herself continually irritated over little things… like the way her visor strap chaffed at her scalp… or how spectators kept pointing their gawky fingers at her… or being made to overhear all those 'bald' jokes from her opponent's caddies. Nothing like this had ever gotten to her before. She was the master at getting into other people's heads… and now their impudence was getting into hers. The round mercifully came to an end with her buried deep in the second tier of scores.

Blaire struggled through sleep that night, and went into the morning's second round with an even greater desire to confront everyone with her displeasure. She was Snake, and they better damn-well take her seriously. With much less subtlety than on the day before, she snapped at anyone who tried to speak with her, and threw clubs for no reason… irrespective of the fines she knew she would receive as a result. Her caddie repeatedly got into her face in order to calm her down, but he need not bother with his warnings. She was well aware that unless she got her shit together, she would fail to make the cut. Yet no matter how hard she tried, the unease within would not settle. By the end of that round, her play had improved marginally... barely well enough to make the cut.

She ditched the visor for the third round in favor of a ball cap that felt better on her skin. From the first tee to the last green, every moment was a battle between Snake, the person she was, and the Flair, the person whose steady professionalism had made her great. Her displeasure at the whole world bounced back into her own face with the urgency to improve her score. In her determination to focus on her game, she sloughed off the presence of all around as if they carried no more significance than that of a dust mite. By the end of the back nine, she began to feel more like her old self... which oddly irritated the hell out of her.

At the beginning of the last round, having spent much of the previous night staring in the bathroom mirror, Blaire finally came to an understanding with herself. She was Snake, through and through, and as Snake, was more than capable of playing the game just as well as the Flair had. And for Snake to have all that she craved... all that she deserved... she would coil up her vengeance and strike at the moment the last putt fell. In the meantime, while in the tournament, she would be smooth and silent... stealthily slithering her way across the course. Snake would happily disguise herself as the Flair while out on the links... if that was what it took for her to win.

By tournament's end, having managed to climb into the top twenty, Blaire conceded to herself that her return to play had not gone as she envisioned. Neither was she satisfied with having sufficiently shocked the world. For the first time in her life, she went out of her way to scan what was written about her. The press, in their papers, websites and blogs, hardly made reference to her... which was far worse than if something scathing had been crafted. One or two did bother to mention that she made an admirable recovery in the Great Lakes Open... and entertained the golfing world in the process with her new 'bad girl' persona.

Blaire had imagined so much more than this. Surely few women could have pulled off what she had done in surviving a near-death experience... yet she had failed to turn that into a dominating performance. She would get even with them in her own time, but for now must face the reality that she still had a very long way to go toward conquering this world.

Early in the morning, Blaire was on a flight heading to the next tournament site. For two months, she competed in a continuous series of WGA events without a free weekend... as was typical in the grind of the tour. As opportunities presented themselves, she pushed herself toward being as offensive as Snake sought fit... except her goal no longer was to outright shock the world. Such brazenness accomplished only a small part of her design. On the course, she concentrated instead on achieving that level of excellence few golfers could duplicate, while in the locker room or off the course, she set about accomplishing her overall plan – to make a mockery out of the WGA... and in the process, bring the whole thing crashing down to her feet.

For years, she had taken pleasure in pitting player against player through combinations of well-crafted suggestions and subtle innuendos. She had a rare gift for deftly extracting a confidence from one girl, and then turning it into a slight against another. Even between best friends, she found ways of tampering with their mutual trust. She did this by staying attune to their feelings. In one form or another, every girl on tour ended up openly displaying their emotions, their hopes and fears, their ambitions and struggles, and even their deepest longings for love. Every such expression was an opportunity for her to drive a wedge into a girl's life. To get at those weaknesses, she sometimes had to put effort into building the façade of a friendship, which usually took a few weeks... perhaps a month... until she was able to discover that one thing worth exploiting.

She thrived on the glorious satisfaction of knowing that she personally had brought about the destruction of a relationship. All those normal people were powerless in combating guilt over having done such a thing... but not her. She felt nothing... except perhaps the gritty, abrasive sensation she often got while meddling in someone's affairs. Sort of like scratching an itch... except relief came in the form of seeing that person's life thrown into chaos. To watch from afar as another golfer's sensibilities quivered in frustration at what had come about through her sweetly secret work of deception... to frustrate the hell out of those who unwittingly got sucked into one of her ploys... that made her feel alive on the inside. Snake wanted more of that feeling. She craved a new kind of prey... and lots of it.

Blaire ended that year on tour with several strong finishes and two major wins. She eagerly went through with the plastic surgery on the exposed portion of her scar in the first week of the off-season, feeling that it was important... even critical... that she regain the hypnotic beauty she had prior to the accident. Not that Snake cared about such things. For her, the subtle sleekness of her scarred head would always be there... only now it would be hidden from the unsuspecting. Having decided months before to allow her hair to grow back, she headed into the new tournament schedule with a cute pixie cut... perfect for creating an irresistible impression of youthful innocence. Her targets were still her competition, but Snake went about it with a renewed intensity... and a plan.

She knew that nearly every golfer had a man in her life... a father, brother, boyfriend or husband who followed the girl around on tour. She frequently crossed paths with these men during WGA events, at tournament venues, at restaurants, and best of all, in their hotels. There were ample opportunities to be alone with just about anyone she set her designs on. In the past, she occasionally enjoyed tinkering with a man's fancy, though never put much effort into it as her mind was on her own tournament play. Now, as Snake, she set about to exploit these men. Overt advancements, she knew, were not her best approach. She could easily derail a single relationship through seduction and an affair, but that would only be one. Too much of that, and word would get around. So she much more preferred the subtlety of strategic flirting. Using her looks and charm, she hunted for targets whose boundaries could be blurred and whose walls could be broken down. All she needed was to get close enough to create the impression that something might be going on... and then let the golfer's jealousy take over.

When it came to caddies, she knew that the lure of sex was not her most powerful weapon. She had known for years that these men were more guarded, as their livelihoods depended upon discretion. She would fire any caddie of hers who got in the sack with another player... and then make damn sure that guy never got another WGA gig. Money, on the other hand, was their weakness, for they had families back home depending on them to cover car payments, medical bills, kid's braces, and all that sort of crap. It did not take much for her to learn which ones were in great need, nor was it particularly difficult to arrange circumstances for her to offer up cash gifts or interest-free loans... whatever worked best for giving off a noble impression of generosity. Nearly all refused, but a few took the bait. Whether they accepted or not was unimportant... just having the news get around that a caddie was being offered money did enough to undermine the player's confidence. A little doubt went a long, long way toward gaining the upper hand on an opponent.

Now... when it came to manipulating the press... not a single thing needed to be changed in the way she conducted herself. As always, she had a gift for bending the truth or offering an outright lie as a means of confusing the hell out of someone in the media. Snake turned out to be far better at this than the Flair had ever been. In a highly targeted manner, she went about tarnishing the reputations of competitors, tournament officials and league representatives... and doing it with a hypnotic smile. After all, the camera simply adored her.

Years before, when she first consented to having Bernie as her agent, all his talk had been about how to challenge the league's grip on women's golf. She, through her cunning, was obviously the best one he had ever come across for doing this, as she, unlike all those young innocents on tour, saw through the league's hypocrisy. But now that she was more popular than ever, Bernie had gone soft on her. The spineless oaf actually wanted her to tone it down.

Whatever the hell that's supposed to mean...

She did much private thinking during that off season on how best to shake up the league, finally coming to the conclusion that to challenge the player code of conduct would be like banging her head against solid rock. The WGA simply had far too much say over player eligibility. Their weakness, however, was their obsession with the wholesome image of the female golfer... which was why they were such prudes over their ridiculous dress code. No cut-offs, no denim, restrictions on necklines, and nothing tight-fitting, flashy, or overtly sexual. There were even rumblings about the league re-instituting a ban on sleeveless shirts. Of course, she could wear whatever the hell she felt like when out on her own... and that she did, personally seeing to it that scandalous photos of herself continued to get plastered all over the web and in the press... but to flaunt the league's conventions while involved in any of their events was to risk fines, suspensions... or worse. Still... all she needed was to find a loophole... just a small window... and she would drive right through their dress code... and make a mockery of the league's good girl image right out there on the course.

In the first week of February, just prior to the start of the new season, a lightning bolt of an idea hit her while watching a women's college basketball game in an airport sports bar. In an instant, she had the player code of conduct up on her smart phone to confirm what she already suspected – she had found an untouchable means of displaying her contempt for the league. It took a bit of a hustle on her part, but she managed to get her exhibition ready in time for unveiling at the first tournament of the year.

A little 'be-my-Valentine' gesture to the league.

From that tournament on, in the locker room, along the fairways, in the private meeting rooms of the league officials, and in the network broadcast booths, everyone was held prisoner to what she, Blaire O'Connor, was doing to the WGA image. And since she was playing better than ever, the fans clamored for more. No one could touch her. She was in complete control. She was Snake, and they were all at her mercy.

If only her mother had remained so. Since that brunch last year, the woman had not returned one call or responded to a single text. Not one congratulations for all the tournaments she had won. Nothing during the holidays, and no birthday card when she turned twenty three. Already five months into the new year, and still the woman ignored her. Even that lazy bastard of an agent had not managed to get through. Her mother had completely gone dark… almost as if she was pretending not to have a daughter.

What the hell kind of a mother does that?

So it was high time she sent a clear message to rattle the woman's cage… and in the process, get even with that pathetic hick-of-a-boyfriend. With a single phone call to her lawyer, Blaire put the full fury of her vengeance into play.

CHAPTER
30

DISTANCE

Throughout the week following that disastrous brunch, Bridget consciously endeavored to turn her eyes toward the future. She was not helpless in this endeavor, knowing that the choice was hers. She was hurt… that would probably never change… yet at the same time was done with being hurt. She had survived one terrible break-up in life, and that gave her confidence to face the pain of another. Already having made up her mind never again to speak with Blaire, the whole brunch now struck Bridget in hindsight as a sadly surreal experience. She had gone to the Butera Country Club expecting to dine with a rather unpleasant person adept at hiding a darker streak behind her mask. That perception got ripped away in an instant. The person she discovered there was someone who was more than willing to tarnish her own reputation at her home club in a show of overt offense toward all those around. This new Blaire had purposefully transformed her beauty into ugliness and her charm into open malice… and to what end? What possible gain could be expected from inflicting such harms against herself?

It had always bothered Bridget that she invested so much more effort languishing over her inability to comprehend her daughter's thinking than Blaire had ever spent in considering the consequences to her own actions. With Lowell's encouragement, she was finally displacing such enigmas from her mind. As the weeks went by after that brunch, her efforts at distancing her thoughts from Blaire were becoming less of a discipline and more of a delight. Her success in this was in no small way owing to her heightened anticipation of each day hearing Lowell's voice and seeing his smile. Whether it was dinner in or a movie out, she found every moment with him to come with kindness and consideration. He listened to her, valued her perspective, and sought her good. Irrespective of where their relationship might be heading, Bridget found herself filled with a youthful excitement whenever she was with him. As a result, a lightness had come over her, both as a brighter outlook on life and as a weightlessness at having been relieved of a great burden. She went through entire days without thinking about Blaire, and on those occasions in which a sorrowful reflection happened to pop in, she found that unpleasantness to be standing at the edge of her awareness, requiring only a little nudge to be pushed out over the brink of disinterest. After all, she was happy.

Not that she was in the least bit ignorant of Blaire's potential for wrecking it all. The cycle of abuse was only in its silent phase. Blaire would eventually reinsert herself… when her appetite for discord once more needed satisfying. That was the way it had always been between them. Blaire would hurt her… and then go merrily along with her own interests… leaving Bridget searching for the slightest overture of softness upon which to restore their relationship. All of those times had been lies. Not once in her memory had Blaire genuinely expended effort to rebuild the bridge between them… leaving Bridget to fret over how she had failed… yet again… to bring lasting change into her daughter's life.

So… for the next time… whenever it was that Blaire finally decided to make contact… Bridget was prepared for the bait that hid well the hook. She was therefore not surprised on answering her office phone one morning to find the cycle restarted.

"Hello, Bridget, this is Alexia… from Mr. Pearl's office. Have I caught you at a bad time?"

"No, now's fine. How can I help you?"

"I'm just calling to let you know that Blaire's appointment won't need to be rescheduled after all. She's still on at ten thirty, so if you could pick her up about an hour before…"

"Excuse me… I'm… not sure what you're referring to. What appointment?"

"The one next Monday, of course… you know… with her neurologist. She's flying in from the East Coast just for this appointment."

"I'm sorry… I don't remember anything about a… neurology appointment."

"No worries… Honestly, I wouldn't be able to keep track of half the things

I'm supposed to do without a calendar app. Blaire actually said you might have forgotten as it's been nearly two months since the accident."

"I really haven't forgotten anything. Blaire just never mentioned an appointment. So… are you saying she can't drive herself because of a suspended license?"

"Oh, no… it's nothing like that. Mr. Pearl got that reinstated almost immediately. I thought you knew…. I mean, she said you did… that her doctor wanted another MRI… and seeing as she got so dizzy after the last one… you know, because of the contrast dye they make you take… she said you volunteered to drive her…."

"Alexia… I'm sorry to spring this on you, but Blaire's mistaken. Please inform her that I'm unavailable next Monday. She'll have to find her own ride."

"Umm… okay… I understand."

"And Alexia…"

"Yes…"

Bridget hesitated, not wanting to expose her family problems to this young woman trying to do her job.

"Never mind… It was nice hearing from you again."

Bridget hung up the phone convinced that she just did what seldom had been done before – break Blaire's cycle of abuse. It had not come about without wavering, as a twinge of concern hit her in the chest when Alexia mentioned the MRI. Since no doctor would order such a thing without cause, it surely suggested that something might be wrong with Blaire's health. Yet Blaire had not called herself. Everything had to be done with trickery, preying upon a mother's instincts. In the past, she would have discarded her reservations and… like a moth to a flame… rushed in on hearing of her daughter's need. The outcome had always left Bridget burned.

Not anymore.

A second phone call from Alexia, not a week after the previous one, sent Bridget over the edge. With an awkward preamble through which Alexia rambled on about what Blaire was doing on tour, the young woman eventually got around to asking if there was a time she could come over that evening to pick up some of Blaire's childhood photos. At least on this occasion there was no illusion that Blaire had set the groundwork for such an exchange. Alexia outright confessed that she had been ordered to head over without calling first… something she swore she would never do. Bridget's response to it all was not her finest moment, especially in taking out her frustration over Blaire's arrogance on the messenger. Without delving into the reasons why, she flatly informed Alexia that *her* photo albums would remain in her possession, then ended the call by not so graciously insisting that no further contact be made on behalf of Blaire.

That whole evening, Bridget sat on her back porch punishing herself for having been rude to Alexia. She knew she had responded more from the surprise of the moment than at any inappropriateness to the call. Truth was, she had been unable to formulate in her mind while on the phone exactly why it was that she still wanted the photos off-limits to Blaire. In the years those albums sat on a metal rack in her garage, Bridget had fought through occasional temptations to reopen the past. Not surprising, the longer she resisted, the easier it became. Maybe that was partly due to a thickening layer of dust that had collected on those boxes. To touch them would leave fingerprints… evidence against herself… but more so, that dirty film served as a constant reminder of Phoenix… and for her to keep her distance from Blaire.

All her life, she had thought in terms of minimizing distance. In every single one of her relationships… whether it be with her parents, her siblings, Mitch, Blaire, or any of her friends… she had always viewed the separation between her and that person as something to be overcome. How else could two people grow close? It was oddly no different than on her daily commute. Distance was something measured against in getting to where she wanted to go… something that had to be conquered in accomplishing her goals. Everything on the freeway… every stratagem and bit of maneuvering… was done in order to make up distance in the shortest time possible. The golf course was the same. Even she, as a non-golfer, understood that a player's success came in accurately judging distance, and having the skill and strength to cover it. The nearer to the pin, the better.

Yet that was not how things had ever been between her and Blaire. Distance, to her daughter, was a trick and a weapon. Whether to separate or draw near, everything was done by Blaire for one reason – to cause pain.

In that moment… and to her great surprise… Bridget suddenly came to realize that all along she had been playing a perverse form of golf with Blaire. Every interaction with her daughter had been teed up beforehand, with her fretting over the best angle of approach, assessing the winds of opposition, taking practice swing after practice swing in scripting her words… and then her ending up changing strategies at the last minute in the same uncertain way an indecisive golfer abruptly switched clubs. She had sought coaching from experts and threw so much effort into becoming a better 'golfer.' In constantly striving to achieve a meaningful relationship with Blaire… and help the girl become a better person in the process... Bridget had kept a scorecard of sorts in the form of her albums. She, like an obsessive golfer, would reanalyze each photo as if it were a stroke on her card, grading each relative to above or below par. She spent hours pondering over her failures... far more time than in relishing the successes... and always with the aim of next time out getting a little bit better at closing in on the perfect score.

All her efforts had amounted to nothing more than playing mind games with herself. Blaire was not some target... some pin Bridget could make chip shots at. Blaire was untouchable. No... her daughter was not a conceptual green for Bridget to reach, nor was she the pin or cup. Blaire was a hazard... and not any random one. She was a murky lake in which Bridget, as the golfer, lost shot after shot... all swallowed up in the girl's deceit. Every failed effort of Bridget's to cover that distance brought a penalty... and over and over she would drop another ball and try again. Not once had she ever been able to cross that expanse of dark water.

Well, I'm not just going to distance myself from her... I'm going to take myself right off the golf course. I'm not playing her game any more. Those boxes of scorecards are going to stay closed up on the shelf in my garage... and not just for my own protection.

As far as she was concerned, Blaire in no way deserved to see any of those albums. Even the thought of her flipping through one with Mr. Pearl... pouring out contempt on the loving way in which a mother kept score... was unbearable. Then there was the ugly prospect of seeing how those photos ended up being used to promote a false impression of Blaire's childhood. Bridget would not tolerate that. The beautiful girl who first took up a golf club at the age of seven was not some cute little angel. At twenty two, she had turned out to be a monster.

A simple text message greeted Bridget when she woke up the morning after Alexia's call about the albums.

wtf mother

She had no difficulty in comprehending the meaning, and in no way was she tempted to respond... for to do so was to senselessly play again Blaire's game of abuse. She ignored the text and went about getting herself ready for work.

Another message came in as she stood in line for her morning coffee.

need photos asap call bp

The 'bp,' she recognized immediately, was Bernie Pearl. Bridget disregarded this message too, paid for her coffee, and set her mind toward considering the impending tasks of that work day. She walked the half block from her favorite coffee shop to the credit union, entered with greetings to her coworkers, and then sat at her desk to discover the next text.

fyi hosting clarity event

Aside from the irony of the misspelling… which nonetheless brought her an unexpected smile… Bridget doubted seriously that Blaire had ever been involved in a single charitable thing in her entire life. Putting the phone on silent, she set herself to work. Near on lunch, she picked up her cell to discover that several voice messages had come in from Blaire. Swiping to the last of these, she hit play.

"It's me… *you're daughter*… again! Why the hell aren't you returning my calls?! You know I need…"

Without hesitation, Bridget ended the playback and deleted that message, along with all the others. With the voicemails, there were also a number of new text messages from Blaire. Most of these were nearly indiscernible owing to autocorrecting errors and Blaire's propensity for employing obscure abbreviations. The profanity laced throughout nevertheless made their meaning clear enough. She scrolled to the bottom of the last one, it being a rather long diatribe against her hypocrisy as a mother. The final line came across as an obvious threat.

Call me now or u regret it donut thing I won drive ur work and male u fade me

Bridget pondered over this for a while before putting down her phone and opening a browser on her computer. Navigating to the WGA website, she went through tab after tab until she found the page for the tournament currently underway. With a significant portion of the field finished for the day, the website nonetheless indicated that Blaire was still out on the course. It was clear that her daughter had been texting and calling throughout that tournament. With a finality made somewhat easier from an intrinsic feeling of her own cleverness, Bridget blocked Blaire's number from her phone and deleted the contact information. She then closed down her computer and went to lunch, content that she would have no further distractions that day. After all, her daughter was in South Carolina.

The holidays came and went without any communication from Blaire… other than a blank 'Season's Greetings' Christmas card sent through Mr. Pearl's office. Even though Bridget was in the midst of an unexpected period of freedom at having cut Blaire out of her life, it did not mean that she was completely free of her. From well before the WGA tour ended in November and onward, Bridget kept receiving sporadic phone calls at work from reporters asking questions about Blaire.

'What part had she played in Blaire's transformation?'

'What did she think about her daughter's persona as a bad girl in a good girl's sport?'

'Was there a rift between mother and daughter?'

'Had Blaire always been difficult as a child?'

To all such inquiries, Bridget respectfully offered no response other than to request that she never be contacted again. Owing to Blaire's heightened escapades on and off the tour, Bridget was also more frequently encountering coworkers, neighbors and acquaintances expressing their curiosity regarding her as the mother of a celebrity golfer. In each case, she responded by politely disassociating herself from Blaire, though sometimes found it necessary to abruptly excuse herself when an inquiry poked too near to the edge of her reserve.

As a result of the unwelcomed attention, Bridget more often than not was on guard when out in public. Not that she was readily identifiable as Blaire O'Connor's mother, but because she did not like being reminded of such. So it was that she found herself at the worst possible time – on Valentine's Day. Lowell showed up at the end of that work day with red roses and a box of chocolates, ready to take her out for dinner… and then maybe a movie afterward. She opted for Chinese not so much for its romantic setting as because it was her favorite… and she was looking forward to seeing him use chopsticks for the first time. The place she liked was more-or-less a dive… which perhaps was why it had the best moo goo gai pan in LA. They took up a corner table and were halfway through an egg roll appetizer when it happened.

"Dude, look… it's… it's what's-her-face."

"Who? Oh… that's O'Connor. What a total head case."

Bridget instantly snapped up from her plate on hearing her own name. The voices, she discovered, were coming from two young men seated at an adjacent table. Discretely turning in her seat, she was surprised to find them looking her way… though not directly. They happened to be gazing above where she sat.

"Seriously, Bro, who cares?! She's like… super hot! Wouldn't you just love to follow that snake head down to where it's pointing?!"

"You'd care if you had a little sister like mine who wants to grow up to be a psycho golfer too."

"Dude… you really need to chill. It's like… totally an act."

"Yeah… sure… whatever you say. I'm still thinking she's a complete nut-job… Pass the soy sauce, will you…"

As the two went back to their meals, Bridget cocked her head about to see where they had been staring. Above and behind her on the wall was a TV currently showing a golf course backdrop before which her daughter stood holding a microphone. Even with the sound off, it was clear that Blaire was answering questions posed to her by an off-camera commentator. Owing to the odd angle at which she was forced to view the screen, it took a few seconds for Bridget to register the overall appearance of her daughter. The first thing she noticed, with a bit of relief, was a patch of short strawberry blond hair decorating those portions of her head not covered by the visor she was wearing. Blaire had decided to regrow her hair. Aside from that, Bridget noted only that Blaire's overall complexion was bright and that there was no sign of the scar… though the visor did block a good portion of her forehead from view. As to the young man's reference to a snake head, Bridget could not make out anything suggestive of such a thing from her vantage point… that is, until Blaire momentarily lowered the microphone to her side.

"What's that around her neck?"

At Lowell's question, Bridget concentrated all of her vision through the eye closest to the TV. For a second, she took the pattern encompassing Blaire's neck to be from a bandana… but then realized that the contours were of the skin itself. After a few more seconds, she came to recognize the thing that started above Blaire's trachea as a rattler's tail. From there, the greater part of it extended downward before curving over her clavicle into a thicker, diamond-banked band that went around her neck at about the fourth or fifth vertebra, coming back to just below its starting point. It then bent downward in a turn over her manubrium, ending there in a beady-eyed arrowhead. The final touch was a forked tongue that protruded from the mouth down toward the cleavage between her breasts. As Blaire was evidently waiting for the commentator to finish whatever was being asked, Bridget unwillingly found herself becoming captivated by how that forked tongue seemed to twitch upon Blaire's sternum with each breath taken.

"Oh my god… it's a… it's a tattoo! A huge snake tattoo!"

Blaire happened to raise the microphone back to her mouth at that moment… likely in responding to a question… once more blocking view of her chest and neck. Bridget noted then a similar snake-skinned band encompassing the wrist of the hand holding the microphone. Whatever words were coming out of her daughter's mouth did not matter, for the stream of them… likely all about her game… were pockmarked with Blaire's mesmerizing smile. In the not-too-distant past, beholding that beautiful smile would have been enough for Bridget. Now, it could not come close to relieving her intense mortification… or answering her unspoken question of why.

"You okay?"

She had not registered that the screen had changed to a graphic of the leaderboard for the tournament underway. Just before turning to answer Lowell, she noticed that Blaire was in the lead.

"Not really. I have a… psycho nut-job… snake-tattooed… embarrassment of a daughter."

"Bridget, don't pay them any mind."

"*I'm* the one who's saying it, Lowell!" She jabbed her eggroll into a cup of sweet-&-sour sauce with absolutely no desire of bringing it to her mouth afterward. "Let's talk about something else. Let's talk about… your daughter."

"We don't have to…"

"I'm serious. I want to hear what it's like to have a normal child."

Reluctantly, Lowell started in on relating a few details about Emmeline's latest contract, but as Bridget plied him with enough sincere-sounding questions, he soon spoke with greater animation. She listened as best she could, yet was unable to shake her feeling of deep dejection. Even without being present, Blaire had ruined the evening.

She struggled to stay engaged through the movie… a romantic drama set in the outback of Australia… as her mind kept straying to dinner. It was not like that was the first time she endured passing references to Blaire not being normal. Whether innocently broached or as outright insult, Bridget was used to it all. It was the tattoo… so like what Blaire had done in flaunting the scar on her head… that would not stop beleaguering her through the movie. Over the years, she had bandied about in her mind a simple question, yet never with the seriousness she was now considering it.

What if Blaire really is a psycho?

Normally, at the conclusion of a movie, Bridget tended to remain in her theater seat all the way through the credits… just in the off chance that the producer had snuck in a small clip at the end. This time, she immediately rose from a desire to get home as soon as possible. They spoke very little on the drive back, made scant plans for the following day, and kissed briefly before parting at her front door. Once inside, she snatched up her laptop from the kitchen counter and made directly for her back porch. The night, being unusually warm for a February in the high desert, seemed the perfect setting to do what she had purposed in her mind all through the movie. After getting comfortable… both in her chair and with the possibility of uncovering the meaning behind decades of hurt… she opened her computer. With a slight hesitation over the wording, she typed her request into the browser and then paused with a finger hovering over the return key.

'*What is a psychopath?*'

She, like virtually every modern TV viewer, had repeatedly been exposed to Hollywood's answer to this question in the form of murderers who destroyed the on-screen lives of other characters. Such individuals were often depicted as being devoid of conscience… sometimes extravagantly. To consider that her daughter might have the remotest potential of being such a real-life horror was beyond her ability to handle… especially since the inevitable conclusion would find her partly to blame.

She nonetheless punched the key, and instantly the internet dispassionately served her up with hundreds of webpage answers to her simple question. She stared at the first of these for some time before clicking its link, as the lead-in sentence already provided a significant part of the answer she did not want.

'*Psychopathy, an antisocial personality disorder consisting of psychopathic or sociopathic behaviors.*'

'*Antisocial*'*… that's Blaire to a tee. She absolutely disdains all people.*

What Bridget discovered from reading these webpages was outright frightening. She found that this chronic mental disorder frequently manifested itself in violent criminal behaviors. From reading many clinical accounts and viewing countless *YouTube* testimonials of hapless victims who had fallen prey to a psychopath, Bridget came to understand that Hollywood's depictions were not far off from reality. The psychopaths she learned about did not seem to be real people. They were more like exceedingly vicious animals in human skin. Yet the devastation these perverse individuals wreaked through their despicable and heinous crimes was so much more tangible… for she personally had lived a part of it. Though Blaire's distorted way of viewing the world seemed not to be far off from that of a psychopath's, a ray of comfort came to Bridget in that she could not remember Blaire having ever physically assaulted anyone.

Oh… but what about that thing with the golf balls? How psychotic was that?! Blaire could easily have hurt someone… maybe was even trying to.

Bridget put thoughts of her ex-husband's mistress-turned-wife from her mind, and focused instead on websites that offered an explanation for the behavioral differences between a psychopath and a sociopath. In scanning one after another, she failed to achieve much clarity between the two terms… that is, until she was able to hone in on one key distinction. Unlike psychopathic disorders, which were linked to true physiological abnormalities, most experts believed that the development of sociopathic traits were brought about from environmental forces, especially childhood trauma resulting from abuse of any kind, death of a loved one, severe hardship, or... *divorce.*

That one word, above all she had read, struck Bridget like a blow to the face. Had Blaire, as a child, adopted a perverse mindset bent on causing pain... all because of the divorce?

It can't be...

To prove to herself that her own failed marriage was not responsible for how Blaire turned out, Bridget rapidly retraced her web search back to a link she had previously glossed over. This particular site provided a list of twenty or so questions developed by a renowned clinical psychologist for the purpose of detecting sociopathic tendencies in children. She went through these quickly at first, and then again in greater consideration, searching back through her memory to a time before the divorce.

Even as a small child, Blaire had never been able to make connections between her words and how they affected others. She relied on false charm to get what she wanted, convinced that no one could resist her. All her ways were aptly described as manipulative. There had never been empathy in her... no care for the feelings or welfare of others. Remorse or regret never guided her actions. She could be impulsive, reckless and irresponsible... wantonly taking serious risks for the thrill of it. If it had not been for golf, Blaire's teenage years would have been spent in complete boredom with all that life had to offer. Worst of all... the thing that convinced Bridget... was that Blaire had always been completely and utterly fixated upon herself. No one else existed in the world except her.

Bridget now faced a startling new reality – that her daughter was deeply and terribly abnormal. The claims of some psychologists that such individuals turned in the right direction could end up doing great things... even in the face of severe social pressures... succeeding where normal people failed... were nothing but hollow reassurances to Bridget. Blaire would never change.

So who was responsible for her daughter ending up the way she had? Too often, Bridget was quick to claim that responsibility, but now... she began to see the past differently. Had she not tried... over and over... to nurture a softness in Blaire? Had she not labored to build friendships for her? Tried to teach her right from wrong? Tried to help the girl see the link between actions and outcomes? Bridget had been there for her daughter the whole time... especially after the divorce... ready to provide instruction, correction and encouragement at the slightest need.

Not Mitch.

In his conceit, he had modeled for Blaire an attitude of contempt for all things... even for the child's own mother. He had indulged the girl's self-focus, exploited her charms for his benefit, and systematically removed consequences to make his own life easier. He had even put up barriers between Blaire and others... none more obvious than golf. In teaching Blaire the game, he purposefully fostered an arrogance in the girl. He showed her how to use manipulation against opponents... and how to play the game within the game. He set up his standard for her like it was some kind of higher calling that only his daughter was worthy of. If it was anyone's doing, it was Mitch's.

But maybe... maybe my working made it worse... all because I wasn't there for her.

From early on, Blaire had failed miserably at making friends with girls her own age... and not at all because she lacked something socially. Blaire could be quite charming... when she wanted to... when there was something to be gained by it. But Blaire always alienated other children... or abused them for her own pleasure.

If only my eyes had been opened to this... maybe I'd have gotten her help... and she'd have turned out... differently.

For that oversight, she now blamed herself. She had persisted in believing that Blaire was only a late bloomer... or that Blaire simply needed help to catch up relationally with other children her age... or that Blaire's tendencies were all just a personality quirk that would eventually be outgrown. Bridget had been in denial... completely consumed with her own performance as a mother... and her longing for a deeper relationship with Blaire.

But had Blaire not grown up with all her needs met... even despite coming from a broken home? Was that not something in a mother's favor? Had she not gone out of her way to further Blaire's interest in golf? And without that distraction, what would Blaire... as an abnormal sort of person... have turned out to be like? Surely far worse...

Bridget, in closing her laptop, unknowingly cast herself into the darkness of her back porch. Her sight, freshly imprinted with a bluish impression leftover from staring a long time at her computer screen, was unable to make out much beyond that of a faint glow coming over her fence from a neighbor's house. It did not matter. Having nothing in the night worth looking at seemed appropriate for the nothingness she felt. She should be angry... or sorrowful... or at least disappointed with herself. She only felt hollow.

As the minutes wore on... with the edges to features in the yard slowly materializing in her eyes... an odd sort of relief gradually sharpened in her mind. Blaire's choices... whether made of her own account or because of 'bad wiring'... were her own. All of those choices were so sadly beyond the redeeming influence of a mother's love. Blaire was who she was... a highly functioning sociopath... and a terribly destructive person Bridget must avoid at all cost.

CHAPTER

31

NEGOTIATIONS

Everything petered down to a halt, for reasons that she… nor any other motorist in LA… could ever figure out. Despite seven lanes available for traffic, the Five had become a parking lot. Although she had nowhere pressing to be… other than at home, relaxing on her back porch… and nothing that evening demanding her attention, she nonetheless could not keep from flying off into a frantic angst over getting things moving. For her, it was not just being forced to shuffle along for miles at a snail's pace. Somehow, she always found herself thrown into a claustrophobic-like anxiety over being confined in close proximity to strangers in their strange vehicles. She never actually worried about them personally… no LA driver would dare step out of their car in the middle of the freeway… though nothing kept them from ramming her car in the rear.

She had spent so much time on the freeway, it really should be second nature to her. Yet the same cycle of emotions always hit her on both legs of her commute. The traffic would be moving along smoothly enough, then… to her disbelief… the flow would inexplicably grind down to a stop-and-go pace. Her astonishment would swiftly turn into indignation toward all those drivers ahead of her who were so clearly responsible for the slowdown. Then, in a frantic search for the fastest way around whatever was causing the problem, she would bargain away her scruples in a mad rush to gain whichever lane seemed to be moving the fastest... even if it meant cutting off other drivers in the process. On finding herself trapped with no alternative other than to wait it out, she would begin the all-too-familiar ritual of second-guessing the wisdom behind having purchased a house way out in Palmdale. Although she liked her quaint little place, she should seriously consider moving... or working different hours at the credit union... or maybe finding a job that did not require an hour-long commute. After about ten minutes or so of grappling with such circumstances... which included being made to crawl along in traffic... she would invariably discover that her mood had fizzled down to a mind-numbing acceptance that she... along with everyone else in Southern California... existed completely at the mercy of the freeway.

This particular afternoon had been grueling enough, what with her being chewed out repeatedly by mortgage holders whose payment due dates were moved up by the credit union in order to accommodate a new accounting system. By the time work ended, all Bridget wanted was to be at home with her feet up and the world closed out... which obviously was not going to happen anytime soon.

At such times of freeway frustration, she would resort to keeping track of the cars in the adjacent lanes as a means of gauging the flow in her own. This was not a game, but instead something of an unarticulated measure of the freeway's fairness toward her. If her lane happened to creep along faster than the others... well... that was only appropriate given how much the freeway still owed her. But if her lane lagged behind, then she would hold that slight against the freeway's account, expecting immediate compensation in the form of her getting to move faster. She adhered to this rigid justice system without compulsion. After all, the freeway never once bestowed on her a single fond memory in all the years it had taken time away from her. So this activity was more of a private grudge match for her... something that went well beyond the normal sorts of complaining LA commuters expressed on a daily basis.

For the moment, her lane was creeping along slightly faster... or less slow, as it were... compared to the one on her right. The greenish pickup she happened to be comparing her pace to was out of sight far to the rear. The lane to her left, equally packed, was making slightly better progress relative to hers. Her marker there, a cream colored van with a bent antenna, had already moved a half dozen or so car lengths ahead. Coming up along side her now was a small sedan loaded down with boxes. She could just make out the head of the driver over the top of a rather large lampshade. Without considering why, Bridget latched onto a notion that this young woman was embarking on something of an adventure in life. Perhaps she just finished college and was passing through LA on her way to an exciting new job upstate... or maybe her prospects had improved such that she could now afford a better apartment in a safer neighborhood... or maybe she met the love of her life. As that car slowly slid by Bridget's, it suddenly became important to her that she confirm for herself the real reason for the change in this young woman's residence... yet a last look into the rear window packed with clothing revealed nothing more. The vision disappeared as quickly as it came, with the spot to her left being replaced by a cable TV installation van whose driver seemed altogether bored.

Odd... after so many years on the freeway, she had never done such a thing before... never called upon imagination to place herself in someone else's car and pretend that she was them... moving on in life.

Glancing back to her right, she noticed that her car was inching up on a van full of kids. Her first guess would have been a soccer mom, except she could clearly see that it was a soccer dad... and with young boys jerseyed for the little league. The man's blinker suddenly came on.

That's a mistake...

One of the first things she learned in driving the freeway was to never use a blinker. Other drivers would be clued in to her intensions and block her out. Bridget eased past the van without the slightest thought of allowing it into her lane. The freeway was the one place where she could exert her will upon others and not feel guilty about it. After all, it was survival of the fittest in this jungle where the niceties of a civilized existence did not apply.

As with many commuters, she frequently turned to music to help her cope with the stresses of highway combat. Unfortunately, her favorite classical radio station was in fundraiser mode... which she considered to be rather unfair to those patrons such as herself who regularly gave. She went to her backup, which was airing an Italian opera of some kind, and then to a different preprogrammed button reserved for the oldies station. A Jimmy Buffet song she disliked had just started, so she continued flipping... largely without satisfaction... until she landed on a local 'all-news' station.

"...the prime minister's delegation is then scheduled to tour several local manufacturing facilities before returning home."

"In celebrity news, four-time Emmy nominee Katie Kleason, star of the popular daytime drama Imperial Wives, has revealed in an interview with Variety Today that this will be her final season with the show. The actress has declined to provide details as to her decision, though recent rumors suggest..."

Bridget punched the button for the oldie's station, but as *Margaritaville* was still on, she reluctantly returned to the news.

"...affair with Daniel Tobias, who played the character Oteria, the young renegade killed off in last season's finale. Ms. Kleason expressed optimism about her future beyond the show, stating that she has several projects worthy of pursuit."

"In sports... attorneys for WGA golfer Blaire O'Connor have announced their intention to file suit against the man who turned a fire hose on sympathizers holding vigil outside Hamilton Memorial Hospital last year. At the time, Ms. O'Connor was recovering from injuries sustained during a drunk driving accident. Her agent, Mr. Bernie Pearl, a recognized sports promoter, issued a statement indicating that fans of Ms. O'Connor have been reticent to offer support for the golfer out of fear of similar reprisals. The target of the suit, a Mr. Lowell Paxton of Winnetka, was recently cleared of assault charges in relation to the incident."

"Turning to the local music scene, bluegrass enthusiasts should expect details this week from the organizers of the annual..."

Switching off the radio, Bridget sat in a daze, hardly believing what she had just heard. Her daughter was suing her boyfriend. Although she continued to inch along in traffic, her mind was racing through the shock of this news. The year thus far had been relatively Blaire-free... except for being confronted with those bizarre tattoos on Valentine's Day. In retrospect, she should have anticipated Blaire getting even for that stupid brunch. Sooner or later, the next shoe was sure to drop... but filing suit against Lowell was like dumping a whole closet load of them.

It was high time that she put an end to her daughter's vindictiveness. Craning her head around, she slowly veered her car into the lane to her right, not so much waiting for an opening as making one. The offended driver laid into his horn... without Bridget yielding the slightest of apologies to him. She continued this same persistent merge across two more lanes of traffic until she gained the exit for the Ronald Reagan, then went about backtracking on the Four-O-Five toward the western fringes of Beverly Hills.

She knew exactly where she was going on this return drive into the city, but had no idea what she was going to do once there. She needed to take her outrage and reshape it into a plan. Unfortunately, all she could think of at the moment was Blaire's disfigured look of contempt toward Lowell at that brunch. The memory of it was more fresh in her mind than compared to the other time the two of them had crossed swords… that being in the elevator where they first met. He had been just as calm then, whereas both times Blaire was…

…completely unnerved!

In an instant, Bridget knew exactly what she would do.

It was eight forty five… well over two hours since leaving work… when she finally parked on the street out front of the building she knew to house Mr. Pearl's offices. Two things confirmed for her that Mr. Pearl was still there. First, the lights were on in his offices on the 12th floor, and second, just ahead of her at curbside was a caterer's van… exactly what she hoped to see. Without an ounce of second-guessing, she grabbed her laptop computer from her bag, walked briskly into the lobby, and strode right up to the after-hours guard at his security desk.

"Hello… I was wondering if I could speak with Mr. Pearl on a rather urgent matter."

"And you are?"

"Mrs. O'Connor… the mother of one of his clients."

"I'm sorry, Mrs. O'Connor, but Mr. Pearl has left for the day. Perhaps you could try reaching him tomorrow during normal business hours."

Having taken in the security guard's nametag on his chest, she cut right across his dismissal.

"Mr. Smits, let me assure you that I'm no stranger to Mr. Pearl. I know for a fact that he's in his office at this very moment… probably surveying the spread he's prepared for his Tuesday night poker game. You do realize that those are well-known among his clients? I'll even bet you've already called up there several times to coordinate the arrival of his caterers." To her immense satisfaction, he glanced down toward his desk phone. "Would you be so kind as to call him one more time? Just tell him that the mother of Blaire O'Connor is down here with news that can't wait. Please mention that this news adversely affects his plans."

"Umm… I'm not sure he'll…"

"Or perhaps I should just stand here until his guests show up."

"No. I'll call him for you. If you wouldn't mind waiting over there in the lobby."

She turned away, not in the least bit interested in overhearing what Smits might have to say over the phone. She was reasonably confident that Mr. Pearl's curiosity would get the better of him… and equally sure that he would want her long gone before any of his guests arrived.

Back when she first learned about Blaire having an agent, Bridget had done some research into Mr. Pearl. She knew, for example, that for years he had hosted a weekly poker game on Tuesday nights for some of the most influential sports personalities in LA. She also knew that he employed alcohol, fine catering, and intentional losses on his own part, all in order to wheedle out tidbits of information about what agent was having difficulties with what client, who was employing what new angle, and what owner, media member or sporting authority was vulnerable to exploitation. None of that really interested her… except to assure her that a man such as Mr. Pearl valued information. Well… she was about to give him some valuable information of her own.

Bridget was only seated for a short time before the security guard came to escort her into an elevator. After activating it with his key, he indicated that Mr. Pearl would be waiting for her in the 12th floor lobby. She stepped in and pushed the appropriate button. As the doors closed and the mechanism jolted into action, she was surprised to find herself calm. Her throat was not dry, and her hands, currently holding her laptop, were steady. She was fully confident that Mr. Pearl was going to be doing all the work.

The elevator came to a stop, the doors opened, and his first words confirmed to her how the interaction would go. She would get her way.

"Mrs. O'Connor… it's a pleasure to see you again. Unfortunately, I don't have much time to speak with you as I have a very important client showing up any minute now… so I'll need you to be brief."

"I'm terribly sorry… I really didn't mean to intrude. It's just that… well… maybe I shouldn't be bothering you with this. I should probably get going."

She turned toward the elevator, knowing for certain that he would call her back.

"No. It's quite alright, Mrs. O'Connor. I have a couple of minutes to spare. Let's have a seat here in the lobby."

"Thank you… and please call me Bridget… because I'm going to call you Bernie."

Her assertion, she was pleased to see, seemed to surprise him.

"Umm… okay. That's perfectly fine. So… Smits mentioned that you had some important news for me."

"Actually, it's for your client… my daughter… but I guess it also concerns you. I heard about the lawsuit…"

She waited for a second to see if he might reveal something, but as he simply nodded, she continued on.

"I thought you should know that I'll probably be called upon by Mr. Paxton's lawyer... you know, to give deposition about what happened at the hospital."

He instantly produced a huge smile, lifting a hand in a reassuring 'stop sign' gesture.

"Bridget... that's not something for you to worry about. I can assure you that your daughter's legal team is more than capable of coaching you through..."

"You don't seem to understand, Bernie. I'll be giving deposition *on behalf* of Mr. Paxton."

"What?"

"That's all I wanted you to know. Now let me get out of your hair..."

She made to rise, though he quickly placed the same hand out toward her, palm-down, as a request for her to stay.

"Wait, I don't understand. What do you mean by 'on behalf' of Mr. Paxton?"

"Just what it sounds like. I assume his lawyer will be asking me about the things I saw and heard around the time of Blaire's stay in the hospital. Things like what you were discussing with your client regarding exploiting Mr. Paxton."

"Bridget, you can't talk about those things. They're protected by agent-client confidentiality..."

"You do realize that you're not my agent and I'm not your client?"

"Don't be ridiculous. What about your daughter? Shouldn't you be considering what's best for her?"

"I can assure you, Bernie, that I'm deeply concerned for my daughter. She's the reason I'm here right now." *Well, not entirely... but that's none of his business.* "I'm afraid she might be getting... how do I put it .. bad advice." Bridget fully intended for the phrase to hang there a bit longer before continuing, but could not resist the urge to get quickly to the true point of her being there. "Oh... and by the way... I should mention one other thing. Mr. Paxton's lawyer will probably be asking me about what happened in that elevator."

"What elevator...?"

She noticed with amusement that his eyes shot over to the one she just came up in, perhaps trying to make sense out of how it had anything to do with Blaire's lawsuit against Lowell.

"Oh, not that elevator. The one Blaire, Mr. Paxton and I were all trapped in for two hours."

"Trapped in… what're you talking about?"

"Surely Blaire's told you about what we went through during that earthquake a few years back?"

"No… she hasn't."

"I'm terribly sorry. Silly me… I assumed too much. Here… let me show you."

Bridget brought along her laptop for this very reason, and as she opened it, the expression on his face changed to astonishment… almost as if he had not noticed it in her hands until that moment. Long ago, she had transferred over from her cell phone the video she surreptitiously recorded over the Pricewater engineer's shoulder. This file sat on her computer for years without being replayed, though she knew exactly the folder it was located in. She even had it queued up before stepping out of her car. Although a bit fuzzy, one could easily make out Blaire standing in a formidable-looking pose over a man seated on the floor.

"This is us in that elevator I was referring to during the earthquake years ago. That's me in the background… and that's… your client freaking out as the earthquake hit. She looks… what's that expression young people are using these days… 'trippy'?"

"How'd you get this?"

"That's not nearly as important as what I'm willing to do with it. If you'd like one, I have an extra copy on a thumb drive…"

With a commanding certainty, Bridget reset the video to play on a loop. This time, she held the computer up close for Bernie, and concentrated on his expression rather than on the screen. 'Bewildered concern' was probably the most apt description she could think of for him. A few times, his eyes shot up to her with genuine apprehension, and it occurred to her that she was experiencing nothing of the kind. Even though she had not seen this video for years… or maybe because of that… Bridget felt strangely disconnected from this complete meltdown of her daughter.

"Actually… this was only the aftershock… which was a good bit milder than the initial quake. Sorry I didn't get a recording of that too. But I think you can tell from the way your client's behaving that this wasn't her finest moment. If you ask me, I think she looks rather weak… and maybe even a bit pathetic. See there… she's standing in an intimidating stance over Mr. Paxton just before the elevator started to shake. Wonder what that was all about? You know, you should probably ask Blaire yourself. Maybe it has something to do with why she's so upset with him… or with me. I really don't know… but I'll let Mr. Paxton's lawyer decide what he wants to do with this."

She closed up her computer with a somewhat formal display of finality, as if the case against Lowell had just been decided in his favor.

"Well… I'm really sorry for wasting your time. I should leave you to your poker game."

Again she made to get up, with him not registering that she had known all along what his 'important' client meeting was all about.

"Wait. I… actually have more time than I originally assumed. Shall we move to my office where we can be more comfortable? We can discuss there what's to be done with this video."

"No… on second thought, I kind of like it here. This seat's really comfy… and I've got nowhere else to go this evening. Besides, when it comes to elevators, you never know who you'll meet."

"Bridget, what's going on? What game are you playing? First you won't share Blaire's childhood photos… even though we've asked nicely several times… and now you want to embarrass her with this video. From all appearances, I seem more dedicated to her success than you are."

"Is that why you took her on as a client… to further her career?"

"Of course! I personally chose your daughter because she possesses the immense potential for opening up women's golf to be so much more than it is."

"If that's your answer, then I can tell you for certain that you don't understand Blaire in the least. So let me give you a piece of advice – get out while you still can. Get as far away from her as possible… and stay away… for your own good."

"Bridget… this… this isn't you. For god's sake, you're her mother! Shouldn't you be acting like it?!"

"Actually, Bernie… I'm not going to answer your question… but I am going to leave you with one of my own that I'd like you to deliver to your client. Ask her this: 'what if?' "

"What if what?"

"Just what if. You're both very intelligent people… there's probably no end to the plausible answers you two might come up with to that question. So… good night, Bernie."

She rose this time and moved to the elevator without delay. As she pushed the button to summon a car, Bernie was at her shoulder, persisting with his questions.

"What else happened in that elevator you're not telling me about?"

She ignored him, but as the doors opened for her to enter, he placed a hand to restrain them.

"I'm not letting you go down until you tell me, Bridget."

To her great surprise, she found herself reaching for the emergency button. The elevator was instantly filled with a high pitched ringing noise that caused Bernie to jump back with his hands over his ears. Exceedingly proud of herself, she terminated the alarm and pushed the lobby button. This time Bernie did not interfere. Just as the doors were closing, she offered him a pleasant smile and a wave of her hand.

CHAPTER

32

A RODEO TO REMEMBER

"And that's when you up and walked out?"

"That's right… and when he tried to keep the elevator doors open, I did that alarm button thing. After that… he just let me go down."

"Clever of you."

"Thanks. The whole thing turned out much better than I expected. In fact… once I got to Bernie… I actually started enjoying myself. I said all the right things at all the right moments… and in the end… it all worked out perfect. No lawsuit."

"For which I have you to thank."

"But now… I'm not so sure how I feel about it."

"What… you'd rather me be sued?"

"Oh, not that! I'm talking about what I had to do to get the suit dropped. I had to… essentially… trick him. I certainly know what it's like to be on the other side of that feeling. I can't tell you how many times Blaire's done that to me…"

"Bridget… you're not Blaire."

"Sometimes I'm not so sure… I know I'm not like her… deep inside… but the whole way to Bernie's office, I found myself trying to think like her… you know… in a manipulative sort of way. Then in that moment when I knew I had him right where I wanted him… I felt… powerful. In all the years that

Blaire's pulled her tricks on me, she's always made me feel the exact opposite – powerless."

"I think maybe you're making…"

"You don't understand – I hate it! I hate how I've allowed her to make me the victim of her warped… despicable ploys. I hate that feeling of frustration I get in trying to figure her out. And there I was doing the same thing to her agent. This's what I'm trying to tell you, Lowell… I actually enjoyed making that man squirm. It felt… invigorating. Like I was sucking energy right off him. I don't ever want to have that feeling again as long as I live."

"But you did it for…"

"It doesn't matter why I did it. I should have gone in there and had a normal conversation… you know, to help him see through Blaire's nonsense… and then appeal to his common sense. Instead… I manipulated him to get what I wanted."

"But all you said was…"

"I know what I said. I lied to him about you and your lawyer. Truth is… I didn't even know if you had a lawyer."

"Of course I have one. Are you forgetting about the fire hose?"

"That's not the point. I wanted to make it sound like we'd already had a conversation when I knew full well we hadn't. Even recording that stupid video in the first place… I did that for the express purpose of one day using it against her… to humiliate her. At the time… I thought I was recording it out of spite because she'd just played a cruel trick on me, but now I know that I did it out of fear… a fear of her. What kind of a mother does something like that?! I'll tell you – a mother who's always been treated like an enemy. I've had that video on my computer for years as an insurance policy… like it was some kind of a secret weapon I could spring on her when she wasn't expecting it. Lowell… every moment with her has been a constant battle."

"War does make a person do things they wouldn't normally do."

"I shouldn't have to be at war with my own daughter! And I shouldn't have to become like her in order to deal with her bullshit! I'm sorry… I really don't like using words like that. I'm just so frustrated with her. She's made me say such horrible… terrible things… things no mother should ever have to say about their child. I hate it! I hate how she's made me compromise my principles. And I hate… baaahh! Lowell, I don't want to talk about her anymore… okay?! Can we just sit quietly for awhile… until I can calm down?"

"Sure, Darlin'… anything for you."

She turned toward her window and watched the hilly contours of the San

Jacinto Mountains flow by. Lowell was taking her on a special trip… something she knew he had been planning for months… and here she was starting out their weekend together by getting herself all knotted up over how Blaire made her feel.

I'm never going to be rid of her.

And I hate having to say 'I hate' to make a point. 'I hate… I hate… I hate…' I must sound like a four year old. I should be above it all… but Blaire always brings me down to the very bottom… and turns me into something I don't want to be. I absolutely refuse to ever curse again because of her.

And I hate this bitter heaviness in my stomach whenever I'm thinking of her. She's so…

Just stop it, Bridget!

Remember – you've forgiven yourself for all those mistakes you made in raising her. That includes every single unpleasant thing you've had to say or do… and everything you've forgotten that you did… and even whatever you might end up doing in the future because of her.

Wow… just listen to yourself. So quick to forgive yourself… and so slow when it comes to… forgiving her.

I do want to… I think.

I just… don't know how.

They had been driving in silence for sometime when, on approaching Palm Springs, it occurred to her that Lowell no longer had a reason for keeping their destination a secret. He had been tantalizing her over the last few months regarding his plans for this extended Fourth of July weekend, but without providing a single hint other than to promise that he would tell her everything once they left the city. Starting out, she knew only that she was to pack an overnight bag, bring clothes for hot days and cool nights, along with sunglasses and whatever else she needed for sitting comfortably over an extended period of time.

"So, Lowell, don't you think it's time you told me where we're heading on this big surprise of yours?"

"I'll give you a clue first. It's got something to do with 'Cowboy Christmas.' "

"That's not much of a clue. Sounds like complete nonsense to a city girl."

"Fair enough. Know how you're always asking me to tell you about my past? This weekend you can ask any question you like… I don't care what it is… and I'll answer it."

"Any question at all?"

"Yep."

"This should be interesting. Okay… here's the first – where in the world are we going?"

"To Frontier Days in Prescott, Arizona. It's a rodeo."

Seriously?! That's the big surprise?!

Before actually saying anything, she made herself pause in order to adjust her expectations… especially since her guesses as to their destination had bent toward something more… refined. Like a getaway at some Palm Springs resort. As she had seen snippets of rodeo scenes in movies… as most everyone had… she could not imagine herself ever attending one. Perhaps it would not be so bad after all… just a bit rustic… sort of like 'Kentucky Derby meets Olympic equestrian event'… with a touristy old-west ghost town feel added in… and maybe a bit of Disney's Frontierland sprinkled around. Not exactly what she would have called the makings of a special weekend together… but really not terrible either, seeing as she would be with him.

"So… we're driving all the way to Arizona… for a rodeo?"

"Don't knock it until you've seen it. It's not just any rodeo. It's the genuine article, going back to eighteen… ahh… something-or-other. I forget. The point is… the rodeo's where I grew up. So you seeing one for yourself is the best way I can think of for you to get an idea of what my early life was like."

"You've competed at this one before?"

"A few times… but I've ridden there more often."

"I don't understand… How does one ride at a rodeo without competing in it?"

"Ahh, well, that'll be a whole lot easier to explain once we get there."

"Lowell… I've never been to one before… I have no idea what to expect."

"Then you and I are in the same boat. This'll be my first one too… as a spectator."

For the remaining hours of their drive, Bridget went about peppering him with questions regarding his past. Here and there, she threw in a few concerning the rodeo, but as they were heading to such a place, she saved most of those questions for later. Overall, she was surprised to find him very accessible when she asked about his time in the National Guard and afterward as he battled through homelessness and addiction. He even seemed rather matter-of-fact on the subject of his divorce and the pain of being separated from his daughter. Only when she ventured into his current situation in LA did he seem hesitant in answering. Not until they neared the town of Prescott did she come to see that the past… painful as it seemed… was something of an open book for him, and he was, in contrast, more guarded about his thoughts on the future.

As it was late afternoon, they checked into their motel rooms so she could freshen up, and then they drove into town. Walking hand-in-hand with him along a packed sidewalk of what he said was Prescott's main street, Bridget felt young again... though not in the bubbly, capricious way that the young women all around her were flirting with their young men. It was more as if all the years that separated her from those women did not really matter. She could put herself in their place... youthful indiscretions aside... and enjoy being with a man she felt very comfortable with. She was pretty sure he felt something similar, as he seemed excited to point out every little detail he could remember about the town – his favorite shops and bars, the courthouse plaza, and the county jail... where he confessed to having spent at least one night. She even thought it rather cute how he built up her anticipation of eating at a famous steakhouse, only to get bemused when he could not find the place right off.

She slept well that night, and in the morning... after a remarkably good eggs and bacon breakfast at a diner... they headed to the rodeo. Not that she was expecting anything as elaborate as the LA County Fairgrounds, but as they drove through a gate in a rickety chain-linked fence onto a dirt-covered field haphazardly scattered about with vehicles... most of which were pickup trucks... she could not help but admit to herself a measure of disappointment in the place. Everywhere was dust, with smatterings of rust and deterioration in much of the fencing and structures all about her. Between where they parked and the entrance to a rather modest-sized grandstand area was a complicated array of holding pens packed with complaining animals... most of which were cows. It struck her as rather odd that those would be one of the first things a visitor might see.

They grabbed the items brought for comfort... seat cushions and the like... with Lowell retrieving a grocery bag from the trunk as the last item.

"What's in there?"

"A surprise. You'll see soon enough."

They weaved their way up to the entrance, and then through a large tent where vendors were displaying their wares of Native American jewelry, leather and wood craftworks, custom western clothing, and assorted rodeo memorabilia.

"Mind if we just pass through? We can come back later if you'd like... but right now... I'd planned to take you around before the events start."

"That's fine with me."

"What do you think of the place so far?"

At first, she was tempted to answer his question with one of her own. Something innocuous like: 'Are all rodeos similar to this one?' She quickly discarded that, as he was surely bright enough to see her hidden meaning. Besides, he had already said several times on the previous day that this arena held a special place in his memory, so in no way would she allow a miniscule blip of her unease to dull his enthusiasm. Her following thought went in a direction she also preferred not admitting. Her 'Derby-Olympics-Disney' presumption was not even close to the feel of the Prescott Rodeo Grounds. What she had seen thus far more resembled 'cattle lot' meets 'flea market'… with a good dose of a county fair's chaos thrown in. Yet every single cowboy-garbed person she passed seemed completely unfazed by the unpleasantness she had latched onto. Groups of kids, couples, and families were bustling about as if in a carnival-like atmosphere. So… she would delay in responding… at least until they came closer to the arena's grandstand. Here, concrete flooring took over, with cinderblock walls between concession stalls showing a recent coat of paint.

"Umm… I'd say this place has a lot of character to it."

"If by that you mean it's a dump… then I agree… but that's what makes it authentic. Just like the people. Come on… let's head over to the main office before we locate our seats. I want to see if I can find anyone from back in the day."

He led her away from the grandstand, in the process passing numerous placards of a cowboy on a bucking horse. Each logo was accompanied by the date of 1888 and the claim of this being the world's oldest rodeo. As they neared a building labeled 'office,' its door opened and a woman emerged. She was clearly on the elderly side, with a bit of that stooped-over shrunken feel to match her gray hair… though Bridget could easily see in her a sort of toughness that went beyond age. As that woman's eyes fell upon Lowell, she straightened up into a stern smile that quickly gave way to a short, mocking sort of laugh.

"Damn. I should call security and have your sorry ass thrown out of here."

"Molly! It's good to see you too."

"It's been a long time, Cub. You sure look fine. Who's this beauty with you?"

"Molly Strickland, this is Bridget O'Connor, my girl… so you be nice to her."

"You bet I will. Pleased to meet you, Bridget."

"Pleased to meet you too. But did you just call him 'Cub'?"

"That's just what my father used to call me when I was a kid. He was one of the first members of the Riders Association. That's a… professional society for rodeo riders. Molly works for them… or used to."

"Still do. So… you two an item, huh?"

Molly's question was clearly directed at her… and she was prepared to answer… but Lowell jumped in first.

"Now, Molly… don't."

"Well, young lady… let me tell you something you need to know. Cub here was quite an item on the circuit. Why, he had buckle bunnies in nearly every county."

"You know that's nonsense, Molly. I was a fair rider at best."

"Hey… remember the time you won bareback at the Days of 47, and that young thing came prancing up to you and stripped right down to her necessities so you could autograph her right on a…"

"Enough, Molly! You're giving Bridget the wrong idea about me. What I *actually* came by for was to see if Kip's still doing the event."

"Of course! No one better than the Hierras… you should know that. Assuming you've not forgotten your way…"

"No… I haven't forgotten. And I'll find him. Say hi to the family for me."

They parted after Molly gave them both a brief hug… along with a wink at her.

"That was interesting… now I've got about a dozen more questions for you. For starters… what's a buckle bunny?"

He smiled… but with a slight wag of the head that revealed he was expecting this.

"It's a rodeo term for a female devotee. Like a groupie. Honestly… I never had much of a following… not anything marginally close to what successful riders have these days. That was just Molly being a tease. I've known her family my whole life. Her father… he passed away long ago… he once pulled me out of an overturned pickup. Let's say I wasn't in a fit state for driving."

"So how'd you get the nickname Cub?"

"Actually… I'm not quite sure. My father called me that for as long as I can remember."

"Well, I think it's kind of cute. I think I'll start calling you Cub from now on."

She was pleased that instead of words he wrapped an arm about her waist and gave her a little squeeze.

"Come on… I want to see if I can find my friend Kip… and then I'll show you what I have in this bag."

With his arm still around her, he steered her away from the rodeo office toward a back lot packed with RVs and campers. He stopped nearly every passerby to ask where he might find the one belonging to Kip Hierra… until they came upon a cowboy stripping himself down to his underwear, casual as can be, throwing his clothes over a fence post. Though Lowell seemed to think nothing of it, she was nearly petrified by the sight.

"Kip? Ahh…. you're likely to find him over at the barn."

The young man pointed off in a direction that Bridget was not in the least bit paying attention to, as her eyes could not be diverted from the rippled muscles all over the man's frame.

Wow! I wonder if all riders are built like this…

She waited until they had walked out of the young man's hearing before whispering her question to Lowell.

"Is that… normal?"

"Sorry… I should've warned you. Any old fence can end up being used by a cowboy as his locker room."

She did not bother correcting his misconception… for she had been thinking only about the way the man was built.

They passed more animal holding pens… one close enough that Bridget could have reached out and tapped any of a dozen or so cows nudging their heads through the bars. She had never been so near to livestock before. All of the westerns she had seen on TV could not prepare her for the smells, the flies, or the muddy hooves. Even the rough-looking wood and metal of the enclosures seemed purposely to be done in the most crude manner possible. Lowell only had to warn her once to watch her step… just as he gently yanked her aside… and from then on she was obsessed with giving every pile of horse droppings a wide berth. On one such encounter, she became somewhat separated from him… just as he was making for a teenage girl who stood outside a huge metal barn… and had to hastily catch up.

"I think I recognize that young lady… though she's a fair bit older than last time I saw her. Hold it here a sec… and watch out for the dirt on that fence."

He motioned toward several clumps of mud that decorated a lower railing where some cowboy apparently had raked clean the soles of his boots. She was so transfixed upon the unpleasant prospect of accidently brushing up against that muck that she did not notice Lowell walking off. When she looked up, he was shaking the girl's hand… and then gesturing for Bridget to follow… before promptly moving into the barn's inner darkness. She quickly moved that way, just as the girl came bounding over.

"Hi. I'm Maria."

"Hello. I'm Bridget."

"So you know Cub? My Tito's told me stories about him. He's about the most famous pickup rider that ever lived!"

"Ahh… I'm sorry… the rodeo's new to me. What's a pickup rider?"

"They protect other riders from getting hurt. They're sort of like… angels." Bridget gave back a nod of understanding, though she had no idea what the girl was talking about. "Cub says for you to follow me inside."

Without waiting for her to agree, Maria grabbed one of her hands and tugged her toward the opening. The girl then led her through the semidarkness over straw-covered flooring and around a series of bends to a long corridor of stalls running the length of the structure. Bright light streamed through an opening at the other end. There, she could see the silhouette of Lowell speaking with another man.

"Bridget, I'd like to introduce you to Kip Hierra… someone I've known and admired for many years…"

"Pleased to meet you. Any friend of Cub's is a friend of mine. I see you've met my lovely granddaughter."

"Yes… she was kind enough to show me in."

"Bridget… Kip here's the stock contractor for the rodeo. He handles every detail regarding the animals… all the transportation, the feed, the care… everything. His family's been doing it for decades. He even raises stock for the sole purpose of competing here."

"You're not suggesting that animals compete in the rodeo too… along with the men?"

"Sure. That's how the toughest bulls get paired with the best riders. Our family… we root for the bulls."

Bridget, who could not quite get her head around cheering for a rampaging bovine, looked toward Maria, whose nod was somehow a more firm confirmation than her grandfather's assertion.

For the next few minutes, as the two men talked about animals, occasionally venturing back into their past experiences together, Bridget stood by silently, not at all feeling comfortable participating in something she knew absolutely nothing about. Finally, as Kip was excusing himself, Lowell held up the bag he had brought from the trunk of his car.

"Before you go, I've got some apples here. Thought we'd have a bit of fun feeding a few horses. Are there any out for the day?"

"Sure. Maria'll show you which ones. Good to see you again, Cub. Don't be a stranger. And you too, Bridget… watch out for this guy."

Maria then took them to a set of small enclosures containing a half dozen horses, pointing out one isolated in its own pen.

"That piebald mare there's got colic… don't give her anything no matter how much she begs. The rest have ligament or laminitis problems, so they're fine."

Lowell extended the bag to the girl. "Mind showing Bridget how it's done?"

Maria shrugged her shoulders, and then pulled out an apple, extending it with a firm grip toward Bridget.

"If you hold it like this, you're likely to get your fingers nipped. Best if you keep your hand sort of flat… and try not to cup it…" Maria turned her hand over so the apple rested freely in her palm. "…then they'll take it without biting you." She stuck her hand through the bars, with the nearest horse taking the fruit right off. "See? Now you try."

Despite the simplicity of what the girl was saying, Bridget was not convinced in the least that the apple presented any more of a delectable-looking treat than did her fingers. On her first attempt, she pulled back too soon, with the apple tumbling to the ground. Being a bit embarrassed by this show of tentativeness, she concentrated on holding her hand absolutely still the second time. Somehow, as the fruit got snatched away, having the animal's muzzle brush lightly against her hand felt strangely gratifying. She did the same thing again and again, laughing with Lowell over how each horse nuzzled their way in… and then sloppily chomped away at the apple. She was having so much fun… moving back and forth along the fence line so the horses had to follow her like puppies… that she forgot herself, and ended up gripping an apple. Just as Maria warned, a horse bit her finger… hard enough to smart but fortunately without drawing blood.

"You okay?"

"Yeah, I'm fine… Like you said… don't grip it or you get bit."

At that very moment, a loud speaker from outside the barn came on to announce the start of that day's events, so they thanked Maria and left for the arena.

In taking up their seats, Bridget looked up and down the length of the grandstand, surprised that the number of spectators was far below what Lowell had implied for this rodeo.

"There's not very many people here..."

"It'll pick up soon enough. They'll run a couple of hours of slack first... before the main competition gets started."

"What's slack?"

His opportunity to answer was interrupted by the announcer's call for all to stand, remove their hats, and direct their attention to the flag for the singing of the National Anthem. She had not noticed it prior to that moment, but all the bunting about the arena... as well as banners along all the guide wires... were adorned in red, white and blue for celebration of Independence Day. It occurred to her... with a measure of sadness... that it had been a long time since she last did anything special on this holiday.

Back in their seats, Lowell turned to her.

"What were you saying?"

"I was asking about the slack."

"Oh... It's a preliminary event. They often get more entries than there are slots for during the evening events, so the slack's designed to handle the overflow. It's open to all comers, free of charge. They run them through pretty fast without fanfare. Those that place earn themselves a slot in the money rounds. I mostly like it because it's low key... and has more young riders getting started out in competition. Let's see... I think we have calf roping first."

The loud speaker came on again to announce as much. In fairly rapid succession, Bridget watched trio after trio of horse, rider and cow bolt out of gates at the far end of the arena, each kicking up a cloud of dust in the process. She had seen cowboys wield ropes lasso-style before, but never in real life and never while attempting to snare something from horseback. When successful... and not all were... she was stunned each time to see the rider launch himself out of the saddle, wrestle the calf to the ground, and then string up its feet with another piece of rope. Several of these episodes took place before she recognized that each rider, right out of the gate, held the second cord in his teeth.

"As you can tell, it's a timed event that takes skill, strength and precision, but more than that... watch the horse."

The next rider roped his calf and then vaulted from his saddle. As he did so, she was surprised to see his horse pulling back on the rope, keeping it taut on the struggling calf."

"That's amazing. They're trained to do that?"

"Along with knowing which side of the calf to charge up on and how close to get. Takes a lot of practice."

"It looks kind of… rough on the calf though."

"Those aren't puppies. Each one weighs as much as a man… and I can attest, Bridget… they dole out far more damage than they receive."

She managed to restrain herself from putting it into words, but nonetheless found it distasteful that any damage should be done to man or beast in the course of playing a game.

"Did you ever do this event?"

"Not often… I was never any good with a rope."

"It looks pretty dangerous to me… even for a professional. So why do they do it to themselves? I mean… I get that it was something that actual cowboys once did… you know, in gathering up their herds and all… but I don't understand why anyone would risk injuring themselves… just to rope a cow?"

For a few seconds, as he stared back blankly at her, she was sure that she had crossed some line by insulting what he held dear. But then, as a sly smile crept over his face, she relaxed in knowing that he was fine.

"Bridget… you have to understand… they don't do it *to* themselves… they do it *for* themselves."

"I don't follow you…"

"In the rider's mind, the rodeo's the best life a person could lead. That goes for their families as well. Personally, I can't think of a better way to travel the country doing what you love doing… what you've been raised to do… and have the opportunity to compete against your best friends. Bridget… there's a connection there that's hard to explain. Besides, what you see in a cowboy's coarseness is only skin deep. On the inside… there's a heart of gold that cares about the other fella."

"Lowell… come on… it sounds like you're exaggerating a bit. From what I know about truly competitive environments… nobody's going to compromise a chance to win just for the sake of… being nice… and looking out for the other guy."

"Okay… I'm not saying that cowboys are saints. They drink and curse and spit everywhere. Hell… some'll cheat you and lie with a smile… and some're as lazy as the day is long. That's not what I'm trying to say. It's more about the… culture. For the most part, it's genuine… and caring. What you see is what you get. Even the god-awful ones'll help a fella out in need… you know, share stock and equipment. That's the thing about the rodeo… you're on your own, but you're never alone."

She was on the verge of further contending with him from within the context of the one thing she was very familiar with – golf – when she noticed a cowboy standing on the other side of the railing below them, waving his hat in their general direction.

"Lowell... I think there's a man down there trying to get your attention."

"Well, I'll be damned... that's Randy Farnsworth... just such a fella as I was telling you about. Haven't seen him in... going on ten years. Hey... would you mind it terribly if I went down to visit for a few minutes?"

"Not at all."

"You sure? Because if you're..."

"Go on, silly. I'm a big girl."

He kissed her on the forehead, and then ambled down the bleacher steps to the railing where the man stood. After the two shook hands, she watched him move along to a gap that opened up onto the track below. As Lowell stood there in the dirt amiably chatting with his rodeo pal, Bridget took the opportunity to consider him from afar relative to all of the other cowboys scattered about the arena. Though older than most, he was nonetheless like them in appearance... hat, boots and jeans... with a big belt buckle.

Guess this is where he belongs...

Without really attempting to make sense out of what she was seeing, Bridget shifted her eyes toward the reoccurring waves of human and animal turbulence flowing past as part of the slack. Intermittently, she would break away from the competition to check in on Lowell and his friend. After awhile, she noticed that two more cowboys had come out of nowhere to join them, with all four casually standing not far off from where all the rodeo activity was taking place. Somehow, the number of them struck a cord of recognition in her.

Like a foursome... waiting for their turn to tee off.

It was such a common sight to anyone who spent time on a golf course, yet why the association had popped into her mind was strange. She nonetheless found herself imagining these four men, dressed as they were, toting golf bags as if they had just stepped out of a country club locker room. The mental image made her giggle. Even though she currently sat before actual men riding actual horses engaged in throwing actual ropes over real live cows, the rodeo still did not seem real to her. It was like something concocted on a back lot explicitly for Hollywood's purposes. Not in her wildest dreams would she have placed herself in such a setting prior to meeting Lowell.

Culture shock, to say the least...

Though she had never been comfortable in it, the world of golf seemed so much more real to her. The contrast was so great that she was on the verge of dismissing all such comparisons as ludicrous… and unworthy of infringing upon her weekend with Lowell… when she suddenly changed her mind and latched onto the idea… just to see how far it would go.

Well… for starters… the golf course is green… whereas everything around here is so… brown.

There was no contest over which of these colors she preferred. Neatly trimmed lawns would always win out over all of the dust and dirt before her. She had always greatly appreciated how greenskeepers maintained a natural aversion against imperfections in their grounds. Any abnormality in the turf got covered over with growing things… or at least cordoned off as being under repair… since the whole purpose was to make the golf course appear beautiful. In contrast, beautification seemed an alien concept to this rodeo. Much before her was in need of repair… especially all the weatherworn plywood signage encircling the arena. The dilapidated feel of the place would surely earn an out-of-bounds in the golfer's way of thinking.

That's another thing… all this fencing. It's so restrictive. Golf courses are wide open… without bars or gates.

Just then, she noticed a cowboy picking himself up out of the dirt and limping off toward the railing she happened to be staring at. It had been a long time since she last saw a golfer get hurt. Golf was a supremely civilized game where strict attention was paid to the course rules… all to keep players safe. This rodeo was clearly in the opposite direction. For both the human and non-human competitors, it was sport at the reckless edge. Even the ground took a thrashing. Every hoof beat kicking up a cloud of dust told her it was so. Sure… a golf club might cut into the fairway, but at least it did so in a graceful sort of 'swooshing' way… especially in how a slice of turf could acrobatically tumble about in the air. Besides… the conscientious golfer always replaced their divots.

As to the overall ambiance of the two sports, she considered there to be nothing better than the dewy newness of freshly cut grass in the morning. It had always been that one sensation she looked forward to when accompanying Blaire onto the course. Now… as to whatever an enthusiast might say was the characteristic smell of the rodeo… she had received a few rather unpleasant nose-fulls of her own to offer as suggestions.

Then there was the obvious difference in the noise levels. The golf course was a place of serenity, whereas the rodeo was a cacophony of chaos. This arena before her was filled with the sounds of animals, riders, announcers and fans, not to mention the backdrop of continuously playing country music. Perhaps the only comfort in all the clatter was that a person had no restrictions against speaking out whenever they wished.

That's because this place is the ultimate in disorder.

If there was one thing she knew for sure that golf was good at, it was order and control. No golfer ever succeeded without those. Everything needed to be done in a specific and highly repeatable fashion. And then there were the rules, the standards and the etiquette… nothing of the sort being apparent in this, her first ever visit to the rodeo.

Her mind was now racing, seeking out more comparisons to be made, feeling rather than knowing that a conclusion loomed somewhere at the end of it all.

Motorized cart versus saddled horse.

The smoothness of a club's grip or the coarseness of rope.

Crisp visors as opposed to dull cowboy hats.

Snazzy-looking shoes versus dirty boots.

Fashionable weaves or beat-up denims.

In all these things, she found her preferences tilting toward the world she knew well… yet did not like.

People were now trickling into the stands at a greater pace than before, filling up the seats all about her. Most were clothed as Lowell was… in western garb… though a few were dressed like her… as if planning to spend a day at the park. To her surprise, those around her went out of their way to greet her, ask where she was from, and politely inquire if this was her first rodeo. In not one person was there a hint of exclusion or condescension that she, as a rodeo neophyte, should have the audacity to occupy a seat in their presence. Their warmth was authentic and welcoming… even though she, so obviously, was not one of them.

And then there were the children – whole families of them – here to share in something that most would never actually experience in real life. In short time, she became enamored with two young girls, not more than eight years of age, sitting directly before her. They wiggled about in their seats with wonder and excitement at every horse and rider team charging into the arena. They shrieked at the failures and sprang to their feet with the successes. And there Bridget was… an outsider… laughing along with them, asking them questions about the rodeo, and telling their mother what well-behaved girls they were. She had never felt this comfortable being with strangers on a golf course.

Unfortunately, it was in this special moment of enjoying these little girls that a cowboy went down hard off his horse and got tangled up beneath its hooves. She saw firsthand how nearby riders quickly came to the cowboy's rescue... exactly as Maria mentioned a pickup man would do... with one leading the horse off and another shoeing away the calf. Bridget's eyes, though, were for the poor man writhing about in the dirt. Before she could fully comprehend what was happening, twenty or so other men... Lowell included... quickly made their way into the arena and collected themselves into a human shield about the downed rider. There, they stayed for several tense moments until an ambulance entered the arena to take the injured man away. As the announcer came on to reassure everyone, the stands all about her burst into a cheer for the fallen cowboy. She was so touched by the whole scene that her eyes actually watered up. Discretely wiping away the moisture, she followed the slow progression of the ambulance out of the arena... just as Lowell happened to take up his seat beside her.

"I hope he's going to be okay..."

"I'm no doctor, but I'd say his knee looks pretty bad. They'll have a collection for him... that's for sure."

"You mean money?"

"Of course. When someone's hurt that badly, folks always chip in to help cover the doctor bills."

"Wow..."

"So... what've you been up to?"

"Just sitting here enjoying myself... taking in all the sights... flirting with these cute little girls here... and comparing the rodeo to my experiences at the country club."

"Why bother doing that? It's like... comparing apples to golf balls."

He immediately burst out laughing as if it was one of the funniest things ever said... which happened to be something she dearly liked about him – no pretense. If he thought something was amusing, then he laughed, and he made no show of trying to hide what he was thinking or feeling... at least toward her.

After he finally got a hold of himself, he started relating what he and his friends had been chatting about... with her straying into one last comparison.

What about the competitors themselves?

Her thoughts instantly jumped to the cowboy who had unclothed himself at that fence. No way something like that would have happened on a country club golf course. Decorum was always sought after by the club member... seeing as many were doctors, lawyers, executives, or some other well-respected professional. They were highly-educated and well-off... whereas all those RVs and campers with their lived-in feel told the story of a far less-refined existence.

Of course… that handsome young man was lean, lanky and muscular. Only someone in the best of shape could do what the riders before her in this arena were doing… whereas to call the average golfer 'athletic' was to stretch the term beyond the bounds of generosity.

Fat's more like it… although that's really not fair to say.

Most country club golfers she knew of put considerable effort into their appearance, as looking presentable… and cultured… was always important. The same could not be said for the cowboy.

Still… there's something attractive about their rugged simplicity. It's… refreshing.

Lowell was now relating a story about how one of those men down there had loaned him a truck for a year. He mentioned that the thing was rather beat-up looking, yet served him well in his travels. It suddenly occurred to her that all her comparisons had been honing in on appearances. Surely there were more important things to consider… such as attitude.

Well… in that case… to be quite honest… I've always had a hard time appreciating the mindset of a golfer. All that 'game within the game' stuff… it's never seemed right to me.

She had no idea if the rodeo was like that. . though nothing in what Lowell had related thus far suggested at it. Still… trying to figure out why people did what they did always muddled up her thinking. She should focus instead on… how the two sports made her feel. It was obvious that in both worlds… golf and the rodeo… she was an outsider. So in that context, summing up golf was fairly easy – it had always made her feel unwelcomed and unappreciated. Now as to the rodeo…

"Hey, Bridget… would you mind checking the schedule for me? When's the slack supposed to finish up?"

At Lowell's question, she snapped out of her musing to awkwardly thumb through the program she had been given on the way in.

"Umm… according to this… looks like… in about thirty minutes."

"Great. I'm hungry. What's say we hit the concessions and then head over to the vendor tent for some browsing before the main events?"

"Sounds wonderful."

She looked back to the program again, realizing for the first time that she had not yet skimmed through her copy. Its front cover was done up with the same bucking cowboy logo she had seen all about the venue. Within were the typical things one might expect to find… advertisements, lists of events and their contestants, bios of selected riders, historical content about the rodeo… and even a scoring sheet for the spectator's participation.

Bridget flipped back to the front cover again and stared at it. Through a good portion of her life, she had held pieces of paper similar to this on nearly a weekly basis. Though every golfer kept their own score, it was not uncommon for spectators such as herself to carry a card along for their own reference. Aside from the details of each hole, when flipped over, scorecards at most courses bore the home rules… the dos and don'ts of being the guest. Yet this program in her hand made a remarkable distinction from anything she had ever been given on a golf course. In a single sentence at the bottom of its cover, she came to see how very different the two worlds were.

'Thanks for coming!'

I don't think I've ever been thanked by a golf course. They always put me on edge… like they're making it clear that I don't belong. Strange… I can't say the same thing for being here. Sure… it's foreign… and weird… but somehow… I feel… accepted.

Wow – the one that looks good, isn't… and the one that doesn't seem so at first… really is.

In a flash, with stunning clarity, it hit her that she had not actually been comparing golf and the rodeo. All along, she had been comparing Mitch and Lowell.

CHAPTER

33

AN OFFERING

Bridget was far too jazzed to find sleep simply because her head was set down on a pillow. Lying wide awake in the dark, she replayed in her mind the happenings from her first ever time at the rodeo. Things had started out awkwardly, what with her being in an unfamiliar environment, but then everything turned around once they were together in the grandstand. From then on, it became crystal clear to her that Lowell was so much more excited about sharing a part of his world with her than he was in indulging himself with reminiscence. That was especially evident by the eagerness with which he went about answering her questions… some admittedly quite naïve. All day long, he consistently demonstrated himself as one of the kindest men she had ever known.

As they watched together from the grandstand, his stories brought her a deeper understanding of what his life must have been like as a pickup rider. He traveled all the time, with his accounts of places and events most often centered around the people – remarkable riders he had encountered over the years, old friends and their families, and individuals he met once but never saw again. Their conversations were not all about relationships, as he frequently explained the ins and outs of the various events. Through his stories, she developed an appreciation for what it took physically to compete as a roper or a rough stock rider. Yet he spoke little of his own accomplishments… despite her efforts to draw him out on these.

Of course, the best part was just being with him. He gave her such a gift in sharing something that was important to him… and not once did she have to be anything other than herself in order to enjoy it… so different than when she had thrown everything at golf in a futile effort to gain Mitch's approval. The difference was so obvious – she already had Lowell's, and that made being at a place as bizarre as the rodeo so very special.

They did the evening's events, and then finished the day off with the city's annual fireworks show… watched from the hood of his car as they hugged their way through a good portion of it. Now back in her hotel room, she had no thought bent toward finding sleep. Turning on her side to cradle a pillow against her chest, she ran through in her mind the things she enjoyed most from that day. Beyond the pleasure of being with him, she concluded that it was actually the feel of the place… irrespective of her initial impressions. It now seemed real… and genuine. Seeing families sharing in the rodeo together… both those in the grandstand and those that traveled with the competitors… was also delight she had not expected. Laying there, she soon found herself wondering whether things might have turned out differently if her family had been 'into' the rodeo.

Probably not… Wouldn't have changed either Mitch or Blaire. They were in it for themselves. Both took what I had to offer and never thanked me… never accepted me for who I am. Horse or club would've made no difference to them.

She was not sure what to do with that conclusion, as it seemed to suggest something terribly sad beyond her control. She tried again to concentrate on the fun… but her mind, pricked by an unseen hurt, kept going back to the question of golf versus the rodeo. Where was she to go from here? She was more than ready to embrace a new life with Lowell… well, close to more than ready… but the day whispered that she was not yet free from the hold of her previous one.

So what am I suppose to do with my anger toward Blaire? I certainly have cause to be upset at her for all the pain she's brought me… and good reason not to forgive her. But… I really don't want to hold onto that. I want to be free of her.

Rather than nodding off into a pleasant night's sleep after a wondrous day with the man she was coming to love, Bridget found herself tensed up over the thought of what it might take to forgive Blaire… especially seeing as she had so many rightful grievances going all the way back to the girl's childhood. To make herself give those up… to release Blaire from what was owed… that would be a heavier price to pay than enduring the original offenses. Putting aside the injustice of it all, Bridget considered it a useless endeavor anyway.

Tell Blaire she's forgiven!? She'd laugh her head off... and then turn it right around on me. She'd end up biting the hand that holds out the peace offering... exactly like that horse bit me.

Lying there in the dark, Bridget knew for certain that it was hopeless to expect anything good in return from Blaire... yet just as hopeless to go on living as she was... with resentment.

Maybe... I need to hold my hurt... differently.

Without a clear idea of what that meant, Bridget fell asleep hoping not to have Blaire on her mind for the rest of her special weekend with Lowell.

In the morning, they took part in the rodeo's traditional Sunday events – a pancake feed and Cowboy Church. At both, Bridget met more people from Lowell's past than she could keep track of. Each and every one seemed to hold him in such high regard... almost as if he were a legend come alive in their midst. In not one case did he shuffle her aside, as he seemed more proud to introduce her as his girl than he was to receive any kind of adoration from them.

Before the final events began, he took her to the vendor tent for a surprise. There, he made her pick out a cowboy hat as his special gift to her... and she was delighted that her choice surprised him right back.

"You want black? Really?!"

"Absolutely... how about this one with the silver band about it? Does it make me look... tough?"

"I think it makes you look cute and sassy."

"I'll take that... and I'll take the hat too."

She purposefully chose not to disclose to him the real reason she was opting for the black felt. While looking at herself in the mirror as she tried on various white and cream-colored hats, she gradually came to view her smile as something not altogether complimentary. Its pleasantness was symptomatic of her compliant approach to so many things in life.

Because I'm always stuck playing the role of the good guy...

Of all the events in this last day at the rodeo, it was the barrel racing that most took Bridget's breath away. This all-woman event completely enthralled her. In every pulsing stride of the horse's muscles and in the rider as she pivoted about in the saddle, straining in the stirrups at each turn, Bridget saw beauty and power combined perfectly together. Even the spray of dirt rising up as each hoof dug in and pushed off was a wonder to behold. Every entry's circuit about the barrels went by so fast, overwhelming Bridget as a grateful admirer of how the rider's flowing hair, along with the horse's main and tail, told a story of speed, strength and agility. More so than any of the men she had watched compete in other events, these women demonstrated a unique bond with their horses… particularly in the way each jumped off at the end to congratulate the animal as if it were an equal partner. That affection and devotion said more to her about the rodeo than anything she had previously observed. Here, amidst all the dirt and upheaval, was a tenderness she had never seen displayed by her daughter on any of their golfing outings together.

Bridget had not planned to spend the drive back talking about Blaire, but as their route happened to be along the same stretch of interstate she endured after that disastrous return trip from the Desert Classic in Phoenix, she found herself telling him all about it… along with many other things Blaire had done to her over the years. He listened sympathetically, and frequently grimaced through the more painful parts.

It was not until they had put the Mojave behind them… with the sun fading over the mountains directly between them and LA… that Bridget came to realize why she was subjecting him to all these stories. She obviously felt it important that he understand fully what he was getting into with Blaire… but knew it was more than that. She needed to hear herself speak her hurt out loud to another person… something she never had the chance to do before. She relived how Blaire had humiliated her in Phoenix, tricked her with the Dr. Fletcher appointment, skipped out on college, stole money from their old country club, vandalized a condo, and generally embarrassed her own mother with a pattern of scandalous behaviors. In getting it all out… fresh as if it just happened… Bridget was preparing herself for something ahead. Somehow, she knew there was a decision looming that required absolute certainty as to what she could remember about what she had experienced… hopefully for the very last time.

It was late in the evening when Lowell dropped her off at home… with her facing an early morning return to work. Bridget nonetheless took to her small kitchen table with pen and paper. She wanted the note to be gracious, yet without neglecting any of the truth she felt was necessary in carrying out her decision. It took longer than she hoped in getting the first line out, and though it did not quite feel right, she kept on going.

> *Blaire,*
> *You've been asking after these for years, so here they are. I*

know you know that they're special to me, so I expect you to treat them well and return them to me when you're done. I have so many things to say to you, but wonder if you'll take any of them seriously. You've hurt me over and over with your

She stopped midsentence, looked at what she had written thus far… and then wadded up the sheet. Nothing good ever came from confronting Blaire. Besides… it now occurred to her what was off with the way she had started that note. It should have been softer… if there was any hope of getting Blaire to ponder on the many things she had done. After a pause over the next blank sheet, Bridget gave her thoughts a second try.

> *Blaire,*
>
> *You're truly a remarkable person. Look at what you've accomplished, and all on your own. Yes, early on I drove you all over Southern California, and you never would have been able to make that first step without me. But even with that, it's been all you're doing. I'm so proud of you.*
>
> *You know I want to be a part of your life, but not at all cost. I'm not willing to take from you what you're unwilling to give. So for now, I offer something to you that I know you want. Please take time to look through them before handing them over to your agent. We've had so many special moments worth remembering. I only ask that you treat these with respect and returned them to me when you're finished.*
>
> *I thought I had lost you when you crashed your car. I was terrified. There're so many things I haven't had a chance to tell you. Things about how you've hurt me. I've forgiven you for those things, but still feel it's important that we talk them through. I want that for the two of us… when you're ready. Know that I love you, and wish nothing but the best for you.*
>
> *Sincerely,*
> *Mother*

This note felt more like her… more encouraging… with a subtle enough message delivered throughout. Deciding that this version was good enough for getting the job done, she went about folding the sheet over… but carelessly such that the paper's edge sliced her finger – exactly in the same spot where that horse had nipped her. She quickly had the wounded knuckle up to be sucked on when the memory came of the way in which she had fed apples to those horses.

When I held on tight… I got bit. I was only safe when I made the offer with an open hand.

She reread what she had written… and realized it was wrong on so many levels. Aside from displaying her old placating self… not the type of thing from someone who had selected the black hat… it occurred to her that she was still gripping the apple. Offering the albums to Blaire in any way other than with an open hand would not free herself… only risk getting hurt again. Even making a point of telling Blaire that she was forgiven amounted to keeping a finger on the apple.

She took a third piece of paper and wrote a single line.

Blaire,
The albums are yours to do with as you see fit.
Mother

She folded this sheet up more carefully, slid it into its envelope, and then wrote her daughter's name on the front. Placing it under her car keys so as not to be forgotten in the morning, Bridget turned out the lights and readied herself for bed.

For most of her life, the garage represented her least favorite space in a house. As a child, she remembered always being annoyed with her father for using theirs as a secondary storage space for his plumbing junk. All those racks of rusted pipe, disassembled valves, beat-up sinks, and cracked ceramics… all of it felt creepy to her. When her first adult opportunity at owning a garage came around, it turned out to be a bigger disappointment. Mitch ended up claiming the space entirely for himself… for the various sets of golf clubs he had purchased over the years, as well as that stupid electric golf cart he bought from a friend. The thing never worked. What with the other toys he got for himself on a whim – exercise machines, weights, mountain bikes, and ski equipment – there had never been room for her to park a car.

When she finally got a garage of her own, Bridget purposed to maintain it completely clutter-free. The only things she kept within were the trash and recycling bins, wall hooks bearing garden tools, and two racks of metal shelving on which she stored holiday decorations and other items of occasional use. For the first year of living there, she had parked her car inside on a regular basis, but soon thereafter began leaving it in her narrow driveway outside. She told herself back then that she preferred starting out the morning by stepping out her front door into a California sunrise, briefly surveying the neighborhood over the rim of a coffee mug, and then climbing into her car for the long commute to work. In reality, she had fallen into the habit of leaving her car in the driveway for an entirely different reason – to avoid sight of the boxes of photo albums on the metal racks dead-ahead as she pulled her car in or out.

On the morning after returning from Prescott, Bridget backed her car into the garage such that its rear bumper came right up to those metal racks. From there, she dragged the boxes… after dusting them off a bit… directly into her trunk, placing a foldable hand truck in afterward. Though she strove to be as impassive as any other cardboard-box-moving chore might entail, truth was… the impending sacrifice saddened her. To give up her photo albums… even though they had sat closed off and unappreciated for years… was nothing short of unfair. Still… it had to be done… and she would go about it with a mindset of freeing herself.

The only reliable address she ever had for her daughter was Bernie's office. In fact, she had absolutely no idea where Blaire currently lived, having never been invited to any of her daughter's residences in the five years since she left home. With just enough time for the detour into Beverly Hills before work, she parked on the street outside the agent's building, unfolded the hand truck, strapped the boxes in, and then inserted fifteen minutes worth of coins into the meter. Clumsily wheeling the stack over the curb and into the building, she rode an elevator to the 12th floor and lugged the loaded cart into the reception area of Bernie's suite. Without fanfare, Bridget deposited the boxes in a pile before the receptionist, handing over the envelope intended for Blaire. She then wheeled out the empty hand truck in the direction she had come.

Back onto the Santa Monica freeway for a relatively short drive into downtown, Bridget kept her mind numb as to her loss. There would be no eureka moment… no cathartic release… no second-thought. The photo albums were already as dead to her as was her daughter. She arrived on time at the credit union, and immediately set about doing the job that was expected of her.

At the end of the work day, right before leaving for home, she received a couple lines of text on her phone from Alexia acknowledging receipt of the albums and conveying her thanks on behalf of Blaire. Genuine or not, the message was far more than Bridget had expected.

CHAPTER

34

PIECES OF PEACE

To her, the first day of the work week was the most hectic. Too many people put off dealing with their financial problems until after a weekend… or maybe it was just her frustration at getting back into the weekly grind. Whatever the reason, Bridget went from customer to customer the whole day, hardly having a free minute to ponder over either her wonderful weekend with Lowell or the monumental sacrifice she made that very morning with the photo albums.

At six, having just read Alexia's brief message, Bridget took a moment to consider what had become of her feelings since the morning. Her mind strayed to the question of what she hoped to accomplish through her offering. Surely she did not expect the gesture to reach some soft spot within Blaire… for to expect that was to expect the impossible.

She left the credit union, walked briskly to the parking garage she entered and exited as bookends to her daily commutes, and navigated her car up to the electronic pay stall in order to scan her parking pass.

Well… I certainly didn't intend the photo albums to be some sort of payment… neither did I give them over with an expectation that they might produce an indebtedness in her heart… if she's got a heart. Besides, the girl holds herself above the notion of owing anybody anything.

As the parking lot gate arm swung up, Bridget concluded that giving away the photo albums was a symbolic gesture. Pulling out onto the boulevard, she slowly progressed through the stop-and-go process of weaving her way onto the Harbor Freeway... the first leg on her commute home.

No... it's more than symbolic. I gave up something special... something I've cherished for years... all without a single expectation... except maybe to free myself... and put an end to so much false hope.

For certain, she left no strings attached to her offering. She neither felt better or worse... only convinced that all her bitterness must cease. She would forgive Blaire, no longer holding anything against her.

As was her practice on the way home, Bridget immediately moved across to the far left lane on entering the Pasadena Highway... well before the many tunnel-like sections to this stretch of freeway... all in order to ensure a smooth transition onto the Five. She hated the unnerving experience of having to change lanes within one of those darkened underpasses.

You know... just because I've forgiven her doesn't mean I'm going to ignore the potential for more trouble ahead. I'm going to stay ready.

Admittedly, something had changed in how she thought about the future. Whether that had anything to do with the albums... or Lowell... or her finally wising up to the effects of her own resentment... Bridget could not say. Only that somehow she felt more... open. Sort of like she had emerged from under a shadowy place to discover a clear blue sky above. As apparent as was the bright California sunshine, it immediately hit her.

How obvious... by not holding on to a thing capable of hurting me, then I'm much less likely to get hurt by it.

Out into the wide expanse of the Five, she fought her way over to the fast lanes, and then settled in for the tensest part of her commute. From there, she went about vying with every other freeway motorist hell-bent on getting out of LA as quickly as possible... before some idiot rear-ended some other idiot and brought the whole thing to a standstill. No way would she allow that to happen to her.

I'm finally making progress in life... so I'm not going to let anything from the past slow me down.

She made the turn onto Highway 14 without having experienced much in the way of congestion along the Five. Even though Palmdale was still a half hour away, her commute always seemed to get better from here. The city of LA was finally behind her... no where to be seen.

Over the dried up Santa Clara riverbed and through the pass... then I'm finally home.

Gaining access to her gated community... and then her own street... Bridget excitedly fumbled through the small storage space beside her for the garage opener. As the door swung up, the first thing she saw within was an empty shelf. Slowly pulling in, she felt freer than ever before... though perhaps still with a touch of sadness.

Outbound Tuesday Morning

Getting a late start heading off to work, Bridget mistakenly departed through the front door and was brought up short by an empty driveway. After a few heartbeats worth of panic over a fear that her car had been stolen, she relaxed on recalling that she had parked it safely in the garage the day before. Backtracking through the house, she got herself into the driver's seat... with the engine on and the garage door coming up... when she realized the door from the hallway had not been locked. Out and then into her car as before, she was halfway down the driveway when it occurred to her that she had left her lunch in the refrigerator. Inside and then out again, she was already tensing up at the prospect of how late she was going to be... and she had not yet gotten herself onto the street.

In her haste to make up lost time, she blew through the tinge of yellow to the last light leading out of Palmdale... and got pulled over for it. The officer cited her for both running a red light and speeding. By the time she was allowed to creep away from the dirt shoulder, Bridget... embarrassed and frustrated... purposed to drive slower now... at least until the patrol car was a good way back in her rearview mirror.

From there on, everything and everybody on the freeway seemed to get in her way. By the time she arrived at work, Bridget was hopelessly late for the morning staff meeting. Her supervisor made a point of saying how inconsiderate that was of her. Now at her desk, she found herself reliving the humiliation she had experienced in being scolded by the patrolman. Resolving to do better, she pushed the issue of being late out of her mind and started in on her job.

Inbound Tuesday Evening

Bridget took an indescribable feeling of disquiet out the door with her come quitting time. She was not aware of anything that had gone particularly wrong that day... no altercations with angry customers... no unpleasant encounters with coworkers... no complaints about the quality of her work. In fact, she had made a good bit of progress on her contribution to the fiscal year-end report. Stepping into her car, the sight of the citation she received that morning… sitting as it were in the passenger seat waiting to be carpooled home… immediately spoiled her mood. She had totally messed up the morning staff meeting by being late.

Straightway, she got stuck in traffic, with the familiar frustration of her commute taking over. No matter what her day had been like, there was the freeway at the end to make matters worse. She could pick and choose with whom she spent time… where she went and what she did… yet twice a day, ten times a week… sometimes on Saturdays… the freeway cruelly demonstrated that she was not in control of her life. She had tried everything to deal with this anxiety – varying her route, listening to music or books on tape, even purchasing a brand new car with all sorts of state-of-the-art, driver-friendly technologies. Whatever distraction she entertained, it eventually wore off… just as the new-car scent had done. Short of moving out of Southern California, she doubted there was anything that could relieve the constricted feeling she got from being held prisoner by the road.

Finally home, Bridget escaped to the back porch, hoping to recuperate there from the hour-and-a-half-long ordeal. She was not a helpless person. Had she not put considerable effort into fashioning this place to be her haven? Had she not also taken amazing steps toward minimizing Blaire's negative influence in her life?

So why can't I do the same thing with the freeway? I just need more… margin.

As she sat there trying to relax… with the first signs of hunger coming on… an odd thought hit her.

Maybe the freeway's not the problem.

All those past reasons of hers for driving so frantically were actually gone. Her job gave her the chance to sit at a desk rather than traipse all over LA visiting electronic stores. No longer did she have an all-consuming guilt bent toward appeasing either a husband or a daughter who cared little for her. Her life was finally her own… and clearly things were looking up. She was in love with someone who was in love with her… and that should be more than enough to dispel her freeway anxieties.

Fact of the matter was… she had been late getting out of the house that morning because she chose to linger on this back porch enjoying her breakfast. She had consumed her morning's margin along with a cream-cheese bagel. And because she stayed up late indulging in a novel, she was slow in responding to the alarm. Her struggles with the freeway started long before she set foot out the door.

She left thirty minutes early, determined not to be late again. Throughout the drive, she kept her eyes out for anything that might delay her progress… construction, accidents, getting stuck in the wrong lane, or any random road hazard. She was especially alert for bad drivers, honing in on those who so obviously did not have their act together.

She saw them all…

…the multitaskers who lived on the edge in bringing their morning preparations along with them on their commute…

…the angry on the verge of exploding at the slightest infringement upon their space…

…the careless who changed lanes without consideration for those around them…

…the distracted engaged in phone conversations or bopping about to the beat of their music…

…the weary who seemed half asleep…

…and so many mysteries hidden behind tinted glass.

Then there were the frustrated ones who maintained a tense grip on their steering wheel, craning their head about in search of every threat and every opportunity. In all of these, Bridget steadfastly refused to see herself.

She arrived to work plenty early, but with an edgy aftertaste. That feeling was so very familiar… of relief in finally being at work, but still stuck in a state of stress that would linger until she had finished her first cup of coffee.

Inbound Wednesday Evening

Having spent nearly the entire day on her feet acting as a backup teller… Bridget entered her car thinking of nothing other than a longing for a glass of wine and a hot bath. For the next hour, she concentrated only as far ahead as whatever bumper happened to be in front of her. She neither endeavored to seek out open space, nor did she allow any to lapse before her. In her driving, she compensated for weariness by applying a purely robotic response developed from years of knowing what lane she should be in, what speed she should maintain, and what turns would eventually get her home.

Outbound Thursday Morning

For her, twenty four hours was as an eternity in the weekly grind. She nevertheless entered her car immediately recalling the tenseness she had experienced on the previous day. She was leaving plenty early again, yet still had an uneasiness over being late stamped upon the forefront of her mind. She was not out of Palmdale before going on the defensive. All of the drivers about her... if they would but get out of her way... and leave the road to her... then every mile would not have to be a battle. All along Highway 14, Bridget fought for control of her lane... while contending against a more unpleasant conflict going on within. She could blame this internal turmoil on the behaviors of others... or having to experience the senseless loss of two hours of life per day... but none of that should turn her into a combative person. She made the choice to be that way. The freeway was not the problem... she was.

But my freeway driving's not a fair way of evaluating myself as a person...

Her mind inadvertently skipped to golf. She had always hated how some golfers played a game within the game... going out of their way to deny others the enjoyment of being out on the fairway. It was not possible that she was like that on the freeway... was it? When she happened to cut someone off... or refused to grant them access... it was simply because she had somewhere important to be. In no way was she *intentionally* bringing someone else's score down in order to make her own look better... just so she could stay in the lead.

Oh my god... I'm actually no better than the worst of golfers!

Moving down the Five through Burbank, alongside Griffith and Elysian Parks, and then onto the Pasadena Highway, her sight naturally turned toward the emerging city skyline... just as had happened on nearly every morning commute in the past. This time something was different. Her usual dread over fighting the last vestige of traffic before reaching the parking garage had somehow lessened... being replaced by a rather nondescript sensation. She actually belonged to this city... and suddenly found herself wanting to do better by it.

Inbound Thursday Evening

Sometime in the late afternoon, Bridget received a phone call from Lowell, and just by his subdued greeting, she knew that something bad had happened.

"Umm... I'm sorry to be interrupting your work day."

"Lowell... what's the matter? You sound really..."

"Ellie died yesterday. Stroke... I think."

"I'm so sorry, Lowell... I'm so terribly sorry. I know she was special. Would you like to meet after work?"

"Thanks... I'd love to see you. To be honest... I wasn't even going to tell you until this weekend... but I just found out that her family's shipping her ashes back east. Even though Ellie's lived here for the last twenty years, they're not planning on doing a service here. It'll be in some small town in Delaware. Bridget… nobody knew her there. I really think I need to attend… if for no other reason than to give voice to who Ellie was during the last few years of her life."

"Would you… like me to come with you? I'm sure I could get time off…"

"No… that's sweet of you to offer… but I'd actually prefer going alone. I hope you understand…"

"Of course… do whatever you need to do. You know I'm here for you."

In the hour following the call, Bridget thought only about leaving work as soon as possible so she could see Lowell. Driving to the nursing home, she took him out to dinner… though they ended up spending little time talking about Ellie, as she could tell that he was still processing the loss. Ellie was not the first resident at the nursing home she knew of to have passed away, but she was Lowell's favorite.

After they finished eating, she took him back to his car, and then made her way home. It was fully dark when she found herself moving through the gloomiest section of Highway 14. A somberness had settled over her mood… partly because of Lowell's loss… but ashamedly also from her having allowed herself to consider the question of whether anybody would remember her with the same fondness.

Inbound Friday Morning

She awoke in sadness over Ellie, but oddly also with thoughts turned toward Lowell's kindness. Sincerely wanting to be more like him, she set out on the morning drive purposing to adopt a kinder mindset. Where previously she had seen herself in competition with everyone on the road, she now endeavored to offer her cooperation to those who frantically strove to get ahead. She drove as if she was giving away her photo albums… with the same approach she had taken in feeding those horses… with an open hand. She yielded the faster lanes to others and curbed her own aggressive instincts.

In short time, she began to see her fellow commuters in a different light. These were not freeway warriors… neither were they inherently evil. In their aggressive driving, they were not savagely bent by an insidious lust for control of the road. They were just normal people… like her… trying to survive the morning commute. The sad truth was… by keeping track of offenses, she had always been her own worst enemy.

"That car cut in front of me … and that driver's following too close… and

that guy had no right flipping me off.

It was all meaningless competition… the very thing she hated about the dark side of golf.

All about her, the Five was packed with harried drivers just like her, so it was hardly a stretch to imagine that many had experienced heartbreak in their lives… divorces as traumatic as hers. Some might be parents struggling to reach a child… just as she had. They had jobs… just as she did… with responsibilities pressing in so intensely that their burdens could not but spill over into the insanity of the freeway. They were living from paycheck to paycheck, grappling with poor health or dangers she would surely crumble under. Maybe some even recently lost a loved one… and nothing in this world would ever be the same. Others were likely a source of pain to their families, friends and coworkers… and here on the freeway, these thoughtless ones went about with the same reckless disregard. Even in the many truckers barreling along with their monstrous loads, Bridget now saw something different – a loneliness spent in hauling over great distances the types of things that she, as a consumer, took for granted.

With a bit of margin in her morning routine, she could now afford the time it took to be considerate. She could be a small positive influence, withholding judgment and offering allowances. She gave and they took, and not once was she dissatisfied with herself. And what did it cost her? She still arrived to work on time… and in a better state of mind… for the freeway never held her captive for long.

Inbound Friday Evening

She left work surprised with herself – she was actually excited about starting in on her commute. Before, the freeway was nothing more than a place she had to be in order to get where she wanted to go. She had always viewed it as wasted time. But in reflecting on the sadness of Ellie's death, it struck her as such a shame that she had ever considered her time on the road… or any time… to be worthless. Life was too precious. She had no illusions that sitting in a car for two hours a day could amount to anything as enjoyable as relaxing on her back porch… or being with Lowell… yet now she saw the time to be like any other moment in life – an opportunity.

Freeway or fairway… neither was something so simple as a stretch of distance that needed to be traversed in getting from a start to a finish. Sure… there were road hazards along the way… just as in golf. The golfer and the motorist both endured the frustrations of waiting on slower ones ahead…

or being taken off course… or having made a simple mistake. Yet the golfer enjoyed being on the fairway as much as they did on the green or tee. They took in the grass… and the sky… and all of the beauty that was open space. Why should it be any different on the freeway?

So it was up to her – the solitary traveler – to view the freeway as the golfer did the fairway. There were interesting things to take in along the way… if she would but look… places to exit and reenter… along with rules and lanes that offered equality to all. In fact, if she were so inclined, she could explore as far as she might care to travel, for there was ample distance to be freely had on the road. But most of all, the freeway gave her such a rare gift – time alone each day to consider herself.

CHAPTER
35

WISH UPON A FALLING STAR

Blaire jolted upright at the alarm's shrill. Responding entirely by impulse, she pitched over onto her side, stretched an arm across the king-size bed, and silenced the thing with a fist brought down sharply upon its snooze button. Flopping back down, she lay motionless in search of the reason for having been awoken. Nothing came to mind... other than the obvious. She was still so very tired.

Ten more minutes... that's all I need. Then I'll get up...

Now somewhat alert, the things of this new day began pressing in on her, each taking hold of a piece of her waking mind. This, she realized, was the shit-day... all those hassles she had to endure in order to do what she loved most.

Golf used to be fun...

That is, until all the league's nonsense got in the way. Item by item, a torrent of a timeline began reconstituting itself in her blurry thinking, forcing her to accept what the day had in store... whether she wanted it to or not... assuming she could but manage to get herself out of bed to start the whole thing rolling.

Instead, she continued as she was – eyes and ears fully open, with the rest of her remaining as still as sleep. The pre-dawn twilight creeping in around the rim of the curtains was insufficient for her to make out anything in the room with much clarity. She nonetheless swiveled her eyes about in search of something capable of making her move. Nothing was all that interesting… desk, dresser, side tables, lamp, chair, TV… all the usual cheap hotel crap she had become familiar with over the years.

Her attention came to rest on something unexpected – a subtle movement taking place nearly overhead. In straining to focus in the gloom, it was several seconds before she recognized the source – a strand of dust-covered spider web dangling from the stuccoed ceiling. As she watched it gently sway… hypnotically waving at her in a pattern of back and forth flexes to the will of some unseen air current… it occurred to her that even though this insignificant little oddity did not belong in the room, it was the only truly distinctive thing here… other than herself. In following how this piece of web fluttered about, its movement seemed to reinforce a notion that she had forgotten of late. Through its carefree ease, the strand reminded her not to be concerned with anything. She was special. No one even came close to her. And in response to this acknowledgement of hers, the thread offered a little noiseless tremor… as if reassuring her with a promise of endless sleep. Blaire smiled and closed off her eyes.

The alarm clock disagreed. More angry than before, it screamed out that she would not be given another opportunity to snooze. She flung the covers off and rose, determined to yank the cord out of the wall. Instead, while gripping the clock in both hands, she reluctantly settled on just turning off its alarm.

Five thirty nine… shit. Better get my ass in gear…

She pulled down the spider strand, momentarily searching for it in her fist before wiping her palm across the comforter. Moving on to the bathroom for a quick shower, her thoughts had already turned back to the day's schedule. She had been over and over every detail with her caddie, and knew exactly where she needed to be and when. Still… a vague dissatisfaction over something about this tournament kept nipping at her confidence… or at least was trying to. In reminding herself of the lunchtime practice session, the annoying little thing came clear in her mind. Her wedge was not playing crisply off this course's strain of zoysia turf. Not nearly enough spin to her liking. That definitely needed to be addressed before tomorrow's first round.

Damn! There's no way of getting there today.

What if… What if I skip out on breakfast with what's-her-face… that'd give me… thirty… forty minutes with the wedge.

She hated altering her schedule for anyone… especially for some idiot greenskeeper from eons ago who happened to have planted the wrong grass. All the work she had invested toward getting into the head of that up-and-coming newbie from… wherever… would be wasted if she stood that girl up for breakfast. Of course, it had only been fifteen minutes spent at last night's party listening to the brat whine about her feelings for some idiot boyfriend she was missing while on tour… but having to endure that ordeal was excruciating enough.

It's not like leaving that twerp waiting at the country club dining room won't accomplish something. 'Oh my! I'm so sorry! Was our breakfast for today?! We'll have to reschedule.' Hilarious! She'll be flustered all day.

Blaire finished up blow-drying her hair while downing a granola bar, then went about dressing, making sure she picked out the shirt and visor with the appropriate logo. Her sponsor expected an appearance at eight thirty for photos before the tournament's requisite clinic at nine. Another morning wasted with some pathetic charity group. She had been fighting an unsuccessful guerilla war against the league, dropping F-bombs and putting on tantrums in order to get out of those ridiculous public relations chores. Everything she did backfired. The more she acted out, the more the fans wanted a piece of her attitude. No way was the league going to allow her popularity to go untapped. Not surprising, Bernie gushed over how pleased he was that her image kept paying off with new sponsorships.

"Power through it, Blaire. Just like your drives!"

Idiot… what's he know about golf anyway?!

All dressed, she looked at herself one last time in the bathroom mirror, feeling a bit sullied that she could not bring herself to wear whatever she wanted to. Fortunately, her snake tattoo could still be seen… part of it, at least.

I swear… one of these days it's going to be cut offs and a tank-top… just to show those morons who's boss.

She knew, of course, that the league was in full control… and the admission gnawed at her.

Seeing as there would be no time for returning to the room, she prepared her garment bag with another golfing outfit… this one bearing the logo of the corporate sponsor hosting the afternoon's pro-am… along with her makeup kit, a dress, heels and hose for the tournament dinner that evening. She tucked a water bottle into the side pocket of her backpack and left the room, heading directly for the hotel parking lot.

Another tournament with a boring midsized sedan. She stood before this one feeling like a bull fighter vainly taunting a milk cow into action. The morons at her travel agency screwed up yet again, failing to get her reservation in early enough to secure a classier car. No matter how many times she told them '*Porsche,*' she always seemed to end up with a piece of junk instead.

Her first order of business on reaching the course was to take a cart out to the opening holes of the front nine for a good look at the dew that had collected overnight. Despite her protests, she seemed more often to get stuck with one of the early morning slots on the first day of a tournament. From there on out, she would be one of the leaders granted later starting times for the following rounds… but tomorrow she would have to deal with the damp greens. With her putter in hand, she went about stroking a couple of balls around in order to get a feel for how the moisture would come into play. Other girls were out there too… but she ignored them… as they did her.

Back to the clubhouse by seven thirty, she checked in at the equipment room to make sure her caddie had done his job. Sure enough, her backup clubs were ready for the afternoon's circus of a pro-am. She inspected them briefly, satisfying herself that all was in order, and then left for the ladies' locker room. Waiting patiently in the private space assigned to her were her tournament clubs – her lovers – safely stowed away. She exchanged the putter for the pitching wedge and three iron, tucking both under one arm before leaving the locker room. Thinking about how good it was going to feel tearing up the course tomorrow, Blaire suddenly came up short on stepping outside. Along one wall were many baskets of tournament range balls, each one embossed with the three letter logo of the home course – Overland Country Club.

What a bunch of incompetent morons! These should be waiting out at the range.

Shaking off her irritation, Blaire wrapped her fingers about the metal loops on two buckets, sixty balls in all, and lugged them out toward the pitching range… vaguely aware of having done something similar in the distant past. She pushed the thought from her mind in moving around the practice green… already occupied by several of her competitors and their caddies. Climbing a slight rise, she came to a stop at its crest.

Shit!

Not being the first one to the pitching range was not the problem… it was whom she would be sharing the area with – Cho and her inseparable father. The golfer looked up briefly and then went back to her practice. Cho Senior, on the other hand, turned his natural frown into a sneer. She could almost read his mind… his daughter had bested her in three of their last eight events together. Nearly as bad, the old man kept such a watchful eye on his daughter that Blaire had not yet been able to get anywhere near her.

She moved past them to a secondary green and went to work. As she suspected, the rough was not nearly springy enough, with each ball sinking in deeper than she preferred. For twenty minutes or so Blaire alternated between her wedge and the three iron in getting a feel for what it would take to pitch and run a ball out of this grass. With ten minutes remaining to freshen up… which meant transforming herself into a god-awful princess for her sponsor… she left the pitching range for the ladies' locker room.

The photo shoot ended up being like every one before it… and likely as every one after. She shook hands, smiled for the camera, and provided totally banal aspirations for the week. Shit like 'I'll do my best' and 'I'm just so happy to represent your brand.' After about thirty minutes of that crap, she felt a tournament lackey touch her on the elbow, directing her to a secondary putting green. It was time for the clinic.

Right off, she noticed that the flavor of the week was inner-city kids, most of whom she was well-aware had absolutely no interest in golf. All of their excitement was simply over having a field trip spare them from the drudgery of school. She scanned the group of children assigned to her, not looking for any who might have an appreciation for the game. She could not care less about taking part in transforming any of these young lives from poverty into a dream-come-true with a single word of encouragement from her, a pro. She was searching for the sick ones. Find them first, and then steer clear. With the others, she might venture close enough for a photo, but no touching… not even a pat on the back. Of course, all they were interested in was seeing her ink. Not one cared a lick about what it took to master the most difficult game on the planet. She signed a few visors… the tournament's gift to each child… knowing full well that most would end up in the trash or be left on the school bus back into the city.

For this particular clinic, she happened to be paired with Schultz… or 'Schultzee' as she was endearingly referred to around the league. Their job today was teaching the kids how to putt.

Totally ridiculous.

Blaire stepped away from the dozen kids clustered about, allowing Schultz's blond hair and pretty face to do the talking for the both of them. She was not a bad golfer… and rather easy to manipulate… perhaps because her English was only marginal. Blaire used that to her advantage, telling Schultz it would be good practice for her to do all the talking. Besides, the kids ate up the German accent. From time to time… as the brats went about whacking each other with their pint-sized putters… Schultz managed a question or two for her… mostly the typical shit about what it was like to grow up in Hollywood.

The girl, like so many of her competitors, never mustered the guts to ask about her bad girl image.

At quarter to eleven, the tourney staff came around to herd the kids toward tents setup for lunch. Without saying goodbye to Schultz, Blaire headed in the opposite direction – toward the locker room for her clubs and another bucket of balls. Her caddie joined her at the driving range, and as per their plan, brought sandwiches from the spread laid out in the country club's dining room. Though he went about downing everything in sight, she ate sparingly, fearful of food poisoning that might ruin her first round.

While she was in the clinic, he took a cart over the tournament course… just as she had done on the day before… and together they went about laying out a strategy for the opening round. She could easily tolerate this guy Curtis as a caddie, as he was not afraid of speaking his mind and had absolutely no patience for the meddling bullshit of the media. Their planning session went fairly well, with only a mild disagreement over how the wind would come into play on the back nine.

She left her tournament clubs with him, taking the spare set he brought along, and headed for the one o'clock pro-am… the league's version of prostitution. She paid absolutely no attention during the introductions, not caring in the least about who was a local celebrity, politician, rich executive, or prominent member of the host club. To her, they were nothing more than all male and all horny… irrespective of how many thousands of charitable dollars they laid down in exchange for being paired with their favorite player. She had been to so many of these events, and knew well what was coming. Some participants were determined to show off, and some were actually delusional enough to think that they could have made it as a pro. Most just wanted to brag about having played along side a WGA star. She was totally used to the innuendos, the occasional touching, and the veiled hopes for something more. As far as she was concerned, these old perverts could cozy up to her as close as they dared, for all she gave them was the privilege of seeing their pride decimated by a woman on the club's junk course.

Today, she was grouped with the owner of a resort hotel and an investment banker… both of whose names went in and out of her memory before reaching the first tee.

Mercifully, the pro-am round… a tedious blur… was over by six, giving her time in the ladies' locker room for a shower and a change into her dinner dress. She then had to endure several hours of these pro-am idiots getting drunk and droning on about their exploits on and off the course. The pre-dinner cocktail party was as boring as ever... as was the long, drawn-out speech by the club president. At least the meal was decent – some kind of small game bird. Tomorrow and onward through the rest of the tournament would be nothing but room service.

As expected, she was interviewed several times during the evening, offering the usual meaningless platitudes about the course, the sponsors, and the league. Through it all, she tolerated so many faceless handshakes, well-wishes from nobodies, and hands laid softly upon her bare shoulders. Her mind had already switched over to the next day. She offered her prediction to a reporter as to the opening round... and then was free. Having gained the country club's foyer, she took out her cell phone and touched base with Curtis. He too was ready for the morning.

Back to her rental, with a short drive to her hotel, she was soon in bed. The room's pillows were pathetic, though she always travelled with her own. She set an alarm, knowing that a call from Curtis would act as a backup. One more brief look over the course distances and her notes before she turned out the lights at eleven thirty.

From wherever it came, Blaire could not say. Perhaps something during that day served as a subtle reminder. Her last thought before falling asleep was so very odd.

I wonder what Mother's doing right now?

"I rather think you're testing me..."

"Ahh... course not."

"You're still worried about me... aren't you?"

"Poof! Don't be ridiculous. Just making sure you don't mind."

"Like I already said... I'm absolutely fine with it. But I am curious as to why this would be something *you* chose to do on our Sunday afternoon together."

"Consider it... me expanding my horizons into something new."

"Well... expand this horizon – I'm totally over Blaire. You want to watch women's golf on TV... then that's fine by me. I'm more than happy to sit with you and interpret what's going on."

"So... seeing her again... that won't cause you any problems?"

She chose not to answer, tipping her head a bit and smiling at him in a more meaningful way than words could accomplish. He turned back to the TV, making a bit of a show out of fussing with his remote like it was the first time he ever used it. She caught enough of those sly little glances back at her to figure out what he was really up to. He was not testing her. He knew what she knew in her heart to be true. She still had a mother's love for her daughter… would still root for her to succeed in life… yet was no longer at the mercy of those old ways of thinking. She did not mind in the least seeing her daughter again… on TV… because she had finally managed to untether herself.

"You know… putting her completely out of your mind won't really solve anything…"

"I'm no longer trying to solve Blaire. Blaire has to solve Blaire."

He gave her a little nod, accompanied by a deeper smile, before turning to a directory of TV channels. That revealed more than he might have intended. He liked her answer… that she was sure of… but for the first time she had a sneaking suspicion that they were actually about to watch Blaire's tournament for him. Of course, that was not something she would point out. Outwardly, he was the rugged cowboy, even though inside was a tender spirit. She would gladly watch Blaire… enduring whatever fleeting hurtful memories or newfound embarrassments that might come… simply to know he cared.

She was absolutely tearing up this course… just as she expected to do. Though the first round had not brought her much separation from the rest of the field, the groundwork she laid in the days prior to the tournament finally paid off in the next two rounds. She slowly crept ahead by getting into the minds of her competition. In carefully planned-out encounters, Blaire strategically went about poking at the weaknesses of those who posed the greatest threat. She nonchalantly asked one competitor about her dying grandmother… right before the girl took to the tee. She made sure of being overheard while raving about how handsome another's husband was… knowing that the girl had witnessed them laughing together in the hotel lobby on the previous night. With outward indignation, she made reference several times to a rumor… one she had secretly started herself… regarding how certain American players kept complaining about how badly the Koreans smelled. She borrowed without returning, promised without keeping, and sympathized without an ounce of feeling. Best of all, no one could lay a finger of blame on her. Blaire was three strokes in the lead at the beginning of the final round… and no longer gave a flip over what anyone else did in the tournament.

The truest sign of her success during the opening holes of this final round was that Curtis left her be. He knew, as she did, that all he had to do was hand over whatever club she demanded and then stay the hell out of her way. For the entire front nine, she maintained a commanding air… not smiling for the cameras… not interacting with the galleries… not acknowledging anyone's existence. It was just her, the course, and her clubs. By design, all that changed on the back nine. As her lead widened by another stroke, she outwardly adopted the demeanor of the grateful victor, smiling, waving, and bubbling over with enthusiasm. Everyone… even Curtis… was eating it up. Not a single thing went the least bit wrong… until the 16th.

She would never admit it, but Curtis happened to be right about the wind. Her drive caught too much air and was pushed off-center by a cross breeze gusting above tree level. As she watched from the tee, her ball landed to the left side of the fairway, bounded into that little slope running parallel to the direction of play, and then veered off into a bunker.

Of course, this was only a minor setback. She was comfortable dealing with such hazards going all the way back to her childhood. In fact, fairway traps were no big deal. With the proper approach, she knew there was always a window of recovery without having to give up too much. Walking out onto the fairway, she smiled graciously for the cameras, yielding to them exactly what they wanted – an acknowledgement that even champions felt the occasional sting of a setback in the game. All along the 16th fairway, she allowed the spectators to catch a glimpse of the master planning out her next shot. This bunker, she already knew, was not so deep as to prevent her from using a long iron to escape. Stepping into the sand, a hush followed her in. Every eye was on her.

With a moment of pause to set her feet and align the shot, Blaire drew back the three iron and swung with all her might. The ball cleared the trap's lip… just as she expected it to… tore out along a line with a slight fade toward the front of the green… just as she expected it to… took its first bounce off the fairway twenty yards before the fringe… just as she expected it to… proceeded along in a series of hops across the lower tier of the green… just as she expected it to… and settled into a gentle roll that took its small white blob of an outline upon a greater pea-green background right up to the cup's lip… just before disappearing within… like nothing she had ever expected it to do. An eagle… from the fairway trap on sixteen.

As the camera view changed from behind Blaire as she swung, with the ball rocketing out from a cloud of sand, to an aerial perspective on its flight, and then to a green-side camera that traced its beeline toward the hole, Bridget let out a scream just as the ball kissed off the pin and fell in. She immediately found herself jumping up and down in Lowell's living room… just as Blaire was doing her own form of celebrating within a fairway bunker on the other side of the country. Yet in the blink of an eye... as by no greater power than that of a mother's premonition... she froze on seeing her daughter launch herself up over the front lip of the trap... and come down to earth limping.

The very weight of herself doubled a sharp, piercing feel in her ankle, threatening to overcome the rest of her with its nauseating intensity. Blaire got off a half step and then crumbled to the turf. Without having the wits to restrain herself, she reached down with both hands to lay hold on the pain... and immediately recoiled onto her side at the agony brought about by her own grip. She was vaguely aware of voices all around her, with Curtis's being the first she recognized... though she was completely unable to open her eyes for him.

"Blaire... you okay?"

"Ankle..."

"What happened?"

"Twisted it."

"Let's see..."

She knew he was trying to be careful, but as he placed a hand on her shin, a sharp surge of pain made her yelp.

"Blaire... this is serious."

"No shit! It hurts like hell!"

With her pain and frustration came a recognition that others were crowding around her... strangers with their cameras.

"Get them the hell out of here!"

He instantly sprang up and began pushing bodies away from her, and though she could make out their questions... 'Is it her leg?'... 'How bad is it?'... 'Can she finish?'... her attention was back on the pain... and trying to hold herself as still as possible.

Stupid, stupid, stupid!

Climbing out over the front lip of a trap was one of the most imbecilic things a golfer could ever do. The eagle made her do it... made her lose her mind. Laying there alone in the grass, an eternity went by in which she experienced again the sensation of her right foot slipping in the sand just as she leapt upward toward a flat spot above the trap. She felt anew that little snapping twinge as her left foot fell short of solid ground, and instead hit the trap's unstable lip. Then came the overwhelming pain... which even now was throbbing its way upward throughout her leg.

Curtis was back… with someone unfamiliar at his side.

"Blaire… Bob Gambling's here… he's the tournament official for this hole…"

"Ms. O'Connor… I've called up a cart for you… and a paramedic… they'll be here in a minute, so just hang tight."

"I'm not quitting!"

"Blaire… you're ankle's already beginning to swell… I don't think you should be putting any weight on it."

None of them understood. None of them got it. The second she sat herself down in a cart, her tournament was over. She would forfeit the round and finish last… and she was no last-place loser.

"Give me an iron… I'll use it as a crutch."

"Blaire… I really think you should consider…"

"I said no!"

The tourney was speaking again, lecturing her about not taking any unnecessary risks. She ignored him, concentrating instead on the pain… turning its overwhelming influence into anger… and directing that anger toward finishing. He was now informing her that she had five minutes to continue with play… or bow out… but then the paramedic was there, telling her the obvious. She had torn something… and needed medical attention beyond his means. She gritted her teeth through his explanations, and then made him do as she insisted.

"Okay… I'll wrap it. I'm going to lift your leg a bit… so you'll need to hold it steady. Can't risk taking your shoe off… I'm afraid we'll never get it back on."

She winced her way through him twirling a bandage about her foot, ankle and lower calf. With only two holes to go… the par three seventeenth and the par four eighteenth… she was determined to make it through. With the help of Curtis and the paramedic, she managed to get up on her right foot… vaguely aware of the imbeciles all around applauding her… and then tested out the left with a bit of weight. Rockets shot up her calf, dampening to a dull throb as she quickly lifted the left back off the turf.

"Gimme a club, Curtis… any fucking club'l do!"

He handed her the same three iron she had used for the brilliant recovery shot. Gingerly spreading her stance… and ignoring as best she could the new throbs of pain in her ankle… she took a three quarters practice swing. As her weight shifted from right to left, she would have fallen to the turf had not Curtis been there to catch her. She had not expected what the follow-thru would cost her.

More carefully this time, she took another swing, keeping her weight on her back leg and using only her arms for power. The swing was ugly… that was certain… but serviceable.

"I can do this."

Getting to the next tee was a whole different matter. The only good thing she could think of was that the eagle meant she would not have to trudge all the way down the hill to the green. As best she could, she hobbled across the 16th fairway with Curtis supporting her the whole way, both of them making directly for the 17th tee. She knew that everyone on the course was tracking her slow progress, with the cameras capturing her every wince. Everybody was staring at her… making light of her pain… or doling out their pathetic sympathies. She wanted none of it… wanted them all to go away. She wanted the galleries emptied and the stage cleared. No one had the right to see her this way… in such weakness and stupidity.

Everything had been going so well… and now this. I can't bare another setback like after the car accident.

Nearly to the opposite rough, Blaire suddenly froze.

"Why're you stopping?"

"Shush."

"Do you need me to…"

"I said shut up!"

She strained to listen, searching through her mind for the smallest hint of a whisper from that dreadful little voice, for she feared that past more than all else. But nothing was there… only pain, irritation and anger… intense, ferocious anger.

"Are you wanting the ball?"

"What?!"

"Your eagle shot… If you want me to… I'll dash down to the green and see who fished it out of the hole…"

"I don't give a shit about that ball!"

"But… Blaire… that was one of the most incredible shots I've ever seen…"

"It's in the past, Curtis. Forget about it. Just… don't leave me. I'll… probably have something for you to do."

She had no inclination toward telling him how much she needed his presence. The past… in the form of her foolishness regarding that trap… was already plaguing her. Every step put her on the verge of screaming out like a little girl… and only him supporting her… bearing a portion of her weight… kept her will strong enough to overcome that weakness.

The broadcast came back from commercial with the camera immediately on Blaire as she muscled her way to the 17th tee. Bridget knew she was gripping Lowell's arm so tightly that she was probably leaving little fingernail dents in his skin. She could not help herself. It was excruciatingly difficult watching her daughter stagger along… every step a chore. The announcers were saying how bad the injury looked… how they doubted Blaire could finish… and what a shame it would be to have that stellar recovery shot wasted. Even Lowell, at her side, was offering allowances for the possible severity of the injury. She had no mind for considering any of that. Her concentration was fully upon the pained expressions on Blaire's face.

By the time she trudged her way onto the 17th tee, everyone there was waiting for her. A tourney standing by said she was up, as Kramer had already gone. Blaire peered down the length of the par three… all one hundred and eighty five yards of it… to where Kramer's ball sat, no more than eight feet from the pin. Looking back around the horseshoe shaped gallery surrounding the tee, she found Kramer standing with her caddie just this side of the rope line, smugly smiling back at her. Blaire recognized the look right off. Kramer was a shark… and there was the smell of blood in the waters of the 17th tee.

My blood…

Dammit! No way I'm reaching that green in one, and that bitch knows it! No way I'm getting better than double bogey on either this hole or the next… not on this piece-of-shit ankle. If she birdies this hole… and the next… then it's a tie… with a tiebreaker hole… and I'm sunk.

"Okay, Blaire… let's focus on keeping it in the fairway. Don't be tempted to muscle it too much with your arms… you'll shank it for sure. Your best bet is a bogey on this hole… and double on the next… that should be good enough to win. Blaire… are you hearing me? You do realize that even after that eagle, you've only got a six stroke lead over Kramer to work with."

She gave Curtis a nod… without having paid much attention to anything he said. Every word of his advice was lost in a whirlwind of pain. She already knew what to do anyway. Still using the three iron as a cane, she limped her way up to the ball he had teed up for her. With a gentle practice swing of the iron, she immediately experienced fresh pain erupting from her ankle. If only it had been the right… then she could put her weight on the left, pivoting off it through the entire swing. She would never be able to do that standing on the right… not and get any kind of power or balance. In retrospect, she should have had the foresight to practice one-footed shots… especially seeing as successful recoveries often decided between winning and losing. She pushed the what-ifs from her mind and once more thought through the swing... not giving a rat's ass for the people waiting to see her make a fool of herself. She took that particular frustration and buried it deep inside, focusing what remained on a spot of turf some seventy or so yards in front of her.

Just get it to that window of green... and let it roll.

The impact was solid enough, yet her drive lacked power. It barely cleared the short-cut section of grass coming off the tee box, bobbing along in a meek roll out to her target landing spot... a mere third of the distance she would normally have gotten from her three iron. There was still well over a hundred yards to go.

Owing to the slight slope out in front, Blaire was forced to backtrack with her three-iron-of-a-cane to the rear of the tee box, and then trudge along the edge of the gallery... which had not moved an inch in anticipation of her passing by. She was vaguely aware of the curses Curtis doled out in order to keep the cameras away... though they were no longer her chief concern. She ventured a quick look to her right... Kramer and her caddie were waiting at the base of the tee box, adopting a slow pace that matched her own.

Shit! That's exactly what I'd do. I'd remain close and taunt the cripple with a cheerful presence.

Sticking with the three iron... both as a crutch and her next club of intended use... Blaire finally came up on her ball. Without much deliberation... for she had little reserve left... she gave the approach shot every bit of her arms... shifting her weight into the pain ever so slightly. As she hoped, the ball took off toward the left side of the green, avoiding the trap that guarded its front, and came to rest within a yard of the fringe.

Puttable.

A smattering of claps came from the gallery behind her, reflecting reluctance in their congratulations. She could relate. That shot was more than decent given the circumstances... but still so very far below her standards.

With her putter from near the fringe, she managed to get her ball within five feet of the pin... dreading what it would take to hobble her way across the green with the aid of her putter. Kramer went next... and sank her putt to birdie the hole. Blaire did not wait for the applause to die down before beginning her slow trek out onto the green. In fact, she was moving toward her marker even as Kramer's ball was on the way to the cup... simply to take advantage of as much distraction as possible.

Because there was no way in hell she could bend over, Curtis had to place her ball and line up the putt. As he moved off, the stage became entirely hers, yet her damaged ankle would not allow her to perform there for herself. Hers was the supreme tragedy. She was nothing more than a prop on this stage… a pathetic puppet dangled out in the center of the green and made to lurch about for the pleasure of others. Despite that pain… and the pain in her ankle… Blaire told herself that she was in control. Her line was simple enough, so she need not concern herself with the script for this part of the play. Yet when the putt was made, Blaire watched in dismay as her ball went a fraction of an inch wide of the mark. A double bogey on seventeen. In one hole, she had wiped out the eagle… with Kramer's birdie taking another stroke from her lead. Now she only had a margin of three.

The slow walk to the 18th tee amounted to the most humiliating experience in her life. Sympathy, curiosity or scorn – it made no difference – she loathed the look upon every face turned her way. Even Curtis was laying the groundwork for her failure, mumbling about it not being so bad to end up in second place after what she had been through. And who could blame him… for if she performed on this 405 yard par four the way she had on the previous hole, then second place would be too good for her. She put the thought out of her mind in considering what it would take to finish this last hole.

At a miserable eighty yards a pop… that'll leave me lying five at the green… and not even necessarily on it.

Three back with one hole to go, Kramer took to the tee sporting all the confidence of a player already in the lead. Blaire did not bother tracking the girl's drive. With her eyes closed, she could tell from the swish of the swing, the resonance to the contact, and the response of the gallery that Kramer's result was truly beautiful.

Her own tee shot… another wretched performance… ended up skipping in and out of the rough some seventy yards ahead. Curtis immediately went about trying to persuade her to go with a fairway wood for the next shot… though she declined without explanation. It made little difference what club she used – there was no power to her swing, so the three was good enough… particularly since this club kept her going. In actuality, it was a bit too long for a cane… and far too short as a crutch… but the three had gotten her out of that fairway bunker, bringing her an eagle in the process, so the three was the thing she counted on to get her out of this mess.

Another pathetic shot… right up to the edge of the creek that Kramer had easily carried with her drive. Blaire was lying two… with well over two hundred yards to go. Her next shot was considerably better, passing Kramer's tee shot by a good margin. But the achievement was short-lived and shallow. Kramer, already on the other side of the creek, took off in a brisk walk toward her ball... leaving Blaire to hobble back across the fairway for the walking bridge. She was not even on the other side when the gallery all about the 18th green erupted into applause. Kramer was on... and Blaire was forgotten.

Now, nobody was paying attention to her struggles. Here she was limping her way along the final hole... and everyone was screaming for more of Kramer. It was all wrong. Blaire was the one in the lead... had led the entire tournament... but these mindless morons were now overlooking their real champion. The pain was there at every step, but she no longer cared as before. She found herself insulted at having been ignored... even though minutes before she had wished everyone away.

"How far is it?"

"A hundred... a hundred ten if you include the head wind... which obviously won't come into play with the way you're stroking that three iron. By the way... you've still got that trap up front to deal with... so you'd better lay up."

"Give me the eight."

"Blaire... you can barely swing... you'll never reach it with that..."

"Curtis... shut the fuck up and get me the damn eight iron like I asked!"

After a brief pause of hesitation, he did as he was told. After switching clubs with him, she noticed him sliding the three back into her bag.

"Keep it out... I'll need it."

This is going to hurt like hell.

She addressed the ball without attempting a practice swing, drew back the eight slowly, feeling a pulse of pain shoot up from the ankle as her weight momentarily shifted to the left... and then, giving up all concern over what would happen next, she took her normal swing. She felt contact... good solid contact... but then the ankle gave way on the follow-thru... and she went down harder than before, writhing about in pain. It seemed like forever before she registered Curtis hanging over her, his face bizarrely alternating between shock and excitement.

"The ball?"

"You're on, Blaire. I don't know how you did it... but you're on. You're even inside Kramer's... maybe eight feet out."

"Shit... it... it really hurts... worse than before."

"Just... just take it easy for a minute..."

"Oh, god... it's killing me."

Somehow, Blaire resisted the impulse to grab her ankle… for it was on fire and heavier than a ton of bricks. Instead, she covered her head with both arms and tried to breathe her way into a duller, simpler pain. That feeling never really came. She knew she should stay lying there in the grass… as that would be the sane thing to do… for any second now she was going to pass out. Yet a stronger urge commanded her to do the exact opposite.

"Get… get me up, Curtis … will you… right now… or I swear… I'm gonna quit."

Locking hold onto his offered hand with both of hers, she was vaguely aware of him sliding a foot up against the side of her right… just before heaving her up. She let him do all the lifting, for her limited focus was on being careful not to drag her wounded left across the grass as she came upright.

"Now… give me the three iron."

For the next few moments, Blaire was completely unaware of anything other than her pain. So why she did it made no sense. As she stood there leaning on the three while her head cleared, she found herself waving an arm about in the air as if acknowledging whatever applause she might be receiving. There was no gratitude to the gesture. She felt only the need of warding off everyone from looking at her… for there was still a very long way to go… and she was not at all convinced of getting there.

Leaning heavily on Curtis the entire way, she finally reached the green… and quickly sized up the situation… though not by assessing the disposition of her ball relative to that of Kramer's. Instead, she took a long look into that girl's eyes, and what Blaire saw there gave her hope… for Kramer was glaring back angerly at her. Turning to the green, she saw that Kramer had a fourteen foot putt for birdie… and she had half that distance to go for bogey.

As before, Blaire closed her eyes. Leaning against Curtis, she concentrated on the hush as the gallery quieted in expectation of Kramer's putt. She heard the plunk of the girl's putter against her ball, sensed the crowd's intake of anticipation, felt a slight flex in Curtis's arm… and then immediately reveled in the mass moan coming from all around her. Not until she heard a second tap, followed very shortly thereafter by the sound of a ball falling into a cup, did Blaire open her eyes.

She easily two putted the eighteenth green to win the Overland Classic by a single stroke. Unlike any tournament she ever won… and there had been many… this one carried with it no celebrations. No handshakes and no post-round interviews either. She remembered only shuffling along to a cart… tourneys shooing fans out of her way… her being sped from the 18th green…

and then being carried through her agony into a waiting ambulance.

An hour later, already pumped up with pain killers, Blaire sat in an emergency room alcove waiting to be x-rayed. Another hour, and she was back on an examination table with another ice pack on her ankle and an orthopedic doctor telling her the bad news – a completely ruptured peroneal tendon. They rewrapped her ankle… much better than before… and gave her a small stock of meds. Curtis somehow got her onto a flight bound for LA later that evening, with Bernie picking her up and arranging for her to see a specialist first thing in the morning. That doctor ended up concurring with the emergency room assessment, making it so very clear that surgery was her only option.

Though nobody voiced it, Blaire sensed in every word and every facial expression from each of the medical experts that this might mean the end of her career.

CHAPTER

36

THE VAGARIES
TO REFLECTION

It goes without saying that mirrors are designed in such a way as to reflect light, though such devices, in themselves, do nothing particularly special. There are, of course, many tricks to refraction – multiple scatterings, concave and convex distortions, parabolic enhancements, dichroisms, and assorted holographic approaches. Elaborate mirrored surfaces that utilize such effects may intensify, disperse, enlighten and amuse, but they can never create light. They only give back to be seen that which is imparted to them. So to behold something that is not quite there, a person must face an entirely different sort of glass.

She was repeatedly assured that the operation was a complete success… and wanted to believe it as true… yet was not so stupid as to expect any surgeon to come right out and admit to having fucked up.

'Sorry, Ms. O'Connor… we made a mistake. You'll be a cripple for the rest of your life.'

She knew that only time… and lots of rehab… would tell for certain. With six weeks of no weight-bearing on the ankle prior to even starting any kind of exercise, Blaire had a long way to go before being convinced that the tendon was fully healed. In the interim, she faced a whole lot of sitting around on her rear doing nothing. Her condo, what with its multitier layout, was unsuitable for getting around on crutches. So while lying in a hospital bed,

Blaire offhandedly commented that a place without stairs would be a hell of a lot easier on her. Bernie picked up on the hint right away and insisted that she stay in his guest house… just as she knew he would. She was already sure the place would be ideal for her – all on one level with a private entrance and direct access to his pool area. He took to the idea with such enthusiasm that he was immediately on the phone arranging for one of his minions to have her things brought over.

After only a week in the guest house, Blaire was not sure that staying there was such a good idea. Sure… she had his hired help at her call 24-7, his pool to lounge around, and the splendor of his view… along with anything else she wanted. But it was Bernie's twice daily appearances that became nearly intolerable, as he was driving her crazy with all his hovering about like she was some kind of china doll.

In truth, it did not much matter where she stayed while her ankle healed. She was completely bored out of her brains without golf… and still had five weeks of being off her foot to go. She made the mistake of vocalizing that frustration in front of him during his visit the previous night… which was why one of his peons was standing in the front door of the guest house with all those boxes of photo albums her lame mother had dropped off at his office.

"Umm… Mr. Pearl thought that maybe… seeing as you have some time on your hands… you could… you know… pick out some really special pictures from your childhood. I have to tell you… he's terribly anxious for you to get some good press while your recovering… so if you could…"

"Whatever. Stack them out by the pool."

She waited for the twit to move the three boxes through to the patio and leave before putting on her bathing suit. Aside from watching TV, the only thing Blaire had been able to do all week with any degree of success was sunbathing… though she felt remarkably stupid lying around in a bikini and ankle brace.

Crutching out of the guest house to the low patio table where the assistant had placed the boxes, Blaire got herself situated in a pool-side lounge chair… which entailed hauling up her albatross-of-a-leg with both hands… and then pulled out an album at random. She was not in the least bit interested in revisiting the past, nor was she going to do Bernie's job for him. As far as she was concerned, he could get his ass down here and pick out pictures himself. She had only one thing on her mind – to amuse herself with the ridiculous amount of effort her mother had invested in these albums. This, at least, would distract her from the pathetic state of her ankle.

Starting at the front, she began flipping through page after page of photos... nearly all of which were of her as a very young child. Every single one fell into the category of 'extremely cute'... and not just because they were of her being cute. All modesty aside... which Blaire chuckled over having none of... she really had been a remarkably beautiful little girl. Whatever expression she might have on... smiling, frowning, or as if caught by surprise... there was not an imperfect picture of her in the lot. She was, beyond a doubt, the most photogenic child ever set before a camera.

In skimming through, Blaire put little thought toward considering the background to any particular picture... whether it be inside or at some outdoor setting mattered not... as her eyes were on herself. She nonetheless noticed that interspersed within the photos of her posing alone were occasional ones of her with either her father or mother, as well as a few with all three together. In none of these pictures did she begrudge having someone else share the stage with her, for they were like props... there to lend some variation to the capturing of her significance on film. With regard to her parents, she registered only that they were so obviously enamored with having her as their daughter, and that she was the reason why this album succeeded in depicting a happy-looking family.

Admittedly, her mother had done a good job in preserving these photos. Each was perfectly aligned on its page, with considerable care having been invested into varying the layout. Many pages had the expected four-corner approach, whereas others were in collages, cascades or crisscross patterns. Blaire put little effort into reading the captions, as most were fairly lame. Still... she could not deny that there was a measure of cleverness to a good many of them... so much so that she reluctantly admitted that her mother actually had an ounce of creativity to her.

Blaire dropped that album back into its box, and extracted one from the second box. She was older in this one... maybe in late elementary school. Just as beautiful as when she was a toddler, Blaire could now pick out a bit of her, as an adult, in these pictures of her, as a grade schooler. Her hair was a bit lighter and longer, but the style was exactly in the way she currently did it. More than anything else, it was her eyes – the eyes of a competitor – that was most familiar... which made perfect sense, seeing as many of the photos in this album were of her golfing. She went page by page, focusing on those photos dealing with her and the game. In each, she experienced an unexpected nostalgia for the clubs she had used as a child and for the golf course she had spent so much of her youth on.

She was nearly all the way through when an odd observation hit her. Going back to the front, she moved through more carefully a second time. As before, she noticed that almost every photo had her in it, either alone or with her father... though occasionally there was one with just him... yet she could not find a single one with her mother in it. The woman had completely disappeared from before the camera. Blaire put this album back and took out another from the same box. The time period was similar... maybe a year earlier in Blaire's life... but yet again, there was not a single photo with her mother in it.

Perhaps this was not so surprising after all. In fact, Blaire now considered the absence of her mother to be rather appropriate, particularly seeing as she was the least photogenic person Blaire knew of... always with a crooked smile or eyes partly closed off as if caught in the process of blinking. Nothing even remotely appealing compared to Blaire's worst display before a camera. Still... that explanation did not seem quite right, particularly seeing as the earlier album had more than a smattering of her mother.

Blaire set this particular volume, and its oddity, aside to take up an album from the last box. She was older in this one... a teenager to be sure. The photos were still only of her, mostly out on the fairways, tees, traps and greens of various golf courses about the city. In a few, she noticed right off minor errors in her youthful approach to the game... not leaning directly over the ball when putting... a slight misalignment in her stance... an off-balance aftermath to a swing. All such lapses were eventually cleaned up by a coach or in her time at the Kensington clinic. She had come a long way since then. Still... she somehow felt uncomfortable being reminded that she had not always exhibited the ideal form or proper mechanics.

Rather than dwelling on past imperfections, Blaire shifted her thoughts to an obvious distinction in this album – her father was literally out of the picture.

Duh! He'd already run off with that bimbo.

Actually, she was the one who drove him off... which, to this day, still made her smile.

As with the albums from the second box, the photos in this one also showed no sign of her mother. Blaire, as a teenager, had the stage entirely to herself.

As it should be...

Strange though... with her mother hidden behind the camera... and her father gone... this collection of photos depicted her as being a rather lonely looking child… which clearly was not how she remembered things. Blaire sloughed off this inconceivable representation in order to hone in on another strange observation – the quality of the captions had changed. They were noticeably shorter and with less of the woman's glib attempts at humor frequently shown in the earlier albums. It was just the essentials – 'Blaire at a tournament in Santa Barbara'… 'Blaire teeing off'… 'Blaire on Christmas morning with her new set of clubs'… 'Blaire on our visit to Pebble Beach.' Inexplicably, she somehow found herself feeling short-changed by her mother… as if the woman had arbitrarily decided to no longer invest the required diligence. She tried pushing aside the feeling by reminding herself how little she cared about these albums. Her mother could do whatever the hell she wanted, and it made no difference to her. Still… in scanning through this particular album… it seemed to Blaire as if her teenage self held to a similar displeasure… or maybe it was something entirely different than her mother's lapsed quality. This teenage Blaire appeared… dissatisfied with herself… with her depiction in the game… and with something else. Perhaps her younger self was looking out of the pictures through the camera lens of time… to where her older self lay lame at poolside… completely bored out of her brain waiting for something to stir.

Blaire laid the album down in her lap and tried to make sense of an irritating little thought poking its way up from the depths of her mind. Being alone had always been the way she wanted things, so why should it now feel off… seeing herself all by herself? If 'feel' was even the right word for it. She actually felt nothing at all… no concern… no self-reflection… not even pity for her younger self. The photos were what they were… empty without her. Why should she want it any other way?! No one merited being in a photo with her. She was superior to them all. Not only did she uncover the secrets of others, but she was the originator of secrets no one else knew. How she discovered her father's affair… How she totally plastered his lover's condo… How she broke up her parents… How she made her money as a teenager… How she seduced and manipulated people at the country club for her own purposes… How she planned all along to ditch college and go pro… And how she was now playing Bernie, the media, the league, the fans, and all her competition.

Her mother had always been so gullible… so disgustingly open… spilling her guts out for anyone who had the stomach to listen. There was absolutely no power in that… and no control. The way Blaire lived… putting herself first… that was so much better than her mother's way.

Yet these photos… by themselves… seemed to tell a different story. In every single picture, she was the one with secrets being revealed. Her little errors of form… hips shifted improperly… an elbow out of place… feet awkwardly situated… a poor grip on a club… were recorded for all to see. Even in the victory poses with a tournament trophy held high, she recognized the frustration in her teenage eyes over mistakes made… over so many bad decisions that kept her from reaching perfection. All along, she had fooled herself – her triumphs were not purely because of her own excellence. Sure… she was superior to her competition… always had been… but that was hardly a suitable standard by which to gauge her uniqueness. These childhood photos, in pointing out her imperfections, argued that her victories had actually come about because of the failings of others… inferior foes who had brought about their own downfall… and not because she had mastered the game. All her life, whenever she posed for the camera, she was actually displaying her own weaknesses. None of these photos showed the beautiful and talented Blaire O'Connor. They proclaimed instead her hidden struggles over how far she consistently fell short… and the painful truth that the game had always bested her.

And her mother… the woman had remained a total mystery throughout… successfully concealing herself and her own secrets from the camera. Yet Blaire knew it was far worse than that. In these albums, her mother had preserved Blaire's imperfections as a little secret of her own. Something to privately relish… and now, at the cruelest of times, to reveal before the whole world.

Blaire lifted the album back up, going to it with a determination not to see what she had previously seen. Instead, owing to her needing to refocus in the bright glare of that June morning, she happened to lock in first on the reflection of herself from off the laminate covering to the page. Her image was not especially clear… more of a gossamer-like representation rather than a crisp depiction of herself. That, she realized, was due to this surface being a poor mirror. Though she should have been irritated with the plastic for doing her a disservice, somehow… she was oddly thankful for the blurry reflection… thankful that the self in there could not see her clearly either… could not recognize this momentary state of weakness she had found herself in. And the doubt… that too was kept clouded from her other self.

Tilting the album ever so slightly, Blaire brought the sun's bright reflection into the very center of the page, burning it up and leaving nothing behind in her eyesight other than an all-encompassing brightness that mercifully cleansed out her thoughts. She then closed the cover and slid the album back into its place, determined to call Bernie as soon as possible… and make him haul all these goddamn boxes away.

37

NO BIG DEAL

"Speculation has been swirling for days regarding reports that three-time WGA Open champion Blaire O'Connor will be..."

Blaire throttled the Lexus over the double yellow line and around a flatbed truck loaded down with shrink-wrapped shower stalls... cutting back close in front as her way of displaying her annoyance. She hated anything interfering with her progress on the road... but hated even more this radio report coming in over the XM golf channel.

"...currently recuperating from successful ankle surgery, was unavailable for comment. Her agent, Bernie Pearl, released a statement to the press this morning requesting privacy for his client, who purportedly intends to take the remainder of the season off before returning to competition in the spring. As per league rules, her card will remain in effect while she's..."

Damn vultures!

Blaire jabbed the knob, silencing the radio. How the media had already caught wind of the situation was beyond her. Someone in Bernie's office must have screwed up... yet again.

This plan of his better work! It's going to cost me months of playing time.

She drove on in silence, wrangling with an unaccustomed uncertainty. It was several blocks before she registered the presence of pawn shops, liquor stores and tattoo parlors lining the boulevard.

This doesn't seem right. Mother would never live in a part of town like this.

After a brief moment of confusion, Blaire realized that in turning off the radio, she had also silenced the Lexus's GPS system. The volume, once restored, greeted her with an insistence that she make a U-turn. Nearly seven weeks since the operation and still she did not feel comfortable enough working the clutch on her Maserati… another frustration. In the interim, she picked up this car as a backup, but was not yet familiar with all its ways. To her surprise, the front tire clipped the opposite curb while copping the U-ey, with her accelerating out of the mishap with even less finesse.

She had never been to her mother's house before… and certainly would not be going now unless it was absolutely necessary. Being forced to meet there… rather than somewhere in the city… would put things on her mother's terms… and Blaire hated that feeling more than the annoyance of getting lost.

Just get in, say what you've got to say, and get out… before you change your mind.

She had been over and over the plan, and knew there was no chance in hell of it working without her mother's cooperation. That was precisely why she was bringing the photo albums back… and not because she had any compulsion toward returning them. They were her way in… a sort of bribe… or peace offering… or whatever. Nothing more than a way of getting her to do what Blaire wanted.

The three boxes of albums, currently sliding around in the back seat, were irritating the hell out of her.

I thought I told Bernie's moron assistant to put those in the trunk!

To say that she was pissed off amounted to the understatement of the century. Tearing up her ankle… having to hobble around on crutches for seven weeks… Curtis taking up with a different golfer… Bernie's incessant presence nagging her… and this latest thing making her show up at her mother's place with hat-in-hand begging for a favor… what else could possibly go wrong?!

She finally located the correct side street, found the development, and gained access to the gated community. Pulling in front of the house, Blaire took note of the obvious – that her mother was not standing out front waiting to greet her.

Shit! She's going to make me ring the stupid doorbell. Fine! No big deal! I'll still make this work out my way.

Blaire maneuvered her way out of the Lexus and up the short walkway. She ignored the doorbell and pounded hard enough to startle anyone waiting inside. Yet her mother answered without the slightest hint of irritation.

"Blaire... how nice to see you. Please, come in. I hope your ankle's healing well..."

Man... she's really playing it cool.

"Doctor's got me putting a bit of weight on it now... but still wants me to go easy on it for another week. At least I've started rehab. Hey... I got your photo albums. They're in the back seat of the car. Can't bring them in myself." Standing on her good ankle, she clanked the crutches together at their base for effect. "It's open."

"Have a seat. I'll be right back."

She didn't even bother asking why I'm here. Doesn't matter... I'll rattle her soon enough.

Her mother's living room was decorated in early American boredom... just matching couch and chairs, each with the same nasty floral pattern, a plain-looking coffee table scattered over with crap, a TV on a stand, and a bunch of cheap artwork on the walls. Sidestepping herself through a gap in the furniture, she dropped onto the couch seriously perturbed that she still had to use these miserable crutches.

As her mother made agonizingly long trips back and forth from the car, Blaire did her best imitation of someone patiently waiting upon another. Each time, her mother placed a box of albums on the coffee table directly before her... without the slightest sign of emotion. The woman actually seemed indifferent to receiving back her precious photos... as well as the fact that her only child had recently been through a very painful operation. No cards, calls or visits from her. Nothing.

What kind of a mother does that?!

The woman was finally coming in with the last box. Those were certainly heavy... Blaire had watched the assistant strain in carrying them out to her car... yet her mother was muscling them about without complaint.

Damn... she's not going to make this easy.

So Blaire turned to her old standby – charm.

"Mother – I do believe you've lost weight! You're so slim! And with your hair up... you look absolutely amazing!"

"I feel good too. I've been working out... I'm glad it shows."

To her immense frustration, Blaire got nothing else other than a pleasant expression and a silence that made clear the next move was still hers.

Fine! Then let's get this the-hell over with.

"I have something you need to do for me. A sort of favor..."

Again, no response other than that annoying little smile. No way was she going to tolerate being treated like this.

"Hello?! Did you hear me?"

"Of course..."

"Well... you going to say something?!"

"I was waiting for a please."

"What...?! Fine! *Please*... how's that?! So... like I was saying... I've got something for you to do... because I'm..."

"When you say it like that, it's evident you don't mean it."

"Mother... can we not make this into a contest. I've got more important things to deal with. Besides... please is just a word."

"No, it's not. It's something every normal person says when..."

"To you... but not to me."

"I fully recognize that, Blaire. To you, it's a device for misleading... another club in your bag of tricks for getting what you want. But to me... it's a show of respect... an acknowledgement on your part that I exist as a person... and that what I want in life might not be what you want. When a person says it the right way, they're putting a piece of themselves on the line in asking for help. To be honest, Blaire... I'm concerned about you. After all these years, you still don't get it. It's almost as if you're..."

"Pregnant."

"...completely unaware of... What'd you just say?"

Before repeating herself, she took a moment to draw out the shock and disbelief flooding in all over her mother's face.

"I'm pregnant."

Maybe she should have lingered a bit longer... Somehow, her mother seemed to relax out of the news way too fast. Like she had bitten into something sour and opted for quickly swallowing the whole thing rather than chewing on it anymore. There was even a hint of a smile coming to her face. Blaire knew that this expression was not humor... her mother never laughed about anything. It was more like... a disappointment deep inside the woman was being covered over by... a breath of perspective.

Oh... I get it! She thinks I'm messing with her. If only it were so...

"I've done the test... I'm definitely pregnant."

That sure wiped away the smile! Oh shit... now she's puckering her lips. Here comes the lecture.

Blaire had been expecting this... more so than any kind of bubbly grandmother-to-be excitement. Her mother could not help herself. She had to make a show out of imparting her useless wisdom whenever an opportunity presented itself.

"You must be… very excited. Congratulations."

Blaire waited, yet nothing more came. The woman just sat there blank-faced. All of a sudden, the absolute absurdity of Bernie's plan came crashing in on her. After she told him about her condition, he immediately made phone calls to his PR machine and came back to say that she should consider going through with the pregnancy.

"Consider it as killing two birds with one stone. You're not likely to get back on tour this year with that bum ankle, so.. you recover while you're pregnant. Just think of the headlines: 'The Flair gives birth!' No outlet could pass that up. The public eats up pregnant sports stars… you know that! They just can't help it… it's like daytime drama. 'Oh my… how ever will she manage career and baby?' Blaire… I'm telling you, it's an absolute goldmine of free publicity. Now… of course… it's your business and your decision… but think on my advice. Don't terminate the pregnancy. Exploit it for all it's worth."

All of that sounded rather sketchy to Blaire the first time around. In playing that interaction back while staring at her mother… it was nothing more than horseshit. Blaire knew, as did everyone on tour, that professional golf offered nothing to women after their playing days were over. No senior tour. No endorsement opportunities. No way to build off past successes. And nothing ended a player's career faster than having a baby. Bernie's plan… though difficult in the long run… would at least keep her in the spotlight while she continued to recover from the ankle injury… and supposedly would make her even more popular than ever once she got back on tour. In the meantime, he promised bookings on morning shows, more commercial spots, and maybe even a cameo appearance from a movie executive who owed him a favor.

"Trust me, Blaire – it'll all come together."

But not if her mother disagreed.

Through all her fears… much of which had lapped around her thinking in the interval between Blaire's call and the knock on her door… she had not once entertained pregnancy as the reason for her daughter's visit. When Blaire phoned that morning to say that she was coming over, Bridget resisted the urge to ask why, as she was sure to receive a lie. Her daughter was always after something. Whatever it was, Bridget had a line drawn in the sand. 'No' most definitely would be the answer. And to better prepare herself, she had rummaged about in the spare room for the notes she made regarding Blaire's sociopathic tendencies. Reviewing those just prior to Blaire's arrival helped her prepare for whatever conflict was coming.

But this certainly was not anything she had expected. So many questions were tumbling through her mind… some intended for Blaire and some for herself. Asking herself whether she was excited did not happen to be on the list, as mortification better described her feelings. Still… she was curious as to Blaire's plans… though 'schemes' was probably a better word for it. Manipulative and controlling – that was the mind of the sociopath. In some ways, Bridget actually felt sorry for her. Blaire could not help it – she was incapable of seeing things outside herself. That was one of the main points she had reminded herself of from those notes.

Oops… I left those out on the coffee table. Thank goodness the boxes are covering them.

"So, Blaire… who's the father?"

Right off, the manner in which Blaire shrugged her shoulders… in that reluctant way meant as an invitation for further inquiry… warned Bridget not to press the matter. It was surely a trap of some kind. She instead switched directions toward something equally pressing on her mind.

"Are you… going to have the baby?"

"I really don't know… it all depends on you."

"Me?! Why me?"

"You certainly don't expect me to have anything to do with it, do you?! I'm mean… raising a kid… that's more your speed."

Unbelievable! She's actually giving me an ultimatum! Agree to take care of her baby… or else!"

"What exactly are you asking? And don't be clever… just come right out with it."

"Okay… here's the deal… if you want me to have this thing, then you'll need to agree to take care of it while I'm out on tour. You've got an extra room here, don't you? I'll arrange for whatever you need… cribs and stuff. Shouldn't take too much… You watch over it for a year or two… until it's ready for preschool or something… and then we'll get together to decide what's needed next."

This was, by far, the worst thing she could have imagined coming from Blaire. To witness such callousness… such disregard… such complete absence of responsibility or concern for another human being… a child of her own… it was more than Bridget could bear.

"Blaire… this isn't a goldfish in a bowl… or a stray cat that you can dump off on someone's front porch. This is a person we're talking about. Your own child!"

Blaire glanced off in the direction of the back porch as if the comment was something obscene… too indecent for her to consider.

"As usual, Mother, you're going to make a big deal out of everything."

"It is a big deal! And you haven't told me who's the father. Maybe you should be asking him and not me."

Theatrically, Blaire made a show of lifting her arms to the ceiling while wagging her head.

"Hell if I know… To tell you the truth, Mother… there've been so many men in my life lately. I can't bother keeping track of them."

"I don't believe this."

"What difference does it make anyway? Are you going to help me out or not?! I'd say it's even your responsibility… seeing as it'll be your grandchild."

Bridget could not help it – she had to lean forward in her chair and hide her face in her hands. Before her, through her splayed fingers, she could just make out the top sheet to a pile of papers partially hidden by one of the boxes on the coffee table. She recognized it immediately – that questionnaire for identifying sociopathic tendencies. It was a reminder to her of who her daughter was. The child within, a mere embryo, was a blank slate… yet one that would surely be written upon with hurt, resentment, and abandonment if this woman were allowed to raise it. That, more than anything else, made up Bridget's mind.

"Yes… of course. I'll take care of the child for you… but only on one condition. It's either all or nothing. When the time comes for the birth, you'll have to decide… because I'll insist on full custody."

Not in the least bit surprised… irrespective of how her insides were reeling… Bridget watched as Blaire made a show of rolling her eyes… just before nodding her agreement. Without another word, Blaire scootched forward on the couch. She had gotten what she wanted and was ready to leave.

While adjusting a grip on the crutch handles prior to lifting herself up, Blaire unexpectedly came to a halt. As a pained expression came over the girl's face, Bridget… at first… thought that something had gone wrong with her ankle. It got tweaked or twisted beneath the coffee table. However, after a few seconds, she realized that Blaire's eyes were focused on the table top. She was reading.

What the fuck…

'1. Does the subject display a grandiose sense of importance when
speaking about themselves?'

*'2. Does the subject readily admit to fabricating falsehoods for
      either purpose or effect?'*
*'3. Does the subject consider themselves to be irresistibly
      charming?'*
*'4. Does the subject approach routine encounters with others from
      the perspective of calculation, manipulation and control?'*

She kept going down the list until a box on the table got in her way. Releasing her crutch, she snatched the sheet up in order to continue reading. A little bell suddenly went off in Blaire's mind… though the sound was nothing more than the metallic resonance of her aluminum crutch clanging to the floor. She recognized this list from somewhere in her distant past. Someone had gone through similar questions with her… and in great detail.

"Mother, what's this?!"

"Umm… what's what?"

She thrust the page across the table toward the woman, fully aware that she knew what it was from the sappiness in her tone.

"This! It's got a bunch of questions on it!"

"Oh, that! It's nothing. Just hand it over."

"Don't lie to me, Mother. I know what this is!"

"You do?"

"He gave it to you – don't deny it! And don't you dare try to shield him!"

"What? Who're you talking about? No one gave that to me. I… I found it on the web. It's… umm… a standard psychological analysis for… for…"

The woman suddenly froze stiff, completely incapable of finishing her sentence.

"For what?! Spit it out!"

"For… sociopathic… tendencies."

How she managed to get the words out was beyond her. To openly admit that she had done research into her daughter's warped ways of thinking was more than embarrassing. She could feel herself shaking from having to admit such a thing to her own child… and from the fear of what Blaire might do next. But there she sat, transfixed on the page… almost as if she were seeing herself for the first time… and perhaps not liking it.

"Blaire… what's the matter? What're you thinking?"

"That bastard! I'm going to kill him."

She had no idea who Blaire was referring to… and was hesitant to ask… though diverting attention toward that subject was better than dwelling on why she, as a mother, had felt it necessary to psychoanalyze her own daughter.

Blaire suddenly released the page to the floor and began groping about for her abandoned crutch. Before Bridget knew what was going on, she was up on her good foot and motoring her way to the front door. Fortunately, owing to what it took to work the knob while balancing on crutches, Bridget reached the door before Blaire could get it open.

"Tell me what's going on. Who were you referring to?"

"Mother, I've heard those questions before. Not exactly like those... but very similar. They were so odd at the time... and I didn't stop to think about them. I just answered. Truth is... my mind was elsewhere. Those questions happened to be the very things Bernie asked me when he was interviewing me... you know... in the weeks prior to me graduating. He said they were... standard interview questions. Mother... he was profiling me!"

"I don't understand. Profiling you for what?"

"It doesn't matter anymore. All that matters is..."

Blaire's lower lip suddenly began to quiver... and it, more than anything else she had witnessed during the visit, stunned Bridget. It had been a long, long time since her daughter last displayed such genuine emotion.

"Blaire... what's wrong?"

"Bernie... he's... he's the father."

CHAPTER
38

GRANDMOTHER
TURNED MOTHER

Leaning against the inner side of her front door, Bridget concentrated on the creaks and clomps of crutches as Blaire made her way out to her car. On finally hearing the engine turn over, she could no longer restrain herself, bursting out crying as she clutched her chest against the pain. Motherhood had always been the essence of her heart, and here her own daughter was showing such disdain... such vulgar repulsion... over the same prospect. Bridget felt absolutely no anticipation of joy... only a sad acceptance that she would become her own grandbaby's surrogate mother.

Looking in toward her small living room, she wiped her eyes in acknowledgement that it was time to be brave. She nonetheless could not yet bring herself to move, and went on staring at the boxes of albums on the coffee table... not having the slightest idea what this new future of hers would look like. At least there was one thing she was quite certain of – she had no interest in revisiting those albums. They belonged to someone else's sad past. Equally, she was determined not to put them back in the garage. Being able to park her car in there without having to see those boxes... or having to face the regrets and accusations they symbolized... that freedom was terribly important to her. Neither would she put the albums back on the shelves in the spare room, seeing as that space might soon be transformed into a nursery.

Guess I'll stack them in a closet...

That decided, her eyes ventured down to the floor… to the single sheet of paper Blaire had dropped on her way out. That was the printout of questions on sociopathic behaviors… the very thing that had affected Blaire so bizarrely. The girl finally managed to pull herself together… swearing out loud that nobody got away with playing her for the fool… and then did her handicapped best to storm out of the house.

In reflecting back on that scene, it occurred to Bridget that her daughter… despite all the unexpected emotion… was still determined to go through with the pregnancy. What if Bernie Pearl refused to agree with Blaire's plan? What kind of a father would he be? Could either of them be counted on to stick it out during the good and bad days? Would they be there when the child got sick… or scared… or had homework… or just wanted to play?

No… it's totally absurd to imagine either of them being a decent parent.

She looked once more at the page lying on the floor… and then to all the other printouts partially hidden beneath the boxes of photos. So typical… her aspirations for a dream-come-true family had covered over the reality of who her only child was. There had been so many obvious signs… like the corners to all those pieces of paper sticking out from under the boxes… yet she had steadfastly kept her eyes fixed upon the falseness of pictures. Hopeful thinking had gotten her nowhere.

She would not make the same mistake again. As with all things Blaire-ish or Bernie-ish, she would only count on them to act supremely in their own interests… even when it came down to the question of what was best for a child. If Blaire did go through with the pregnancy… and that was a big if… gave birth and passed the child on to her… then Bridget would be a fool not to expect one of those two snakes… the mother or the father… to one day come slithering back. She needed to be prepared for that day… if for no other reason than the baby's sake.

She pushed herself away from the door, scooped up the single sheet of paper from the floor… along with all those scattered across the coffee table… and made directly for the trash bin in her garage.

Throughout the first and second trimesters, Bridget purposefully restrained from poking about with questions regarding whether Blaire was taking care of herself and the baby. Neither did she offer suggestions for helping Blaire cope with the challenges of being pregnant. At least through the assistance of Alexia, Bridget was able to make sure that Blaire showed up to her various checkups… even got her signed up for a birthing class… but never actually attended any of those appointments with Blaire.

Yet the appointment of Blaire's that Bridget was showing up to this day was different – it was not medical in the least. She also knew it to be different for another reason – Bernie was supposed to be there too. Strange as it might seem given the circumstances, she had not laid eyes on the man since that day the elevator doors closed on his befuddled expression.

Wow... that was nearly two years ago.

Unfortunately, Bridget's first glimpse of him across the parking lot, just as he and Blaire got out of the back of his luxury town car, sent an unexpected pulse of revulsion through her insides. The thought that this man was the father of her unborn grandchild disgusted her.

Having arrived before them... and not wanting to remain inside alone... Bridget opted for waiting by her car. At times like this, she found herself bemoaning her tendency for arriving early to appointments. It would have been easier had she appeared after them, then... in being late... she might have been able to avoid exchanging pleasantries with the man who had gotten her daughter pregnant.

She was doing it again... contemplating for the hundredth time how in the world her daughter had become mixed up with someone like Bernie Pearl. He was much too old for her... too pudgy... and far from her type... whatever that was. So what if he was rich... Blaire had her own money. Perhaps Blaire took advantage of him for a different reason... or maybe he took advantage of her.

Unlikely. Nobody takes advantage of Blaire.

Bridget looked up in time to see Bernie give Blaire a hug... and then he got back into his car. In complete confusion, she watched it drive away... and then had to hustle over before Blaire could enter alone.

"Where's he going? I thought he needed to be here too..."

"Something's come up. He'll get back when he can. In the meantime... let's get this over with."

They turned together through the smoke-tinted glass door into the offices of Blaire's attorney, with Bridget noting how Blaire arched her back in compensating for the baby she was carrying.

"You feeling okay today?"

"I'm in no mood for mother-daughter time... so no small talk. Herb's heading right back to pick me up."

"Who's Herb?"

Blaire did not respond, instead offering their mutual last name to the receptionist. The woman greeted them and then motioned to a waiting area. Blaire, however, seemed determined to remain there drumming her fingers on the countertop.

She's going to stand here... in her state... just to make the receptionist nervous... or maybe to avoid talking with me.

"So, Blaire... have you settled on any names yet?"

"What?"

"Names for the baby."

"Oh... Bernie's handling that detail. I've got more pressing things to attend to."

"It's not a detail, Blaire. It's a person."

"Mother... don't think I won't reconsider my agreement if you insist on meddling."

Bridget threw up her hands and turned away, heading for the waiting area... and a seat without a view of her daughter. Outwardly, she worked hard at maintaining an idle manner, nonchalantly picking up the nearest magazine, while inwardly she was seething. It was one thing to be treated rudely... it was another to have Blaire go out of her way to repeatedly show disregard for her own unborn child. After a moment of pause, she made herself calm down... especially after noticing that her clinched fists were crinkling the magazine. The fact of the matter was... the very reason she was here centered around her sparing this child from Blaire's contempt.

"Ms. O'Connor... Mrs. O'Connor... if you'll follow me. I have everything ready."

Bridget looked up to see Blaire's lawyer, Mr. Sanchez, standing in the doorway of the small consultation room she had been in on her previous visits to hammer out the details of the custody agreement. On entering, she was relieved to see papers laid out on the table, ready to be signed.

Blaire... after waddling her way backward into a seat... snatched up the nearest pen and began incessantly clicking it, making it so very clear that she cared nothing for the explanations Mr. Sanchez was offering as a prelude to the signing.

"I think I have everything spelled out according to everyone's wishes. Now, as a reminder, the agreement doesn't go into effect until..."

To Bridget's surprise... and obviously to the lawyer's as well... Blaire grabbed each stack, one-by-one, and began signing where indicated for her to do so. Mr. Sanchez went on as best he could... from which Bridget gathered that he was accustomed to being treated brusquely by his client.

"Umm... until birth. That way, you, Ms. O'Connor, have an opportunity to void the agreement. These things do happen, so having a..."

With a bleep from her cell phone, Blaire raised a stop-sign gesture to her lawyer... and then awkwardly slid forward in the chair so as to push herself up into a standing position.

"Is everything okay?"

"I'm done here. Herb's waiting outside to pick me up."

Blaire offered no further explanation on leaving the room. Even before the snap of the closing door, Bridget had turned her concentration to the contract, making sure that the wording was as agreed upon. She signed the various copies... just as Blaire had... yet felt uneasy on finishing.

"So... is it a problem that Mr. Pearl's not here to sign when we do?"

"Not at all. As long as he signs... which I'm fully convinced he intends to do... everything should be fine. He called a few hours ago to say that he was too busy today. I'm sure he'll be by tomorrow or the next... when he's free."

That made no sense. Had he not, just twenty minutes ago, idly stood in the parking lot hugging her daughter? Suddenly, Bridget got that nauseatingly familiar feeling of being played.

For Blaire, the half year prior to giving birth amounted to a constant drag. Being pregnant was like grating cheese – easy at first, but as the chore progressed... and the hunk of cheese got smaller... she had to slow everything down and take care not to hurt herself. Except the difference was obvious – the hunk inside her was getting bigger and bigger.

Through all those months of sitting around, she worked hard not to think about the thing growing within her. She absolutely refused to wonder what it might end up being... boy or girl... or how it might look... or by chance what part of herself it might come to own. She repeatedly told herself to ignore the thing kicking away at her insides. It was of no greater significance than indigestion... or gas... or maybe a muscle cramp. She needed to do what was best for herself, and that meant not caring about this thing. A time or two during those months, she did catch herself asserting in her thoughts the notion that having a baby was necessary in order to show the world the full spectrum of her toughness. She was the most distinctive woman to have ever lived, so how could she be that without demonstrating to everyone how easy it was to snap right back from having a baby?! Of course, she knew that all such rationalizations were a phony excuse for having gotten herself pregnant... and staying that way. She would never purposefully do anything to inconvenience herself. That was just stupid. She had terminated other pregnancies without a second thought, so why not now? What made this one any different?

Somehow it was… and not because it had anything to do with Bernie. He was a real clod, and in no way better than any of those other men. Yet even as she stood in the guest house bathroom staring at the positive test result, she knew she would go through with this one. Not because it was some kind of ridiculous 'turning of the page' event in life. That shit was for weaker minds. Pregnant or not, she was still the same person… the only person.

So… maybe she was doing it for… her. Not really 'for her' as much as 'because of her.' And not because dumping a baby on the woman's doorstep would be a particularly delightful prank to pull. Having to endure the hell of being pregnant would never be worth that. But maybe… just maybe… this was her way of giving the woman a chance at the second child she never had. The one *he* repeatedly denied her.

And maybe this one'll end up being… better for her… than me. And maybe then she'll finally leave me alone… and I can be free.

One of the more frustrating aspects of being pregnant was having to behold herself in the mirror… though she avoided doing that whenever possible. Her other self in there too often responded with frustration over what she had gotten herself into. Blaire knew exactly why. It was all because she had been bored while recuperating from ankle surgery… and needed some excitement… and Bernie was there in the guest house, drooling all over her… and she made the stupid decision of seducing him… and not because she wanted to give him what he had long been yearning for. She simply needed something to break up the monotony… bad ankle and all… and managed to enjoy the experience a bit. But then he was back for more on the next day… and the next… and it became as boring as hobbling around on crutches. She put an end to that… but not before it was too late.

All that other shit about being pregnant… the wearing of baggy clothes, not being able to sleep at night, sporadic pains in her back and tailbone, eating like a pig, and the answering of asinine baby questions from the press… not to mention total strangers… none of that was as bad as getting sucked back into her mother's life. Just because she was doing this baby thing for her did not mean that she had to tolerate having the woman around. That was why, early on in the pregnancy, Blaire did everything she could to avoid contact with her mother.

Rehab had been a great excuse for a while. In that sliver of time after the ankle was deemed sound and before her body began to show, she was finally able to put some work into her swing. But too many of those precious days ended up being wasted because she felt like barfing. Sure… Bernie arranged for some talk show appearances along the way, but she shut him out completely sometime late in her second trimester after he suggested she consider posing pregnant. No way was she going to have her protruding midsection smeared about in the press… naked or not. In fact, she was determined never again to be depicted on film in any way other than perfect.

The real fact of the matter was… Blaire had never been more bored in all her life. No alcohol meant no bars or nightclubs. But even if she stuck to ginger ale, she doubted seriously whether anybody wanted to party with a pregnant whale. Being so big, she found it impossible to swing a club… or get into her sports car… or do anything even remotely exciting. She tried watching tournament play, but all too often found herself screaming at the TV because of some bonehead move on the part of one of her competitors. It was so very odd… she had never before gotten worked up over someone else's sloppy play. For some unknown reason, she found herself tuning in to daytime soaps, but became so disgusted with the ridiculous displays of brainless drama that she hurled her cell phone into the screen. She could afford a new plasma… but somehow decided to go without. She ate… and slept… and tried to recreate in her mind every round of tournament golf she ever played. Hole after hole, she imagined herself on each tee, straining to recall how it had gone… stroke by stroke. The tedium was torture.

When her water finally broke, Blaire found herself being hustled to the hospital by Bernie's driver… seeing as Bernie was out of town. From the moment the heavy contractions started, the entirety of the experience more than galvanized her against ever getting pregnant again. She spent agonizing hours alone in the birthing room, laboring through the decision to have this baby for her mother. Out of spite… and fear of being nagged throughout the whole birthing process… she refused to call the woman.

Without warning, everything suddenly went wrong. Her OB/GYN was all in a panic because the baby had somehow gotten itself into extreme stress. Before she knew what was happening, Blaire was being knocked out with general anesthesia for a rush Caesarian delivery. She awoke in a special care unit with absolutely no idea of what had happened. A nurse informed her that she had given birth to a perfectly healthy girl, to be brought to her as soon as she was transferred to a normal recovery room. She was asked for the name… and struggled to remember what Bernie had selected. It was his mother's name… Eileen… which Blaire managed to mumble out, making the nurse write it down herself. An hour later, after having been moved, she was presented with the hospital's certificate of birth bearing the name 'Irene O'Connor.' Blaire affixed her signature to the document, not caring one way or another.

Now the nurse's cheerful self was all over her about bringing the thing in. Blaire redoubled her show of grogginess, and still the nurse persisted with what surely would have come across to another woman as a reassuring tone. Not to Blaire. She closed her eyes, feigning sleep. In short time, the nurse was back again with a bassinet on wheels. Before getting her face turned away, Blaire mistakenly caught a glimpse of a pink thing poking through a blanket.

"Of course you want to see your baby! She's beautiful!"

"I'm not interested. Take it away."

"Trust me… just hold her in your arms and everything will change."

Out of the corner of her eye, Blaire sensed the woman scooping the thing up. There was no way she was going to hold that thing. It had already demanded too much from her, and she would not risk it laying hold on more. As the nurse drew near with the wad of wrappings, Blaire crossed her arms as tightly as she could… which unexpectedly pulled on her IV tube, sending a twinge into her wrist. She concentrated on that small pain, allowing it to be the voice speaking through her.

"I don't want it…. and I don't know how I can make myself any clearer."

"Oh, dear, you're just suffering from a very early onset of postpartum depression. It happens all the time… especially to first time mothers. You hold her and I guarantee you'll feel much better."

No way was she going to fall for that.

"Take your psychobabble bullshit… and that thing… and get the hell outta here!"

To her surprise, the nurse did not respond… but neither did Blaire turn her head about to witness how her words were received. Her eyes remained fixed on the wall. In the silence, she picked up on a faint gurgle from the infant… and cursed herself for having not plugged her ears. But then came the warbled squeak of wheels moving across the floor. The nurse was finally gone with the bassinet.

Blaire relaxed her arms back to her side, but kept herself hardened. She had made her decision and would not change. Now, the only way to fully seal it for certain was to hate… to hate the man who had gotten her pregnant… to hate the child who had interrupted her life.. to hate the mother who was so needy… and to hate herself for giving in. Yet somehow, the hate was not working the way she needed it to. It still connected her to the child. She needed something else... a very different stance.

You know... it's not a person... it's a thing.

No more significant than a... bug... or a worm.

Just a prop... and a really nasty one at that.

It doesn't belong on the stage of my life. It'll just mess up my play.

Actually... it doesn't really exist. Not like me.

Only I matter. Only I truly exist.

She repeated such things over and over in her head, allowing them to flow in and fill her. Slowly, they took away the rage, replacing it with a stronger, more powerful influence. She imagined the assurance of it to be coursing through her veins, borne along by some mysteriously translucent fluid hanging in the bag at bedside. Drop by drop, all ties to that baby soon dissolved away with the beautifully numbing influence of indifference... with sleep becoming the final argument to seal it.

Her doctor appeared shortly after she awoke... perhaps on schedule or perhaps in response to an alert from the nurse. Right off, Blaire wanted to know when she could be discharged. He declined to answer, but instead began lecturing her about what she should expect emotionally and psychologically in the aftermath of Caesarian childbirth.

What the fuck?! And I thought the nurse's postpartum shit was lame! This guy's actually claiming that I'm suffering from post-traumatic stress syndrome! From giving birth?! He's got to be kidding!

"So you see... in some ways... it's perfectly understandable that you should associate the stress of what you've been through with your baby. It's a very normal response."

"Good. Glad we got that cleared up. Now if you don't mind leaving, I'm tired."

"So... are you willing to give it another try... holding your baby? You must realize that she needs to nurse... and your body needs that too."

Blaire would not respond, facing away as before. None of them could possibly understand the line she had drawn in order to protect herself. Everything depended on her not crossing it.

"Lowell... I just got the call... Blaire's... well... she's already had her baby!"

"You're kidding?"

"No! She didn't even let me know she was going in. And it's worse... she's on her way here now!"

"She's already left the hospital?!"

"Lowell, she gave birth three days ago! It's a girl, by the way… Irene… and I can't wait to see her… but…"

"But what? Is the baby okay?"

"Yes… as far as I know."

"Then what's wrong?"

"I don't know if I'm up to this…"

"Bridget… you're all the child has left"

"Not that! You know I'm excited about taking her. It's… facing Blaire as she hands the child over that concerns me. I wish you were here with me…"

"No problem. I'll head over."

"Don't… not yet at least. Not until Irene and I have had some time to ourselves. You won't get here before Blaire arrives anyway. Wait… I hear a car out front. It might be her. Let me call you back later. Wish me luck…"

She hung up the phone and dashed to the front door. Through the peep hole's distorted view, she recognized Blaire coming out of the back of a limousine parked at curbside. As Bridget got the front door open, she saw that the driver had already come around to remove the infant car seat, with her heart skipping a beat on first seeing the swaddled form of a newborn. With Blaire leading the way, the driver carried the car seat up the walk.

"Blaire – are you okay? You were supposed to call me when…"

"I checked myself out."

After an awkward moment of hesitation, the driver made to hand the car seat to Bridget, but Blaire snatched it away with a curt nod that dispatched him back to the car.

"Allow me to take Irene. You really shouldn't be carrying anything after your…"

"I'm fine, Mother. Don't nag. Well… are you going to let me in… or do we do this on your front porch?"

She stepped aside so Blaire could enter first, but found herself looking back toward the driver as he was reentering the limo.

"Bernie's out of town."

Not knowing what to make of Blaire's disregard for her own condition… or of her being chauffeured about by Bernie's driver… or the driver's matter-of-fact indifference… or even of Bernie not making an effort to be there… Bridget opted to let it all go and follow her daughter inside. Blaire went only as far as the threshold to the living room.

"Okay… umm… then let me show you what I've done with the spare room. I think Irene will be very…"

"I can't stay, Mother. I've got an appointment with a trainer to discuss upper body conditioning… and then I'm getting another opinion on my…" She paused, clumsily gesturing down with a finger to trace a line along her lower abdomen. "…stitches. My guy says to wait four weeks before doing anything. That's total bullshit."

Bridget stood there completely stunned, not knowing in the least what to say or do.

"You know… we don't need to have a ceremony, if that's what you're waiting for. I'm only here to drop the kid off… like we agreed."

Bridget noticed then that Blaire, in gesturing down with the same finger, did not lower her eyes to look upon Irene. For whatever reason, she knew in a flash that a falsehood was coming.

"Don't worry, Mother… I'll be by to check on her later."

The opposite was so very obvious. Her warped daughter was desperately anxious to leave… and never come back.

"I'm at a total loss to understand you, Blaire. You've never borne the responsibility of another… I know that all too well. But this… this is… this is really sad. One day, Blaire… I hope for your sake… you'll look in a mirror and be shocked at what you see. You have no idea what you're giving up. This baby is your future, and you're selling it so very cheaply."

"I didn't come here for a lecture."

"No… I'm sure you didn't. As in countless times before, you're only going to do what you think is best for yourself. So… do what you came to do."

Bridget stood there in a strained silence… right up until the point at which Blaire abruptly stuck out the infant car seat toward her. The extension of Blaire's arm… which could not have been good for her incision… went too far, forcing Bridget to hastily cradle the entire thing in her arms instead of being allowed to grasp it by the handle. After a moment of panic in which she sought and found balance, Bridget looked up to see a twisted grin fade from off Blaire's face.

"See that you take good care of her."

Blaire immediately turned about and was gone.

The days to follow were surreal to Bridget. With a lack of sleep and much weariness, she often found that the past and present got twisted about in her mind such that the certainties of caring for baby Irene often got themselves tangled up with the vagaries of having once done so with a baby Blaire. In time, she came to focus her emotion toward enjoying the discovery of Irene.

The baby was not overly fussy, possessing a remarkably even temperament that was easily entertained. Beautiful too, with strawberry blondish wisps of hair… just like her mother's… and the same smile and cute little button nose. By the way Irene instantly relaxed in her arms the very first time, Bridget knew that this baby would be a cuddler.

As wonderful as Irene was, she still required a constant level of effort… like any other baby would… making Bridget tired all the time. She hardly slept… or ate… or even showered. Lowell made frequent visits… bringing her takeout and flowers, doing shopping for her, and even babysitting so she could take a nap. All his assistance only barely took the edge off her exhaustion.

As the weeks went by, she slowly found herself getting into the swing of being a mother again. With improved stamina, she got by on less sleep and finally managed to establish a daily routine. Maybe she would even try going back to work in a month or so… part time only… assuming she could identify a reliable daycare facility near her workplace.

As things with Irene gradually became easier, Bridget found that only one overarching stress hung over her – Bernie had not yet signed the custody papers.

None of her dealings with Bernie Pearl had ever been easy. From the beginning of his involvement with Blaire, he promoted a separation between his client and her mother. So… Bridget willingly kept to herself and left her adult daughter in the hands of this agent. This situation, however, was totally different. Irene was over a month old, and neither parent had come by once to see her. So for the sake of this precious infant granddaughter, Bridget was more than willing to entangle herself again within the world of Bernie Pearl.

The baby equipment was loaded into the back of her car, she had the diaper bag fully stocked, and Irene was already strapped into her car seat.

"You're sure you want to go through with this on your own? I'm more than happy to come along and help."

"I can handle it, Lowell. Besides, being alone… and looking terribly helpless… it's all part of my plan. Trust me… it won't work if you're there with me."

It was the morning of the first day of what she had dubbed 'Operation Attrition' – her plan to wear down Bernie Pearl. She drove to the high rise that housed his business, parked in the garage across the street, and then lugged Irene and the equipment into his building. She had been there twice before, yet was still uncertain as to the overall layout of the main lobby. She was pleased that her sketchy memory had not failed her. There was a ladies' room, a water fountain and some seating… everything she needed.

At first, as she entered, the security guard eyed her suspiciously… likely because of all the baby equipment… but did not approach until she began unfolding the portable crib.

"Excuse me, ma'am. Can I help you?"

"Yes… that would be very kind of you. Would you mind finishing this crib for me? I can never quite figure out how to get it set up." Which was not the case… though she had a role to play. "If you could put it over there by the…"

"That's not what I mean. What're you doing?"

"Well… I'm… setting up a crib, of course."

"You can't do that here. This is an office building… not a…"

"I'm sorry… I forgot to mention that I'm here waiting for someone."

"Who? Never mind… that doesn't matter. You'll need to…"

"I'm waiting for Mr. Pearl. You see… this is his daughter."

Bridget pointed to Irene, still strapped in her car seat. The man stared down at the baby, most likely trying to figure out if this could possibly be the daughter of the building's most prominent occupant… and a notoriously single one at that.

"Umm… maybe you should just go up to his office. He's probably waiting for you there."

"No. Actually… he doesn't even know we're here. But this is where I'm going to meet him."

Bridget turned her back on the man and continued to make a show out of struggling with the crib's assembly. When she next looked up, he was at his station making a call, but was back to her shortly… a bit more formal than before.

"I'm sorry, ma'am. Mr. Pearl's out of the office today and won't be back for a few days."

"Thank you for finding that out for me." She began unstrapping Irene from the car seat, making the process seem more labored than it actually was. "So tell me… do you happen to have a microwave somewhere nearby? I was going to heat up a bottle with the hot water in the ladies' room, but a microwave would be considerably easier."

"Did you hear what I said?"

"Yes, of course."

"I'm sorry, but if you don't leave immediately I'm going to be forced to call the police."

"Please do… and while you're at it, call the Los Angeles County Child

Support Services too. Tell them that the infant daughter of Mr. Bernie Pearl has been abandoned in the lobby of his office building." She fought down the impulse to smile at the startled look developing on his face. "Tell you what… I'll wait right here while you make those calls."

He stood there befuddled for a few seconds before returning to his station. Already, the first of the morning's arrivals to the building were passing through the lobby. Their perplexed glares… sometimes disapproving… did not discomfort her in the least. They were actually part of her plan.

The security guard came back after a few minutes.

"Mr. Pearl's on the phone. He'd like to speak with you."

With Irene now in her arms, Bridget went about rummaging in the diaper bag with a frenzied haste.

"Ugh… not right now. I think she needs changing. Tell him I should be free later on if he'd care to stop by."

"I already told you… he won't be coming in today."

"That's too bad. Please tell him I'll be here until six… in case he gets free. If not, tell him I'll be here tomorrow… and every day afterward… until he finally comes to see me."

Off he went, but was soon back with the building manager. That man repeated everything the security guard had said.. including the threats… but Bridget held her ground, knowing that no one would dare forcibly remove the daughter of Mr. Bernie Pearl. Both men eventually returned to the security desk where they consulted together in whispers. She gave them no further mind, as all her attention shifted to Irene.

The hours of that first day wore on uncomfortably. Bridget made no effort to dull the sights, sounds or smells of an infant's presence in the lobby. She wanted every person passing through to take note. For the few who dared to complain, Bridget was quick to tell them that this was Mr. Pearl's child, that she was waiting for Mr. Pearl, and that if they had issues they should take them up with Mr. Pearl. Not once did she yield. After all, this was a battle of wills – a tired-out grandmother's versus that of a very influential sports agent.

Bernie did not show up that day… or the next… likely expecting her to cave in. At the end of each of those days, Bridget packed up and left the way she came. On the third morning, she was once more bright and early in the lobby, and once more endured the stares of those arriving for work. It was not until the late afternoon that Bernie finally decided to show up, approaching her directly through the building's front doors.

"Bridget, if you insist on keeping this up, I guarantee you, child protective services is going to take this baby away from you. Is that what you want?"

She was absolutely prepared for this.

"There's a more important question, Bernie... is that what *you* want? This is your child, not mine. But I'm sure they'll be asking me questions about why you've abandoned her to the lobby of your building for the last three days. You can bet I'll tell them that you knew she was here, but did nothing. I wonder what the radio folks down at KGGQ sports will have to say about this when I call them? Or maybe I should skip the locals and go to one of the national outlets? You know... I heard an interesting rumor somewhere that you're trying to negotiate some big deal in professional soccer... wonder if this will get in the way?"

"What is it you're after, Bridget? If it's money, then you can forget it."

"Have your lawyer bring over the signed custody papers right now... and I'll leave for good."

"There's surely more to it than that. What's the catch?"

"There's no catch. The contract already states that I'll not lay claim to child support from either you or your client. You do realize, Bernie, that without your signature, I can petition the court for child support from you? You'll be paying from now until she turns eighteen. But if you sign full custody over to me, just as your client's done, then the law will be on your side."

She noticed him run a finger around the inside of his collar, and knew she had him.

"I'm going to need some time to think about this."

"Why? So you can figure out an angle to play? No, Bernie – you've had all the time you deserve. Why you haven't signed before now is beyond me."

"It's... personal."

"By that, I gather it has more to do with Blaire than with this baby of yours. You know, you're only deluding yourself if you think you can control her through this child. The fact that she signed right off has got to tell you something."

"Well, what about you?! Why'd you agree to..."

"I'm not the one you should be worried about. I'm going to tell you the same thing I told you over two years ago – get out while you can."

For the first time, he softened, sinking his chin to his chest.

"But... I care about her... and would have thought you did too."

"She doesn't care about you or me... or this child for that matter. She's incapable of caring about anybody but herself... or didn't you take seriously the results of that psychopathy assessment you did on her eons ago?"

"How'd you know about that?"

"It doesn't matter. What matter's, Bernie, is that you're messing with fire… and she's going to keep burning you."

He still had his face down toward the lobby's carpeting, so Bridget, sensing the moment, softened her voice.

"Bernie… you must see that this is what's best for you… to free yourself from a rather embarrassing situation. I'm not saying you've done this sort of thing with any of your other female clients, but just imagine the impression this will leave in the media if everyone finds out that you're the father of Blaire's child. Besides… you must be close to my age… much too old to be saddled with the responsibilities of raising a child. Let me take this burden off you."

Within the hour, Bridget went about packing up the baby equipment for the third and final time. She put the remaining items in the diaper bag, placing on top the manila folder that contained her fully signed copy of the agreement giving her sole custody of her granddaughter. Nestled within her car seat, Irene had napped the whole time she waited for a courier to show up from Bernie's lawyer. The infant's resilience was impressive.

That night, Irene slept for five hours straight… the very first time… and Bridget took it as an encouraging sign of better days to come.

CHAPTER

39

SHOWERS

With each swirl of wind, Bridget savored the feel of cool, damp air coming at her from across the pinewood decking. Grabbing fists full of the quilted blanket, she pulled the edges together around her as one might do in closing off drapes against a draft. She did not mind the cold, being plenty warm when wrapped up… despite not yet managing to maneuver her slippered feet beneath the quilt's tails. The crisp tingle of morning just so happened to be her time. Lowell was making coffee, and would soon bring her out a cup.

She was fully aware that the sun had risen, in agreement with the almanac's account, though a layer of dull purple clouds blocked her sight of it. She did not mind the sky being overcast either. Somehow, the low canopy gave her a sense of security unlike anything possible from the bright glare of Southern California. The thought made Bridget smile.

No car horns or sirens… just the songs of birds mingled with the soft splatter of rain on the roof.

For in those sounds, she found a kind of warmth that no blanket could ever provide.

A steady shower had gone on all night, though she slept far too soundly to be disturbed by it. Like the camper who sets up their tent in the darkness, Bridget rose early in anticipation of discovering what newness this morning's light might bring. In the months they had spent here, the sweetness of this air went far toward purging from memory the smog of LA. South Dakota was not a place she had ever envisioned finding herself. At first, there had been the nightly fears that wolves… or bears… or some other creature of the dark might break in… yet it was not too long before she came to realize that life in the wilderness was far more secure than in her previous gated community. Already, the scattered woods about this ranch house felt like a shelter to her. Though many aspects of living in seclusion were still foreign, she had quickly come to embrace the purity of the prairie. But whether it be tropical paradise or lonely plain, Bridget no longer derived peace of mind from what was seen or felt… but instead from what was known.

Her life as a mother could not be condensed down so simply to a grade of success or failure, as if all things must rest in a delicate balance between realized happiness and reluctantly swallowed sorrow. To the best of her ability, she had made every effort to reach her daughter. She remained terribly sad for Blaire, but had also come to accept that which was true – how she felt about her daughter mattered not. Blaire's life was Blaire's, for good or ill… with Bridget finally making a mother's supreme lifetime sacrifice of yielding to that choice. So rather than linger on the pain, she concentrated on embracing the new things in life. A crib situated in a small room through the wall behind her was one of those. She leaned her head back against the wood paneling as a reminder not to re-immerse herself in the past. The statute-of-limitations had long since expired on those feelings of guilt.

Her eyes came to rest on another object of encouragement. A favorite sight of hers from this porch was a not-too-distant mesa, with its perfectly smooth line marking the horizon and rugged cliffs all about its sides. On clearer mornings, the rising sun lit up the portion facing her, but on this day clouds hung at the table top… almost as if the sky's shades of bluish gray emanated from the mysterious regions above. She squinted so as to blur the effect, and imagined instead that the heavens were being supported by that huge hunk of rock. More often, though, she would sit on this porch and contemplate how the flattop once marked the level of the prairie, but wind and water partnering together with time had decayed what once was… leaving only this lonely stretch before her. She knew that nothing would be left of it with more of the same. Yet there it stood, with horizontal streaks persisting in beauteously layered hues of rust, brown and chalky yellow. It was not letting go and giving up, but neither was it fighting against what would inevitably be its end.

Despite the distortions brought on by the weak current of rain, Bridget could easily make out places where massive sections had fallen off the sides and contributed to alluvial slopes about the base. All that rubble and scree marked the most recent faults in that proud monument's form. Other failings in the distant past had been spread out onto the adjacent prairie by the slow workings of time… some of which had become covered by small stands of pine. She would often sit on this porch pondering over those features, and imagining herself telling the mesa not to be ashamed of what was becoming of it. All that erosion was transforming it from one stage of its life to the next… and it need not be afraid of the future. Her feelings of admiration toward it would remain strong irrespective of the deterioration it was experiencing. Though it crumbled all about its edges, the rock… in that moment… was at the height of beauty. It was special… a blessing.

She held up her left hand at arm's length, allowing her eyes to gradually shift focus from the mesa beyond to the rings on her finger. Somehow, she felt newness of life despite the many years already misspent. It was not just the diamond… or the gold band… neither very different from the ones she had previously worn. Yet these new ones had a very different feel to them because the man who gave them to her was genuine. He loved her fully… and she loved him in the same way. That had made saying 'yes' to him as natural as breath itself.

The front door rattled, and Lowell emerged with two mugs and a smile.

"How's the morning?"

"Beautiful as ever… and peaceful."

"That it is."

"Irene still asleep?"

"Like the little angel she is."

He sat down beside her, their shoulders slouching together as each sipped while taking in the pine-and-prairie feel of their home.

"Thank you for moving us here."

"Anything for you, Darlin'."

A thousand miles away, from Blaire's perspective, the same kind of rainy morning had all the makings of a shitty day. The night before had been difficult enough. Despite repeated complaints, her room's air conditioner had not been fixed properly. Whereas on the previous day when the fan only eked out a weak stream of air… and the temperatures held in the nineties… now, after some idiot repairman had gotten his hands on it, the blades clattered away with an incessant grind… no matter what speed was selected. It was absolutely impossible to sleep with that racket, but if she turned the fan off, the muggy heat of a Texas night soon had the room broiling. She chewed out the guy at the front desk without getting an ounce of satisfaction, for there were no other rooms available. It was equally clear that hotel maintenance would not be responding to her calls. The best she could do all night was cram ear plugs in and clutch a pillow over her head.

On autopilot, Blaire went through her morning routine in preparation for the tournament's final round. After dressing, she downed a carton of 2% milk and a cold English muffin... along with a handful of chewable antacid tablets... then gathered up her belongings and headed out. Dragging her carry-on and garment bag to the curb, she hailed a taxi. Her tight cash-flow situation had necessitated foregoing a rental, and though this was not the first time she went without, having to repeatedly cab-it added an especially humiliating twist to what was supposed to be a triumphant comeback.

Of course, her bad mood went well beyond the lousy hotel accommodations... or being jostled about in a cab by someone who barely spoke English. Neither was it related to all this rain that had come out of nowhere in the early morning. The reality was... she had barely made the cut on Friday... and done little on Saturday to improve her ranking. She was at the bottom of the pack, and had earned herself one of the early tee times on this dreary spring morning. Undoubtedly, she would be paired with two other losers rather than have the pleasure of going mano-a-mano with one of the leaders later in the day.

Finally at the clubhouse, she threw herself into her pre-round preparations, trying to harness the intensity she had routinely displayed in her earlier years... though not much of anything was there other than irritation. Closing her locker, she made her way out to the course, passing by a cluster of girls gathered together in their collective Sunday morning tournament ritual. They ignored her, and she ignored them... or tried to. Of late, she found herself begrudgingly envying girls like these, though not because they were younger than her... with their entire careers ahead of them... and she was struggling to regain the form that had once earned her the nickname 'the Flair.' The real reason was that they seemed happy... and Blaire hated happy people... for she had no such power of her own. For whatever reason... whether through brainlessness or some inexplicable gift of insight... the way those girls pleasantly went about life gnawed at her. It was like they could compete as intensely as she could, yet were free from the burden of having to be first... though many of them often were.

Her rent-a-caddie was waiting outside... just as grumpy as on the day before. Though he supposedly was familiar with this course, it being where he normally worked, she found him to be totally worthless for anything other than carrying clubs. In fact, he did far more talking about the quality of her previous shots than he ever did regarding strategy for the one upcoming.

She spent the next half hour familiarizing herself with the speed of the practice green and getting loose with a bucket of balls at the range… then made her way to the tournament starter. The guy, obviously from the host club too, completely ignored her in providing her caddie with the go-ahead for moving to the first tee. Blaire gave the idiot an earful, as he should be addressing her, not her help.

The other two members of her designated grouping were already there. Each curtly shook her hand before moving off to re-form their own private twosome within the threesome, making it so obvious that neither cared to associate with her.

Little prima donna bitches… who needs them anyway?!

The meager collection of spectators gathered at the first tee for their group was entirely the friends and family of those two girls. Blaire expected that was as good as it would get given the foul weather. It had been a very long time since she last played alongside a throng of 'Blaire the Flair' fans. Not since before the ankle injury. Of course, it was absolutely embarrassing not to have anyone clamoring for her autograph or begging her to acknowledge their devotion from the gallery. Her fall had been far.

Screw them all… I'm better off without those annoying distractions.

She took her turn teeing off… a decent drive, though nothing spectacular… and then headed out on the fairway ahead of her idiot caddie, who consistently lagged behind with a lazy pace. That was fine by her… except she was paying him to do a decent job… which obviously meant being available to talk about golf.

As in the previous rounds, on hitting the fairway, she found her thoughts being dragged backward into a consideration of the past… and where things had gone bad.

I don't get it… how could something so trivial as coming out of a bunker the wrong way send me spiraling?

She could not have seen that coming… no one could… so surely it was not her fault. After all, it was not like she could see into the future… which obviously no one could. So twisting her ankle in the way she had… no one could have avoided that. And how was she suppose to recover from giving birth any faster than she had. No one could. It was all so unfair to expect her to have done better than what no one could. And it was equally all wrong… what with her greatness… to find herself ending up being like everyone else… like all those 'no-one-coulds.'

Of course, she was fully aware that few golfers made a go of it after having a baby, but had always thought that was due to them being too far out of shape… or maybe having a bizarre love of motherhood replace their desire for the game. No one bothered telling her that pregnancy spreads the hips and shifts the body's center of gravity. She sensed it the very first time she took to the range – her swing had changed. That beautifully smooth and hitch-free flow from right to left was now so very clunky… and the difference had nothing to do with the ankle. That eventually had healed. After months of working at it, she finally found a way to compensate with a more compact approach. It was enough to get her back on tour… though her power was completely gone.

She shook off the thought in order to line up her approach to the first green. In the past, she would have been at least twenty yards closer on this hole… using an eight rather than a six. She took her stance, trying not to think about what she had lost without finding any gain. Her shot came off fat owing to the rain-soaked turf. Even without seeing it land… or because of that… she knew the ball had not carried the front trap. The sand in there would be wet, obviously making it difficult to get any kind of decent lift with the wedge… which likely meant a poor recovery and a two-putt for a bogey.

Shit… first hole and I'm already down a stroke.

Her comeback on tour had fallen far short of her expectations. It took a month before she made her first cut… and then many more months before making a cut became something even remotely certain. In the whole year back, she had failed to finish in the top ten on any tournament. The league, she was sure, would love nothing more than for her to drop out… except… no one seemed all that bothered by her anymore. They no longer rose to the bait of her tricks. She used to be able to throw a tantrum and get the tourney officials all worked up… but lately… they just ignored her. Truth was… nobody seemed to care one way or another that she was back on tour.

There her ball was… lying in the very center of the trap. Her moron caddie just stood beside her staring down at it… so she spun him around and snatched the sand wedge out of her bag. Gingerly stepping down in, she was surprised to find the trap so deep that nothing could be seen from the bottom… not even the top of the pin.

"Hey, you – go do your job. Lift the pin up so I can see where it's at."

He trudged off without a word. She waited there in the damp sand for what seemed like forever before the top of the pin happened to poke up above the front lip of the trap... and then go right back down out of sight again.

Moron! Doesn't even have the brains in his head to know that he's supposed to hold it up until I say so.

Doesn't matter anyway... I'm not getting out of here with any kind of... flair.

On every side, the rim was well above her head... so high that all she recognized was sand, a ring of grass, a dark sky... and how very deep in she had gotten herself. Her career was supposed to take her into the heights of celebrity and beyond. To be alone, at the very top, was the way of the champion. But now... even though she had the stage all to herself... the audience had left her. Not a person on the course could see her. She was at the bottom of a trap... and just as alone.

She ground her feet into the sand, working hard to disregard a notion that she had somehow gotten herself caught in a pit of her own making. She had absolutely no one in her life. The fans had abandoned her, the league had become bored with her antics, and her competition... along with their families... were steering clear of her. Everybody was treating her like she was some kind of a worm... rather than a snake.

She took the shot... and knew right away from her caddie's grunt that the ball would end up far from the pin. She climbed out, not caring if the guy ended up doing his job of raking out the trap.

Bernie's not doing his job either.

The endorsements were gone, and the media attention had dried up. In refusing to return her calls or text messages, Bernie was making it painfully clear that he had moved on to other projects... younger women in their prime. Everything he had promised... everything she had claimed as her own... it was all a lie... just a flimsy backdrop to her stage. To him, she was nothing more than a prop that had served its purpose and needed to be moved off. He had taken over her script and was rewriting everything. She had thought herself to be in full control... to be untouchable.

But he certainly out-Blaired me.

The tournament cycle would not return her to the West Coast for nearly a month, but then she was determined to hunt down the bastard... and force him to make good on his commitments. Walking out to her ball, it lying a good forty feet from the pin, she took relish in the idea of confronting him for his betrayal. But in reality... she knew that any plans she might come up with would be as far-fetched as this upcoming putt. Somehow, she no longer had it in her to kindle the fires of revenge. Not that she was incapable of making him squirm... or that he might not deserve it... only that she was coming to distrust her satisfaction of it. Payback had always been so sweet, bringing her that sense of superiority... but what was the good of it now? Even if she sent him crashing to his knees, she would still be at the bottom... all alone.

She somehow managed to two putt the green and avoid a double bogey. Seventeen holes to go... and she was already so very tired. What little sleep she got last night was disrupted by a stupid dream. She found herself inside a huge bubble, with a crowd of people gathered around outside. Every single one of them had their backs turned on her. She was screaming with all her might, yet not one paid attention. Then the bubble began to shrink... and in terror she frantically went about poking and punching at it... desperately trying to get out. The thin barrier flexed, but would not break. She awoke in a panic of suffocation to the irritating grind of her room's malfunctioning fan. Laying in bed afterward with the weight of the dream on her, she never managed to fall back into sleep.

The damp to this morning was not allowing her to warm up, which made getting through the front nine pure drudgery. The forecast for the back nine called for more rain, along with periods of lightning – the golfer's bane. Looking up toward the sky, she stepped off the ninth green awkwardly and caught a spike on the rough. The ankle twinged, and she immediately experienced a surge of fear that she had reinjured herself. Putting her left foot down hesitantly, she was relieved at having absolutely no pain. Moving up to the clubhouse, the thought that she might have to go on living like this... afraid to take the next step... could not be shaken off.

Of course, Bernie was not the only one to have forsaken her. Her own mother had broken all ties with her. No phone calls. No messages. No updates on the baby. When Blaire finally had enough of being ignored, she headed downtown to confront her at her workplace... only to find that the woman had skipped town with the cowboy. Both of them had moved to some god-awful place in the middle of nowhere, taking the baby... *her baby*... with them.

What the hell kind of a mother abandons her own daughter like that?!

Suddenly, Blaire was brought up short by an unsettling realization – that she was precisely that kind of mother. She had abandoned her own daughter... and in a far greater time of need. Yet despite the startling nature of this recognition, she was not surprised that she felt nothing in the way of regret. Her decision was what it was. Still... there was something not quite right about feeling nothing. No obligation. No guilt. No empathy. No connection at all. That baby was just a thing. Surely that was not the way of a mother. All of Nature provided a different model... of mothers sacrificing everything on behalf of their offspring. But no matter how she strained her thinking, she could not find herself anywhere in that pattern. She had considered her way to be so superior… but now, it almost seemed as if something was wrong with her… and not the other way around.

The tourney at the tenth tee was rushing her to get started, as the bad weather was coming. The front nine had dropped her two strokes… though her mind was no longer on golf. She lost another with a pathetic performance on the par three 10th.

Just get it over with.

The sky flashed as she was putting out on the 11th, and then opened up with sheets of chilling rain. Their meager gallery scattered, with her and her group scarcely reaching a shelter off the 11th green. Normally, the organizers would have carts ready to hustle players to the clubhouse, but the rain came on suddenly… and the tourney rep at the 11th said the carts were needed to get the leaders in first.

Even though the shelter had a foot-high gap about the base allowing air to flow through, she still found the space to be stuffy. With barely enough room for the golfers, their caddies, the two tourney spotters and a puny little standard bearer, Blaire moved to the opening and claimed it as her own. To no surprise, her caddie went off to associate with his own kind, leaving her be.

Leaning against the wooden frame, Blaire stared out into the rain. It was intensifying, with periodic flashes that conveyed an obvious warning to anyone carrying clubs. She glanced back toward the 11th fairway and noticed a small group of spectators clustered beneath some trees… though the deluge soon obscured their forms. The green of the golf course was slowly fading into the noisy gray of this downpour. Soon, even the chatter of the shelter's other occupants became drowned out by the pounding of drops on the roof.

To her annoyance, occasional swirls of wind carried mist through the doorway. At one point, an intense gust forced her to tilt her head down, with her visor providing only a meager protection for her face. It was then that she noticed a large puddle outside the opening, extending right up to her feet, it being fed by the roof's run-off. She could just make out a crude reflection of herself in the midst of the many interconnected rings from raindrops pelting the surface. It struck her as odd that she preferred this distorted view over the clearer reflection that might come about if the puddle was still.

There was so much more wrong in her life than her game being off. This lack of feelings… something she had always considered to be a strength… now confused her. All her efforts at manipulating people by exploiting their feelings… it had never really brought her any true feeling of her own. Sure, there was always the utter delight found in controlling someone… until they wised up and no longer took the bait. Then she had to find a new target… another prey… and those were becoming so much harder to locate. It was like having a ravenous appetite… with absolutely nothing to eat. Besides, all her mind games were wearing her out and distracting her from the game she loved.

This was still not her main problem. All her life, she had contempt for normal people, thinking herself so very far above them. But what if not being able to feel anything for anyone actually made her less than normal? If that was true… if she was actually abnormal… then she was the most pathetic person of all. How was she to make up a deficiency she had always considered to be a strength? She had nobody in her life, and was absolutely incapable of connecting with anyone on a meaningful level… and equally incapable of having the kind of happiness that came from filling a void she never knew was there. She was a prisoner to that void… trapped within a bubble that was herself.

At that moment, a change in the wind caused the rain to be swept away from the opening, allowing the puddle before her to still. As Blaire looked down into its quieted surface, the sky suddenly lit up with lightning, making her reflection perfectly clear. Except upon the puddle's mirror was not herself… at least not the person she was today… but instead something of a phantom from the past… a young girl staring up at her. In a heartbeat, Blaire recognized the visor on that girl's head, for it bore an oddly distinctive emblem from the past. The girl also seemed to recognize her, for she smiled back. Yet it was not at all a pleasant-looking expression. Blaire had smiled like that so many times… and fully recognized its meaning. Immediately, she found her very worth draining down her body and out her feet, being sucked away by the image in the puddle. For the girl in there was smirking… not *with* her .. but *at* her.

Overwhelmed, Blaire fell back from the puddle, for this reflection… unlike any she ever beheld before… had nothing but contempt for her. This younger self had taken the full measure of her, the adult, and found the result so very lacking. She was deemed a fraud… a blurry replica of the perfect design conceived so long ago on a very different glassy surface.

The wind, mercifully, took up its previous tack, with the puddle once more becoming decorated by rings and ripples. Blaire stepped forward and waited, but the girl in there did not reappear. The surface before her remained nothing but a clouded window.

All of a sudden, she realized that the puddle was not just a window – it was *the window*. Not one she could see beyond, yet still one she somehow knew could free her from this trap that was herself. And nothing else mattered but finding a way through that window… for it was her only shot at recovery.

Fully fixed on the puddle, Blaire flinched at the feel of someone poking her shoulder. It was just Sandbox… one of the other golfers in her party. As the girl came into focus, Blaire struggled to remember her actual name.

Katrina… ahh… Thygesen.

She was one of those talented European newcomers… a wave of young teenagers hitting the tour… all strong, smart and extremely attractive.

"Snake! Did you hear me?! Spotter says the radar's clearing. This'll pass over in fifteen minutes or so."

"Blaire."

"What?"

"My name's Blaire… not Snake."

"Okay… whatever."

Blaire, fully expecting the girl to go away, returned her concentration to the rippled surface before her.

"Is something wrong? Why're you staring at that puddle?"

"I have a daughter."

"What?"

"I have a daughter."

"I know that. Everyone knows it. Snake… I mean Blaire… you're practically old enough to be my mother."

"She's real."

"What?"

"My daughter… she's real. She exists."

"Ahh… yeah."

Blaire delayed until Katrina had turned away, and then crouched down to the puddle's edge. Picking up a meaningless little thing, she gently moved it to beneath the hedge that bordered the opening. Then, hesitating for just a second, she stood back up and stepped directly into the middle of the puddle. Whether anybody was watching her, Blaire cared not to know, for she remained there with purpose… waiting for the cold water to fully seep into her shoes, soak her socks, and take away her pride. Not expecting it, she suddenly found herself feeling lighter… so weightlessly bouyant that she seemed to glide across the puddle's surface and flow out with the many rivulets that ran down the cart path toward the 12th tee. The asphalt beneath her spiked shoes felt all wrong, so she followed the water's course off the path and into the wet grass, delighting in its spongy feel. All about her was the sound of pouring rain, and she was completely alone in it. Yet the feeling was different than before… from when she stood by herself in the bottom of that sand trap. She somehow found herself having a longing that could not be understood… yet so indescribably strong that all her disdain for this world immediately dissolved away. Lightning flashed overhead, and Blaire took it as a sign. Closing her eyes, she lifted her face to the sky and allowed cold droplets to fill her eye sockets, collect in her ears, and run down her already soaked body. This shower took her warmth, and in return bathed her with new sight.

I've been such a fool.

The rain mixed with her unseen tears, and both washed her clean.

She played the remaining seven holes of that final round completely wet, not bothering to take advantage of the time provided for players to change clothes. Instead, she wanted to shiver… to be cold… to have an inkling of what it must feel like to be treated as she had treated others. From the 12th tee to the 18th cup, her mind was fully occupied in compiling a list of people… real people… she had hurt with her cruelty and deception. She had considered those people to be nothing more than things… just props on the stage of her life… but somehow now understood that life's play had so many actors than her. At the top of this cast list was her mother… followed closely by an infant dumped as refuse into her grandmother's arms. And the memory of the face in the puddle was the punctuation mark to each name on this list. For when the image was taken away, the first thing Blaire saw in the puddle was a worm, writhing about as if drowning. She had considered her own baby to be no better. Yet Blaire was that worm… and nothing was more important than saving herself and her child.

She put together her best back nine of the year, birdieing several of the remaining holes and nearly eagling the 15th. She moved up six spots to finish twentieth in the tournament. Having holed out on eighteen, she thanked Katrina and the other member of her party, paid her caddie the flat rate they had agreed upon… tipping him beyond what he deserved… and made for the locker room without delay. Even before removing her wet clothing, Blaire was on the phone to her travel agent, rearranging her itinerary. She quickly showered and dressed, then gathered up her things and hurried out of the locker room, not caring in the least what became of her clubs. Snagging the first available taxi out front of the country club's main doors, she relaxed in its backseat on getting a favorable ETA from the driver. She had just enough time to make her new flight.

CHAPTER

40

TURNING

On the edge of the couch, Bridget switched off her cell and carelessly dropped it to the coffee table. The rather loud thud it made should have startled her… would have under normal circumstances… but the conversation she just finished was far from normal. Before trying to make sense of it, she called for Lowell to come into the room.

"You won't believe this… but I just got off the phone with Blaire."

"Really? How'd she get your number?"

"No idea… I didn't ask… I was far too shocked…"

"Why? What'd she want?"

"She phoned from the airport in Dallas. Lowell… she's coming here."

"What?!"

"She'll be here tonight… and she wants to speak with you."

"Me?! What the blazes for?!"

"She wouldn't say… only that it was urgent. Lowell, she's up to something. She said 'I love you.' She's not said that to me since… since… well, not since she was in kindergarten. And then she wanted to know how Irene was doing… and all I could say was 'fine.' She even asked about you."

"What do you make of it?"

"I really don't know… I guess… we'll just have to wait."

For the remainder of the afternoon and into the evening, Bridget moped about the house constructing worst-case scenarios… all of which centered around Blaire trying to take Irene away. She would never allow that to happen… and neither would Lowell… but that kind of determination never kept Blaire from making an unpleasant scene.

Because she could not face doing nothing at all, Bridget spent several frustrating hours pouring over the custody agreement searching for loopholes… all the while bemoaning the fact that the lawyer who drafted the document could not be reached on a Sunday. Lowell eventually took the papers away from her.

"You're getting yourself all worked up for nothing. We have no idea why she's coming. And we can certainly contact the lawyer in the morning if we need to."

As logical as he was being, she could tell that he was nervous too… especially by the way he wore a rut in the carpet with all his pacing. That was far from his style… which told her that the situation was as bad as she imagined it to be. As the hour drew near, he moved out to the front porch in order to head Blaire off when she showed up. Near on eleven… with the sound of a car moving in on the gravel drive… Bridget took to a corner of the living room and waited tensely, trying to imagine from all her years of being duped what Blaire might now have up her sleeve.

Because of things the credit union HR person let slip, Blaire already had their address. Some remote town in South Dakota. So from the moment she left the tournament venue, Blaire's biggest concern was how to persuade her mother that she meant no harm. She had to say things over the phone that she had never said to her mother before… and with all the sincerity she could generate. Unfortunately, she had to end the call abruptly, seeing as her flight out of Dallas was already on the runway. She easily caught the puddle-hopper out of Denver, and arrived in Rapid City after dark. Halfway through the hour long drive to their house… it being somewhere out in the boondocks… her GPS inexplicably failed, forcing her to pull over and study by dome light the map she had gotten from the rental car agent. Carrying out a secret plan had always been so clear… so invigorating… but not this time. She had no idea how she was going to be received… or even if her message would come across as remotely believable. That was critical… that she at least be believable… as even she doubted what she had to say.

From the flights through to this drive, Blaire struggled with a notion that her mother had left LA for the sole purpose of escaping from her… and here Blaire was showing up uninvited to her new place in South Dakota. Even that sounded sketchy to her, so certainly her mother would be on guard... as would the cowboy. Would their distrustfulness prevent her from having the opportunity to speak? Would they slam the door in her face... or maybe never even bother opening it? She needed to stop thinking about such questions... for their answers would be what they were. Instead, she should focus on not getting herself lost down some godforsaken back road to nowhere.

Her GPS eventually came back on, confirming that she was in the right place, and in a short while her headlights panned across a mailbox bearing the name Paxton. As she turned in, her heart rate suddenly jumped. She had arrived... but not yet figured out everything she needed to say. Through a stand of trees, a ranch house came into view... with him sitting on the front porch waiting for her. She turned off her headlights in time... so the glare would not wake the baby... and parked beside a pickup truck. There was no more time for planning... she just had to do. Quickly out of the car and up the porch steps, she was determined to be the first one to speak.

"Hello, Lowell. I'm... sorry if I've kept you up... but this couldn't wait. Mind if we talk out here?"

He nodded, but said nothing on motioning her to a folding chair next to his... one that just so happen to place himself between her and the front door. In times past... in another life... she would have gone right inside without waiting for his approval.

"I... umm... wanted you to know... I'm not here to cause trouble."

"So you're not trying to take Irene away?"

"Hell no! I mean... no... I would never do that to her. You two... you're the best thing for her. I... actually came for... for your advice."

"My advice? What do you mean?"

She could tell he was surprised just by the way he suddenly leaned back in his chair... yet was evidently still on guard because he had his arms crossed. She knew she did that to people... put them on the defensive... and had always thought it a fine thing. Not now. She had no desire to outmaneuver this man. But how was she to get him to understand, when even she did not? How was she to feel what he was feeling... when she had never managed that with anyone before? Rehearsing her lines on the flight over had been nothing more than a game... a meaningless distraction... because even doing something so simple as telling the truth was completely foreign to her.

"I'm... not very good at this... and I've got a lot of ground to make up. I want your advice on how best to... beg my mother for forgiveness."

He sat there with mouth ajar, unable to say a word. She had expected this too… expected him to be stunned… to not believe her. In preparation for this very moment, she had done much thinking on what she knew about him… about what he was like and what he might appreciate hearing from her. In her few interactions with him, he had always seemed to value directness. No beating about the bush or sugarcoating. From the research she had Sanchez's PI do on him… back when her motives were less pure… she learned that he had been a rodeo rider… which likely meant he had done crazy shit like stare down bulls ten times his weight… or ride deranged broncing bucks… or fling himself off a saddle onto a set of horns. She used her imagination to fill in the rest – a lifetime of hard living. Maybe even the ridiculous kinds of cowboy barroom fights that ended with him waking up on the concrete floor of some jail cell. She learned that he had seen war, fought through divorce and addiction, and recently was reunited with a daughter of his own. How he ended up working at a nursing home was still a mystery Yet here he was enjoying a second chance at love… with her mother. All in all, there was little in life he had not struggled through. Now, sitting before this man on his front porch, she suddenly found herself facing someone not too different from herself. A competitor… someone with whom she had no idea how to become a friend.

"I don't know what to tell you, Blaire…"

She waited him out, believing he eventually would… but was surprised when he remained silent… waiting for her to say more.

"I'm… being completely sincere, Lowell. I really want to make things right between us."

"Okay… if that be the case… then let me ask you something. Are you willing to face the past… your past?"

"Yes… that's already begun."

"And you're telling me that you're ready to start over and start right?"

She did not understand why… and did not try to… but found herself bowing her head… almost as if she was following that question down toward the wood decking at her feet.

"Yes… if… if you two are willing to give me that chance…"

"And that's both as a daughter and a mother."

"I… really don't know what that takes… but… yes… both of those things."

"And you'll put an end to all the manipulation, all the lies, and all the preying upon others… especially your mother?"

What he was asking of her, she had already asked of herself… and had no idea how she was to accomplish it. In every way, she only ever looked at others through her lens of control. To find some way of giving that up… to be different than the only self she had ever known and enjoyed… would be near on impossible. She nodded… and then waited.

"Okay… I'm not going to ask what's come over you to bring about this change, but I expect she will. So I'll give you the best advice I can think of – be absolutely truthful with her no matter how much it costs you… and be completely accepting of whatever she gives you in return."

That, Blaire could do, seeing as she spent the last ten hours doing the same things with herself. She nodded again… at which point he rose and moved toward the front door. It was appropriate, she knew, to thank him for his honesty, yet had no way of knowing how to do that… outside of the hollowness of simply saying so. For reasons she was not quite sure of, she extended him a hand… assuming a shake to be a gesture with which he could relate. To her great surprise, he wrapped his arms about her instead… but not the gentle, lingering kind she frequently offered to a man she wanted to unnerve. His was firm… and perhaps fatherly… especially in how he ended it by patting her on the back. It made her feel… ashamed of herself… if such a thing was a thing. In no way did she deserve such kindness… not from someone she had only ever wrangled with.

"I don't know where to start."

"Just do it. Any place is better than never."

She nodded, drew herself up, and turned to the front door, yet paused in indecision as her hand touched its latch.

"Go on in. You'll see her right off."

Blaire gave him a weak smile… more as a way to bolster her own courage… and then moved inside. The décor in the living area before her was surprisingly modern… not rustic in the least. She noted a creamy colored couch… most likely leather… glass-top tables and stylish lamps… all about the polished stonework of a cold fireplace… and then her eyes fell upon her mother, sitting in an armchair facing the door. Blaire immediately recognized the posture – her mother was ever so slightly rocking with hands balled up together on her knees, all in anticipation of experiencing something unpleasant. She had probably never been aware of it, but Blaire… as a teenager… had experimented with what circumstances could best throw her into this state. Generally, anything that involved conflicted responsibilities did the trick… like asking her to take off work for some stupid high school tournament.

Blaire had no such desire in that moment. In fact, she wanted to get to the heart of the matter as soon as possible for her mother's sake… and for her own.

She pointed to the ottoman directly before her.

"Mind if I sit here?"

"Go ahead."

"So… I guess you're wondering why I've… ahh… barged in on you like this."

Her mother said nothing… just sat there silently… yet still slightly shaking. Blaire knew that plainspoken words needed to come now… and she had rehearsed so many of them on the drive over. She closed her eyes, purposing that the first of those words should come forth from the darkness within.

"Mother… all my life I've treated you with disrespect and disdain. I've never shown you anything remotely close to the… love you deserve. I've been a fool… but hopefully one that can change."

She opened her eyes, trying to add to her words a sincerity that her own lack of feelings had always deprived her of.

"I can say it for certain now, Mother… that I so admire you. You're the strongest person I've ever known… because you've put up with me when no one else would. You're giving… and supportive… and someone I can scarcely ever hope to be like… but I want to try. I want to ask for your forgiveness… and an opportunity to start over new with you."

Without really knowing what she was doing, Blaire found herself gently lifting her mother's hands from off her knees and holding them in her own. They were warm… and trembling. But then, to Blaire's great shock, her mother pulled away, leaving an empty shell out of her own hands.

"Blaire… I accept your apology… and I forgive you. In fact… I forgave you long ago. But I still want you to realize something… that doesn't mean I trust you. You've played these kinds of tricks on me before…"

"I know… and I'm sorry. I don't deserve your trust. All I can say is that I want to change. Mother… I'm not normal. There's… something really wrong with me. I don't… feel… like normal people feel… and that makes it hard for me to… know how to change myself."

"Well, that's where you've got it all wrong, Blaire. It's not a matter of changing. It's a matter of… turning."

"I… don't follow you…"

"People don't change. Not really… Not at the core of who they are. I'm not saying that they can't make little improvements in themselves. It's just that… we are who we are. But I believe a person can… turn. They can turn from one thing to another. From putting themselves first to putting someone else first.

And in the turning… I think people end up getting changed… depending, of course, on what they turn to. That's the key part, Blaire… deciding which direction you're going to face in life. You have a lot of work ahead of you to repair the damage you've done. Are you going to face that… or turn away? You know… you can have all the right feelings… or none of them… and it really won't matter. All that really matters is which way you've turned."

Well if that's it… if that's what it takes… then I can do this.

"I think I see… So… Mother… there's something I need to… turn to. About Phoenix…"

Blaire waited through several heartbeats, both preparing herself for what needed to be said… and hoping that her mother might receive it.

"In that moment when I first saw you… across that green… I… I hated you. I'm sorry… but it's true. My whole life… I've never wanted to acknowledge how much in debt I am to you. I couldn't… because to admit that was to admit that I was lacking… and that I owed you something for all your sacrifices. For me… to do that… it was like… like death. So… I allowed that same hate to carry over into the shot… the one that hit off the lip of that trap. If I'd been half the professional I claimed to be, I would have first stepped away from that shot… cleared the hate out of my mind… and then put that ball exactly where I wanted it to be. But I couldn't… because I was too proud to admit that my hate made me weak. It's all because of my ridiculous pride that the shot fell short. It wasn't your doing at all. But I took it out on you… because I was too embarrassed to admit to myself that I was not the woman I claimed to be. I hurt you so deeply… I humiliated you in front of everyone… all to protect myself. And the irony of it all is… from that moment on… I've had to continue in the lie… or everyone would know that I was a fraud. Mother… I'm so terribly sorry for hurting you. Can you… can you ever forgive me for what I've done to you?"

She made to interrupt, but Blaire was determined to keep going.

"I'm not finished, Mother. There's so much more I need to hold myself accountable for. Terrible things you have no idea about… But let me start with what you said to me… on the day that I… dumped Irene on you. That I would one day look into a mirror and be shocked at what had become of me… and what I'd given up to keep up the lies. Those things were all true. They've haunted me… slowly boring a hole in my brain… and I haven't been able to get them out. I don't know what kind of a mother I can ever be… surely not one as caring and gentle as you… but I want to try. Will you… give me a second chance?"

Bridget tensed up of a sudden, for she could hear that Blaire was already out of her car and up on the front porch with Lowell. Nothing of what they were saying could be made out from within the house... only that neither was yelling at the other. That, she credited to him and not to Blaire. She was fairly confident that he would not allow Blaire inside... not unless he was absolutely convinced she meant no harm... which Bridget could not in her wildest imaginings conceive as possible. But then the knob jiggled... and Blaire entered, pausing there at the front door. She watched her pan about the room, critiquing the place... obviously searching for an advantage to take. Whatever she had come to say, Bridget wanted it said quickly... so Blaire would be gone as soon as possible. In no way was she going to fall for another of her tricks... not with the fate of Irene in the balance. None of what was about to happen could be counted on as real. No way Blaire had come all this way for a noble cause... to restore what she had broken... for that was far from Blaire's way. Blaire always went to great lengths in deceiving.

So don't be moved by anything she says. Not by her charms... or her false tears... or her spectacularly worded promises. And definitely don't give in to her threats.

Bridget patiently listened, but much more so sought out those little signs of deceit in Blaire. A well-scripted speech, with eyes flickering up to see how the words were being received... or a huge winning smile that covered over a more genuine smirk... or a little twitch of self-satisfaction in her shoulders over a plan that was unfolding as expected. Those grandiose hand gestures Blaire gave were always meant to distract. She would draw near for a false show of closeness... right before casually leaning away in that critical moment when the snare was set.

But what came across instead was unlike anything Bridget had witnessed before. Blaire's words were halting and unsure, and she spoke with her head down and back bent. Throughout, she did nothing with her hands... not until she reached out with unusual gentleness. Bridget wanted so desperately to accept those hands... but knew better.

Then came the unimaginable... a sincere sounding apology for Phoenix. More than an apology... Blaire offered an absolute acknowledgement of both her weakness and how terribly hurtful her actions had been. Bridget wanted to accept that apology too... to embrace it for no other reason than the rarity with which it was given... but first, she must know for certain.

"Blaire... I appreciate your words. They seem... sincere... and I want to believe them. But I have to ask you... are you here to claim Irene?"

Immediately… and just as forcefully… Blaire began wagging her head about. To Bridget, she looked pathetic, and so very far from charming, what with how her lips were sucked in, her head inclined toward her lap, and her shoulders slouched forward. Not a very compelling performance… which somehow made it all the more convincing.

"Then what about Bernie? Is he going to…"

"Bernie doesn't care about Irene, I can assure you of that. He says he loves me… but he loves himself more. I guess I can't fault him for that… I've treated him horribly. I knew he was enamored with me from the very beginning… and I went out of my way to rub it in his face. I didn't care a bit about how it made him feel. Only that I could control him through it. But to be absolutely honest… I have no way of knowing, Mother. Maybe he'll show up one day… but I doubt it."

"So… what is it that you want, Blaire? Why have you really come all this way?"

The question seemed to catch Blaire by surprise, for her eyes began darting about the room.

"For this."

"This what? What're you saying?"

"I want to… prove myself… to you and to her. I can't promise I won't fuck up… sorry… I mean, mess up. You were there for me as a role model and I rejected everything you tried to teach me. So I wouldn't blame you if you said no. But… if you can… if you will… I promise to try. I promise to try like I've never tried for anything before. I want to be part of your family again. But… beyond that… I really don't know. All I know is… it's my only shot at… at any sort of recovery… and knowing what it's like to be… normal."

"You do realize there's absolutely no way I'm giving you custody… no matter what you do."

"I'm not asking for it. I'm only asking for a chance to… be her mother."

"Blaire… being part of a family… it means putting others first. Are you going to do that with both Irene and me? And what about Lowell? He's part of this family too. You going to put him before yourself? Nothing you do is going to work if the answers aren't all yes. And how do I know you'll treat me with respect? When things get difficult, how do I know you won't quit?"

"I never quit."

"Really? You quit on me."

Fully expecting defiance, Bridget was surprised to see her look down in acknowledgement. That was something… but not enough, particularly seeing as Blaire was a master at knowing how to respond.

"You know, Blaire… no one can begin something new until they've first quit something old."

"I know. I've already made my decision to retire from the tour and…"

"That's not what I mean. Truth is… if you choose to re-enter family, you'll feel like quitting every day. But you should know that raising a child isn't a competition. It's not you versus Irene. It's you loving her… loving us all… and allowing yourself to be loved in return. Does that… make sense?"

"No… I mean, yes… in concept. But for me… it's always been about me versus me… you know… trying to be the best I can be."

"But Blaire, if you're striving for perfection in raising a child, then you've already failed because you're striving for the wrong thing. A child is far from perfect. Irene may be a year old, but she's still a baby requiring so much work. She's plenty cute… but those moments won't add up to all the crying and fussing… and all the chores… and all the diaper changing you'll have to do. You'll make such a mess of things that getting through the day sane is achievement enough. But the greatest achievement will be Irene herself."

"I know… I want to do this… I really do… He told me to be truthful. So the truth is… I'm scared. I can't do this alone."

"No, you can't. Few can. That's why it's called family."

In the brief silence that followed, Bridget suddenly came to realize the very thing that would tell her for certain whether Blaire was being sincere. Without further pause, she offered this final test.

"Would you like to see Irene?"

"Can I?! Really?!"

"Of course… come on."

She led Blaire down their hall to the small bedroom she and Lowell had set up as Irene's nursery. At that moment, the room was bathed by the soothing softness of the pale blue night light Lowell had suspended beneath the ceiling fan. Somewhat to her surprise, Blaire did not seem to notice this, nor did she take time to consider anything about the room… not its furnishings or decorations. She strode past the well-stocked changing table and small dresser… paid no mind to the walls decorated in a motif of wild flowers whose petals seemed swept about in swirls by an unseen wind. She went directly right up to the crib, not glancing once at the overhanging mobile of dancing bunnies. Her eyes were fully upon Irene, peacefully lying there in a canary-yellow sleeper.

"Oh, Mother… she's… she's so beautiful!"

"Would you like to hold her?"

"But… she's sleeping. I shouldn't wake her…"

"She'll get over it. Her mommy's here… that's more important."

Blaire, taking her eyes off Irene for the first time, hesitated for a moment… almost as if asking for reassurance with a single glance toward her own mother… and then slowly reached both arms over the rail. Inches short of touching Irene, she abruptly drew back.

"What's the matter?"

"I've… never held her before."

"Never?! How's that possible? Not even when you left the hospital?"

Blaire said nothing, but by the way her mouth crinkled about at its edges, with her head wagging in little jolts to the right and left, Bridget saw there what she had never seen before – shame.

"Just do it. I'm here. There's nothing to be afraid of."

More cautiously this time, Blaire gently laid her hands on Irene's hips… placing them there for so long that Bridget could not tell whether she was giving Irene a chance to wake first… or perhaps was still gripped with indecision. Taking hold of Blaire's wrists, Bridget directed them… fully aware that her daughter was not objecting to being controlled.

"Here… let me show you. Just place one hand beneath her head and neck… helps if you spread your fingers so you're supporting a bit of her shoulders too… and then slide the other under her bottom from the opposite side… that's it… and lift. Perfect."

Irene came awake with the stunned suddenness that Bridget had seen on many occasions. She might burst out crying any second… or might remain silent for the next several minutes trying to figure out her surroundings. Either way, Bridget was not concerned, as she was much more interested in watching Blaire hold her own daughter for the first time.

"Now gently press her against you… same side as the hand on her head… that's right. Keep the other one under her bottom… that way you support her and at the same time hold her close to you."

As Irene's head came up against Blaire's shoulder, Bridget was stunned yet again, for Blaire gently laid her lips upon Irene's hair… just as the tears began to flow… not from Irene, who smiled in recognition of her grandmother… but from the stranger of a mother who was holding her.

"I'm sorry, Mother… I'm so, so very sorry…"

"Save your words for later. We'll have plenty of time to talk. Just be with her now. Come… sit over here and rock her. She loves that. Tell you what… I'll go make her a bottle… and then after, we can change her together."

"Yes. And, Mother… thank you. Thank you so much."

Bridget kissed her daughter on the head… exactly as was done to Irene… and left for the kitchen with a tear and a smile.

41

PRACTICE

Her eyes were not on the ball, as she concentrated instead on the features of the swing more revealing than its outcome. She checked to see if each joint to the arms was bent, straightened, and re-bent at the proper times... for where the elbows were kept... for the shifts in the feet, hips and shoulders... and whether the head remained still and focused throughout. Even before the swing was done, Blaire had a mental list of things requiring work. At least contact had been made... that she knew from the thwack of the club as it whooshed through the air... and then she picked up the sizzle sound of a ball in-flight... a thing she always enjoyed hearing... right before a sharp crack made her blink.

"Damn."

"Watch your language."

"Yes, ma'am... but you can't blame me. It was like it had eyes for that tree."

"Yeah... sure. I've heard that one before. Try it again, but this time nice and easy. Don't bully it."

She heard again from behind that gentle tittering noise... the one that had been going on ever since she got him started taking practice swings. Blaire did not bother turning about... seeing as her eyes needed to be on her pupil... though she caught him winking in that direction before returning to the task she had given him of hitting a line of balls with a three iron. He muttered out another 'yes, ma'am'... most definitely to tease her.

"And stop saying that."

The giggling intensified… so much so that Blaire came about to face its source… without the slightest sense of irritation. Despite how the boot heels were locked into a lower rail, the little girl's denimed legs wiggled about with so much energy that Blaire was surprised the tiny frame managed to stay put on the fence. Somehow, the way those strawberry blonde ponytails bobbed about from under the pint-sized cowboy hat gave the impression that they were cooperating in trying to unseat her little girl from off the top rail.

Actually… not a bad job of braiding. I'm getting better at it.

Yet the most distinctive thing in Blaire's mind was the smile cutting across that freckled face… a face she had come to cherish.

Too soon, she was brought back by the whoosh-and-whack sounds of her student's next swing, except this time the ball kept to the ground, sending up a linear spray of dust. As it petered out some thirty yards away, she heard him utter a long, drawn-out 'darn'… so clearly his way of making a point within a point.

"You're not enjoying yourself?"

"You know… I only agreed to do this because your mother…"

"You mean your wife. And don't point a club at your coach – it's bad form. And stop making excuses."

Blaire paused here, allowing Irene's giggles to better make her point.

"Another… keep your elbows locked at the moment of impact… that way you don't pull up on it. And remember… keep your head still. Don't be tempted to lift it early. There's plenty of time after the follow-thru to find your ball. Besides… that's what your gallery's here for."

Irene immediately piped up with an enthusiastic 'that's me,' just as Blaire knew she would… which earned the little girl another wink and tip-of-the-hat from Lowell.

His next swing managed to produce aerial flight… except with a much more left-to-right trajectory than desired… terminating with a loud metallic clank and a sharp ricochet.

"Ouch! That was pretty terrible… even for you, Lowell. I didn't think it possible anyone could slice that badly. Probably left a dent in that shed. Golf's harder than it looks, isn't it?"

"Harder than an old bull's…"

"Watch your language. You'd do better to concentrate on your swing."

"You can do it, Cub. I'm sure of it!"

"Then why you giggling so much?"

"'Cause you're funny…"

Lowell went to wink again, but Blaire was ready this time. Side-stepping between him and where Irene sat on the fence, she brought him up short with a frown… which immediately made him turn back to the task.

"You know… what you're saying about how I'm supposed to be standing… it doesn't feel right to me."

"Really? Because you know so much about it? Think it's got anything to do with those ridiculous things on your feet?"

"Where's a cowboy without his boots?"

"For an hour a day… when you're under my thumb… you're not a cowboy – you're a golfer. Tomorrow, you're going to Competitor's World for a pair of spikes."

He started to object, but Blaire cut him off.

"Irene."

"Yes, Mom?"

"How's about going into town with me tomorrow to make sure this old fool buys some proper golf shoes. We can get frozen yogurt together after."

"Yippee!"

"On him, of course."

She got him with that one. No way he could resist lavishing treats on Irene. Yet when he turned back to the next ball, he made no effort to raise the club into a swing. So… perhaps it was time for a bit of encouragement.

"Okay, Lowell… I really think you can do this. You've got many of the essential mechanics down… you just need practice to fine tune them. You know… I should thank you. You're actually helping me become a better coach. I think I'm pretty good at teaching kids and high schoolers how to play, but the pinnacle of any golf instructor's ability would be if they could transform a crotchety old bastard into…"

"Watch your language."

More giggling came from behind her, though Blaire ignored it.

"…a golfer who can drive, chip and putt… then they can teach anyone."

"Well… 'teacher'… this one's not working right."

He extended out the three iron… but without pointing it this time.

"Works fine for me."

"The whole mess of them work for you."

"Okay… Maybe you're not a long iron kind-of-guy. Here… try this instead."

"What's this? A number seven, huh?"

"A seven *iron*."

"Right… seven iron."

"Now play it back a little bit in your stance .. that's right… and don't be afraid of taking up some turf. That's what it's there for. Same gentle grip as before. Wait… let me see what you've got there."

She made a quick inspection of how his fingers were folded about the club, satisfying herself that he had not forgotten the previous day's lesson.

"Good. Now… slow back… still center… then fluid all the way through. Power into the pivot… and show me the sole of your boot.

He took his stance and swung into more solid-sounding contact than before. The ball shot off in an arc… just as any good seven iron should do… landing some ninety yards away.

"I like that one."

"Not bad… for an old fart. Let's see you try it again, except this time I want you to…"

Her cell phone suddenly rang, interrupting her instructions to Lowell.

"Sorry… I need to take this."

She moved off to speak privately, yet kept an eye on him, seven iron in hand, as he stuck his tongue out toward where Irene sat on the top rail. Blaire was not surprised in the least to see Irene return the favor… and then snort out laughing at the commencement of a comical exhibition from him. He was waddling around like a penguin while twirling the iron about its club face as if it were a cane. The routine went on through several figure eight patterns before it came to a finale with him making something of an elaborate swirling bow… at the same time as he tipped his cowboy top-hat. Irene instantly began clapping and calling for an encore. In response, he went into a Vaudeville-like dance – both hands over the head of the iron and the grip-end thrust into the ground. There he was, swaying back and forth with a ridiculous swoon on his face… and Irene doing all she could not to topple off the fence from laughter.

She's so happy… and that… makes me happy.

Blaire needed to pay attention to her caller, but still found her thoughts straying back to the familiar conflict she had contended with on nearly a daily basis over the past six years.

Everything about being a mother had been as difficult as her own mother said it would be. So many times, she found herself stuck between her old self… who knew exactly how to take advantage of someone's feelings… and a new self who was trying to embrace those feelings as her own. Early on, she was unable to make much sense out of that internal conflict… but somewhere along in Irene's third year, she decided that she could feel whatever way she wanted to… or feel nothing at all… so long as she never turned from her place in the family. Sometimes that meant making herself do what she did not want to do… and in the end, she came to consider that as nothing all that different from what a normal person had to do.

Irene was still laughing at Lowell's antics, and for the umpteenth million time, Blaire found herself without the ability to feel about life the way her own little girl seemed so adept at feeling. Joy, empathy and concern… all those things Irene had mastered by the age of four… Blaire, thirty years older, had absolutely no clue about. But she could imitate Irene… imitate Lowell and imitate her own mother… and with imitation, begin to understand. Irene was such a snuggler… and totally unaware that her own mother had no inclination toward such affection. Her daughter loved soft things… soft words and soft feelings… so Blaire turned herself in that direction too… and somehow found that she did not need to fake it every time.

Well… all that was fine and dandy, but it was high time that their foolishness ceased. Lowell was now plucking at the seven iron like it was some kind of a banjo. Still speaking on her cell, Blaire took several steps in their direction and stared bullets at him until he got the message. Sheepishly, he shrugged his shoulders and returned to the line of golf balls. From there, he managed to loft three more half-decent approach shots into the horse pasture before her call was over.

"You guys… I just got the Klimpton twins… boy and girl. That makes a dozen for the summer. Not bad."

"Congratulations."

"Good job, Mom!"

His next attempt was another bad slice.

"Lowell… don't be tempted to grip the club too tightly. It might make you feel like you've got control, but it doesn't make the shot any better. For the best result, you have to allow the club face to flow freely through the swing. Let it pivot along with your hips."

"Thanks… I'll work on that. Are they any good?"

"He's going to be a handful. Middle school boys drive me crazy. Pretty sure he's only coming to ogle my figure."

"Mom! Really?!"

"I'm only joking, Irene. Truth is… I don't think he cares much about golf. The girl seems pretty serious about learning. Got some promise."

"Hey, Mom – just like you when you were a kid."

"That's right, Angel. Maybe someday you'll take up golf too."

"Maybe…"

"But I think you'd rather be on a horse…"

Irene's smile widened, as Blaire knew it would.

"Well… that's fine with me. But I'm going to teach you anyway… just so we can have our own little thing to do together. Doesn't look like anyone else around here's going to be picking up the game anytime soon."

"Hey! You see me here trying?!"

"Then let the club face do what it wants to."

Blaire watched several more swings before returning to the previous subject.

"They're going to be fun to work with…"

"Who's that?"

"The twins. The girl's got real fire… and I think the boy's going to end up enjoying it once he gets started."

"You know, Blaire… everyone in town says you're the best coach."

"That's true, Mom. Everyone knows it."

"Thanks, Angel… but don't be fooled by this guy. He's only saying that to butter me up because he knows everything eventually gets back to your grandmother."

"Darlin'… that ain't at all the way it is. I'm… proud of you."

Without warning, she found her eyes watering up at a feeling she had never understood… and still could not… though she knew full well its meaning. She was grateful.

"Hey you three! Dinner's ready. Time to come in."

Though they were a good distance off, she easily recognized the joy with which Irene catapulted herself off the fence into Lowell's arms. Her granddaughter was only there a second before turning to Blaire, nestling herself beneath an arm. And to see Blaire take that arm… along with her other one… and wrap those about Irene in a hug… even lift her off the ground in the process… that was enough to make a mother smile.

She waved them in… and all three waved back. With Irene in the middle, they turned together up the dirt road toward the house… all happy… simply because she was the one calling them home.

THE END.

ACKNOWLEDGEMENTS

The characters of Bridget and Blaire would never have come into their fullness without the many hours of thought, effort and interaction invested into them by my wife. Thank you, Pam! You're awesome!

Thanks to my brother, Mark, for all those ridiculous conversations meant to distract during our many torturous hours together on the golf course. Those were the inspiration behind both Bridget's sour attitude toward golf and Blaire's 'prop-ish' outlook on life.

Many thanks to Ed Moore for sharing his extensive knowledge and insights into the world of professional golf. Blaire is a richer character because of him.

Thanks to Karol Kowalski for help with Polish.

Thanks to Bond for trudging through two drafts of this novel for me. Thanks also for her firsthand insights into the Prescott Rodeo Grounds

Wikipedia – where would I be without you?

BOOKS AND RESOURCES DRAWN FROM IN PREPARING THIS NOVEL:

"Behind the Chutes – The Mystique of the Rodeo Cowboy," by Rosamond Norbury.

"Chasing the Rodeo," by W.K. Stratton.

"Rodeo Girl," by Linda Eisner (photo compilation).

"Good Parenting Through Divorce," by Mary Ellen Hannibal.

"What Your Divorce Lawyer May Not Tell You," by Margery Rubin.

"Desert Storm: Dreadnought," by Joseph B. George.

"Lucky War: Third Army in Desert Storm," by Richard M. Swain.

"Superquake! Why Earthquakes Occur and When the Big One Will Hit Southern California," by David Ritchie.

The amazingly candid account of the transformation of 'Jess,' a professed narcissitic sociopath (https://truthlover5.com/2012/12/07/profile-of-a-sociopath-charming-manipulative-grandiose-lying-narcissitic-authoritarian-secretive/comment-page-2/#comment-5379)

The Psychopath Checklist (PCL), readily available in various forms on the web.

Google Maps.

Chapter images were obtained from the following public domain sources:

- Arizona Manual of Approved Signs of the Arizona State Department of Transportation (https://www.azdot.gov/business/engineering-and-construction/traffic/manual-of-approved-signs)
- The Manual of Uniform Traffic Devices of the United States Department of Transportation (https://mutcd.fhwa.dot.gov/services/publications/fhwaop02084/index.htm)
- Wikimedia (https://commons.wikimedia.org/)

AUTHOR'S CONTEMPLATION

(Spoiler alert)

Bridget is a story of conflict between two women - Blaire, a callously single-minded daughter, and Bridget, an empathetically over-invested mother. Each struggles to be at peace with who they are in relation to the other. Their individual peace journeys are explored through two distinct settings - the golf course and the freeway. Blaire is the golf course - something beautiful that hides something perilous... and Bridget is the freeway - always burning in a frantic drive forward. In combination, the characters and settings display something of the quandary behind peace. Blaire's pursuit of peace (if she would stoop to call such a thing a thing) is governed by a simple law - me first and only, whereas Bridget's pursuit of peace is tethered to the choices of others. Neither is at peace because neither gives freely. Bridget's offerings are bound up in expectation and obligation, while Blaire's are shrouded in deceit and cruelty.

As both characters discover, achieving peace can be as frustrating as playing the game of golf or getting stuck in freeway traffic. Peace, after all, is not such a simple concept. There is inner peace, peace of mind, peace with the past/present/future, peace in relationships, peaceful settings, peace as an experience or lifestyle, peace between adversaries, and peace with God. Peace, or lack thereof, can be linked to a place, a condition, a circumstance, a realization, or a decision. Peace is different things to different people. In a way of acknowledging this complexity, the story employs multiple voices - primarily Bridget's and Blaire's, with bits of Mitch, Lowell and the narrator's scattered interjections added in. The accounts jump back and forth in time as they contradict and confuse, yet collectively demonstrate the difficulties encountered in finding true peace.

Perhaps God's name could be added to the list of voices searching for peace. Strange... before starting in on this novel... I never gave much thought to the possibility that the God of all universes could ever *not* be at peace. Surely ultimate power brings ultimate everything! But in crafting beings with the ability to choose, he has willingly conceded aspects of his own peace to the choices of others... unfortunately resulting in a world as deeply disturbed as our own. Yet God is at peace because he has made the ultimate free-will offering of himself... to be accepted, rejected or ignored.

Personally, I find that peace is lost or found in the turning. Despite our best intentions, we humans are not very good at changing ourselves. We struggle for control and resist being controlled. The tighter the grip, the harder it is to let go… just as it was for Bridget with her photo albums. She was never free until she gave up the hold her daughter had on her. Only when she offered the apple with an open hand did she avoid getting bit. In this sense, the apple is symbolic of control… the fallacy of knowing what is best for ourselves and others… and to this, we grip ever so tightly. To be at peace, I believe the apple needs to be offered back to God. In turning over control to the one who holds peace in his open hand, we are somehow changed… and the things that oddly once seemed so important no longer are.

Peace… against such things there is no law.